Thanksgiving Breakfast

John Fitzgerald

ISBN: 147916822X

ISBN 13: 9781479168224

Library of Congress Control Number: 2012917484

CreateSpace Independent Publishing Platform, North Charleston, South Carolina

Dedicated

In loving memory of Mary,

My Children & Grandchildren:

To Daniel who pointed the way.

To Molly & Sisie, who paved the way.

And to

Pammy Sue ... In every way.

Special thanks

To

Erica Kester & Phil Whitbeck.

Forward

In northeastern Pennsylvania about a hundred miles north of Philadelphia is the small community of Clarks Summit. Nestled on top of one of the Blue Ridge Mountains, it's a picturesque little village with narrow streets shaded by large maple and oak trees. It was founded by William Clark, a veteran of the Revolutionary War. He fought at the Battle of Bunker Hill and spent a winter at Valley Forge with General Washington. For his service he was granted eight hundred acres in the Abington wilderness. He built a log cabin there in 1799; one hundred years later a school was built. In 1911 the borough of Clarks Summit was incorporated.

For thousands of years, the Indians roamed this area; but in the late 1800s, the major influences were coal mining, farming and the railroad. In 1913 Clarks Summit was scarred by what was known as the "big cut." A deep ravine was dug through the town to accommodate the construction of the largest concrete structure in the world at the time: the magnificent Nicholson Bridge. Like so many other changes in Clarks Summit, the ravine still has a subtle but powerful effect on the community that an outsider may not notice.

The natural barrier of the mountains separated Clarks Summit and the Abington area from Scranton, the major city in the area. This environment also set Clarks Summit apart and isolated from the adjoining coal-mining towns of Dunmore, Moosic, Throop, Olyphant, Old Forge and Dickson City as well as the farming communities of Chinchilla, Newton, Dalton and Waverly.

Before Interstate 81 was built in the 1960s, State Route 6/11 was the major highway, feeding a steady stream of cars and trucks with a variety of state license plates through the heart of town. It was fascinating to watch the large tractor-trailers hauling loads up and down the Clarks Summit hill on their journey to customers throughout the country. At night, while lying in bed, you could hear the straining of the lonesome diesel locomotives as they pulled the long trail of freight cars to mysterious destinations. The movement of commerce through our little town amplified the sense of adventure to a young fertile mind.

Clarks Summit was a wonderful place to grow up. It was like Mayberry; although we didn't have Andy Griffith, we did have a few Barney Fifes. On State Street we had a pharmacy, a movie theater, a variety of shops, a few bars and the Summit Diner.

Everyone knew everyone. It wasn't until later in life that I realized I had grown up with Irish, Italians, Polish, Germans, Welsh, Catholics, Lutherans, Baptists, Jews, and various kinds of Protestants. As kids we didn't notice any difference; they were our friends and neighbors. Our fathers all had jobs of seemingly equal importance although some were paid more. We knew the shop owners and employees of each business. We knew every schoolteacher and policeman, the people who worked at the gas stations, and even the town drunk, although some of those positions would change with the times. Respect for others was the unspoken community code we adhered to. We may not have liked everybody, but we respected everyone. To our innocent minds, all the girls and women were virgins . . . including our mothers.

Growing up we didn't have much money; for us kids there weren't any jobs except cutting grass in the summer, raking leaves in the fall, and shoveling snow in the winter. But we didn't need much money. Back in the 1950s, movies were twenty-five cents, candy bars a nickel and a Coke was six cents. My parents' cigarettes were seventeen cents a pack.

Though we may not have had much money, we did have a lot of freedom. We could explore the surrounding fields, mountains, streams, and lakes, and investigate the boundaries of life. In the summer we would sleep outside, talking and dreaming under the distant stars. We were able to build lifelong friendships that remain as genuine today as they were more than fifty years ago—providing some of those old friends don't read this book.

Growing up in this area was a beautiful, enjoyable experience. It was a fun time to be born and a fun place to grow up. There have been so many fascinating characters in our town, with so many entertaining episodes. I chose to share just a glimpse of our life with some of these stories. The setting is real, many of the incidents are real, and the characters are combinations of the unique cast of characters I grew up with. Some of these people are more recognizable than others, and all were enchanting.

Chapter One

1963

This would be an out-of-the-ordinary Thanksgiving weekend, and the festivities would begin the Wednesday night before Thanksgiving. In the home at 513 Highland Avenue, you could hear the TV blaring with Walter Cronkite on *The CBS Evening News* at 6:30 p.m., followed by *Leave It to Beaver* and the popular *The Beverly Hillbillies*. Life was changing in this little community and the world.

Alex Flynn was home from college and preparing himself for a reunion of sorts. Standing in his bedroom as he finished dressing for the evening, he offhandedly asked the image in the mirror. *So here I am taking a personal inventory of myself,* he thought. *I'm a freshman in college, and I really don't know who I am. Who is Alex Flynn?* He took into consideration all of his physical features as stated on his driver's license: six foot one, one hundred and sixty pounds, with blue eyes and dark blond hair.

Not bad to look at, but not considered attractive by most girls, he thought to himself. Perhaps it was his long face or the fact that he was not as funny as most of his close friends. Because of his poor eyesight, Alex was required to wear glasses; therefore he couldn't play sports and didn't have an athletic body. Without any scholastic achievements, teachers considered him not too smart, but he did have a curious mind and a deep interest in people, all kinds of people.

If I were born in a different family, how different would I be? Alex pondered for a moment. *Even my name would be different.* His mother had named him after a cat. As a small child, Alex remembered that strange-looking cat, his mom's favorite pet. She loved that cat so much, but one day it went out and never returned. The loss of that strange cat changed his mother's whole outlook on life. She became distant, cooler, and seemed to lose her interest in life. Alex wondered if she often thought what her life would have been like with a different husband and different children.

"What difference did it make? I'm me," Alex said as he dressed. He was growing aware of the changes in life that lie ahead. He was in college now and starting on his life journey to who knows where. If only he could make that journey together with his dear friends, all on one team. But he knew they must each travel their own trail. Even so he hoped they could somehow stay connected. However, they had already begun the separation process and were each going their own way. It was like looking at the road map out of St. Louis, knowing they all were traveling on different highways, heading in various directions. Only God knew where they'd end up. Tonight at O'Connor's Alex was going to ask them for a commitment to strengthen their friendship, and hopefully they could remain connected no matter what lay ahead.

The night was cold with a light drizzle. Alex had to park his car a few blocks from Grove Street High School. He joined the other people walking toward the school parking lot where a pep rally and bonfire were already in progress. Alex was surprised by the size of the jubilant crowd, celebrating the annual community ritual. It was a euphoric occasion, like a homecoming for many of the former high school friends. The purpose of the rally was to unite the community and school in sending the high school football team off to the game with thunderous support.

Alex looked around the mass of people as he searched for friendly faces without much luck. The crowd was much larger than he expected, considering the rain and cold. In the center of the parking lot, the large bonfire was ablaze. The heat could be felt at a long distance. Alex recognized some faces in the crowd and acknowledged those he knew, but he decided to remain alone in the crowd and kept his spot until the right people presented themselves. He could hear the high school band marching up Grove Street. As it drew closer, it got louder. Everyone started moving to the center of the parking lot as the triumphal band marched in, playing the school's alma mater. The crowd cheered and applauded loudly.

The cheerleaders led the parade into the parking lot, followed by the band, fire trucks, floats, and local politicians in convertibles. The grand marshal of the parade was Bob DeAngelo, the head football coach. The procession marched from the volunteer firehouse on State Street through the small village, turned up Grove Street, and then continued for a half mile to the high school parking lot.

More than a thousand people assembled in a large circle around the raging, twenty-foot-high bonfire. They backed away as a green tractor slowly made its way, pulling an empty hay wagon, and stopped in front of the powerful fire. Principal Graham, wearing a long, dark parka, emerged from the crowd and stepped on the wagon to address the fans.

With a megaphone in hand, he yelled, "I want to thank you all for coming out tonight. This night is special. Tomorrow's game is special. We all have just gone through a difficult time, but tonight we're not going to dwell on what happened last week. However, I ask you now to please bow your heads for a moment and say a prayer for the family of President Kennedy and say another prayer for our country." Everyone bowed in silence.

After a minute Principal Graham lifted his head, looked over the audience, put the megaphone to his mouth, and yelled again, "We are here tonight to support this fine football team. So now let's talk football." The crowd went wild with cheers and revelry. The band started playing the Notre Dame fight song. It was an enthusiastic, festive atmosphere. No one was quiet, and after a few minutes, the principal continued.

"When it comes to football, there's no one more qualified to talk about it, and there's no one more qualified to coach it, than our own head coach, Bob DeAngelo. Who wants to hear from our coach?"

Principal Graham had the timing and skill of a vaudeville performer. Everyone was yelling and cheering, and the band was applauding. Coach DeAngelo waited out of view behind the wagon. When the roar and applause was pitched just right, he made his way up onto the wagon. He was dressed in a dark overcoat, with a white shirt and tie exposed as if he were dressed for business. He walked across the wagon toward Principal Graham. With both hands high in the air, fists closed, the coach wore a smile of determination.

The men shook hands, turned, and faced the crowd. Principal Graham handed the megaphone to the coach, smiled, and pointed toward the cheering multitude. It was quite a sight. The large fire roared in the background, reflecting a reddish glow on both men as they stood out on the cold, dark night. After a few moments, the principal left the wagon, and the coach stood alone, basking in the adulation of his supporters.

Coach DeAngelo was small in stature, only five feet four, but he was a dynamic speaker and motivator. He understood destiny, hard work, and planning. The school board paid a lot of money to recruit him and gave him whatever he wanted. Standing alone on the wagon, he looked like Napoleon addressing his troops before the Battle of the Pyramids. Everyone quieted down. As the coach was about to speak, he discarded the megaphone.

Holding his head high and looking over the heads of those he was addressing, Coach DeAngelo extended his right arm and pointed to the sky. "I'm here tonight to tell you that these are the best young men and this is the finest team I have ever coached," he yelled out. The cheers and yells were instantaneous and thunderous. He looked all around, taking in the spectacle. "Tomorrow we play the game of the year," he continued. "We will be representing this school district and this community. When we go on the field of play tomorrow, we will be thinking of the tradition of this great event. We will look up at the stands, and we will see your faces, we will hear your voices, and we will know we have your support. With our effort and your support, we will win tomorrow." The crowd went wild. "We will represent you well." The roar again erupted, and the coach began to introduce the players.

Alex moved along with the crowd toward the blazing fire. As he walked along, he spotted Johnny Thompson. Alex could pick Johnny out of a crowd of a thousand people. They had been friends since third grade, and they lived in the same neighborhood. They camped out in their backyards as small children; they shared ghost stories and family secrets, and discussed everything from girls and frogs to God and religion. Each was aware of the other's strengths and weaknesses. They had a special understanding with each other. In their own way, they were closer to each other than to any of their family members.

Johnny stood six feet tall with wide shoulders, a thin waist, and muscular arms. He walked with a special stride, chest puffed out and head cocked; some would say he walked around as if he owned the place. His large shoulders were the result of hard work as a child and dedicated training as a star athlete in high school football and wrestling. He wore his sandy-colored hair in an odd flattop manner, up and to the side. The hairstyle resulted in his nickname, "Wedge Head." It was a secret name and rarely, if ever, used in his presence. Johnny had one physical problem he was sensitive about: his complexion. As a child, Johnny developed skin problems that resulted in a teenage embossment. He had deep pits in his face and large pimples that seemed constant.

Nothing he tried—including trips to the doctor, home remedies, and using a scrub brush on his face for hours—had much success. Nothing relieved the pain or the shame of his blotched complexion. Although he went through high school with a quick wit and sarcastic attitude, as though nothing troubled him, Alex knew how ashamed Johnny was of his face.

Johnny came from a strict Protestant family. They were God-fearing people who worked hard and didn't drink alcohol in front of others. They went to church on Sundays, praying for the sinners, the sick, and the shut-ins. The Thompsons were proud of their church affiliation but had contempt for Catholics with all those kids and Jews with all that money. They expected their children to go to school, work around the house, and hold a part-time job. Johnny and his brother cut lawns in the summer, raked leaves in the fall, and shoveled snow in the winter. Johnny's dad worked for the A&P food stores. The job didn't pay much, but it was a job with security. Money was so tight that the Thompsons didn't have enough income to justify operating a car. Mr. Thompson walked to work every day in rain, sleet, or snow, a mile and a half each way. He also walked home for lunch. As a family they walked to church. In poor weather, Mrs. Thompson's sister would drive the family. Because Mr. Thompson walked so much, he kept his tall, lean physique, and his white hair gave off an air of dignity. Mrs. Thompson baked pies to help with the family income. It took long hours and hard work to make what little money she could.

Johnny strolled across the parking lot hand in hand with his girlfriend, Melody Brown. He was dressed in a stylish, yellow rain parka, and Melody was dressed in a matching green parka with the hood up due to the light mist. They were a handsome couple and obviously very much in love.

Melody was a well-proportioned girl, almost as tall as Johnny. Her brown hair was puffed up in a fashion that made her face appear smaller. Large brown eyes and an innocent warm smile were her most attractive features. She was shy and meek, like a quiet, slow-flowing mountain stream; but below the water's surface, she was as hard as a rock.

She came from a hardworking family. Her father had a small, struggling construction company, and her mother, Mrs. Brown, worked part-time to help with the strained income. They were strict Southern Baptists. There was no drinking or swearing and no working on Sundays. For Melody and her sister, there was no dating until they were sixteen and then only on special occasions with a proper chaperone. In the presence of her parents, Melody was a perfectly behaved daughter who smiled sweetly and was considerate of others. In the presence of others, she was independent, quite open, and enjoyable to be around. Although she gave the impression of holding dear to her church values, the only values she adhered to were not working on Sundays and being absolutely devoted to Johnny.

Melody and Johnny had been secretly dating for years. Her parents had no idea that when she spent the night at a girlfriend's house she was actually sneaking out with Johnny. Over a period of time, Mr. and Mrs. Brown eventually allowed Melody to go out officially on a date with Johnny, partly because of his close association with his church. However, they kept a keen eye on the couple's activities with many restrictions to ensure that nothing sinful happened. Through deception and ruse they were more involved than her parents ever suspected.

Alex waved his arms high in the air to get the attention of Johnny across the parking lot. Melody spotted Alex first, waved back, and alerted Johnny. The three ran through the crowd toward each other.

"Hey, Johnny," Alex said, shaking Johnny's hand, then reaching out and smiling at Melody. "Never shake hands with a pretty girl; you must always kiss her." He then embraced Melody and kissed her on the cheek.

"Nice to see you too, Alex, but remember I'm the jealous type. I'm watching to see how tightly you squeeze her," Johnny said jokingly.

"How is college, Alex?" Melody asked as she looked directly into his eyes.

"It's different, a lot harder than I thought," Alex said with a concerned voice. Almost as an afterthought, he asked, "How does your father like having Johnny working for him?"

Before she could answer, Johnny blurted out, "I'm the best worker he has. If he works with me, I'll build that business into something big."

Melody smiled and said in a joking tone, "Right now I have two very strong men in my life, each trying to keep me from the dominance of the other."

"But I'm winning, Alex, even though both parents are against me. Oh yeah, her mother likes me even less than her father. But that's okay; soon I'll have all the family's women loving me and the father respecting me," Johnny said confidently.

"Sounds like the two of you have your future planned out," Alex said.

"We know what we are doing, and we're trying to keep everyone else in the dark," Johnny replied.

"Speaking of the dark, where is everyone? Have you heard from anybody? I was hoping to see some of the A-team tonight at O'Connor's," Alex said.

Johnny was quick to answer as usual. "I saw Nancy Bishop at the gas station, and she said she had some things to do but would see us at O'Connor's tonight. I called Phil Whitman too, and he said he was going to try to make it to the rally tonight. If not he would see us at the bar later."

"How about Danny Fredrick?" Alex asked meekly.

"I don't think anyone has talked to him recently, at least I haven't," Melody said, glancing toward Johnny for comment.

"I haven't either, Alex. I'm sure he'll be around tonight. They say the Wednesday before Thanksgiving is the busiest night of the year at the bar. There will be drinking and a crowd, so he'll be there," Johnny added with a smirk."

Has anyone heard from Jerry Weaver? I hope he can make it in this weekend," Alex said in a serious tone.

"Nancy said he was at Fort Benning, Georgia, finishing up jump school. He is now a genuine Army paratrooper," Johnny said.

"The hoopla here is about over. I'm getting cold and wet, so let's get to O'Connor's. This could be a fun night," Alex said, shivering.

"You just want to get to the bar to have a few drinks," Johnny said and laughed.

Alex looked over at the fire and yelled to the loving couple, "Okay, Johnny, I'll see you and Melody in a few minutes at O'Connor's."

"We'll be there in a little while; I have to run over to Doc Stones for a few minutes," Johnny said as he squeezed Melody. She looked into his eyes and smiled.

Alex knew that Doc Stones was an old dirt road that led to nowhere but was a great isolated spot for young lovers. Alex said with a chuckle in his voice, "I understand John; I guess something just popped up."

O'Connor's Bar was located next to the Summit Diner on State Street. Viewed from the street, it looked like a white farmhouse with an extended porch. It was a picturesque scene with large oak trees towering over the house, which sat back fifty yards from the street on an elevated parcel of land with a stone wall in front. There was a small parking area in the back with a side entrance. The hidden parking was convenient for those who preferred their cars to remain out of sight, away from the scrutiny of the good citizens. The rear entrance was also convenient for illegal Sunday liquor sales and the flock of underage drinkers who were afraid to use the front door.

The interior of O'Connor's Bar was as unique as the ownership. Upon entering the place, customers were impressed by how clean and comfortable it looked. It seemed like a large recreation room at a friend's house. The long, dark red mahogany bar had eleven wooden barstools, and the walls consisted of yellow, knotty pine planks from floor to ceiling. On the wall attached to the house, a large square window was installed so Frances O'Connor and her sister could peek through to monitor Frances' husband, Eddy's drinking. Illuminated beer signs furnished the only glow in the dimly lit room. Behind the bar were three shelves displaying whiskey bottles. Above the shelves was a long, wide mirror. There were a few side windows for light, and on the walls hung old black-and-white pictures and some framed billboards. One picture was of "the greatest fighter of them all, Jack Dempsey," according to Eddy. In addition to the bar there were six small tables, each with four classic barroom chairs.

Frances kept the place immaculate. In the restrooms she placed newspapers on the floor near the toilets to catch any inadvertent spray and put out scented candles near the sinks to clear the air. Eddy was the bartender, but when he was out Frances took over. This gave her the opportunity to add water to the whiskey bottles when no one was looking. When they were together, it was a battlefield of insults. Eddy usually had the upper hand until his sister-in-law, Liz, appeared and added verbal support to Frances. Even Eddy couldn't fight the two of them. Insults were not limited to O'Connor family members. Both Eddy and Frances had a reputation of insulting whomever they chose. That was one of the reasons the place was so easy to keep clean; many potential patrons didn't like being insulted, so there weren't too many customers. Eddy and Frances were fussy about the clientele but not too finicky about the fact that most of their satisfactory customers were underage drinkers. No cursing was allowed, and if anyone disagreed with the management, he was subject to ridicule and expulsion. The real lure of O'Connor's was not the ambience or the service but the fact they would serve almost anyone with any type of ID.

The only food available was pickled eggs. And there was no jukebox or any other type of music. The only entertainment was Eddy and a large black-and-white TV set high above the bar. Eddy was in sole control of the TV. Before the development of the remote control, changing channels was done manually. Watching Eddy change a channel was an amusement in itself. Climbing up on a stepladder, he extended himself as far as possible to change to one of the three networks. As the evening progressed, Eddy's intoxication would make the channel-changing process even more precarious and humorous.

From a barstool, you could sit and gaze out the large picture window on the right side of the bar and witness the changing of seasons. In the summer you could spot local townsfolk walking uptown to the movie theater on a warm, starlit evening. In the autumn you could witness the turning of the leaves, watching them change color and fall from the large trees. They would start floating and spinning as the wind directed them to their place for the winter to be covered with layers of snow. The cold, harsh winter nights were perhaps the ideal time to sit at the bar. Perched on a stool, you could sip a shot of whiskey while watching a winter storm, as trucks with snowplows made slow progress up State Street. The few pedestrians brave enough to be out at night walked by quickly, all bundled up. The high winds blew the snow back and forth, swirling into drifts. Many nights Alex would sit and sip a shot of Rock & Rye whiskey, enjoying the warmth of the bar and staring out at winter's magical display.

Eddy O'Connor's unique personality was known throughout the area and had made him kind of a folk hero. His black hair was streaked with gray. He stood five foot six, weighed ninety-six pounds, and had a humped back. Eddy had fought in World War I; he was wounded at Cantigny, France in 1918, when he was struck with shrapnel from an artillery shell. When the shrapnel was removed, the field doctors gave a piece of it to

Eddy. Upon returning to the States, he had it dipped in gold and made into a beautiful tiepin. At times he was kidded about being shot with a tiepin gun.

Out in public he always wore a three-piece suit bought in the 1920s. In the summer months, he wore a white Irish linen suit with a white panama hat. He looked as if he just stepped out of an F. Scott Fitzgerald novel, perhaps a neighbor of *The Great Gatsby*. While bartending he wore a white waiter's jacket that exposed his oversized tie and gold tiepin. Eddy had a glass eye, and while sitting behind the bar, he would take it out and polish it to the horror of first-time customers. When he spoke in heated conversations, he would cock his head and stare intensely with his good eye for effect. Eddy had a keen wit and strong opinions, and he expressed them openly. He felt Roosevelt should be canonized; this Democrat was the savior of the workingman. Eddy lived through the tough times of the Depression, Prohibition, and war. Although now in his mid-seventies, he was quick on his feet, retaining the agility of his younger years as a boxer. He never looked back with regret; his wit was contagious, and he was quite lovable.

Alex parked his car behind O'Connor's. Walking in alone he knew this would be an exceptional night. This might be the last time the A-team, our high school clique, would all be together. A lot had happened since graduation. In just five months since receiving their high school diplomas, everyone had started on their own path of life. But tonight they would be together again to enjoy each other's company.

As he entered the crowded barroom, Alex could see many familiar faces in the crowd; his attention was focused on a table in the center of the room. Sitting there was Danny Fredrick with his apparent date. Alex didn't know the girl, but she had long dark hair and strange, eccentric-looking clothes. For Danny, though, this look would be desirable.

Of all the people in the close-knit group, Danny was the most independent. He seemed to walk to the beat of a different drummer. He was tall and lean; his hair was always cut short but always looked unkempt. Jeans, sandals and a buckskin jacket were one aspect of his style of dress. Soft-spoken and strongly opinionated, he was the voice of conscience for the group. He was not a member of any sports team nor did he participate in school activities. His passion was music; the guitar was his instrument of choice.

Like Samson's long hair, music was Danny's strength. Danny was popular and respected mostly for his musical talents although he had his share of critics. Alex was fond of him and appreciated his sense of independence and refreshing viewpoints. Alex and Nancy Bishop would often smooth over many of the misunderstandings he created with his outspoken and marginal views.

Danny had one younger sister who was his total opposite, very shy. Their father worked for the state in some nondescript job. Their mother was sort of a recluse; no one ever saw her out in public. She would answer the phone and the door when friends called though. Danny was now attending the University of Scranton, a local Jesuit college.

"Over here, Alex," Danny yelled and waved his right hand high in the air.

Alex made his way through the crowd, shaking hands with some of his old friends and acquaintances. Some he hadn't seen for quite a while. Finally arriving at the table, Alex extended his hand and with a large smile said, "Hello, Danny, you are looking good." Then looking directly at the girl with the long hair, he added, "You're looking good too."

"Easy, Alex. This is my newest love; her name is Ida Freeman. I met her at college."

"I thought the university didn't allow girls on campus," Alex said.

"Times are changing, Alex. There are girls at the U, and soon there will be guys at Marywood College," Danny said with a musical tone in his voice. "I can see big changes coming because we need big changes in our society."

"Yes, we'll discuss that later, but for tonight we are supposed to have fun. We may not see each other for some time, so let's enjoy the night and let Atlas carry the world on his shoulders for a while," Alex said. He then took the initiative to talk to Ida.

"Welcome to O'Connor's, Ida. I hope you enjoy the evening. I can promise you it will be interesting if nothing else," Alex said as he took a better look at her. She was very pretty, with her black hair hanging beyond her shoulders. She wore glasses and a very serious look on her face, which gave her an intellectual appearance. Alex had seen pictures of this beatnik type of girl in magazines, but this was the first time he met one face-to-face. She was intriguing to say the least.

Danny yelled out, "Over here, Phil!"

Alex turned his attention from Ida to the door; he could see Phil Whitman talking with a few friends as he made his way to join Alex and company.

Phil was built like a fireplug: short, stocky legs; powerful shoulders; and a large head. He started on the varsity football team as a tough lineman. He was physically strong with a poker face that seemed to hide all his emotions. He possessed a strong image of integrity, which was the center force that held the A-team together. He had the ability to see both sides of an issue, and with his warm and pleasant personality, he was able to develop close friendships with various factions in the class of 1963. Phil was popular with a congenial sense of humor. Although he dated often, there was no one special.

His father drove a milk truck at a time when home delivery was as common as cable TV is today. His mother worked as an assistant to the school administrator; she was well informed about her son's school activities. Phil worked hard for the grades he received although he was rarely on the honor roll. His mom persisted in directing Phil to attend college. Her desire was to have her son return to his alma mater as a respected teacher. Although Phil was attending a state teacher's college, his heart was not in teaching. He was more interested in exploring the world.

Phil made his way to the table, and Alex and Danny were on their feet when he arrived. There was the usual backslapping and greetings along with the introduction of Ida. Phil realized there was a shortage of drinks at the table, so he excused himself to make a beer run.

"Phil is quite a character, isn't he?" Alex said, looking over at Phil as he brought some beer from the bar.

"Yeah, he's okay. He's one of the few people I know who lets you express your own opinion without expressing his opinion in a better light," Danny said as he looked over at Ida who remained motionless.

"Here's beer for my men," Phil said in a hardy voice as he returned to the table with four glasses of beer on a small tray. "And ale for the fair maiden," he added in a joyful voice as he handed a beer to Ida.

They all sat down, toasting to the good times. Alex sat a little uneasy knowing he had to bring up a subject that might raise some suspicion, but he felt he had to. "I wonder where Nancy is? I thought she was going to be here tonight."

The words barely were out of his mouth when Phil smiled and said, "There's your answer Alex; she just walked through the back door."

Nancy Bishop was a very pretty girl with short, dark, cola-colored hair, always styled in the latest fashion. She was blessed with bright turquoise-blue eyes and a very light, smooth complexion with some scattered freckles. She had a friendly smile and a pleasant personality. When she had a conversation with anyone, she looked directly into his or her eyes. Almost everyone liked Nancy. She came from a well-to-do family. Her dad was vice president of a rather large manufacturing company. He showered his daughter with an abundance of worldly goods, and they shared a close father-daughter relationship. She possessed an air of decorum. Her wardrobe consisted of prestigious brand-name clothes. Although she dressed smartly, she was always quick to notice and compliment classmates when they dressed in something snappy.

Nancy was a cheerleader full of enthusiasm, a writer for the school newspaper, and usually played a major part in the school productions. She was very popular with the faculty and her classmates. She dated many different boys; however, there was no chemistry with anyone in particular. Her favorite person was Alex Flynn. They were close friends but for some reason didn't date each other. Although she participated in most of the high school activities, she also devoted a lot of spare time to church commitments. She went to Sunday school and sang in the choir. If she were Catholic, the convent would be her aspiration. However, being raised a Methodist, her secret dream was to become a missionary or at least work with the poor and less fortunate of the world.

Life had been good to Nancy, but she didn't take it for granted. She was sensitive toward those less fortunate, never mentioning her parents' club memberships nor the various vacations to appealing sites of the world. She told Alex that her father's favorite brother, William, was killed on Christmas day in 1944 at Bastogne, Belgium, during the Battle of the Bulge. Each Christmas her father would toast his brother with tears in his eyes as he thought of that horrible winter. He once confided in her that he was in one of the lead troops that entered the Nazi concentration camp at Dachau, Germany. Of all the terrible things he saw during the war, nothing was as frightening as what he saw at the exterminating facility. Nancy shared some of her father's trepidations about this world.

College life was a new experience for Nancy. Even though she chose a Christian college for girls, her social life was more traumatic than expected. For Nancy living in a dormitory of girls from different backgrounds and aspirations was an education in itself. She soon discovered that life in the dormitory and the exposure to different ideals opened up a whole new world—a new kind of freedom, a new independence, an environment of unchecked opinion, and a new cosmos opening up the opportunity for learning and growing. She had changed a great deal in the five months since high school.

Nancy quickly made her way over to the table. She was so excited. This was the first time she had seen everyone since graduation. She hugged everybody at the table except for Ida. She felt Ida was intruding into her territory. With a forced smile, she extended her hand and said, "Nice to meet you, Ida. How do you like the Abingtons?"

Ida responded in a cool manner. "Danny told me so much about all of you. I now get to meet you in the flesh."

They all sat down, talking profusely. Alex's eyes and attention were focused on one person now. "What would you like to drink, Nancy?"

"A bottle of Budweiser," Nancy answered as if automatic.

Alex was shocked. Did she really mean a bottle of Budweiser beer? "A bottle of Budweiser beer, Nancy?" he asked for confirmation.

Nancy looked at Alex with a large smile and said matter-of-factly, "Yes, Alex, a bottle of Budweiser beer, with a glass."

Alex sheepishly walked to the bar to retrieve the beer for Nancy, even though he was in shock. He wondered just how much college had changed Nancy. On his way back to the table, he was joined by Johnny and Melody who had just arrived.

"A bottle of Budweiser for Nancy and the company of Johnny and Melody for the rest of you," Alex said laughingly. There were greetings and the usual frolicking as they all sat down at the crowded table.

"Melody, I see you and Johnny are still together. I guess that makes your mother very happy, doesn't it?" Phil asked half-jokingly. Phil and the rest of the A-team knew the real truth.

"Phil, you need to find someone so you can be as lucky as Johnny," Melody joked.

"Yeah, Phil. When you grow a little taller, you may find out there are a lot of women out there," Johnny quickly added.

"One thing's for sure. Knowing you're not out on the prowl, I may have a better chance finding one," Phil said, not wanting to verbally duel with Johnny.

"Do your parents disapprove of your relationship with Johnny?" Ida asked.

Everyone laughed out loud, joking and snickering. Ida was a little embarrassed, not realizing the humor of her question. Johnny and Melody just quietly smiled. Johnny was thinking of something to say as they all waited for his reply.

Johnny looked at Ida and remarked quickly, "When we first started going out, her mother didn't like me. After we'd been dating a while, this acne problem I have had all my life started clearing up. Well now she thinks she knows what cured it."

They all started laughing, except for an embarrassed Melody, who said, "Now, Johnny, you don't know for sure if that's the reason."

"You're right, Melody, but your mother sure thinks it is." Over the laughter Johnny added, "And that's why she's so suspicious, and that's why she hates me now."

Sitting on the table was a pack of Lucky Strike cigarettes. Nancy picked up the pack, took one out, and lit it up. Alex's eyes opened wider. He asked Nancy, "So now you drink beer and smoke? What else has college life taught you?"

"They taught her to smoke free. Those are my smokes!" Danny yelled out.

"For heaven's sake, they're a quarter a pack," Nancy said as she lit up, taking a deep breath and inhaling the smoke. "Don't worry, I'll give you a penny for the cigarette later," she said as she exhaled.

"I remember when a pack of cancer sticks was only seventeen cents," Johnny blurted out. "That was when I started. Of course I was only in the fifth grade."

"Things certainly are going up. In some places gas is thirty cents a gallon," Phil said. "But that's on the turnpike, which is always a little higher."

"The high cost of living doesn't affect Nancy," Alex said as he glanced over at her. "She drinks bottled Budweiser at forty cents instead of draft beer at fifteen cents."

They all started to chuckle and shouting jeers at Nancy. She looked somewhat embarrassed. Smiling as she lifted her glass of beer, she said, "There's a reason for ordering bottled Budweiser. I discovered if you go into a bar and order a draft beer, the first thing they do is card you. When I walk into a bar, I go right up to the bartender, look him square in the eye, and order a bottle of Budweiser, no questions."

Phil jumped in quickly with a comment. "It's a good thing you didn't try that with Eddy; he'd take an eye out and polish it." They all broke into laughter, except Ida, who didn't get the local humor.

"Well, Nancy, college life seems to have a corrupting effect on you," Alex said in a condescending manner.

Phil chimed in, "Remember what Mae West said, 'It takes two to corrupt one.'"

"I think it has a liberating effect on me. If I were the only one here smoking and drinking, I would agree college corrupted me, but you are all smoking and drinking. Let's face it, we're not in high school anymore. We're adults, and we can make our own decisions about what our world is going to be like," Nancy said in her defense.

"To free speech," Danny yelled out, lifting his glass of beer in a toast.

They all toasted with their glasses raised high."Vive la France," Phil yelled, and the others joined in the cheering and drinking.

Ida sat back taking it all in. As an outsider she sensed the changes taking place among these close friends. Danny had told her how close they all were. They learned to ride bikes together, attended their first school dance in seventh grade together, walked to the Comerford Movie Theater on Saturday afternoons in elementary school and to the Friday night movies in junior high, and also learned to drive cars together, which led to their first steps of independence. They were closer than family. Like many families time and space had an effect on them. Add in a new environment, new friends, and the fact that they were now adults with valuable opinions different than their parents.' How would these changes affect their close relationship?

There was a sudden commotion at the front entrance, and everyone's attention was focused on who was in the doorway. Alex stood up, trying to peer over the bobbing heads. Right away he recognized it was Jerry Weaver in his wintergreen Army dress uniform with his newly earned jump wings pinned on his chest. He looked handsome, and the uniform fit like a glove. It looked like a scene from a John Wayne movie with the hero coming home from the war. Jerry, however, was not coming home from a war. He had completed basic training and was headed to infantry school to follow his dream of jump school at Fort Benning, Georgia. A crowd rushed over to congratulate him and welcome him home. Jerry was the first to go into the military service after high school. As a uniformed soldier, he was kind of a novelty.

He was of medium height and build, and being athletic in high school, Jerry made the varsity football team his last two years. He also made the varsity track team running the mile. His best time was five minutes and seventeen seconds. His father was an industrial salesman, moving to the Abingtons when Jerry entered sixth grade. He grew up looking like a soldier with his short black hair neatly trimmed. Always well groomed, Jerry kept his shoes shined and his car clean. In high school he let everyone know he was going into the Army after graduation. He once told Alex that he wanted to make the world a better place where peace and freedom would flourish. These were not idle whims to Jerry; these beliefs were at the core of his being. He lived in the shadows of those ideals. He practiced what he preached; he was an outspoken critic of racism and prejudice. He had no fear defending anyone who was weak, and he had no fear of battling any bully. He was like a white-hatted, Saturday afternoon cowboy hero.

Alex looked over at the scene, smiling just to see that Jerry was receiving a joyous reception. Jerry was a likable person with a happy-go-lucky personality. He was in his element, standing there shaking hands, laughing, and telling funny war stories. Everyone who knew him liked Jerry. His round face beamed with enthusiasm and good will. A few of the girls had crushes on him, but for the most part, he was not a hot number as far as the females at school were concerned. Throughout high school he had one girlfriend, Ruth Ann. No other girls appealed to him. He was more of a guy's guy. His personality, friendship, and keen sense of humor made him very popular. Although lighthearted, Jerry had a very serious temperament.

After a few minutes of shaking hands and telling jokes, Jerry made his way to the table of the remaining people waiting to greet him.

The group was on their feet when he arrived at their table. He made his way around shaking hands and patting shoulders. Guys didn't hug each other then. Respectfully he shook Ida's hand but kept a special greeting for Nancy at the end. He kissed her on the cheek and gave her a bear hug, lifting her off her feet and spinning her around.

They all sat down as Jerry gained his composure and pulled out his wallet. Taking out a twenty-dollar bill, he handed it to Johnny and said, "Let's have some suds. Johnny, would you mind getting us some liquid A rations?" Johnny grabbed the money and went to the bar.

"How was basic training?" Phil was first with the questions.

"It was a hoot," Jerry said quickly, then thought for a moment. "The idea is to bring you in, break you down. First off they shave your head, give you oversized uniforms, scream at you, belittle you, and demand you do disgusting jobs like cleaning grease pits, scraping floors on your hands and knees, and working ungodly hours on KP cleaning pots and pans. We were doing all this even before we learned to march. Then we started to train; we became a unit of men joined together for a purpose. Gradually they build you up to something better than you thought possible. We completed basic training in six weeks, and at the end we at least looked like soldiers. Then it was off to the next phase of training. For me it was advanced infantry school. That's where you really become a fighting soldier, firing M60 machine guns, M79 grenade launchers, and 3.5 bazookas."

"How about jump school?" Alex asked.

"What was it like to jump out of an airplane?" Nancy's perky voice rang in. "Were you afraid on your first jump?"

"I wasn't too afraid on the first jump. We went through three weeks of training, learning how everything works. We were even dropped from a 250-foot tower. So on the first jump, I knew everything would work okay. But when you jump out and the chute opens, you look down at the ground and see the ambulances parked with the big Red Cross on them. I thought if everything worked so well, why did they need so many ambulances? Well, they need them because so many people do get hurt.

"Ya know, I was more scared on the fifth jump than I was on the first. But I will say it was quite an experience. We have so much equipment on that you can't walk; you have to waddle. When the C-130 is in the air and they open the doors, the wind is screaming. It is so loud you can't hear yourself think. You stand up, the plane is pitching and swaying, the jumpmaster is yelling out commands and using hand signals. Then all of a sudden you are shuffling to the door of the aircraft. There is a tremendous, deafening sound of air turbulence, the prop blasts, and the parachute deploys. You bounce around for a few frightening seconds, then the chute opens, and you are suspended in midair. All is quiet; the only sound is the low purr of the plane going off in the distance. For a few minutes, you hang in the air;

it is the most tranquil silence I have ever felt. Then you slowly, quietly fall to earth. It's quite a rush."

"That sounds like a unique experience. It's almost worth joining up for the thrill of it all," Danny said, looking at Jerry with envy.

"The only problem for you, Danny, is they would cut your hair, and you'd have to get up rather early each morning," Phil said jokingly.

Johnny returned with a tray of beers, which included a bottle of Budweiser for Nancy. "These should keep us happy for a while." He put the tray down and handed the bottle to Nancy. "For the princess."

Jerry reached over, grabbed a glass, raised it, and yelled out a toast. "To the A-team. Whatever the physical distance we're apart, may we always be close in spirit."

They all lifted their glasses and cheered the toast. Ida stood for the toast, searching the excited faces as they gleamed at each other. She had never witnessed such intense affection among friends. They were all young and naive, choosing different paths of life. She wondered if they would remain impervious to the changes that lay ahead.

"Jerry, now that you are in the Army, how do you like it?" Nancy asked. "Is it what you thought it would be like?"

The question sparked Jerry's attention. "To tell you the truth, the training was better than I thought it would be. There are a lot of things I didn't necessarily enjoy doing, but for the most part, it was a challenging, unique experience." He thought for a moment as he took a sip of beer; all eyes were wide, waiting for him to continue. "The most fascinating part was the relationships I have had with the guys in my platoon. It was amazing how close we became in such a short time. There were so many people with all kinds of backgrounds and educations. Many of the guys were drafted, some even married with children. They complained but did their jobs."

"How did they all get along? I mean those Southern rebels and coloreds. Just because they put on a uniform, did it make that much of a difference?" Phil asked.

"I can't answer for the rest of the Army, but in our company there were racial problems. Our platoon sergeant was black, and so was the first sergeant. The rebs may not have liked it, but they didn't complain," Jerry said.

"Enough about my experiences, what have the rest of you been up to?" Jerry said, looking around for a response.

"I'm the only one working. The rest are in college," Johnny started off.

"During our first semester in college, President Kennedy was assassinated. It's been like hell ever since. What's happening to this world? It's so confusing. I don't know if I can concentrate when I go back to school," Phil said sadly.

"I was in class when he was shot," Nancy said as she put down her glass of beer. "I didn't know anything about it. I was walking across campus to lunch when some girls came running out of the Student Union building crying. One girl dropped her books but kept running. The place was wild; people were running around saying, 'Oh my God, oh my God.' I finally got someone to tell me what happened. President Kennedy had been assassinated. I just stood there not knowing what to do. I felt sick to my stomach. I made it back to the dorm and called my father. He wasn't a Kennedy man, but he was very upset. He jumped in the car and drove right down to get me.

"It was a real shocker, like when Buddy Holly was killed almost five years ago. He was my first idol. His music was our music—'Maybe Baby,' 'Peggy Sue.' He was exciting, shy, and outgoing at the same time. I had a real crush on him," Nancy said solemnly. "I remember my grandfather died a few weeks before Buddy's plane crash in Iowa. I loved my grandfather very much, and I still miss him. I cried a lot when he died, but I am ashamed to say I cried a lot more for Buddy Holly, even though I never met him. As hard as Buddy's death was to take, it was an accident. To have the president murdered is frightening. I kept thinking that if they can kill the president, none of us are safe." Nancy sat quietly, reflecting on what she just said.

"Of course I'm still in high school, so I shouldn't be in a place like this at my age," Melody said daintily, scrunching down and looking around, hoping no one noticed her. "But I remember I was in Mr. Powell's typing class. All of a sudden, there was an announcement from the principal, Mr. Graham. His voice was very serious as he said, 'Students and faculty, the news has just reported that President Kennedy was assassinated in Dallas, Texas, about noontime today. Classes are canceled. The school buses are being brought in. Those who don't ride the bus can leave when they are ready. We have set up television sets in the auditorium so those remaining can watch the coverage.' I went to the auditorium to watch the news on TV. When I saw Walter Cronkite with tears running down his face and his voice cracking as he announced the president was dead, that's when I started to cry. It was really something. Both students and teachers were sobbing. I never saw anything like it. As I was crying, I thought to myself, why is this hurting so much? I didn't even like him, and my parents said they'd never vote for him."

Johnny put his hand on Melody's shoulder and then looked over at Alex. In a voice of compassion, which was rare for Johnny, he said, "I was in my car. I had just pulled up to the stop sign on Center Street and Winola Road. I turned on the radio, and there was a news bulletin breaking, saying President Kennedy was assassinated. I just sat there; I couldn't move. I was numb, in shock. It was weird. There was dead silence, nothing moved, and for a few seconds it felt like the world stood still. That's when I thought of you, Alex. I know how much your family loved Kennedy. Your dad with those bumper stickers, 'Let's Back Jack,' and 'All the way with JFK.' I remember your house had Kennedy signs all over the front yard. I thought, it's going to be real hard on Alex and his family."

They were all quiet at the table, waiting for the purging to continue. Phil spoke next. "I was in my English Lit class when one of the professors came in. Without saying a word, he walked over to our professor and whispered something in his ear. Our professor looked startled, said something had come up and that he'd be right back. They both walked out the door. We thought something was wrong but didn't have a clue what it was. After about ten minutes, our professor came back. He said President Kennedy had been shot and wounded in Dallas, Texas. Classes were canceled, and the faculty was watching the news on TV in the student center. They would let us know of the developments. We all left the classroom and went over to the student center, but the faculty guarded the doors. Only they were allowed in to watch TV. By the time I got there, it was announced he was dead. Every few minutes someone would come out and announce another detail. After a while I went back to my dorm, packed up, and drove home. It was the longest two-hour drive of my life."

"Ida and I were in the coffee shop down in Scranton," Danny said quietly. "We had just finished a late breakfast when a city cop came in all excited. At first I thought they were giving away free doughnuts. He was rambling on to the owner, throwing his hands in the air. I then noticed the cop had tears in his eyes. The owner of the coffee shop became all disturbed, and when he went in the back to the kitchen, I could hear his loud voice speaking to his wife. He then brought the radio out from the kitchen and plugged it in. He turned up the volume so we could all hear. We still didn't know what was happening. That's when we heard the president was shot, and then a few minutes later, they announced he was dead. I sat and watched the cop and the owner standing there crying. The wife came out from the back, and all three sat down at a table weeping. When we got up to leave, the owner waved us on; they didn't even charge us for breakfast."

Ida perked up, adding, "Danny and I sat through that ordeal with neither of us saying a word. I thought, how could anyone be so mean and vicious to kill President Kennedy? I thought of his two small children who are about the same age as my nephew and niece."

"I was on a machine-gun firing range that morning," Jerry said as he picked up his beer and took a long sip. "At eleven thirty we broke for chow. After we ate we had a class lecture on the bleachers. We were all sitting and waiting for the afternoon session to begin when the drill sergeant came out to address us.

He stood for a moment looking up and asked, 'Are there any Republicans in this group?' A few guys stood up and said, 'Yes, sergeant.' The sergeant then said, 'Well, you gentlemen will be happy to know the president has been shot.' We thought it was a cruel joke. No one believed him. He then continued with his regular lecture. A little while later our company commander came out and announced training was canceled. Then we marched some eight miles back to our barracks.

"When we got back to the main base, the entire base post was standing in formation. By now the rumor had spread through the ranks that the president had been assassinated. I thought as I looked over these tens of thousands of soldiers, with millions more stationed all over the world, all sworn to protect the government, how could something like this happen?"

Jerry picked up his glass again, this time finishing the remaining beer. He then continued, "The battalion commander told us officially of the assassination. He then told us to pack up everything; we were restricted to the barracks. The entire military was on 'red alert status' until further notice. We went back to the barracks not knowing what to do. The coloreds really took the death of Kennedy very hard. There were a lot of tears and moaning; they seemed to love him. The rebels didn't say much, and they didn't shed any tears. I tried to call home, but it was impossible. Lines to the pay phones were over fifty guys deep."

"November 22 started out as a great day; it was a warm, sunny morning. I had plans for the entire weekend," Alex said and looked over at Nancy. "I even had a date for the big football game. It was going to be a party weekend, Lehigh versus Bucknell. About noon I was walking across campus on my way to check on some beer for the party that night. A friend came running from his dorm. Once he spotted me, he ran right over. He told me President Kennedy had been assassinated. I couldn't believe it! I just stood there thinking, how could something like this happen? I thought of Lincoln's assassination, but that was a hundred years ago before they had the Secret Service. I remembered reading somewhere that the president was starting to campaign for next year's election. He was going somewhere with Mrs. Kennedy, but I forgot he went to Texas.

"I went back to my dorm, grabbed some clothes and books, and hitchhiked home. A Catholic priest gave me a ride all the way to my house. The way he carried on you'd think they had killed the Pope. My family took it very hard. When I got home, my entire family was stunned, silently watching television. I have never seen my family so upset about anything. We all were glued to our chairs for days, watching every event on TV from Dallas to the White House. I even saw Ruby shoot Oswald. My family is still sulking around the house in grief."

"Johnny, would you get us another round of beers?" Jerry asked. His voice was lighter.

"Yeah, I'll get them; there's still money from the twenty you gave me earlier," Johnny said as he made his way to the bar.

"I wonder how this is going to affect us," Alex said as if thinking out loud. "I mean Johnson is now the president. Things probably won't change much."

"Things will be different. Do you think Johnson would put on his PF Flyers and run down to Birmingham, Alabama, to get Martin Luther King out of jail like Kennedy did?" Danny asked. "Kennedy was almost our generation; he was young and energetic, and the future looked bright."

"Before I came home on leave, an old drill sergeant told me the Army was expanding and drafting a lot of people. He said there must be some long-range plan for the buildup. Maybe it's Germany. Remember this summer Kennedy made his speech at the Berlin Wall, proclaiming, 'Ich bin ein Berliner'? 'I am a Berliner' is a direct challenge to the Soviets who just built the wall." Jerry paused for a moment then added, "I believe Kennedy wanted to draw a line in the sand and say no more Communists taking over countries. I think the focus is on Asia, perhaps Laos; but if I were a betting man, I would put my money on a country called South Vietnam. They are fighting a Communist guerilla force called the Vietcong. There's an ongoing, small but significant buildup of American personnel and equipment being shipped there, nearly twelve thousand advisors so far."

"I read Dr. Tom Dooley's book, *The Night They Burned the Mountain.* It was about Vietnam and the mountain people," Nancy said.

"You mean you heard the song, 'Hang Down Your Head, Tom Dooley'," Phil said without anyone laughing.

"It was a very sad book about how the Communists brutalized the people," Nancy said with added concern. "He was a navy doctor who stayed over there working with the refugees. I think he died a few years ago."

"I read the same book, Nancy," Jerry said, looking directly at her. "You should read his other book, *Deliver Us From Evil*. It's a beautiful, moving book—again about the plight of the Vietnamese."

"Do you really think they send regular Army troops to South Vietnam?" Phil broke in again with a serious voice, looking at Jerry for an answer.

"We need the troops here to enforce the law," Danny said sarcastically. "Kennedy had to send troops to Alabama to force Governor Wallace to admit black students to college. We should clean our own house before we start cleaning someone else's."

Johnny was back with more beers. He started passing them around and, in a humorous voice, he said, "I heard you talking about changes. Well, I don't care who the president is, even if he is a Democrat. Melody and I are going to tie the knot soon anyway, and that's not going to change. I just bought a new Chevy 409 four-speed. And the payments aren't going to change till it's all paid for."

"These drinks are paid for, so let's drink up. Tonight is not about world events; it's about friendship," Jerry said in a loud, cheery voice.

Glancing around, Alex could see that everyone was enjoying the evening. This was a night for good conversation and laughs. He could see from the corner of his eye that Jerry was enjoying the close companionship of being at O'Connor's. As the evening progressed, the crowd got noisier, and conversations went from talking to nearly yelling.

Ida sat drinking in the beer and the stories of this group. Danny reminisced about the times he siphoned gasoline from his father's state-owned automobile and put it in his own car. Mr. Fredrick couldn't understand why he was getting such poor mileage. Unfortunately this free gas program came to an end when Danny's lips became horribly infected. Danny and his father made a visit to Dr. Wagner's for medication. The doctor believed the infection Danny had contracted was due to lead poisoning, perhaps from gasoline. He prescribed a messy, jelly-like ointment to be applied on his lips, which restricted Danny's romantic backseat escapades for a while. It created even more problems for Danny when Mr. Fredrick ran out of gas late one night and realized just how Danny had contracted lead poisoning. The punishment that followed was swift but not effective.

Jerry started kidding Phil about his good eyes during football practice. It seemed Phil needed snow tires for his old car, but he didn't have the money for new tires. One of the football team's drills was to high-step through discarded tires. While running through the tire drill, Phil spotted some tires that would hold air and fit nicely on his car. So after football practice one night, he and Alex went to the practice field under the cover of darkness and gathered up two slightly worn snow tires for Phil's car. It was the joke of the high school that the discarded tires became so valuable to a certain team member on and off the field.

Nancy told a funny account of how shocked she was when they all attended a party at Phil Newman's house. Phil's poor, widowed mother decided to go away to visit her sister over the New Year's Eve weekend. Phil hosted a party that began about noon on New Year's Eve and lasted for three days. When Mrs.

Newman returned from her holiday, the house was a wreck. Her prized German knickknacks were broken and crudely glued together. There were stains on her Persian carpets and burn spots on the hardwood floors.

The neighbors complained to the three-man police force that Newman's home appeared to change into a teenage brothel for the weekend, with people going in and out twenty-four hours a day, drunks lying on the porch, and frolickers relieving themselves in the bushes on the sides of the home. When the police chief arrived early in the evening to evaluate the situation, Phil invited him in for a drink to discuss the problem. The chief of police enjoyed the discussion and the drinks, partying through the night. After spending the night at the beer bash, the chief had other pressing problems for the next few days.

The stories continued with humorous descriptions of past feats and debacles. Ida was amazed how unbelievably funny the stories were. She liked the story they told of late summer nights after the A&P closed; the store would leave hundreds of watermelons out front unguarded. This was when the members of the A-team were most proficient. They would drive by slowly, jump out of the moving car, gather up three or four watermelons and then race off to Dr. Stone's for a watermelon party. Watermelon parties in the cornfields were a great time. How this group didn't have any permanent damage from broken bones, or remained in school and kept out of jail was amazing. One string of connection running through the stories was the bond they all had. They didn't always agree on certain subjects, but they all seemed to laugh together.

As the night progressed, the crowd started to thin out. Jerry noticed the bar now had empty stools and said, "Let's adjourn to the bar and talk to Eddy."

They all made their way to the bar, and Ida and Nancy sat down on two barstools. Eddy was sitting directly behind the bar facing the two girls as he patiently washed glasses and dried them with a white towel. Eddy perked up to take care of his two pretty customers. With his glass eye partially closed, he stared at the girls with his good eye and asked, "Would you lovely ladies like a drink?"

Jerry, who was standing behind the girls, said, "Yes, they would like a drink, Eddy; that's why they're sitting at the bar. And so would the rest of us. So would you pour us some of your watered-down beer?"

Eddy cocked his head, looking directly at Jerry, put up his open hands like an old boxer, and started yelling with a smile, "Now wait a minute! These young ladies were here first. I will take their order first." Eddy smiled at the girls. "Now what would you like?"

"Draft beers, if you please, Mr. O'Connor. Would you join us with a drink yourself, sir?" Nancy said with a smile. "When you have time, would you kindly serve the riffraff behind me some of that watered-down beer?"

"Yes, ma'am, I'll get your drinks, and we don't water down the beer either! And yes, I will have a drop of the creature with you," Eddy said as he got up to get the beers. After all the drinks were served, Eddy sat down and poured himself a shot of PM whiskey—jokingly called Polish Moonshine. Eddy stood, lifting his whiskey, and said, "First one today." Everyone laughed. "To your health and good fortunes." He then gulped the shot down followed by a glass of beer.

Then Danny asked, "Hey, Eddy, show Ida the gold tiepin." Danny looked over at Ida and said excitedly, "You really ought to see it; it's neat."

Eddy leaned over the bar with pride to show his prized tiepin. "I was wounded in World War I. The doctors cut this out of my body and gave it to me as a souvenir. When I came home, I had it dipped in gold. Isn't it nice?" Eddy said with pride.

This was the moment Jerry was waiting for; Eddy had heard it all before and was anticipating a reaction. "Eddy, I just completed many weeks of military training. We watched air bombardments and trained with rifles, machine guns, bazookas, mortars, artillery, and even flamethrowers. Of all the weapons we trained with, including all the weapons of this century, I never heard of such a secret weapon. You are the only one I've ever heard of who was shot with a tiepin." Everyone burst out laughing.

Eddy stood silently, smiling. He was used to the carrying on. He enjoyed the young, quick-witted Turks. It was like he understood their youthful humor; it kept him in spirit. He turned to the girls. "See what I have to put up with? Now if I were fifty years younger, I would be taking you girls out to a nice place."

About this time Alex returned from the men's room. He spoke loud enough for everyone to hear. "Hey, Eddy, I was just in the men's room. I see Frances finally changed the newspaper in there. I didn't finish reading the old one. I wanted to find out if there were any survivors on the Titanic." Again laughter.

Nancy chimed in with her newly gained independent wit. "In the ladies room is a more recent newspaper. According to the headlines, it looks like President Franklin Roosevelt's going to run for a second term."

Johnny broke in, "We have to get going. I better get Melody home soon; I don't want to take any chances with her parents churning up the waters in the sea of love."

"We all know where your sea of love is located, Johnny, at Dr. Stone's. We've seen your Chevy rocking on that sea." Phil injected his humor again as everyone chuckled.

Melody blushed. Johnny put his arm around her, saying, "That's okay, honey; we have each other, and they have their beers." He then looked at Phil with a large smile on his face. "Remember, Phil, you can sip a beer all night, but you can't kiss a beer good night."

"Yeah, Phil, I've seen some of the babes you've dated," Danny jumped in. "And the beers have better-looking heads."

The bantering continued for a few minutes, back and forth, and the humorous verbal insults danced. Ida was witness to a rare and wonderful display of friendship, caring, acceptance, respect, trust, and love. This group thrived on each other's presence. She enjoyed every physical expression and every word they spoke.

Jerry lifted his glass, putting his arm around as many as possible and asked, "Is everybody going to the breakfast tomorrow?" In unison everyone yelled, "I'll be there."

Jerry walked to the bar and raised a hand in the air. "Eddy, would you pour us each a drop of the creature?" Looking at the bottles on the shelf, he requested, "A shot of Rock & Rye. I'd like to make a toast."

Eddy put seven shot glasses on the bar and slowly, meticulously poured out the shots as the A-team watched in amazement. When his ritual was complete, everyone held a shot.

Jerry stood back a few feet from the group. He was swaying a little from all the beers he drank, but he stood erect looking intensely into the faces of those he loved. "A toast, as we embark on our journey through life, may our friendship endure through time and our experiences. Let us recall where we came from and who we once were. Till we meet again here, or we meet again in the hereafter."

They all finished their drinks, and Johnny announced again his need to depart quickly. So he and Melody left.

Alex put his arm around Jerry and Nancy. It was apparent the beer and whiskey were having their effect on Alex. He stood embracing them as if he didn't want to let them go. In a surly voice, he said, "These are two of my favorite people in the world. We need to stay together no matter what."

Jerry enjoyed the attention although he was slightly embarrassed. He smiled at Alex and then at Nancy, saying, "Why didn't you two ever go out together? I know you both love each other. While I am out defending freedom in the world, I'd like to know you two are happy."

"We do love each other," Nancy said, looking first at Alex and then smiling at Jerry. "But we have a special relationship, too valuable to jeopardize on a romantic fling. And besides I think I have found my mister right, my alpha man. He's a wonderful guy. I know both of you will like him."

Alex's facial expression went from a warm smile to a forced smile. No one would even notice the difference but for one feature: his eyes. They changed from wide open to focused, as if he was trying to think of something witty to say. Perhaps it was the booze, the late hour, the joy of being together, or Nancy's announcement, but whatever the reason Alex couldn't think of anything to say.

Jerry sensed the strain, and his quick reaction clicked right in. "Tell us more about this Mr. Wonderful; where'd you meet him? How do we know he is good enough for you?" he asked in a joking voice.

Alex gained his composure, trying to give the appearance of being genuinely interested in the new love of her life. "So tell us all about this guy; if you're happy, we're happy."

"Well, I met him in college." Nancy was quite excited to tell of her first love. "His name is Rodney Williams. He's a junior, studying to be a minister, and after graduation he's off to Princeton to complete ministry school. Everybody loves him. He sings in the choir and is a member of a very popular college band. He's tall, dark, and handsome. All the girls at school adore him. As they say, he's a big man on campus. But he loves only me."

"Just how serious is this relationship?" Alex asked.

"I think he may be the man of my dreams; I think I'm in love," Nancy said as if thinking it up as she was talking. "He's everything I want in a guy. He's a lot like you guys, the salt of the earth: good, honest, caring, and fun to be with. He's going places; he has plans. We will see how things work out when I get back to school. But I can tell you one thing, I do love him."

Jerry sensed a seriousness coming about, so he decided to change the mood. "Enough of the romance talk. Let's have another drink." Jerry looked over at Eddy, yelling just loud enough for Eddy to hear. "Bartender, how about another beer?"

Ida sat quietly at the bar observing the group. She was smitten with all the guys. Although she was with Danny and liked him, she knew the others were great characters to be around. She grew up in a high-rise apartment in Chicago and had attended private girls' schools. The friendships depended on your family status, like who your father was. The environment was cool, dignified, and aloof. She had never experienced the warmth and humor of a group of friends like these. She could see herself dating any one of these guys. She sat at the bar fantasizing over which guy was the most interesting, which one would be most successful, which one would be the most fun to be with. As she was daydreaming, Tom Wilkinson walked in the side entrance.

Tom was considered the wildest of the group. He was average looking, of medium height, with dark hair. The only noticeable feature was a two-inch scar above his right eye. As a child riding his bicycle at night, he ran into the back of a farm wagon, splitting his head wide open. He was not supposed to be out that night, so he self-treated his head wound. When it healed an ugly scar remained. Tom was in one of the peripheral groups, considered a part of the B-team. He was the best known of the group because of his many antics. As a small child, he was the daredevil of the group. During the winter he would walk out on the ice, jumping up and down to see how thick it was. At age fourteen around two in the morning, he would steal his father's car and drive through the deserted countryside for a few hours at a time. The Wilkinson family was large, five boys and three girls; Tom was stuck with middle child syndrome. He was noticeably different from the rest of the family: mischievous, and curious with polite, pleasant manners that endeared him to others. Even those close to him grew frustrated with his escapades but still enjoyed his company. He tried out for various sporting activities but didn't have the natural ability or desire to make any of the teams. During his school years, he was notorious for his shenanigans outside the school grounds. Tommy was well liked, but many of his classmates kept their distance due to his reputation as a crazy character.

Tom quickly walked over to Nancy, Jerry, and Alex, injecting himself into the trio. He was late because he had to work extra hours at the gas station. He was also fixing something on his Jeep, an old 1945 Willys army surplus. It had a snowplow, which Tom used to clear driveways in the winter. The rest of the year the jeep provided the coolest set of wheels for partying. All that was needed was a case of beer in the back, and then it was off to the rough country to party where no one could interfere. High Tower power lines ran through the mountains nearby, and the service roads were rough and treacherous, but a four-wheel jeep could traverse this beautifully forested terrain. Tommy was the guide to many isolated parties in the wild.

The four stepped to the bar for another beer. Tom ordered this time. "Eddy, could we get a beer before the price goes up?"

"Now wait a minute, I have other customers," Eddy chuckled, as he threw his hands in the air. He then poured four beers.

"I guess you like the Army, Jerry?" Tom asked as he reached for his beer.

"I do. How about you, Tom? Have you decided what you are going to do?" Jerry asked as he picked up his drink.

"The way I see it, Jerry, there are three options for me: One, work in a factory or in construction. Two, go to college. Three, join the military, considering the fact that there's a draft, and I may be drafted in a few years anyway." Tommy took a sip of his beer. Then glancing over at the others, he continued, "I don't have the grades or the money for college. I'm not making very much money working in construction, so I might be joining the military too."

Nancy piped in. "Tommy, I think you are smart enough for college. It's a shame you don't have the money or the grades for a scholarship."

Ida and Danny walked over, joining in the conversation. "Didn't your parents talk to you about preparing for college?" Ida asked.

Tommy was surprised that Ida injected her unsolicited viewpoint. Danny also noticed the surprised look on the faces of others. "Ida's from Chicago, Tommy. She grew up in a different environment than ours." Danny paused a moment, adding, "You see Ida, my parents didn't talk to me about college or much about my future. That's my responsibility. My father worked for his paycheck. Providing for the family was his responsibility. Feeding us and keeping the house clean was my mother's job. No, there was no talk about college.

Alex spoke next. "My father still talks about how tough it was during the Great Depression. There were no jobs. My grandfather lost the family farm, and he never got over it. My mother had to quit high school to work as a maid," Alex said quietly. "Then my dad went into World War II. He was gone for more than three years. Although he never talks about it, I know it still bothers him. My mother has her friends. My father has his work and a few friends. On the weekends they all get together and drink a lot. They seem to give us a lot of advice when they talk so loud among themselves. I guess they want us to hear what they are saying, so they can teach us without answering any questions. Last year my dad bought his first new car, a Buick station wagon. That was a big deal in our house. They buy us things too, the stuff they didn't have when they were kids. They think that's important, but they don't take much notice of what we do or who we really are."

"Yeah, my dad's a salesman. He's always working, so he says," Jerry said. "The only time he came to watch me in sports was when I played varsity football. He never showed up for any other sporting event. I knew what I wanted to do, and he neither suggested nor advised." He paused for a sip of beer. "I think he was upset that I joined the Army. Even though he was in the war, he didn't comment on my joining up. I remember the look of anguish on his face as we shook hands good-bye, and I went off to basic training." Jerry's voice cracked. "But he didn't say a word."

"Maybe because my father is a doctor," Ida broke in again. "He plans everything in advance. We discussed what schools I would attend. My education was laid out a long time ago. I threw them a curve ball when I decided to go to a Jesuit college in Pennsylvania."

"I'm glad you did." Danny put his arm around Ida.

Tommy took a real notice of Ida for the first time. She was pretty, smart, and well-spoken. He was impressed although she was not the type of girl who would usually attract him. There was something about her though. But she was Danny's girl, at least for now. There was a stringent code among the group, and coveting another's girlfriend was not permitted. But admiring them was okay as far as Tommy was concerned.

"I'm glad I decided to come to this get-together." Ida paused and continued, "You all seem to get along so well. It's rare to see friendships last so long."

"We have our differences, don't we?" Alex said, looking at Danny and Jerry. "Our little group is a band of individuals. We don't all see the same solutions to the same problems. In fact, sometimes we don't realize the same problems exist."

"I see the world a lot differently than I did six months ago," Danny said quickly. "I came from a hardworking family; we all went to church on Sunday and prayed. My dad didn't talk much about the world, and Mom said less. On my first day in college, the history professor started out by saying, 'I'm an atheist and believe in a Communist form of government.' He stood there in front of the class, the most educated man I'd ever met and I imagine the smartest too. He shocked me into reality. Everything I was raised to believe flew out the window. He lectured about a new world, new freedom, a philosophical approach to life that emphasizes love, peace, respect for the planet, and respect for each other."

"I believe in love, peace, and freedom, Danny," Jerry said as he went back to his beer. "But I don't believe they come about by sitting around listening to folk music and staring at a lava lamp. I believe in what President Kennedy said: 'Let every nation know, whether it wishes us well or ill, that we shall pay any price, bear any burden, meet any hardship, support any friend, oppose any foe, to assure the survival and the success of liberty.' To me this means helping to spread freedom throughout the world in a uniform, not with a guitar."

Danny became vehement. "I believe in the Peace Corps, Jerry; you believe in the Marines. I believe peace is the way to resolve differences. I believe in a new world of freedom, honesty, and justice, where a man isn't judged by the color of his skin. I am looking forward to a truth that seeks inner vision and peace."

"I've heard it all before, Danny. Don't trust anyone over thirty! If it feels good, do it!" Jerry said loudly. "You're seeking the truth by following your current guru, Bob Dylan, and his latest big hit, 'Blowin' in the Wind.' Yeah, he's so truthful he doesn't even tell us his real name, which is Robert Zimmerman. He's a young Jewish boy from Minnesota."

"Now now, guys, take it easy," Alex interrupted. "You see, Ida, both of these guys believe in what President Kennedy said in his inaugural address, helping 'those people in huts and villages struggling to break the bonds of misery.' He also said, 'Only a few generations have been granted the role of defending freedom in its hour of maximum danger.' We want the same goals, but how we achieve them is the question."

"It's been a long day for me," Jerry said, almost yawning. "I think I'll have one more and be done. Eddy, could you run over here with a beer?"

Hearing the raised voices, Nancy and Phil moved up the bar. "What's going on here? Looks like Cain and Abel are at it again," Nancy said in a joking manner.

"They're analyzing Kennedy's inaugural address again," Tommy replied.

"Just remember, ask not what your country can do for you, but what you can do for your country," Nancy said as she joined in.

"That's exactly what I am going to do," Jerry answered quickly.

"You're already doing that now, Jerry. You're serving the country . . . in the Army!" Phil said.

"I've decided that when I get back from leave, I'm going to volunteer for Special Forces," Jerry said calmly.

Phil seemed confused. "My uncle was in the Special Forces. He played tuba in a marching band."

"That's Special Services. They entertain the troops. Special Forces are called Green Berets. President Kennedy personally authorized only them to wear that distinctive attire. Mrs. Kennedy chose the Green Berets as pallbearers for the president. 'Liberate the oppressed' is their motto and their mission. I talked to a Sneaky Pete, as they've been called. He worked with the mountain people in Vietnam. He said working with the Montagnards was the best experience of his life. These people just want to live in peace. They got caught in a war of aggression and were brutalized by the Communists; they don't like the South Vietnamese much either. Helping these people preserve their way of life is something I want to do."

"Isn't that kind of dangerous? I hear that even advisors are being killed in Vietnam," Ida said tenuously.

"I'll be careful, but I'm really doing it for the money. In Vietnam you're paid combat pay, an extra sixty-five dollars a month," Jerry said with a chuckle.

Danny added regrettably in a sarcastic voice, "I read one general said, 'I know Vietnam is a small war, but what the hell, it's the only one we have.'"

"All right, let's not start again," Alex interjected quickly. He felt it was a good time to change the subject because he wanted to know more about the change in the lifestyle of his secret love. "So Nancy, are you still going off to the missions when you've finished college?"

Startled by the inquiry, Nancy answered thoughtfully, "I don't think so. Like Danny, college life has opened my eyes to a much larger and complicated world. I don't know what I want to do right now. I've changed, and my priorities have changed. Things that I never even thought of now seem so important. I have a lot of thinking to do before I decide what I want to be."

"Well, I haven't changed my mind; I still want to be an engineer," Alex said confidently.

"I'm going to finish this beer, even though it isn't a Budweiser," Nancy said as she picked up her glass. Then glancing at the group, she asked, "Is everyone going to the breakfast at Shadowbrook?"

They all answered affirmatively.

Alex stood erect like a priest with a chalice. He lifted his glass and waited for everyone's attention. When they were quiet, he offered his emotional toast. "To our friendship and the optimism of our youth. May it carry us through the adventures of our life to the wisdom and wealth in our healthy retirement. And may we always remain honest, caring friends!" Everyone said, "Hear, hear," as they lifted their drinks. Even Eddy joined in the toast.

Chapter Two

1963

Alex was up and dressed early, excited about the morning's adventure. His mother couldn't understand why anyone would go out for a big breakfast on this day. This Thanksgiving morning was cold, damp and dreary. It was the least appealing time of the year. Autumn was over, and this bleak time of the year was an interim before the winter season with all of its snowy activities. After autumn's brilliant colors, the early winter pause was a letdown any way you looked at it. As he drove toward Clarks Summit, Alex noticed the drab hillside, now barren of the greenery that concealed so much during the summer months. The charcoal trees were now stripped of their uniform leaves, exposing their naked limbs. Glancing about the countryside, he noticed the weathered rocks, scraggly underbrush, and decaying leaves that were visible on the dirt floor of the exposed woodland. The plush green fields of grass and hay that danced and waved in the summer breeze had faded to a pale green and stringy tan. The tall, green cornfields of summer were reduced to bleached stubs, cut so short they looked as if they were sliced by a lawn mower.

Alex always enjoyed the fall when the cozy smell of burning leaves wafted through the afternoon air. There was something special about the enthusiasm of football fans supported by the sound and fury of the high school marching band. Warm, sunny October afternoons with cool evenings and cold nights were all part of the formula for this beautiful time of the year. Witnessing nature's magnificent transformation from summer green to pumpkin orange and crimson red with a touch of purple was a wonderful gift for those who appreciated it. Only an artist of Jack Frost's stature could accomplish this annual miracle.

Alex was on his way to pick up Nancy. They had decided some time ago to attend the breakfast together. Alex was in high spirits for the morning drive. He felt content knowing he'd be alone with her. They could once again talk openly, just the two of them, like they used to. Alex knew they were more than just friends; they had a very close relationship, almost a spiritual connection. But last night at O'Connor's, Nancy showed a different side. Perhaps she was in a bad mood, or maybe it was the excitement of the evening. He hoped to learn more on their drive up to the breakfast.

At 7:30 a.m. on the dot, Alex was in front of Nancy Bishop's home. As he pulled into the driveway, she was waiting at the side door. She was striking with her black hair pulled back. Ever the model of collegiate wholesomeness, Nancy wore an open, camel-hair car coat over a maroon turtleneck sweater; short, dark green plaid kilt; matching knee socks; and shiny penny loafers. Alex had to admit that she looked sexy. His heart raced, and he couldn't keep his eyes off her.

Nancy ran out the door and jumped into the front seat. She was in a happy, bubbly mood. "So your father let you use the family wheels this morning? That means you must be in good standing," she said jokingly.

"When I told him I was taking you, he threw me the keys." Alex was also in a jovial spirit. "I had to promise to get the snow tires put on this weekend."

"We should have a lot of fun today, seeing some of our old friends and starting our own tradition," Alex said as they drove off.

"Alex, do you mind if I turn up the radio? I'm waiting to hear the Beatles' new song, 'I Want to Hold Your Hand.' It's a cool song," Nancy said and reached for the radio.

"I liked the first one, 'All My Loving,' but the Beatles are a little too far-out for me with their long hair and weird clothes. Well, I guess a lot of people like that music. I heard they're coming to America in February to be on the Ed Sullivan Show," Alex said. After thinking for a few moments, he added, "I still listen to folk music, like the Kingston Trio, the Limeliters, and Peter, Paul and Mary. Their music tells a story without a lot of yelling and jumping around."

"My taste in music has changed," Nancy commented. "I guess my life has changed a lot too. I'm glad I grew up here, but I'm happy to get out of this town. There's a big unexplored world out there, and I want to be a part of it. To have an influence in this world, you have to have passion, brains, money, or power. That's why I'm in college—to prepare myself for whatever the future may hold."

"What about the missionary work you talked about so much? Isn't that the reason you chose the girls' seminary? Have you changed your goals in life already?" Alex asked as he stared at her for an answer.

Nancy sensed the seriousness of his question. "Look at the road, Alex. We don't want an accident before we get there." She wanted to divert the questions until she felt confident enough to answer.

"Alex, we have always been honest with each other. I'll try to be honest with you now. My life is all screwed up. I'm confused about what I want to do. The reason I chose a small girls' college was because I knew I'd be lost at a big school, and honestly I was afraid of the competition at a large campus. In high school I was a big fish in a small pond. So when I went to college, I wanted to remain a big fish but in a slightly larger pond. I've had a pretty easy life growing up. Now I have freedom, but I can't escape responsibility."

She paused, staring out the window. "Do you know how hard it is for me to do my own laundry? I've already ruined half my clothes. In addition to that, some pervert exposed himself to me in the Laundromat one night. What a frightening experience that was. When I got to college I started going to the keg parties almost every weekend. Let me tell you, living in a dormitory with girls of different cultures and backgrounds is a real eye-opener. That's where I learned to smoke and drink, from those good Christian girls with Christian values of love and acceptance of their fellow man. That is as long as their skin is the same color, and they interpret the Bible the same way. Some of these girls are really characters. They walk around campus dressed in raincoats with only bras and panties underneath. A few of them wear hair curlers almost everywhere, even to class. Now my father is mad at me because I don't write to my mother enough, and he complains when I ask for money. All I want to do is get good grades and get out of school, but I have a long time to go."

"You and me both," Alex said as if in deep thought. "I don't know if I'll be able to make it through college. Money is going to be tough, and I'm not really prepared to handle the difficult classes. My study habits are terrible; I know now that I should have studied more in high school. Right now I look at college as my job. I go in every day and work hard, hoping that someday there'll be a sheepskin."

"It's not the studying or the grades I'm having problems with," Nancy said as she turned up the radio. "Oh, here's 'Moon River.' I've always loved this music. I think it's the theme from the movie, *Breakfast at Tiffany's.*"

They listened for a few minutes to the tranquility of the violins and soothing chorus. Nancy spoke in a thoughtful voice, "Alex, my whole world is upside down. Everything I believed in six months ago has changed. I still love my parents, but my feelings have changed. I'm no longer Daddy's little girl, and the world is different from what I thought. My father is successful at making money but not much else. His main concern in life is business and family. He is a materialist. My mother has few interests outside the family; I can see that my mother wasted her life as a glorified servant. At college my eyes have been opened quite a bit. And now I find myself, for the first time in my life, really in love. Ron has awakened feelings in me I didn't know existed. I know it's hard for you to understand the commitment we have to each other. It's a love that generates energy, and I believe that this love reaches out to those who would have a universal acceptance."

Alex was keenly curious about her commitment; he decided to be tactful when asking the $64,000 question. "I understand a lot has changed in the last six months. It has for me too. But I hope our friendship hasn't changed. I know you love this Ron, and college is a broadening experience. Maybe I don't have the right to ask, but just how far have you gone with him?"

"Why, Alex, you do have a dirty mind," Nancy answered quickly with a laugh. "Put your mind at ease; I'm still a virgin. Although I must tell you, we've have had some romantic trysts in the pine forest. The moonlit walks were a beautiful experience, and I must confess, there was a lot of sexual excitement. In fact, one night we got so hot that when I got back to the dorm, my skin was covered with goose bumps. I went to the dorm nurse and explained where we went. Her face turned red, and she told me not to worry; it was a natural occurrence. The girls in the dorm explained it to me later, and we laughed about it."

Neither spoke for a few moments. They just listened to the radio. The disc jockey started talking about his favorite recording artist, Roy Orbison, and his new hit, "In Dreams."

Nancy's head perked up. As if thinking out loud, she said, "I sometimes wonder if this life is all a dream, our whole existence just a dream. I've often noticed my thinking is so different than what I say. Frequently I'm dreaming and thinking at the same time. It's rather confusing. It's like trying to watch two movies at the same time. Maybe college life is driving me crazy. What do you think, Alex?"

"I don't know what to think, Nancy." He paused. "Your life has changed, let's face it, and you're growing up. Hell, we're all growing up, some quicker than others. But adulthood is not just a word; it's a way of life. The way I look at it, we're on the roads of life, and today you and I are in the same car going in one direction. On Sunday you'll be back at college and so will I, but we'll be on different roads. By Monday night each one in our little group will be traveling in different directions in life. Where these roads lead us or how the journey will be, no one knows. You and I have a wonderful relationship. Don't take this the wrong way, but I love you in an inimitable way." He caught himself being too serious. "Now that's a fifty-cent word. Inimitable. It means impossible to imitate because of uniqueness. That's the name for our relationship. I want it to remain inimitable. I want you to know that no matter how crazy you think you are or what you do, in dreams or reality, I will always want to be near you."

Nancy looked over at Alex with tears in her eyes. She put both arms around his neck, squeezed him firmly, and then kissed him on the cheek. "That's the sweetest thing anyone has ever said to me. I could just cry." She then sat back, gathering her thoughts. "I've always loved you, Alex, so much I wouldn't allow myself to jeopardize our friendship. I know you will always be there for me. Sometimes I wish I loved you differently, but I don't want to take the chance."

"I know," Alex said quietly. "Let's not get all mushy now. Just remember we're inimitable. And today we're going to have a lot of fun."

Nancy smiled but said nothing. She just sat there staring out the window as the countryside passed by.

Tom needed a ride, so Danny and Ida were happy that he joined them on the twelve-mile drive to the town of Tunkhannock where the festive event was taking place.

The three fit comfortably in the front seat of Danny's '59 Chevy, with Ida sitting between Danny and Tommy.

"How do you like Danny's car?" Tommy asked as soon as he pulled away.

"It seems very nice to me," Ida replied.

"Don't let him get it over ninety-five miles per hour," Tommy said.

"Why is that Tommy?" Ida inquired.

"Because the design of the '59 Chevy has the rear fins on the sides like little wings. Under the right conditions and high speed, the rear of the car will actually lift off the ground."

"I don't believe that, Tommy. You made that up." Danny was a little annoyed.

"I read an article about the design of the car. It said the side angle fin acts like a wing. At high speed and with the proper updraft, it can lift the rear of the car, causing an accident. That's why the state police would never purchase a '59 Chevy. They had all the other models except the '59." Tommy was resolute.

"Now where's this place we're going?" Ida asked as they drove north.

"The place is called Shadowbrook Farm," Tom interjected quickly. He always enjoyed exploring the natural beauty of the rolling hills and fishing in the local streams. He also enjoyed learning as much as he could and loved to regale his friends with stories. "It's a restaurant on the banks of a beautiful stream, where it empties into the mighty Susquehanna River. Tunkhannock is an Indian word for 'meeting of the water.' Shadowbrook was just a dairy farm at one time. The farmer started selling milk at a roadside stand back in the 1930s during the Depression. After the war he opened an ice cream parlor. In the fifties he added a restaurant and put two large fiberglass cow heads on the roof. Now they're putting in a golf course." Tommy paused, reminiscing for a moment as he stared out the car window, and then continued, "When we were kids, my parents would sometimes take our family on a Sunday afternoon drive for some of the country's best ice cream. Cherry vanilla was always my favorite. Things seemed simpler then. The ice cream cones were all we really wanted."

Ida gazed at the road ahead. "I guess you want more than ice cream cones now."

Tom sat quietly thinking, and then said, "Yeah, I do. But I don't know if it will bring me as much enjoyment as that pure white vanilla with bright red cherries. Nobody made better ice cream than Shadowbrook. Just sitting outside licking a double-dipped sugar cone and looking around that beautiful green valley with the stream running through . . . made it taste even better."

Danny piped in, "You're going to have more fun this morning than eating an ice cream cone. Just think of everyone who will be there. I'll bet a couple of your old flames will be looking for you."

"I doubt that, Danny; you were always the ladies' man. The girls used to chase after him, Ida," Tommy said in a relaxed voice. "I'll bet he's a hit on campus, isn't he, Ida?"

"He's caught me," Ida said jokingly.

"I figured he'd fit right in at college," Tommy said as he looked over at Danny. "He likes being around smart people or at least being around people that think they are smart."

"I do like being with intellectual people." Danny was getting his dander up again. "I like to discuss ideals, war, and peace. We discuss paying taxes to the government that subsidizes giant corporations, mostly to large war contractors. The draft is used to supply the military with the poor to expand our economic system in impoverished countries."

"I thought you were interested in music. It seems to me you're listening to a pied piper. You should be wary of strangers playing magic rhetoric. You don't know just where the piper may lead you children," Tommy said in a cool manner.

"Tom, you don't know what you're talking about. I'm the one in college. I am quite capable of knowing what's happening in the world. That's the problem with this world. The establishment is leading you townies like sheep." Danny was on a roll. He had his mind set; he was confident. "The freedom and peace movement is going to change this world. We will stop the war efforts of imperialists."

"You're right, I'm not in college. I know I'm not a smart as you, but I do understand a little about history, Danny," Tommy said quietly. "I read some. I've read about the meeting in Geneva, where North and South Vietnam were created. I think it was Mao who said, 'Half a loaf is better than none.' It reminds me of Korea. The Communists settle for half a loaf of the north and then try to conquer the other half. The North Vietnamese Communists got the north and are using the same playbook, but the playbook cover is changed to read civil war."

Before Danny could answer, Ida jumped in quickly. "We're going to a breakfast party, so let's not argue politics this morning."

Danny wasn't going to let it rest. He barked out quickly, "That's you, Tommy, a simple mind with a simple explanation."

Tommy was quick to raise his voice again, saying, "Just remember, Danny, you don't learn much if you only learn from one source. You're smart enough to cross-reference." He paused for two seconds and added, "Then again, maybe not."

"Please, will you stop your bickering? You're fighting like two brothers." Ida was getting frustrated. "I'm feeling as if I'm an umpire at a shouting match. Let's change the subject and enjoy ourselves! Danny, turn up the radio. I think that's Peter, Paul and Mary, singing 'Five Hundred Miles.' Listening to the mild sounding background music, she suddenly realized how strong her feelings were for both of them. This guy Tom, the townie, had something to his character she admired. She couldn't understand her sudden, strong feelings for him. Perhaps the way he handled himself on an intellectual level, arguing with Danny, or the way he carried himself. She noticed that at O'Connor's last night. It certainly was not because of his looks, although he wasn't bad to look at either. For some strange reason, she felt very comfortable with him. She was torn sitting between them, not knowing what to do. Best to be cool; what will be, will be.

"How much farther is this place?" Ida asked, partly to change the subject before they started arguing again and partly to distract her own feelings for now.

"It's over this next hill, then down around the bend, and we'll be there," Danny said as he seemed to concentrate on driving.

"Will there be many people for this breakfast binge?" Ida asked.

"Oh yeah," Tommy said as he let out a huge gasp. "You'll see more early morning drinking today than some people see in a lifetime. The crowd will be as varied as the scenery. There will be both extremes of the money spectrum: dirt-poor farmers barely making a living, and trust fund kids like the Bealons and the Chamberlains, coupon clippers who never worked a day in their lives and who have so much money that their children won't have to work either."

Danny piped in, his voice indicating he was in a lighter, cheerier mood. "There will be some interesting people, all right. Remember what we used to say, Tommy? 'The doctor's kids are lazy, and the preacher's kids are crazy.' That's the fun of it all. To see what happens after high school."

The parking lot was partly filled when the trio arrived. As they walked across the parking lot, Tommy commented, "Look at that new Corvette; I think it's a '64 Stingray Coupe with a 427 engine. I wonder who it belongs to." Danny was more interested in an old girlfriend he spotted. Betsy had dumped him a few years ago for a football player. She still looked beautiful to Danny, and Ida noticed his eyes following her as she entered the restaurant. Ida knew if Danny was a successful musician, women groupies would be part of his life. It was something else to consider in their relationship; times were changing, and you could not own another person.

The dismal weather conditions didn't deter the spirit of those attending the breakfast at Shadowbrook Farm. The early morning buffet began at eight, and the open cash bar started serving at eight fifteen.

Jerry Weaver was already at the bar dressed in civilian clothes and talking with a few older fellows. They had graduated a few years before and now were making their own way in life. Apparently Jerry was the first one of the group to arrive. Danny told Ida and Tommy that he wanted a table near the bandstand. A group called the Aztecs, a popular local band, was scheduled for the morning's entertainment. So Danny went to stake out a table while Tommy and Ida went to the bar for drinks. The restaurant filled quickly as more and more guests made their way into the large banquet area. Phil, Johnny, and Melody arrived together, and spotting Danny's table, went directly to join him.

"I can't believe how many people are here," Melody said as she looked around.

"I'm surprised at the number of teachers that are here," Danny replied.

"Yeah, most of those teachers are the ones who flunked me at one time or another," Johnny said sarcastically. "Now they'll expect me to buy them a drink. Well, they'll die of thirst before I'd buy any one of them a drink."

"They'd probably prefer dying of thirst than sharing a drink with you, Johnny," Phil said, catching him off-guard.

"I don't have to be nice to them; my mother doesn't work for the school board," Johnny replied with his quick wit.

Looking over to the bar, Phil smiled and quickly commented, "Johnny, if your mother had to be nice to everybody you offended, she would have to give out more gifts than Santa Claus."

Before more verbal battling could erupt, Alex and Nancy walked in the back door. Their entrance got everyone's attention. Standing together they looked like the perfect couple. Alex noticed the hands waving in the air and started walking toward the table. No one seemed to notice the brown package he was carrying in his right hand.

The large, round table was at capacity with chairs squeezed around it. The group was just getting comfortable when Jerry walked over with two large pitchers of beer.

They decided to drink a few beers and then gravitate toward the buffet table for scrambled eggs, fried potatoes, bacon, and Polish sausage. The table conversations were loud with lots of laughter. Johnny and Phil put on a show of witty insults, all in good fun. Most of the conversations were about the attendees—who was married to whom and who was really with whom. After a few beers and a trip to the buffet, everyone was settling in, becoming more congenial. Ida remained somewhat distant, observing the interaction. "Hide the beer; here comes Mr. Cotter," Phil said in a low voice.

Ida looked over and saw a tall, well-built, gray-haired man, in pretty good shape swaying as he strolled from the bar to Danny's table. He held a mixed drink as he ambled carefully with a determined look on his weathered face.

Winfield Cotter was the civics teacher. He taught all classes, so no one graduated without advancing through his rite of passage. He was from the old school, both literally and figuratively. He joined the school system before the evolution of modern classrooms and believed in corporal punishment. He was a powerful man with a temper; his trademark was the large ring of keys he always kept near. If he got mad at a student, he'd throw the keys at him. Fortunately no one was ever hit at a high velocity. All the students had a humorous, healthy respect for him and his keys. He was also a real teacher; being a highly decorated soldier in World War II, he taught by direction and example. He cared about his students and enjoyed telling stories of his life's experiences.

"Good morning, students," Mr. Cotter said in a slurred voice as he approached the table.

"Good morning, Mr. Cotter. Will you join us for a drink?" Phil politely asked.

Mr. Cotter looked at the pitcher of beer and said, "Beer, huh? What the hell, why not? Yeah, I'll have a beer with you." He sat at the table, finished his drink, and had Phil hand him a fresh glass of beer.

"First one today," Mr. Cotter said as he took a sip. He slowly looked around the table. "I can't believe it. It seems you were all in my class just a few days ago. From high school to adulthood, it all happens in one night; it's called graduation. For you kids it's like jumping into a pool of cold water. Now you have to swim. You have no choice, and you'll have to swim the rest of your life. And I get to see the progress some of you will make as the years go by. I hope you'll keep in touch with us back here."

Everyone at the table was dumbstruck as if they were back in school. He took another drink of his beer, again looking around the table, then out on the main floor. "You all were friends all through high school, weren't you? With the exception of the pretty, dark-haired girl, right?" He smiled, looking over at Ida. They all responded positively. "I remember when you all started eighth grade together—the girls so gawky, silly, and shy, wearing white bobby socks. And you young guys, kind of smart-asses, dressed in blue jeans with your short-sleeve shirts rolled up, thought you were a big deal to be assigned to the high school building. Everything went so fast. I tossed my set of keys a few times, taught a few classes, and then all of a sudden I was chaperoning your prom. Those same girls changed so quickly, and all of a sudden they were beautiful young ladies dressed in stunning evening gowns being escorted by young gentlemen in tuxedos. Being a witness to the transition is the part of teaching I love.

"You are all very lucky. Look around you," Mr. Cotter said as he pointed to the crowd. "I don't care where you go, what you do—college, the military, marriage, or whatever. You'll never again find the bond of intimacy and acceptance like you have with your high school friends."

Nancy was the first of the group with enough nerve to say anything. "I think we were fortunate to have great teachers like you, Mr. Cotter. Your classes were always a lot of fun, and we learned a lot too."

"You're not saying that just to get a better grade now, are you, Nancy?" Mr. Cotter jokingly asked. "It's a little too late for that."

"Your classes were a hoot, Mr. Cotter," Jerry chimed right in. "And your flying keys kept us ducking."

"Sometimes I wish my aim was a little better cause you were a sweet target, Johnny," Mr. Cotter said laughing.

They were all laughing as Mr. Cotter poured himself another beer. He glanced over at Tommy, who was standing off to the side. "Tom, you always puzzled me for some reason. I've seen a lot of kids through my years who never worked up to their potential, and you were one of them. But I suspect in your case there's more to it." Mr. Cotter took a large gulp of the beer. He glanced over at Tommy, then turned his head and stared at the beer in his hand as if he were trying to solve a problem. "There are a lot of smart people who for one reason or another never explore the potential they have, but they seem content and that's okay; that's their choice. But you, Tom, you have shown that you have an inquisitive mind. I know for a fact you enjoy using your God-given brains to acquire knowledge. You're not afraid of learning the truth, but for some reason you don't read books; that's the confusing part. To be successful, and I believe you want to be successful, you must read books. I can't understand why you don't realize it."

Tommy was embarrassed. He stood silent as the conversation spotlight was on him. All eyes were looking in his direction, but Ida's attention was the most spirited. He shuffled his feet back and forth, shifting his weight. He bent his head toward the floor, reaching up with his right hand to scratch the back of his head. "You're right, Mr. Cotter. I do enjoy learning as much as I can, and you can learn a lot even without books. I don't have the time or the desire to sit around all day and read books that are way too thick to begin with. I've gone through life so far without ever reading a book cover to cover. Now I'm not saying I'll never read a book, but I just don't see the need to do so now."

"Thank you for being honest, Tom. You've helped put some of these pieces of the puzzle together." Mr. Cotter sat for a moment, not saying a word. The old teacher took another sip of beer and sat back in his chair. "I know we're not back in school now, and you don't have to listen to an old goat like me anymore. But try to visualize this silly parable. For an inquisitive mind, reading books is akin to roots growing in the earth. In plant life the roots grow deep, growing stronger in the earth and drawing nutrients that are converted to energy to perpetuate the strength and life of the plant. In the intellectual life, the reading of books deepens one's knowledge through the experiences of others and converts this knowledge into enlightenment and understanding." He paused for a moment to sip a little more beer and continued, "For a plant to continue to develop, its root system must grow deeper, seeking more and more nutrients. For an inquisitive mind to develop, it needs to embrace knowledge through books and experiences. If the root system stops driving deeper in the earth, the plant will shrivel up and die; similarly if you don't read books, your mind shrivels up. I don't ever want to meet any one of you in the future and find you have a shriveled-up mind. Remember, your mind is the most valuable asset you have in life. Your body will grow old, round, and wrinkled. But you can keep your mind sharp, and a sharp mind is always valuable to society."

Tommy didn't say a word; he stood quietly, thinking and shaking his head as if in silent agreement. Ida didn't say a word either, nor did she take her eyes off him. She sensed that both she and Mr. Cotter shared the same intuition. There existed a rare, unique trait in Tom that set him apart, like a diamond in the rough that needed to be cultured.

"Mr. Cotter, can I get you another beer?" Phil asked to help the conversation along.

"No thank you, Phil. I wouldn't want your mother to find out you've been feeding me drinks." They all laughed. "I must get going now. Thanks for the drinks and the morning conversation, and thanks for being good kids." He got up from the table. He and Tommy smiled at each other, neither one saying a word.

"I kind of wish we'd had more teachers like old Potbelly Cotter. He is one of a kind," Phil said with admiration.

"That's because he never poked his strong finger in your breastbone or threw his keys at you. You were one of his pets, or he was afraid of your mother," Johnny said.

"Johnny, you were considered one of his pets. I remember Mr. Cotter saying he thought you should be in a cage," Phil said as everyone laughed.

"You have to admit he was a fun teacher," Alex joined in.

"I like him a lot more than the new history teacher, Mr. Katz," Jerry said in a cool voice.

"Why didn't you like Mr. Katz?" Danny asked.

"Because of the opposite reason you do like him, Danny," Jerry said quickly. "He teaches class with an attitude of intellectual superiority. I think he has contempt for our way of living. He's not a real teacher; he took the job to beat the draft. He'll teach until he's old enough so he cannot be drafted, then he'll be off to his real career of making money."

"You don't know that for sure," Danny replied.

"You're right, Danny, but I do know he is different than the other teachers. I had him in one class. I didn't like the way he taught, with his subtle sneers and condescending comments about America in World War II. I'm sure he has his own agenda of ideas for a better society, but he doesn't come out and say what he's thinking."

"Enough about our old teachers. Did you see Bean Newman over at the bar? He is arguing with Punchie Fuller," Phil said.

"I bet they're arguing about the process of nuclear cold fusion," Johnny injected with a laugh.

"If that's what they're arguing about, Johnny, I'm sure they could use your expert advice on the topic," Phil shot over for effect.

"You better watch it, Phil. I may give you some advice you won't want to hear," Johnny rebuffed with a snarl.

There was silence. No one was about to enter that verbal playground. That's when Ida's attention perked up. "Which ones are they?" Ida asked as she looked inquisitively toward the bar.

"The tall one with the loud laugh," Alex said, "is Bean Newman. He's tall and skinny, over six foot five. We called him 'Beanpole' or 'Bean' for short. He was quite a character. Everybody knows him, especially the police for some of his antics. He's hosted some wild parties in his time, and if his mother ever finds out, he'll be disowned. The other one is Bobby Fuller, known as Punchie. He was quite a high school football player and had all kinds of scholarship opportunities, but right after he graduated, he became a father and married the mother for a short time. He loved the physical competition of sports, especially the cheering crowd, so he entered the world of boxing. He's pretty good. I think he's had about ten or eleven fights, and so far he's won them all."

Alex paused for a moment and smiled as he looked over at both of them, throwing their hands in the air, laughing loudly as if they were the only people in the room. "They are both real characters, and when they're drinking firewater, there's no telling what they may do. I remember one night, after one of Bean's parties; he and I went down to Scranton half-drunk at three in the morning for breakfast. He walked into Yanks Diner as if he owned the place. He sat down and loudly ordered a quart of orange juice, a dozen scrambled eggs, a pound of bacon, and a loaf of bread, toasted. There were a lot of staring eyes at the diner, but he ate the entire order. When he finished, he got up, gave a big tip, walked out and left the place leaving a lot of gawking, curious customers."

"Hey, there's Jake the barber over at the bar," Phil said as if surprised.

"I wonder why he's here," commented Danny as he looked over. "He doesn't strike me as the partying type. I know he enjoys all the gossip and what's happening in town. He must know half the people here. He's been cutting my hair for the last couple of years."

Johnny looked at Danny, whose long hair hung over his collar. "To me, Danny, it looks like it's been a few years since you had your hair cut," Johnny interjected with one of his quick, humorous jabs.

"Well, Johnny, speaking of haircuts, it looks like it took him a few years to sculpture that flattop to match your head," Danny replied jokingly with a quick counter jab.

Phil broke in, "I remember when Jake opened his barbershop about eight years ago. I was one of his first customers. He was just moving in, and I was delivering papers for the Scranton Times. I asked if he wanted to subscribe to the paper. He said he would. So I signed him up and had my hair cut at the same time."

"To cut the hair on your big head he probably gave you an estimate first," Johnny said, laughing.

"Maybe he did, Johnny, but he told me after he cut your signature flattop, he took a picture of you and sent it to Ripley's Believe It or Not," Phil said and had everyone laughing. He then added, "And Ripley's sent it back and said they didn't believe it." There was even more laughter.

After a few minutes of laughing and joking, Alex said, "I have been going to Jake's all through high school. He's always been nice to me, and he always asked what I was doing. He seemed to be interested in what was happening." He then looked at Phil, asking, "So Phil, Jake has been cutting your hair since he opened?"

Phil was silent for a short time, thinking what to say. Everyone suddenly became interested in this delayed answer. "Well, I don't go to Jake's anymore," Phil said in a serious voice, as if there was some diabolical reason he no longer frequented this much-liked barber.

"Why is that?" Alex asked, seeking the hidden secret motive.

Phil drew in a breath, as if preparing the group for this great explanation. "Well, when I was in tenth grade, I decided I wanted a flattop. I went in and told Jake what I wanted, but he said he couldn't do it. I asked why." Phil paused as everyone intently listened for the answer. "He said, 'Because your head is too crooked.'"

Again there was loud laughter. "To see all the terrain of your head, he must have used an aerial photo shot," Johnny said in a loud voice, laughing hysterically.

"Hey, Tommy, isn't that one of your favorite teachers, Mr. Collura, over at that far table talking to that group?" Alex asked, thinking for a minute. "Remember when he brought into class old Mr. Huffmeister, the janitor? He told us how he worked at the age of eleven as a mule boy down in the mines. As a small kid, he worked ten hours a day in the mines, sometimes alone in the black pits with only a dim candlelight to show the way. And he told how the miners had to crawl on their hands and knees on rocks in the monkey veins to load the coal by hand. Man, those were tough times."

"Yeah, that's his favorite teacher all right. He's the one who grabbed old Tommy by the neck and almost punched him out," Phil said in a sarcastic voice.

Ida looked over at Tommy, concerned. "Is that true Tommy? Did that teacher really grab you by the neck?"

"Yeah, he did. He grabbed me by the neck and cocked his hand up in the air in a fist. I thought he was going to punch me right in the face," Tommy said quietly. "But I had it coming."

"What did you do?" Ida asked

"Well, Mr. Collura was my history teacher in eleventh grade," Tommy said as he picked up a beer to sip. "One day in class we were discussing the War of 1812. I was whispering something to someone across the aisle. Mr. Collura spotted me and asked me a question about the war. I didn't know what to say. So I told him I didn't know the answer, and I didn't care what happened over a hundred years ago, and I didn't care about history anyway. History had no influence on my daily life."

Tommy took another sip of beer and continued, "I just got the words out of my mouth, and a second later he was down the aisle in a rage, grabbing me just the way I described. I sat there staring up at his fist. Then he started speaking in a very determined voice, his hand shaking, his voice quivering. He said, 'I'll tell you why history is important. I had friends in foxholes in Korea who didn't know why they were there. I don't ever want one of my students waking up in a foxhole somewhere in the world not knowing why they are there. If you know your history, you'll know why you're there. That's why history is important.'"

Tommy paused again, sipping his beer. "He was all shook up about the incident. I felt kind of bad about it myself. After all, he knew more about the world than I did, so I apologized to him and the entire class the next day."

"How did he treat you after that episode?" Ida inquired.

"We talked privately," Tommy said as if thinking of the conversation. "He told me one of the reasons he went into teaching was to help his students understand the world better than he did when he was in high school. He said no one knows where we're going to be in ten years. It's important to know some history of where we came from."

"I'm really enjoying this weekend," Ida said thoughtfully. "I guess it must be nice to have a get-together each year so you all stay in close contact."

Alex answered Ida's question. "Not everyone comes to the Thanksgiving breakfast; most of the locals don't even come. I asked Jim Dougherty, who lives here, if he was coming. He said no; his friends are local, and he sees them often enough. He can't see any reason to get up early on Thanksgiving to see people he doesn't care about."

"Well, I hope our little group will be here as often as we can," Nancy said in a strong voice.

"I agree," Danny seconded.

"Me and the little woman will be here," Johnny said as he put his arm around Melody. "You can count on that."

"That all sounds good," Alex said. "But who knows for sure when we will all be here together again." He reached under the table and picked up the brown paper bag. From the bag he pulled out an exquisite, dark green leather journal. It was the size of a school textbook with gold-edged pages.

"I know not all of us will be able to be here each year, so I bought a journal for those who are here. They can write in the journal the things that are happening in their lives. Whenever someone is in for the Thanksgiving breakfast, they can read what has taken place in their absence. Then they can put in whatever they wish about their own journey through the perils of life."

"Let me take a look at this journal," Danny said as he reached for the book in Alex's hand. "What happens if I write something in it now and I become a famous musician or folk singer? It may become a collectible to my fans. I may not want certain information leaked out, if you know what I mean."

"The way you're heading, Danny, the certain information you don't want leaked out may be your whereabouts from the cops," Johnny said with a smirk.

"Johnny, we don't have to worry about what you write in the journal," Danny said as he flipped through the pages, "because no one could read that chicken scratching you call handwriting. But I would like to see what Mr. Brown would write in the journal about you. I'm sure it could be used as evidence at his trial if he ever finds out the truth about you and Mildew."

"I think having a journal for the group is a great idea," Nancy said. "I have a diary at home that I've kept since sixth grade. It's a lot of fun to open it up from time to time and read it. It brings back the memories and feelings of what I was doing when I made the entry."

"Yeah, I think it's a great idea too. We will be able to keep a written history of our little group. We'll find out who kills who, right Johnny?" Jerry Weaver said jokingly.

"Should we choose someone to keep the journal and update it, say, on a yearly basis?" Nancy asked.

"I don't think one person should be responsible for keeping the journal. If he or she is negligent or something happens to this person, then there will be no journal at all. Plus one author will put a personal viewpoint on what goes in. I think whoever is in for the breakfast once a year should have the opportunity to read it and put in whatever they want. If it's the groups' journal, it should be written by the group," Danny said, trying to persuade the others to his viewpoint.

"That sounds like a good idea to me," Alex said quietly. "We can leave it in the care of someone, but all entries would be made on Thanksgiving day by whoever is in town attending the breakfast."

"What happens if there's no more Thanksgiving breakfast?" Phil asked. "What will happen to the journal?"

"I bought the journal with the hope that this could be something we could keep for the rest of our lives," Alex said as his passion rose. "If for some reason they stop doing this annual event, let's say any three members of our group can decide how to try to keep the tradition alive. But for now, let's try updating it on Thanksgiving."

Phil Whitman raised his hand and asked, "Who will keep the journal? We want someone who will be here each year. This journal may be a treasure to us later in life. Maybe we should have a trusted outsider keep it for us. That way there will be no temptation to alter what we put in it. As in a diary, there may be powerful personal entries as time goes on. Our lives may change dramatically, and one of us may want to change or destroy some pages. If this journal belongs to the group, I think it should remain as pure as possible. Any tampering would destroy the value of something as sensitive as it may be someday."

"How about Jake the barber?" Jerry asked in an excited voice. "He has been living here for a while, and he loves the town, so he's not going anywhere. He can keep it at his shop with the understanding that the journal comes out only once a year on turkey day."

"Once a year, that's about how often Danny gets his hair cut," Phil said with a laugh.

"Yeah, once a year, Phil. That's about how often you have a date," Danny zinged back.

"Well, everybody, what do you think we should do?" Alex asked.

"This journal is your idea, Alex. I believe we should follow your suggestion. I think it would be nice if we all wrote something in it today. If Jake agrees to keep it, we'll turn it over to him when we leave. Whoever is at this event next year can add whatever they want to it. As time goes by, I hope to add some interesting pages myself," Jerry Weaver said matter-of-factly.

Everyone seemed to nod in agreement. Alex picked up the journal from the table, staring at it as if it were the sacred Bible. As he fanned through the blank pages, his eyes searched for a glimpse of the stories yet to be written. "Okay, from this date on, this will be the official journal of the A-team. We will write our names and date on the inside cover. I will write a simple bylaw stating that the journal is to be opened once a year. In the event that anything happens to the breakfast or to Jake, any three members can decide the fate of the journal. Does everyone agree?"

Everyone at the table agreed, saying "yes" and nodding their heads affirmatively. Ida sat quietly, regretting she was only a guest and not a member of the group. Suddenly out of nowhere, Tommy made a strong recommendation. "Considering our special guest this weekend, I would like to include Ida, so she too can contribute in the journal. She has already fit right in and will bring a fresh viewpoint to our group. That is if she remains in the area or returns for the Thanksgiving festivities."

Nancy was caught off-guard by such a blatant attempt to have a newcomer admitted so easily; she also resented the open reception Ida had received so far. Melody Brown was not thrilled with the idea of another female in the group either. She didn't trust women who were not a close friend or a member of her family. However, the male members seemed pleased with the proposition of Ida joining the group. After this, the entire group would no longer be together on nightly excursions but more on an annual get-together. One more attractive female would add to the enjoyment of the events.

"I don't know, you're all so very close; it may not be fair for me to be considered a member. You all grew up together; you know each other's families, all your memories are of each other. I think you're the finest group of people I've ever met and the funniest. If I were Nancy or Melody, I would probably resent a new female being added to the group. I don't want to cause any problems or dissension. It was very kind of you to offer, Tommy, but I think I should decline," Ida said sadly.

"You're right, Ida," Nancy said quickly. "I do kind of resent how easily you fit right in. But that means everyone seems to be comfortable with you, including me, and I think it would be nice to have another female in the group. Who knows what you may write in the pages. Not being from around here, your viewpoint will give us a different perspective in the journal."

"Ida, I think it would be nice to have you in the group," Melody said in a meek voice. "Just remember, Johnny belongs to me." Everyone laughed.

"Who else would have him?" Phil bellowed.

"Thank you, Nancy and Melody, that was very generous of you both. If the gentlemen don't object, I accept your invitation to be an honored member of your group and a contributor of the A-team journal."

Ida wasn't finished with her acceptance speech yet. She cleared her throat and said loudly, "As my first act as an honored member, please follow me to the bar. I will buy a round of drinks for the entire group. And I do mean drinks, not just beer but whatever you want." There was applause as they started moving toward the bar. "Dear Dr. Daddy, I need more allowance," Ida said laughingly as the group moved along.

They were all at the bar with various drinks. Melody was drinking her first whiskey sour; Johnny stayed with beer. Danny wanted to have a rusty nail; he had heard his father talking about this drink made by mixing Drambuie and Scotch. Nancy and Ida both ordered Johnny Walker Red on the rocks. Alex was shocked at what the girls were drinking and just ordered a Bacardi and Coke. Tommy and Jerry both ordered a shot of Southern Comfort with a beer chaser.

"A toast to our newest member," Tommy proclaimed loudly.

They all lifted their drinks as they yelled, "Hear, hear." While the drinking was going on, Alex made his way down the bar to talk to Jake the barber. Alex wanted to make sure Jake would be the host for their journal and would adhere to the bylaws of the journal.

John J. Masco was Jake's Christian name. He was a distinguished-looking man of medium height with the standard black Italian hair. He carried himself like a successful businessman, and spoke and dressed like a well-educated person. Jake fit right in with the assembly of partygoers. He had just finished talking to Dr. Johnson, the town's oldest dentist. He was pleased to see Alex approaching him. "Greetings, Alex. I was hoping to see you here. Are you having a good time? Can I buy you a drink?" Jake asked in a cheery voice.

"I have a drink, thank you anyway, Jake."

"Are you sure? I'm just about to order another one for myself, how about one?" Jake asked.

"Okay, Jake, a Bacardi and Coke," Alex answered reluctantly.

Jake was back in a minute with the drinks. "So Alex, how is college? I bet it's a lot harder than you thought," Jake said. "By the way, have you ever made any headway with Nancy Bishop? I know you've been interested, and she is quite a girl."

"Thanks for the drink, Jake. College is tough, but so far I can handle it. Nancy Bishop and I are and have been friends for a long time. I'm afraid that's all it's going to be, for now anyway." Alex took a sip of his rum and Coke. "Jake, I have a favor to ask of you." Alex discussed the details of keeping this sacred trust. Jake agreed to keep the journal as a distinctive responsibility. He knew most of the group, and he felt it was a unique way to serve his adopted community.

After some small talk with Jake, Alex returned to the group at the bar. Alex was pleased that everyone had received his idea so well. He wanted to make sure to have each person make an entry in the journal this special day. Who knows when or if they would all be together again.

The A-team was in high spirits with drinks in hand, talking and laughing loudly at the far end of the bar when Alex rejoined them.

"Everything is set with Jake. After our celebration this morning, I will turn the journal over to him. He promises to keep it safe and bring it to the breakfast each year." Alex paused. "The journal is over on the table. Let's make sure each one of us writes something in it this morning. It doesn't have to be much, just a little about yourself and something brief about your hopes for the future. You can go to the table by yourself and write what you want in private. Who wants to be first?"

No one said a word; they stood there with blank faces. It seemed like a solemn request to write something so profound so early in the morning when they were all under the influence of alcohol. Surely becoming serious would interrupt this festive mood and writing something heavy could cause immediate sobriety.

"Let me be the first to write in there," Johnny said as he put down his drink. "While the rest of you stand around hemming and hawing, trying to think of something smart to write, I'll tell it like it is and what I think the future holds for me and my gal. And I'm not worried if you want to read what I put in there. Because you all said you can't read my chicken scratch anyway."

After his announcement Johnny walked over to the table where the journal was located, sat down with pen in hand, and started to write.

Hello Journal,

My name is John G. Thompson. I graduated from Abington High School in June. Even though I caused a lot of trouble in high school, those were the happiest times of my life. I didn't want it to end. I would be happy back in school if I could have the same people with me. But my life has changed, and so has theirs. I have a good job working for Melody's father. I love Melody and hope soon she will be my wife.

I don't know what the future has in store for me, but I am sure it includes Melody and me being together. I hope this group remains friends, but I can see strong personalities developing that will put a strain on these relationships. It will be interesting to watch. We all like each other, but as we grow older, I see us growing more distant. I like living in Clarks Summit; it has all I want out of life. It will be a great place to raise children.

It will be interesting to see who, if any, out of our group will make a mark in the world. Some think it's getting the right job and marrying into the proper family. I believe it's hard work and knowing how to achieve the goals set. We will see how it all turns out.

John Thompson

Johnny didn't take long to complete his entry. As he finished Johnny stood up, and Melody walked over to the table. She wanted to follow right behind him and check on what he wrote. She also wanted to be alone as she made her entry. Johnny attempted to hang around, but she shooed him off, saying this was going to be her words, her way. Johnny acquiesced, complaining to himself as he walked toward the bar to join the rest of the group.

November 28, 1963

Dear Journal,

My name is Melody Brown, and I am seventeen. I live at home with my parents and one sister. Johnny and I came up to the breakfast together this morning. My parents don't know where I am. If they did I would be in big trouble. I love Johnny Thompson. I think we are going to get married sometime in the near future. Nobody knows for sure except Johnny and me. He's a good person; he's funny and hardworking. I know the future is going to be good, although seeing Jerry in a uniform sent a scare into my heart. I remember my uncle, who was in the Korean War; my mother said he was never the same when he came home. I hope nothing like that happens to Jerry. He is such a nice guy.

I love these fine friends here. I hope they will all be at our wedding. I hope my parents will be there too.

Melody Brown

Tommy was the next one to venture over to the table to record his message in the journal. He sat down, thinking about what to write. He didn't know where to start. He picked up the pen and was astonished when it started to move in his hand.

November 28, 1963

Tommy Wilkinson here; I'm nineteen years old. I am working on road construction. I feel dumb writing in the journal. But here goes. I hope the future is happy for all of us. For me, I don't have any idea where I'm going or what life has in store for me. I believe others will judge us not by what we write but on how we live our lives and what we accomplish. I suspect our successes will be highlighted and bragged about, and our failures will be kept a quiet, glossed-over secret. But the experiences are what life is all about.

I'm happy to have grown up with such a great group of friends; I hope we can all remain close. We are just beginning our adult lives; I'm sure we'll act differently and have our own separate goals in life. My goals are not set in cement. I want a better life, and I will strive to get it.

I don't know what the future holds. I know it means going into the military or going to college. Without any money I guess the Army is in my future. I'm not as gung ho as Jerry, but I don't expect to make it a career. I do have a little fear. If Vietnam does grow into something big, I do want to be there.

Let's hope everything goes well, and we all come back each year and write our success stories.

Tommy Wilkinson

Alex stood a short distance from the table, staring at the closed journal. He realized the journal would be the future-binding element of this little group. It would be a lifeline to keep them connected in a unique way. They would now record some of their treasured activities in writing instead of telling them to each other in person. On the bright side, by writing in this journal, perhaps everyone would undertake a deeper sense of purpose that was difficult to express verbally. He believed if they all wrote with an honest heart, the journal would be filled with large, cursive scribbling of exciting, happy events as well as some pages stained with tears of sadness. But more importantly he hoped they would open the window to their inner beings to share what they felt in the pits of their souls. Would this happen? This was truly an experiment in time and circumstances to see what the bond of friendship could produce over a long period of time. How long would their relationships last? What was the impact they had on each other? The pages of the journal would unveil the mystery as they went off in different directions at different speeds at various altitudes.

Sitting down slowly and reaching for the pen as if he were writing an epitaph of a close friend, Alex started his entry.

November 28 1963

On this cold morning, my name is Alex Flynn, and I'm a nineteen-year-old freshman at Stroudsburg teachers college. Nancy Bishop and I came together to the annual Thanksgiving breakfast. So far we're having a great time. I am grateful for the great friends I have. We have a little group called the A-team. In this group are Nancy Bishop, Johnny Thompson, Melody Brown, Phil Whitman, Jerry Weaver, Tommy Wilkinson, and Danny Fredrick, plus a new friend, Ida Freeman. She's a friend of Danny's; we'll see if she remains and adds to our journal.

I don't know exactly what to write on this first occasion. This journal is a neat way to keep in touch with each other. I doubt if I'll ever have the same deep-seated friends I have now. We are independent of each other, but we have a special bond that is hard to describe. Time will tell how strong that bond really is.

Jerry is a soldier now. I wonder if any others will be wearing a uniform soon. There is a lot of turmoil in the world. The Russians built the Berlin Wall. The situation in South Vietnam is bad. We need to fix the racial problems in this country. I think President Kennedy was right with federal aid to education to make the school systems better. I believe education is the key to the brightest future.

I know we will be going our separate ways from now on. I know I will make new friends, but I couldn't ask for better friends than I already have. I hope the future will be exciting for all of us, bringing us as many happy days as we have experienced so far.

As I write today, I have mixed feelings. We are together, and that makes me happy. It's knowing that we will be separating that makes me feel sad. This group has made my life worth living. I will miss being with them. I do love them all . . . Nancy, a little bit more.

Alex Flynn

"Why don't you go before me, Ida?" Danny asked, showing his concern for her to join in. He wanted Ida to be comfortable so she would contribute something in the journal.

"I don't feel right," she said as she looked around at their faces. "This is your journal, but if it's okay with everyone, I'll write about how delightful this weekend was for me," Ida added as she strolled over toward the table. "And maybe something else."

Dear Journal,

This is November 28, 1963. My name is Ida Freeman from Chicago, a partying town. I'm now attending the University of Scranton, "Tha U." This weekend I was invited by Danny Fredrick to attend a few parties and meet some new people, and to share Thanksgiving dinner with the Fredrick family. So far this has been one of the happiest times of my life. I have encountered some fabulous people, and I hope I've made some new friends. I met this group of people last night at a bar called O'Connor's; what characters they all are. This morning we are again together for a liquid breakfast at a place called Shadowbrook. It is a beautiful setting, and we're having a blast.

The future I see is rather frightening. We just lived through the Cuban missile crisis, almost going to war with the Soviet Union. The Berlin Wall is dividing a city and is the symbol of a divided Europe. This open wound in Germany could cause a European war. There's also war brewing in Vietnam. For the first time in my life, I know someone who may be shipped off to fight in a war. His name is Jerry Weaver. I just met him, and he is a great guy. My fellow classmates and I are against war. Our parents and authority in general are not listening to our voices. I know some big changes will be needed to make this world a better place. I know the youth of our nation are working to get ready for a change. I am hoping to march with Dr. Martin Luther King next year. He is a great leader who is making great changes. It is an exciting time to be alive. I am studying hard in college, and I want to help make a difference in this crazy world.

I hope that this weekend will be the beginning of new and lasting friendships. I very much like the people in this little fraternity. They are sincere, kind, and witty. I enjoy being with them. They kid each other a great deal, making fun of their own individual characteristics. It's a joy to watch the interplay of verbal assaults with a loving sense of humor. The girls' school where

I came from is so different. My friends and I were members of an exclusive clique. We grew up together, we all dressed alike, talked alike, dated guys alike; there was no individualism in my circle of friends. I don't think we ever were honest with each other. We were more concerned about how we were accepted in this clique than I wanted to believe. My eyes have been opened by a group of individuals who love each other, not because they all agree on everything but because of their individual personalities. I feel closer to this group in one weekend than to all the friends I had for years in Chicago.

I am grateful for this time spent here getting to know them. I do wonder what will happen to them all. Most are in college, one is in the army, and the others are working. Who knows what will happen to any of us. They care about each other. I hope to keep in contact with this group; they are special people who have changed my life. Who knows, just maybe we'll be lifelong friends.

Ida Freeman

Ida sat for a few minutes reading over what she had just written. She was surprised and pleased at the depth of feeling she entered in the journal. She almost wished to erase those personal sentiments she exposed that were now part of the record. But for some strange reason, she felt refreshed and had a clearer understanding of her own makeup, an insight into a portion of her life she didn't know existed.

"Are you finished, Ida?" Danny's voice rang out as he walked over to the table to add in his entry. "You were only supposed to write *in* the journal! Not write a journal!" He was kidding her about the amount of time she spent writing in the journal and then taking the time to read it over.

Danny sat at the table alone. He was tempted to peek at what took Ida so long to write. But he chose not to read it. He wanted to write with a clear mind and an unbiased attitude. His words would create something worthwhile that would seem avant-garde when read years from now. Danny didn't know what he was going to write, but he knew it would be noteworthy.

Thanksgiving morning
Danny S. Fredrick

This is a special day. I am here at Shadowbrook enjoying the company of my close friends. We are here for our first Thanksgiving breakfast. Later Ida Freeman is coming to my house for our big turkey dinner. I am a freshman at the University of Scranton, majoring in history and studying music. Although I enjoy college life, I am drawn to the music world. If I could make enough money playing music, I would quit school tomorrow.

I believe music reflects the mood of the people. Our music is changing from the good times of rock and roll, dancing around the clock, to folk music that examines the deep-rooted psyche of our society. "We Shall Overcome" is the theme for ending racism and poverty. Dr. Martin Luther King is leading the Negroes for their rights. He was jailed in Birmingham, Alabama, for protesting. But he made one heck of a speech in Washington when he said, "I have a dream." That's when he sat with President Kennedy. He is making progress. President Kennedy is dead, so as students we must join in his cause. Bob Dylan is the spiritual spearhead of peace and harmony in the world. His music has already sparked the energy of our generation. He's right: "The times they are a-changin'." Just over a year ago, we almost had a nuclear war with Russia over missiles in Cuba. That war was narrowly averted. We must stop the next war by any means possible. The nonviolent student peace committee has already made a difference with the march in Washington, DC. We will not be controlled or intimidated by big government, the large military industrial complex, the oil companies, or any other authority that is hampering our freedom.

What I believe may be difficult for others, including my close friends, to understand. We are living in a new world where we have to take on the responsibility for equal rights for all people, a world without war, and a clean environment. It will take courage and dedicated people with strong resolve to ensure these changes are made. I believe we are witnessing an emergence of a strong conglomeration of young people dedicated to taking whatever means necessary to achieve these objectives.

What the future holds I can only speculate, but I'm not afraid.

Danny Fredrick 11-28-63

He put down the pen, closed the book, got right up, and walked directly to the bar to join the others.

Phil ordered another drink and then said for everyone to hear, "Me and my beer will put a few words of wisdom in the book. I imagine scholars will be studying these pearls for centuries."

"It will probably take us half that long just to understand what you wrote," Johnny said with a laugh.

Phil walked beer in hand, over to the table to complete his ritual.

11-28-1963

Phil Whitman

This is kind of uncomfortable for me, writing my private thoughts like this. Especially knowing someone else will be reading this. But here goes. I honestly think I'm an all right guy. I try to get along with everyone, with a few exceptions. I work at it, but who knows? Maybe my future will be in dealing with relationships. I really wish I had a steady girlfriend because I'm not that strong on my own. I take a lot of kidding about it although I think I hide my feelings pretty well from my friends.

I don't know what the future will bring, but I'm kind of worried about the commotion in Vietnam. Confrontations seem to be building up between the US and the Communists, and last year with the Cuban missile situation. I'm worried about my brother who recently enlisted in the Marine Corps and is now in Parris Island, South Carolina. I am very concerned about my very good friend Jerry Weaver, who just finished jump school. Those two could be right in the soup if a war breaks out. Right now I'm in college, but that's not going great either. I wish I knew exactly what I want to do with my life. Here's hoping that everybody in the A-team lives a long and happy life, and that we all get back to O'Connor's someday soon.

Phil put down the pen, grabbed his beer, and went back to the bar without saying a word.

"Who wants to be next to write their words of wisdom?" Alex asked as he glanced around, searching for the next author. He noticed Jerry Weaver at the bar, talking and laughing with Phil Newman. They seemed to be enjoying themselves. Alex didn't want to interrupt the fun Phil and Jerry were having, but Jerry heard Alex talking and looked directly at him. Alex nervously asked, "Jerry, you haven't been over to the diary table yet. Would you like to take your chances?"

"Okay, I'll write in that book if you promise not to laugh at what I write," Jerry said with a light chuckle. All eyes were on Jerry as he walked slowly across the floor. Even though he was not wearing his uniform, he moved like a soldier. He seemed so young and humane to be a warrior. What would he write? Would these be his final words? Would he leave a message to be read later with tears? Each one had his or her private thoughts as to what Jerry would leave in the journal. After all, he was different in so many ways from the rest of them, and he was living in the real adult world.

Thanksgiving Day 1963

Jerry Weaver, Private First Class, United States Army

Thanksgiving is the right day to begin this journal. I am very thankful for all I have been blessed with. I have a wonderful family that I love very much, an outstanding community to live in, with a great school system. I have been surrounded all my life with true and caring friends, a rare and valuable gift of this life. I will never forget how much they all mean to me. When I'm far away from this area I love, my heart and mind will return to State Street surrounded by these wooded green hills. I will visualize the commerce going on in the small shops, and I will hear the laughter of my dear friends. I will see their beautiful, glowing faces joking and screaming. I will again be thankful for all my memories of these happy times. I will not live in the past, but when I visit there, I will draw strength from knowing how wonderful life can be. I don't know what lies ahead for me, but I will judge it against the glorious times spent growing up here.

I have chosen the career of a soldier. Some people choose to be a fireman, some to be a teacher, a doctor, or a lawyer; each choose their profession for their own particular motive, knowing full well the advantages and disadvantages of any given career. As a soldier I consider myself a defender of freedom and our way of life. I write these words not as a trite slogan but rather as a motto to guide me. I am proud to serve our country with some of the finest people in the world. I'm proud every time I put on my uniform. I understand clearly I may be called upon to fight in combat with the possibility of being wounded or killed. I grasp the weight of such a reality. I do this, not out of pride or righteousness, but out of love for the people and places I hold so dear. I've seen other parts of the country, and I know just how lucky I am; I couldn't ask for a better town or a better set of friends. I look forward to a long and exciting career. But if the gods of war take my life, I would gladly go knowing I helped protect the way of life I had the good fortune to experience growing up. I finish these thoughts with a note of thanks to all that have made my life such a joy.

I look forward to being with you all soon. Let the party roll on!
Jerry Weaver

The crowd started thinning, but the A-team remained intact drinking and talking. It was evident they didn't want to separate, but there was a football game to attend, and this weekend was a family-oriented holiday. Although there would be other parties over the weekend, they knew other motives and forces would divide them. Phil noticed Jake the barber was still talking to someone at the far end of the large room, yet he kept glancing toward Alex, trying to catch his attention.

"Hey, Alex, I think everyone has written in the journal," Phil said solemnly, not wanting to be the one to end the party. "Do you think we should turn it over to Jake? He looks as if he wants to leave."

"Yeah, you're right, Phil," Alex replied quietly and looked over at Jake. Alex waved his hand in the air. Jake noticed and replied by waving back. He then started walking toward the group. "He's coming over now." Again Alex's voice was noticeably heavy-hearted.

When Jake arrived at the center of the group, he was met with smiling faces and warm hellos. "Jake, I think you know most of our group. But let me introduce you anyway." Alex went on to introduce each person to him.

Alex picked up the journal and held it close to his chest; it certainly was more than symbolic of how much he thought of this book. "Jake, we have a monumental request to ask of you. Will you faithfully take responsibility for keeping this valuable Thanksgiving journal in your custody?" Alex asked, sounding like a minister at a wedding.

Jake stood erect, emitting a serious image. He spoke slowly in a somber voice. "I will carefully carry out the task we discussed earlier, Alex." Jake paused, looking around at the assembled group, all eyes staring at him. "Which means I will keep this journal locked in a safe place. Once a year, at this breakfast, I will make it available to any member of this group. Your names are all on the inside cover. At the end of the party, I will retrieve the journal and return it to its secure location until the following year. The journal will not be available except on Thanksgiving. If there ceases to be a Thanksgiving party, or if anything happens to me, then any three can decide what to do with the journal."

Alex looked around, searching the faces and waiting for a comment. No one said a word. In an authoritative voice, Alex said, "Are there any questions? Is everyone in agreement on how the journal will be handled?" Again no one said a word. They all seemed to sense the magnitude of what was happening.

Alex, holding the journal in both hands, placed the book in Jake's outstretched palms. To an outsider it looked like Alex was handing over a signed treaty with pomp and ceremony.

"Jake, we put our journal in your capable hands for good keeping," Alex said with his voice cracking. "Let's pray all the entries we make will be stories of good times, exciting adventures, and successes beyond our dreams. I hope this journal will be a thread that keeps us connected."

Jake was always a man of few words. Even in the barbershop, his manner of conversation was mostly asking questions, listening, and then adding a word or two of his own. On this solemn occasion, he was no different and simply said, "I will keep the journal safe. I wish you all a very nice Thanksgiving." He then put the journal under his arm and walked away, leaving the group standing spellbound for a few seconds.

Breaking the silence a voice yelled out, "I still have some money left; how about another round of drinks?" It was Ida with a second wind.

"Only if you're buying," Johnny replied, seconding the motion.

"Johnny, that's the only way you drink," Phil shouted.

"Phil, you ought to ply the girls you met this morning with some whiskey," Johnny zapped right back. "If one gets drunk enough, maybe she'll go out with you."

"Drunk or sober they probably wouldn't go out with you, Johnny," Phil retorted quickly. "At least their parents wouldn't let them. Oops, I forgot, neither will Melody's." There was loud laughter as they moved toward the bar for the round of drinks.

Tommy strolled next to Ida with a smile on his lips and said, "You're a woman after my own heart, Ida. You're beautiful, witty, and you buy drinks. Now if you would only say the Rosary for me, you'd be an Irishman's dream girl."

"Is that what your dream girl is like, Tommy?" Ida said freely. "I'm Jewish; I don't say the Rosary."

"Well, three out of four isn't bad," Tommy replied and quickly added, "make that three out of five, you're Danny's girl."

Ida was silent, her eyes staring at the floor. She lifted her head, smiled at Tommy and said, "I could learn to say the Rosary. Who knows, I may go for a perfect score."

Tommy was caught off-guard by Ida's direct approach and her modern, cosmopolitan, unabashed form of womanhood. He was dumbfounded; he didn't know what to say or how to act and just followed his instincts, continuing directly to the bar.

Ida slapped a fifty-dollar bill on the bar and yelled with a laugh, "Drink tender, a round of beers for my friends!" They all chuckled and were somewhat surprised at the witty barroom humor Ida displayed. Everyone ordered a final drink and was still in a joyous mood, talking and laughing. Alex, Jerry, and Nancy were huddled together in the midst of the group. Their conversation seemed to be of a serious nature.

"Who knows, Jerry, maybe the next time we see you, you will be a sergeant, a lieutenant, a captain, or a general or something," Alex said with a degree of respect, looking proudly at PFC Jerry Weaver.

"I have to finish my training first, and then we'll see what happens. It will be interesting to see what unit I am assigned to and where I will be stationed," Jerry said, smiling over at Nancy. "But who knows, I might see Nancy here doing her mission work in some Third World country."

"Let's hope we're always on the same side," Nancy said without thinking.

"We'll always be on the right side, Nancy," Jerry said with a smile.

Johnny and Melody muscled in a few words. "Jerry, do a good job in the army, make the world safe for dormancy if Uncle Sam comes looking to draft me," Johnny said jokingly. "I won't have to wear a dress or hide in the hills."

"Now you take care of yourself, Jerry," Melody said in a concerned voice. "Why you joined the army I'll never understand, but you are in my prayers."

"If Uncle Sam asks me if he should draft you, Johnny, I'll tell him to take you after they draft the blind and the crippled."

"Yeah, the army wants fighters not lovers," Johnny interjected.

Melody spoke right up with a sly remark. "Johnny, you're good at both."

Phil piped in with, "Melody, if your father ever finds out about you loving Johnny, he'll be doing a lot of fighting, okay?"

"Well, we don't know if you're a good fighter, Phil." Johnny picked right up on the challenge. "But judging by your track record, we all know you're not a good lover."

"Who knows, by the time I get back in town," Jerry said looking at Johnny and Melody, "you two may be married, and Phil, you may be engaged."

"You expect to be away a long time then, Jerry?" Alex said jokingly.

Danny made his way over to join in the conversation. He seemed quite sincere in his manner and his voice as he said, "Jerry, I wish you the best of luck. We've been friends as long as I can remember. I think we both want to make this world a better place, don't you?"

"Yes, I do, Danny," Jerry said warmly. "We may disagree on how to make this world a better place, but that's what makes this country great. We have the freedom to choose the method. But deep in our hearts, yeah, I believe we both want what's good for mankind. I'll do what I can, and I'm sure you'll do what you think is right. You've always had a passion in what you believed in. I hope your music brings you all the success in the world. Who knows, maybe I'll go to one of your concerts someday. You have a wonderful musical gift; don't let it get wasted."

While Jerry was talking to Danny, Tommy maneuvered his way over to talk with Ida. He didn't know what to say, except that he felt something for her and wanted to see her again. "I hope you had a good time; I enjoyed your company. I guess after this weekend its back to Tha U for you."

"Yes, we have classes on Monday. I'm not hard to find on campus. I'm usually hanging at the student center," Ida said quietly, then asked in an evocative manner, "Will I see you again?"

Tommy thought for a moment and replied, "If they don't throw the townies out of the student center, I might stop by for a Coke and some conversation . . . that's if I can find someone to talk to.

"What topics do you like to discuss, Tommy?" Ida asked coolly.

"Love and war," Tommy replied quickly in a humorous voice. "They both evoke strong feelings. And you can justify any action depending on your own viewpoint."

"I'm sure your viewpoints would be interesting," Ida said thoughtfully.

"Yes, interesting," Tommy said and paused, looking to her side as Danny approached. "Here comes Danny. It may be interesting to talk to you again; maybe I'll stop down by Tha U."

"I'll make it interesting," Ida said quickly and then turned toward Danny. "Tommy and I were just discussing college life. He may stop down the student center and see what it's all about."

"You should, Tommy; in fact, you should be in college now," Danny said like a lecturing uncle. "You're one of the smartest guys I know. I don't know why you're so stubborn."

Tommy was embarrassed. In a mild voice, he said, "Well, Danny, there is a little problem of money. I don't know now, but we'll see what happens. Who knows, maybe someday I'll be wearing one of those funny little freshman beanies." Tommy had been accepted at a few colleges, but his family couldn't afford the tuition. He was working, trying to save enough money for college but so far with little success.

"That's the last call for morning alcohol," the bartender yelled out.

"Our final toast of the morning," Alex yelled.

The group gathered with glasses in hand, looking at Alex for direction. Nancy was whimpering and fighting back tears. Jerry was sober, not flexing a muscle, his face frozen. Johnny had his arm around Melody. Danny had his arm around Ida, and Tommy was standing next to Phil, both being stoic. Everyone was still . . . except for Ida and Tommy whose eyes kept drifting toward each other.

Alex was in the center of the group. He stood tall, head held high. With a trembling hand, he raised his glass, readying himself for the toast. His eyes were glassy but not due to alcohol; he was fighting back tears. With his free hand he wiped his eyes, and from his pocket he pulled a piece of paper. He blinked, trying to clear his sight as he glanced at the crumpled paper. His voice cracked as he read his toast.

Until we meet again . . .

May we be gallant in foresight to see where we are going,

May we learn from hindsight to see where we have been,

May we investigate insight to discover who we are,

May we be blessed with friends to share the experience of life.

They all lifted their drinks and took a large swallow. Danny pulled out his harmonica and started to play "Auld Lang Syne." Everyone began to sing, joined by the remaining patrons still hanging out at the bar. It was a special moment, one that would burn into the memories of all those singing.

Chapter Three

1969

The weather report called for a cold, rain-soaked Thanksgiving weekend. Perhaps the pep rally and bonfire would be canceled this year. It didn't matter much to Alex; he had decided to skip the high school event altogether. This year's festivities would begin with drinks at O'Connor's on Wednesday night. After all, he now had a real job, his first since graduating from college. Although his money was not flowing like a river, he had plenty of cash, more than enough to enjoy an unpretentious celebration. An evening of drinking and reminiscing seemed like a good idea, along with the opportunity to catch up on the news from the old friends who still lived in town. Alex always smiled when he thought of Eddy and the good times he and the A-team shared at his favorite bar. There were many fond memories of all the laughs, the pranks, and the stories that were part of the magic found within the walls of

O'Connor's Bar. Alex hoped he could capture a few more good memories, but he knew it all had changed.

On the Wednesday night before Thanksgiving, O'Connor's was crowded and noisy.. Alex chose to go in the front door with confidence now that he was old enough to drink legally. There were new unfamiliar faces at the bar. Alex didn't recognize many of them, but that was all right; it was still a friendly atmosphere. He walked slowly up to the far end of the bar, saying hello to a few people he knew. Eddy was in his usual spot, sitting behind the bar polishing glasses.

"Bar keep," Alex yelled out enough to startle Eddy, " I'd like to buy everyone a bottle of Colt 45 Malt Liquor."

Eddy slowly raised his head, staring with his good eye, and smiled. "Oh? So you want to buy everyone a Colt 45, do you, Mr. Moneybags?" Eddy got up and started walking to the far end of the bar, shaking his head. He smiled at a few patrons who were excited at the thought of a free bottle of Colt 45 Malt Liquor. (It's a heavy beer.)

"Well, I just don't have any Colt 45 in stock!" Eddy said as he walked down the bar. Then he added with a sarcastic, humorous jab, "But you already knew that before you ordered! If I had a real Colt 45 revolver behind this bar, I'd use it on you, Moneybags."

"If you would fire the gun as fast as you serve the drinks, I'd die of old age before you could shoot me," Alex replied jokingly.

Eddy was shaking his head, looking down the bar at another customer as he said, "I hear Johnny Carson is looking for new comedy writers. You should go out west and apply."

"Oh, I forgot, Eddy; I thought I was in a real bar," Alex said with a laugh. "All right then, just give me a draft beer . . . in a clean glass. And fill it up. Never mind all that foam at the top."

"All that chatter for one glass of beer?" Eddy said as he went to pour the beer. He looked at two disappointed young guys sitting at the bar and commented, "He always orders a round of Colt 45 knowing I won't carry that stuff. I only sell quality drinks."

"Would you like a drop of the creature, Eddy?" Alex asked, knowing the answer.

"What time is it?" Eddy asked. He glanced over at the window into the kitchen to see if anyone was looking. At times Frances still peeked from her favorite window, checking to see if Eddy was drinking any whiskey.

"It's time for a drink, Eddy. It must be midnight somewhere," Alex said.

"Maybe I'll have a little Polish Moonshine," Eddy said as he bent over to pour himself a shot of PM Whiskey.

"Eddy, have you seen any of my old friends lately? By now they must all be successful doctors, lawyers, or crooked politicians."

"Chatterbox Johnny comes in a few times a week. Now that he's married, he's an expert on marriage," Eddy said as he picked up some dirty glasses. "I'd sure hate to be his wife."

"Well now, Eddy, maybe if you listened to him and followed his advice, you could make your own marriage an experience of marital bliss," Alex said jokingly. "Just think how happy you and Frances could be. Why, you both could be throwing kisses at each other instead of ashtrays. I'm sure you could find enough happiness to sprinkle a little extra love dust over on your sweet, pleasant, lovely, little sister-in-law, Liz. Just think of it, Eddy, this place could be a barroom of love."

"Why don't you listen to Johnny yourself; maybe he'll tell you how to marry! You're old enough, but I doubt if you're smart enough. It's going to cost a lot of money to get someone to go out with you," Eddy said quickly.

"I can't get married yet, Eddy; I'm not as lucky as you. I haven't found a wealthy woman with a beautiful sister who will buy me a bar and put me in business. Then I could sneak drinks all day and hobnob with the big spenders of the town," Alex said as he drank his beer, knowing this ribbing got Eddy's gander up. "No, Eddy, I think it is more noble that I devote myself to full-time employment, making this world a better place for the little people."

"Little! That's the amount of work you're capable of doing! I know you'll never get a humped back from hard work," Eddy shot right back. "Your next day of work will be your first day of work."

"Why, Eddie, I remember in college reading a lot about working." Alex said loudly, joking.

Before Alex could say any more, Eddy cut him off. "Yeah, yeah, yeah, you and working hard. That's all you can do is read about it. On a real job you wouldn't last till the morning coffee break." Eddy stood erect, holding up his hands as instruments of verbal accent. His voice went to a higher scale. "When I first went down in the mines, we worked twelve hours a day, six days a week. It was dark when we went down and dark when we came out. The only day we saw the sun was on Sunday because the mines were closed. Now that was work," Eddy said as he finished his shot of whiskey.

"Johnny works harder than that for his father-in law," Alex said with a laugh.

"And he even works on Sunday."

"Don't tell me about how hard Johnny Thompson works; his father-in-law calls him 'Blisters'!" Eddy said loudly.

"What?" Alex asked in a puzzled manner.

"Yeah, they call him 'Blisters' because he shows up after the hard work is done," Eddy said sarcastically. They both laughed.

"If Johnny Thompson ever went down to the mines with his big mouth, he'd never come out," Eddy said with humorous emphasis.

"Speaking of hard workers, Eddy, have you seen Phil Whitman lately?" Alex asked.

"Another hard worker!" Eddy yelled. "Yes, sir, he comes in here a couple times a week. That hard worker is a schoolteacher. He works a few hours a day. I hope those kids are smarter than he is, but that won't take much."

"Who's been talking about me?" a voice rang out. It was Phil; he had just come in using the side entrance. As a noted schoolteacher in good standing, he didn't want the fine towns-people to see him enter a gin mill.

"Good afternoon, Mr. Whitman. Are you here looking for some of your students?" Alex asked with a warm smile.

"No, my students fancy a little classier place. They prefer the company of a slightly elevated social clientele," Phil said jokingly. As he walked over to greet Alex, the smile left his face and he added, "To tell you the truth, I wish I would see a student in here drinking instead of the stuff they are smoking and using now."

"Well then, what did you come in here for?" Alex asked as if he knew the answer.

"I came here for some brain food and to read the newspaper. Eddy, pour me some brain juice as I go into the men's room to read the floor," Phil said in a loud voice.

"Well, Phil, I'm glad your book learning at school hasn't changed you too much," Alex joked with a country accent. "After a day of chasing those young'uns around the classroom, you might say you deserve a drink.

"Eddy," Alex yelled, looking behind the bar to find the proprietor. "Pour this fine pillar of the community a glass of your most expensive, domestic draft beer. And for this festive occasion, a clean glass, please."

Alex waved Phil toward the bar and continued with his humor. "Nothing's too good for the educators of our young. They take their place on the stage of history, educating tomorrow's world leaders with no thought of personal gain or vanity. But for now these young brains of mush await in awe for your guidance, wisdom, and direction, which will inspire them on their journey into the brighter life, stiffened with courage to face the unknown future."

"I thought you were going to be an engineer not a half-pasted poet," Phil said, smiling, as he sat at the bar.

"Ah, Phil, where is your appreciation for the warmth and wit bestowed upon you from one of your long lost friends? One who visits so infrequently but thinks of you so often." Alex continued to speak in a higher voice, "Has your tenure as an educator got you down? I would have thought looking up the miniskirts of all those young female students would make you a very pleasant teacher, although I admit it would be quite distracting and hard on the eyes."

Phil laughed, then asked "Eddy, where's my beer?"

Eddy finished up pouring his beer and as he handed the drink to Phil, he said, "I only have two hands to work with."

"Well, if you used your hands to work with, instead of using them for talking, you'd probably pour a lot more beers," Phil jested. "Now Mr. O'Connor . . . Alex here . . . is an engineer. He studied in college all about efficiency. He could help out if you would listen to him."

"I don't need him to help me out; I don't need you to help out," Eddy said as he raised his voice and both hands, pointing them in Phil's direction. "In fact, I just may help you both out . . . the door." Eddy walked away, talking to himself about how smart everybody thought they were. He mumbled, "If they are so smart, why aren't they rich?"

Phil and Alex were quiet for a few moments as they drank their beers. They knew Eddy was a lot of fun, but like playing with a puppy, they didn't want him to bite.

"So tell me, Phil, how is life treating you? Things should be pretty good for you. You've got a job here teaching at your favorite school. You are lucky. There are not too many college grads who can find a job in this area."

"You're right, Alex, I was lucky to get a teaching job. My mother did help me. That's the only way anyone can get a job around here. You have to have a good connection to a school board, hospital, or a relative who is on the government dole. This area used to be known for anthracite coal mines. Anthracite is considered the hardest coal giving off the highest heating value. But when the economic changes came about and the mines closed, gone were many of the jobs and supporting businesses. There's no other industry here to replace all those jobs, and there's no new industry coming in. So jobs are hard to come by."

"Teaching must be fun?" Alex asked, not understanding why Phil wasn't happier.

"The kids are much different now than when we were just a few years ago," Phil said in a concerned voice. "Drugs have changed the whole makeup of the kids. They used to drink a little, party a little, keeping it low profile but having lots of fun. Nowadays they keep to themselves. There's no humor; they do drug parties and sex orgies."

"It's changed that much in a few years?" Alex seemed concerned.

"Remember in high school, Alex? There may have been maybe two girls that put out."

"Yeah, I remember, and neither one of them would go out with us," Alex said as he took a sip of his beer.

"Now it would be hard to find a virgin in the junior or senior class. And some of the girls are putting out in the eighth grade because everybody that's 'cool' is smoking the weed called marijuana. It's having an effect in and out of the classroom. That's not good," Phil said sadly as he drank his beer.

"I saw a lot of kids smoking weed in college. Not everybody but a lot of them, and some were friends, but I managed to stay away from the drug scene. The druggies were all too quiet and introverted. They didn't like to party hardy like I did. I had enough troubles with boozing without getting involved in drugs," Alex said solemnly

"Is that what has you down, Phil?" Alex asked, trying to get a feel for Phil's mood.

"Well, there is one other thing, Alex, and it's really opened my eyes to how life is." Phil took a large gulp of beer. "Remember a few years ago when I pulled Richard Garble from the creek at Little Rocky Glen?"

"I know the place you're talking about; that used to be my favorite place to swim. From the highway bridge, it was a tough walk down that rugged trail through the narrow, deep ravine.

It is a beautiful area with those large pine trees and the giant boulders with high rock ledges. Yeah, some of the ledges were over thirty feet high. I remember the roar of the white water crashing over the rocks and racing into the deep green pools of water. To think of us jumping off those ledges, we had to be crazy then," Alex said as he picked up his beer and took a sip. "But I forgot all about you pulling Rich Garble out of the water."

"It happened about four years ago." Phil took another sip of beer then put his glass on the bar. He stood for a moment, staring at the glass.

"I remember it rained most of the week. On Sunday the sky was clear, and it was a hot day, not a cloud in the sky. So a bunch of us decided to go to Rocky Glen for a dip. It was a sunny, carefree July afternoon. I had been swimming, jumping, and diving off some of the normal ledges. I noticed the water wasn't its typical clear, light-colored green; it was muddy, and you couldn't see beneath the surface. The water level was high because of all the recent rain. After a while I got tired and was sitting on the edge of the river taking a break.

"I noticed a guy on the opposite side picnicking with his young wife, and they had a small baby wrapped in a blanket. After he made his wife and baby comfortable, he climbed down to the water's edge. I casually watched as he made his way onto a rock ledge just a few feet above the water and, without hesitation, dove in. He was under the water for a short time. I noticed his heels surface first. I thought it looked strange to see his ankles floating in the swift current, then I observed the small of his back with his bright-colored bathing suit. I was confused about what I was seeing.

"Then the rest of his torso appeared, drifting in the muddy water. I was trying to understand what I was witnessing when I noticed the back of his head surface; he was floating face down. His entire body seemed immobile, being carried by the rushing river. I stood up, sensing that something was terribly wrong. I saw him raise his head out of the water, and when he did, blood was pouring down his face. I dove in and swam as fast as I could to reach him. The current was very fast because of all the rain. When I got to him, I grasped his shoulder to keep him above the surface. I struggled to keep his head above water as I tried to cling to anything, like a tree limb or a rock that would keep us from being carried downstream. On the edge there is no shoreline, only rocky ledges. We were being carried downstream very quickly. I was finally able to snatch onto a tree root. I was struggling to keep him afloat and looking around for someone to help us. I heard him moaning in pain, 'My head, my head.' I told him, 'You'll be okay; you just have a cut on your head.' That's when I glanced over and saw the top of his head. It looked as if you took an orange and punched it. He had a large T-shaped gap right though his scalp clears to the skull. I could see the crack in the skull with stuff oozing out."

"Eddy, could we have a few more beers?" Phil asked. He was in a serious mood; this was no time for kidding. He continued, "I held him in my arms in that cold, swift-flowing water. Some other people came down to help. They said we shouldn't move him, just keep him quiet in the water until the rescue people could get there. I knew it would take an hour or so for the volunteer firemen to reach us. I said we had to get him out of the water. We did the best we could. We lifted him up on a ledge and wrapped him in blankets and towels until the fire company arrived. They carefully packed him onto a stretcher. Then we had to carry him a half mile up the trail on the edge of the cliffs to the ambulance."

"I never heard the details before, Phil. That had to be tough," Alex commented quietly. "But it was a good thing you were there to save him."

Eddy arrived with the beers, setting them quietly on the bar. Phil picked up his beer, staring at it for a moment, and then looked over at Alex. "Was it a good thing, Alex? I talked to his friend John Goyna a few months after the accident. He said that had been Richard and his wife's first outing after their baby was born. The little girl was only six weeks old." Phil picked up his beer, taking a large sip.

"John went on to tell me that Richard had suffered a severe fractured skull and a broken neck and now was a quadriplegic. He had no movement below his chin. His wife has since divorced him, and he is now institutionalized for life. I wonder, Alex, was it a good thing I was there? Or would Richard have been better off to suffer the brief pain of drowning that sunny Sunday afternoon, instead of living a tormented life as a spirit in an unmovable body?"

"There must be a reason for it, Phil. I don't know what it is, but maybe someday we'll find out why," Alex said with compassion as he too picked up his beer to drink.

"Oh, there's a cosmic reason I saved him all right. I was in court this week. There's a lawsuit because a farmer named Wingate owns the land. Remember we used to have to pay to park in the field when we went swimming? Legally the farmer is liable for the injury. Thus a lawsuit resulted, and I was called as a witness."

"Was Rich there in the courtroom?" Alex asked in earnest.

"Yes, he was there," Phil said remorsefully. "Rich seemed so alone with his attorney and a few of his family members who kept their distance. It was quite a scene in that large courtroom. It looked like a TV set for *Perry Mason*. It was very sad; the widowed farmer didn't have insurance for this type of tragedy." Shaking his head, he continued, "It was a real calamity. The lawyers conducting this case were shameless. They fought like cats and dogs, yelling insults at each other; one even called the other incompetent. I thought they were going to come to blows and physically hit each other. The farmer's lawyer screamed at Rich's lawyer saying he was cold-blooded and only interested in the money. Rich's lawyer pleaded with his voice cracking and said, 'Look over at my client strapped in a wheelchair. He's a vegetable.' Both sets of lawyers were so corrupt, and I kept looking over at poor Richard sitting motionless in a wheelchair, his head propped up, hearing everything, and not being able to respond. Then at 4:00 p.m. the judge said, 'Court adjourned.'"

Phil picked up his beer, taking a big gulp. He stared at the whiskey bottles on the shelf behind the bar.

Phil continued speaking in a low, meaningful voice. "I sat there in the courtroom after the judge left and watched as an attendant slowly wheeled Richard out. I sat quietly, reflecting on the courtroom antics, and I watched as both sets of lawyers began clearing the papers on their tables. As soon as it was quiet, I heard one yell to the other:

'Tom, what time does this cocktail party start?'

'It starts at 6:30, so make sure you and Sue are on time.'

'Don't worry about us being late. It's not every day a son is admitted to the bar.'

'You know, I may want to talk to Jack about joining our firm.'

'Let's wait until the kids get married before we push him into either firm. And besides, you already have my oldest son over there now.'

"Both men walked out of the courtroom together laughing and discussing the upcoming evening festivities. And the next morning they would be back in court playing that legal charade. One of them will be wiping tears of injustice from his eyes as he pleads for mercy, and the other one will be raising his fits in moral outrage at the injustice of it all. In reality they'll perform a recital in the courtroom, without any emotional honesty or ethical commitment. For the first time in my life, I saw how corrupt our legal system is."

"I understand what you're talking about, Phil. Welcome to the adult world," said Alex as he picked up his beer, taking a long drink. "Things were easier when we didn't know as much."

"You're right, Alex. Things were easier then, but let me tell you one more depressing story. I was working as a volunteer at the Bobby Kennedy campaign when he was killed. I couldn't believe it could happen to another Kennedy. What a tragic time for that family. We were all surprised when Jackie Kennedy married Aristotle Oasis. Who could blame her? I guess she needed a strong man to help her for a while. During that time I was disillusioned; I didn't know what to do, and I even considered going into the Peace Corps. But that's all changed now."

"It sure has been a tough time," Alex said quietly. "Last year Martin Luther King was assassinated in Memphis, and all those riots followed. Half the cities in the country were in flames. I thought they were going to burn down the country."

"Did you watch the Democratic convention on TV with the antiwar demonstrations? The Chicago police had their hands full with all those students and peaceniks. They threw thousands in jail before it all ended. I remember watching as the cops punched out Dan Rather right on TV. He was in the convention hall trying to make his way up front. A security agent got in his face, knocking him down. Dan got back to his feet, and then started yelling up to Walter Cronkite, 'Did you see that, did you see that, Walter?' That was the only funny part of the whole convention," Phil said, his voice picking up as his spirit rose.

"Enough of the depressing stuff, Phil. How about some good news. Any news if anyone is coming in for Thanksgiving? Alex earnestly asked.

"I got a letter from Tommy; he might be in. You know he just got back in October from his a tour in Vietnam. He's now stationed at Fort Bragg in the 82nd Airborne. I've only seen him a couple of times when he was home on leave. He's changed a lot; he still has his odd sense of humor but is somewhat quieter now, with a wild streak that's something else."

"I guess being a teacher has its advantages, Phil," Alex said, picking up his beer as if to offer a toast. "You don't have to worry about the draft."

"Before you drink to that, Alex, just remember you're not a teacher. That means you're not draft exempt, so how do you stand with the draft board?"

"You're right, Phil. At any time now I could get a letter from my 'friends and neighbors who have chosen me.' I do have a high draft number. I don't know if I'll be drafted or not. So I will enjoy life to the fullest, and we will see what happens."

Alex heard some commotion at the front door. "Hi, Tommy. Welcome back, Tommy, when did you get back?" Tommy Wilkinson was making his way down the bar greeting different people with warm handshakes, smiling and joking like a politician running for reelection. He was wearing civilian clothes. Alex looked closely to see if he noticed any corporeal change. Sporting a short cut, military hairstyle, Tommy had gained some weight and appeared in excellent shape with a masculine image. Alex was a little disappointed that Tommy was not in uniform. After all, Tommy had just completed serving a combat tour in Vietnam. Surely he was awarded some medals and ribbons for his service. He should be proud of his experiences and achievements. Everyone should be aware of his sacrifice and his service to the country. Tommy was of this new generation of veterans. Up until a few years ago, the thought of a combat veteran conjured up an image of the potbellied old men who used to hang around the VFW (Veterans of Foreign Wars). The one feat that bonded the VFW members wasn't the horrors of war but the social enjoyment of drinking together in a private club. Tommy went to the VFW a couple of times but felt uncomfortable. He seemed too young to join a club whose members were at least twenty years his senior and who fought in a big war and won the big victory.

Tommy finally made his way to the end of the bar to join Alex and Phil. He was happy to see his old, dear friends. Embracing both of them in a big bear hug, Tommy said with a great deal of enthusiasm, "It's great to see both of you guys. I just got in tonight and was hoping we'd team up and have some fun!" He looked over the bar, smiled at Eddy and yelled, "Hey, beer tender, how about a bar?"

Eddy's gray- and black-haired little head peered up from behind the bar. In his Irish brogue with his hands pointing at Tommy, Eddy said, "Now wait a minute! I have other customers. They want service too!" Eddy paused for a moment, then quickly asked in a mild, friendly voice, "What would you like, sir?"

"Well, Eddy, I'd like steak, mashed potatoes with lots of gravy, and a green salad," Tommy said, laughing. "But if I wanted that I'd be somewhere else. So while I'm here, Eddy, let's all have a drink. And if Frances isn't looking, we will all have a drop of the creature."

Eddy went on his way to make the drinks. "Tommy, it's great to see you. It's been a long time since we toasted a few," Alex said as he looked with pride at his mature dear friend.

"We've both been educated in the last few years: you and Phil with your college degrees and me with my worldly experiences, not to mention some of the places I've been to," Tommy said as he looked down the bar for the drinks he just ordered.

"Tommy, why didn't you wear your 'war suit' tonight?" Alex asked in a disappointed voice. "I would have liked to see what you look like in your dress greens with all your combat ribbons. Now that I am a taxpayer, I want to see what I'm paying for. And I'm sure some of the young chicks here would fall all over a conquering hero."

"I doubt that, Alex," Tommy said in a somber tone. "Not unless I had a pocketful of pot. Wearing an army uniform isn't what it used to be. Most people are kind and go out of their way to be friendly. But the long-haired hippies and the intellectuals in their beads and dirty clothes with their smug sense of superiority don't take kindly to men in uniform. Nothing upsets the peaceful serenity of those sweet, kind, music-loving daydreamers like a man in a military uniform. You should see the hatred in their eyes as they curse and yell obscenities. So off base I seldom wear my war suit."

Eddy appeared with the beers and shots of whiskey. The foursome picked up their shot glasses as Tommy proposed a toast. "Through the lips, over the tongue, look out stomach, here it comes." They all swallowed the whiskey in a gulp. Phil wanted a more relevant toast. The three friends were together again, and that required a meaningful expression of appreciation.

As soon as the glasses hit the bar, Phil asked, "Eddy, could we have another shot?"

They were all quiet as Eddy poured the shots of whiskey. "Thank you, Eddy," Phil said, pushing some money toward him. "Now I'd like to make a toast: It's good to share good drinks with good friends and to Tommy in gratitude for his safe return."

They had the shot glasses to their lips when suddenly Tommy added to the toast, "To those still in the nightmare, may many return home safely." Alex noticed Tommy had tears in his eyes as he downed the drink.

Tommy, Phil, and Alex adjourned to a corner table so they could talk and drink privately. As they drank they conversed about the old times and caught up on what was happening and who was doing what to whom. After drinking a while, the stories were funny, the mood was jovial, and all three were talking and laughing loudly.

"Tommy," Alex said in a serious voice. "I don't know if you want to talk about it or not, but I'd like to hear from someone who was there. What was it like in Vietnam?"

"All right, Alex," Tommy said as he took a sip of his beer. "I can tell you what I know and some of the experiences I had. First let me explain: The unit I was in is the 173rd Airborne Brigade. We were stationed on the island of Okinawa. In October of '64, we knew we were going to Vietnam. We were the first unit issued the new M-16 rifles. We started extensive jungle conditioning, using helicopters in training operations. All of our equipment and uniforms were updated for jungle warfare. But President Johnson wouldn't make any military moves until after his presidential election. When he was safely sworn in, he issued an order to have the 173rd be the first Army combat troops committed to Vietnam. However, he put a stipulation on that commitment. We would be sent in on a TDY status or in military terms, temporary duty yonder. Our mission was to go in and secure a base camp near Bein Hoa. We were to go out on operations known as search and destroy missions. If we received heavy causalities, American troops would not be sent to the jungles of Vietnam. Because we were on temporary duty status and not really assigned to Vietnam, Johnson could merely say that our temporary mission was completed. So back to Okinawa we'd go. We did perform our duties well, sustaining low casualties. It was then decided in Washington that Americans could fight in the jungles and more troops would be sent in. Then came the big buildup of American ground forces."

"So it was because of you, Tommy, all those guys are over there now?" Phil asked jokingly.

"That's right, Phil," Tommy said as he picked up his beer and stared at it for a moment. "I remember one hot sweaty night sitting out in the boondocks; we had a landline set up to headquarters. I was on the phone pleading my case to Washington. I could hear my favorite song, 'Downtown' by Petula Clark, blaring in the background. I said, 'Look, Mr. President, we need to stay. The people are friendly, and I need the extra combat to pay off my gambling habit.'"

"Was it that much fun, Tommy?" Alex asked in a serious voice. He knew Tommy well enough to know it would jolt him into straight talk.

Tommy quickly leered over at Alex. "I'll fill you in a little. Let's have some more drinks; this may take a few minutes."

Phil moved vigorously to the bar to secure more drinks. Tommy sat gathering his thoughts. He didn't want to spill his guts, nor did he want to cheapen anything that he saw or took part in. His experiences were not the same as seen in old war movies. He wanted to be honest, explaining his feelings about serving in Vietnam. But how could he express the impact of what he witnessed? The carnage of war, the destruction caused by warring forces? Tommy searched for the words to describe the brutality of the killing, and the bravery and heroism of those suffering solders still fighting over there. How could he describe the barbaric conditions of prolonged jungle operations, moving in stifling heat and tall elephant grass with no air circulation, and always wet, plagued with insect bites and leeches? How could he explain that the heat was so unbearable that sweat would pour down his face until the salt burned his eyes? The nights without real sleep followed, causing perpetual fatigue and exhaustion. They lived in constant, heightened alertness and fear of sudden explosions, ambushes and booby traps, always waiting for a shocking surprise along with a host of other wartime perils. That was the living hell of Vietnam. It was a remote world to be understood only by those who experienced it. The sound of whirling helicopter blades embedded a unique feeling for all those who served in Vietnam. There was more he wanted to talk about, like his emotional aftermath. Tommy was reluctant to reveal his private anguish of recurring nightmares, his volatile reaction to a sudden noise like a door slamming or a popping balloon, his inability to concentrate on any subjects for a period of time. He was aware of his apparent subconscious desire of self-destruction. These emotions and more were now a part of Tommy's private world. But Tommy couldn't share the horrors. It would seem so unreal or fabricated, and he didn't want to have a reputation of telling "war stories." So he decided to talk about what they could understand.

Phil was back with two pitchers of beer. He poured the glasses full, then sat down and waited for Tommy to begin.

"What is it like in Vietnam? Well let me tell you. I think it's the hottest place in the world. For me the heat was so unbearable. I remember after being there just two days, I thought about accidently shooting myself. I looked down at my foot and thought long and hard about getting along without a big toe. At the time, if you were wounded or shot yourself by mistake, you'd be sent back to a hospital in the states. The military has changed all that now."

Tommy picked up his fresh beer, took a large sip, and continued, "The country itself is beautiful with bright, plush, emerald-green fields and mountains. It was something to see, driving down a country road you'd see the Vietnamese bent over working in the peaceful rice paddies some as large as lakes, harvesting rice as they had for centuries. It was a special feeling seeing them wearing their distinctive 'non' hats—that look a little like umbrellas—to protect them from the sun or rain. It would be a great place to visit if there was no war going on, except for the heat." Tommy paused, taking a drink of his beer.

"You might say it's a schizophrenic war because it's the craziest war ever. Pretend for a minute this is Vietnam. We're here in Bein Hoa not Clarks Summit, and all the area north of us is Vietcong territory. Twenty miles away is not Scranton but Saigon. In between is Indian country or an area controlled by the Vietcong. If you're lucky enough to get an overnight pass, just imagine going down to Scranton on any given night. And every night in Saigon is a Saturday night. All the bars are open and packed. Soldiers are everywhere, chasing beautiful, young Vietnamese women and spending lots of money on Saigon tea like it was colored water . . . and that's what it was. If you like, you can spend the evening on the roof of one of the better hotels, enjoying a few drinks and looking out over the bright lights of the city. While up there with your bar girl, you can see fireworks going off in the distance with the high-air explosion of artillery flares falling beautifully to earth. Then you can watch the 50 calibers shooting red-hot traces off on the other side of the Mekong River. A C-130 might fly by dropping flares a few miles away to light up the countryside that's under attack. Some nights the big 155-mm howitzer cannons are firing. Although they may be miles away, you can feel the booming and the rumbling impact of those big guns. After a few drinks, and if no one has tried to blow up your hotel, you might take your honey down to your room for rest and other Asian delights. The next morning you may find yourself riding in an assault helicopter twenty miles from downtown Saigon off to Indian country, War Zone D area, a Vietcong stronghold.

It's like partying in Scranton at night, and the enemy headquarters are just a few miles up the road somewhere in the fields around Tunkhannock. You might spend a day in the bush, then hop on a helicopter, and be back in the bars for cocktails at five. There's no front line or safe area, but it's one hell of a war."

Tommy sat back comfortably, looked around, and then continued, "And remember, if you're ever drinking in a bar in Saigon or anywhere in Vietnam, always sit in the back of the bar facing the front. If the VC throws a grenade in the place, they throw it from the front door. They usually can't throw it too far, so the safest place is in the rear; just hit the floor. And don't run out, because they usually have a second explosion targeted to get the gathering crowd of spectators."

"What's it like in the jungle, Tommy?" Phil asked.

Tommy knew he couldn't possibly explain what it was really like to a boonie rat. It was just too much, so he decided to explain as best he could. "Phil, let me explain it this way. Just visualize yourself as a high school senior in Debunk, Iowa. The largest building you ever saw was your high school or local hospital. Let's say you graduate in June and join the army in July. Off you go in a Greyhound bus to basic training—eight weeks of basic training, six weeks of infantry training, and then you're given orders to go to Vietnam. You're taken to an airport for your first ride on an airplane. There she is, a gigantic blue and white Pan AM 707. You've never seen anything that big before in your life; it has giant wings and it flies. You get into this fantastic flying machine for a trip to Vietnam. You have a few meals, a few drinks, and you watch a movie. I mean this plane is something else. Twenty hours later the plane lands in Vietnam. When they open the aircraft doors, the heat of Vietnam implodes into the cabin. You can hardly breathe. There is a strong, irritating smell of the Orient combined with 99 percent humidity. You grab your gear, move out of cramped rows of seats, and make you way to the exit. The beautiful, well-dressed stewardess pleasantly smiles and says welcome to Vietnam, have a nice war. See you in twelve months."

"Now you go off to war, scared to death. You are assigned to an infantry unit. That's when you learn what hell is really like. You're a new guy, resented and trembling with fear. After a short orientation and training, you're off in a helicopter on a search and destroy mission. That's when you find out there are levels of hell, and you just entered the frightening lower level.

"If you're lucky you won't get wounded, but you will see a lot who are wounded and killed—healthy, fun-loving, good-looking guys. Some will go home in body bags, some without arms or legs, many broken and disfigured. You may not remember their names, but you will never forget their faces. I remember one operation we were on; we had taken some casualties. Later on I was walking down the trail, and we passed the body of a guy I knew. He was lying on his side, his one arm extended on the ground. I noticed his wristwatch and wondered if he bought it himself or if some loved one bought it for him? I glanced down at his jungle boots covered with blood and mud, and again I thought, what was he thinking this morning as he laced them up? Did he know that in a few hours they would be cut off his dead body? I knew he was dead, but his family didn't; they were back in the world, living their everyday lifestyle, maybe at church praying for him. They wouldn't find out for a few days, and then their lives would change forever. You'll wonder why he was lying there and not you. Then you might think that you could be next to be killed or wounded. But you'll soon understand that everybody is wounded, some more physically than others. You see the terrible portrait of death. And sometimes you start to have strange feelings about death. Like I'm going to die someday anyway; it may be better than the life I'm living now. Maybe death isn't all that bad, no more fear or pain. After all, it's final, quiet, and peaceful. But you snap back to reality.

"You're forced to live in barbaric conditions you never dreamed possible just a few months before. You learn to hump through the jungle, forgetting about the future. Perhaps you give up all hope of going home. After a while you become a hardened combat veteran. It no longer feels morbid carrying a heavy body bag across a rice paddy; it becomes just another job that has to be done—even though it's someone you know that's in the bag. You'll meet the funniest and the bravest people you'll ever know. You'll see acts of bravery go unrecorded, guys volunteering to go down in tunnels, guys dragging wounded comrades through raging battlefields. You will never forget watching the bravest of the brave, the 'dustoff' evacuate choppers with the bright Red Cross on them, swooping in to pick up the wounded and dead, many times in the middle of a battle with a barrage of flying lead all over the field. You'll experience horrors, laughter, and heartbreak, but mostly horrors and heartbreaks. And you will bring those experiences home with you. You will never get over the constant sound of helicopters inserting and lifting off; gunships just above treetop level roaming the countryside searching and firing; and the constant flights of 'dustoff' choppers on their heroic lifesaving missions. Then you'll meet garrison commandos telling war stories, claiming victories, wearing underserved ribbons and medals. But there will be no victories. If you're lucky, after twelve months that beautiful stewardess, immaculately dressed, will be standing in the door of the 707 bird of freedom, for a first-class flight back to the world.

"You'll leave Vietnam by yourself and come home by yourself. Let's say you get on the freedom bird on Wednesday; by Friday night you may be back in Debunk, Iowa. You're back in your local pub relaxing and sipping on an ice-cold beer. You are not worried about a thing, just sitting there in that cool air-conditioned bar nibbling on pretzels. As you sip the beer, you think of your friends and wonder what they are doing, the friends you left behind. But in your gut you know what they are doing right this very minute: they are still there humping in the jungle, slopping on mosquito repellent, fearing the sweaty nights, and listening for alerting nighttime noise and the rotor blades of huey gunships overhead. They're just trying to make it through another day of a living hell. And you know some of them will never make it home alive. You wonder, will Jimmy White make it back home, or Sergeant Sweat, or Paul Coleman, or any of the many guys you think about? What will happen to them?

"You're sitting in a bar without a care in the world—no snipers, no bombs, no copters overhead—but this is when you start feeling guilty. You ask yourself, should I have stayed there with them until we finish it? How can you explain those crazy feelings to anyone? You feel restless, you've got to do something, and so you go for a walk."

Tommy picked up his beer, taking another drink. "Now your old friend Clyde Kadiddlehopper comes strolling up the street, not a care in the world, whistling a happy tune, and he spots you. Old Clyde is mighty happy to see you. He runs up to you and says, 'Phil, where have you been? I haven't seen you in over a year. Wait till I tell you what's happening around here. You won't believe it! We're going to get a McDonald's here next summer! And that's not all. You remember Frankie Flathead? He married Betty Big Boobs! He got him a good job down at the hardware store. And Johnny Lockjaw, well, he just bought himself a brand-new Ford pickup truck that cost almost three thousand dollars! Can you believe a pickup truck costs three thousand dollars? I can't believe it, three thousand dollars for a pickup truck! Oh yeah, Phil, how's the Army treating you? Yeah, someone said you were in Vietnam. How was it?'"

Tommy picked up his beer again, looked over at Phil and asked, "Phil, what was your question again?"

"I understand, Tommy," Phil said somewhat sheepishly. "I don't know if we're getting a McDonald's or not. And I don't desire to know the price of a pickup truck. So let's have some more drinks and have some fun."

Alex walked over, joining in. "That's the best thing I've heard all night," he said, holding up his glass as if to make one of his toasts.

"Speaking of good things, has any one heard from Nancy?" Tommy asked.

"I haven't heard from her in a long time. She just stopped writing to me," Alex said sadly.

Phil was reluctant to speak. He kept looking down at the table and then raised his head, looking at Alex for a reaction. "Nancy sent me a short note. She will be in for the weekend. Without her husband."

"Husband!" Tommy yelled, turning to Alex for confirmation. "What husband? When did this all take place?"

The expression on Alex's face was pure shock. He sat motionless for a moment. "Don't ask me. I had no idea. The last time she wrote to me she was having some trouble in school. She was unhappy, but she never mentioned anything to me. What's the story, Phil? Why didn't you say anything about it?"

"I didn't know how to tell you, Alex. I know how much you felt for her. I knew this would be a shocker. I just wanted to find the right circumstances to tell you." Phil was saddened by the turn of events; he knew the close relationship Alex and Nancy had shared. "She dropped out of college and married some guy she met in school. He had already graduated and was in law school. In fact, he has exams this week, and that's why he isn't coming in with her for Thanksgiving."

"If Danny were here, he'd be singing, 'The times… They Are A-Changin'.' I guess we are a-changin' too." Tommy spoke as if he were carrying a lot of weight on his shoulders.

"You said she's coming in for the weekend," Alex said as if he were thinking out loud. "Did she say anything about tonight? Is she coming down here tonight?" Alex was getting excited.

"She'll be here tonight," Phil said in a reassuring voice. "I spoke to her this afternoon. She is all excited about seeing whoever is here. She sounded great."

"Is she pregnant?" Tommy asked.

"No, I don't think so," Phil replied quickly. "She met this guy in college, fell in love with him, and they ran off and got married. No big wedding. Just the two of them."

"Is this the minister guy she was in love with?" Alex asked.

"No, this guy—Jim is his name—is studying to be a lawyer," Phil said.

"A lawyer, for Christ's sake!" Alex was astonished at his own language; he usually didn't curse. "I thought she was marrying a minister and going off to a mission somewhere in Africa. I hoped she'd see what the real world was like. But I didn't think she would become so mercenary to run off and marry a money-grabbing ambulance chaser."

"So who's buying the drinks?" a loud voice rang out. The three heads turned quickly to see Johnny Thompson standing by their table. No one said a word for a moment. "What did I do, interrupt a confession? Ah, you guys wouldn't know what real sins are anyway. I know you're all Catholics. Never mind, I'll buy the drinks, which should put you in deeper shock."

Johnny buying drinks put everyone in high spirits. With the drinks and the light conversation, everyone joined in shaking hands and reminiscing about good times. They all sat down, getting reacquainted with each other and telling stories of the last few years.

"It's been a long time since we all have been together," Tommy said with a light voice. "And now that you're married, Johnny, we probably won't see Melody out in public."

"In private or public, she loves me just the same!" Johnny replied quickly.

"Just when did you get married, Johnny?" Alex asked. "My wedding invitation must have been lost in the mail."

"You're invitation wasn't lost, Alex. It wasn't sent because you wouldn't have come anyway. It was going to be a Presbyterian wedding, which meant the Browns said no booze at the reception," said Johnny as he cocked his head, looking directly at Alex. He continued his harangue. "Now, Alex, would you have been there if there was no booze?"

"You're right, Johnny." Alex said in a mocking, convincing way. "How very thoughtful of you. At your own wedding, the celebration of your highest achievement in life, you put my feelings first in your heart. At this event of joining together in marital bliss with your one true love, you thought of me. You kept me in mind, what consideration of your dear friend. Your thoughtfulness helped eliminate the possibility of my discomfort at a dry wedding reception, and for me, being at a wedding without booze is like attending a funeral without a corpse." Alex raised his glass as if to make a toast. Without saying a word, he drank the glass empty.

Then all at once, she was standing there, all sure of herself, her head in the air. Roy Orbison's words were singing in Alex's mind as he fixated on Nancy, who was standing at the entrance searching for her friends. Nancy was alone, strikingly dressed in a camel-hair overcoat with a large fur collar. Her hair was long and sinuous, and she was still as beautiful as Alex remembered. She spotted them and smiled, waving vigorously; then she hurriedly her way to their table.

"Hi, everybody," Nancy said as she reached them. The four guys were on their feet. Phil hugged her first, followed by Tommy, then Johnny. Alex savored the moment; being last he felt he could hold her the tightest and the longest.

"Well now, Nancy, how is married life suiting you?" Phil asked.

Before Nancy could answer, Tommy jumped in, "I would say married life suits you fine, Nancy. You look great."

"Where's your husband, Nancy?" Johnny asked in a sarcastic voice. "Is he afraid to be seen in public with you?"

"No, Johnny, that's your wife you're thinking about," Phil said jokingly. "And who would blame her?"

"I know you're looking for a wife, Phil," Johnny said loudly. Everyone cringed as he continued, "You might find her in the library; look under the title, *Little Women*."

"I see your charm hasn't changed much in the last few years," Nancy said in a joyful tone.

Alex stood motionless, waiting but not knowing what to say. He was confused and in disarray. How could she change her life so much without letting him know? She was a very special person in his life. All of his secret desires and dreams were now shattered. Somehow, someway Alex believed Nancy and he would be together. He was willing to wait until she completed college and had her fair share of dating, but in the final analysis, she would realize that Alex was her true love. Alex still loved her, but now she shared another man's bed along with his last name. How could this be? Alex knew his love for Nancy hadn't changed, so he would have to wait and see what opportunity presented itself in the future. He knew they would be together someday.

"I understand that best wishes are in order for the bride," Alex said in a cool voice. He kissed Nancy lightly on the cheek. "And to the groom, congratulations."

Nancy and Alex stood for a moment staring at each other. Nancy was showing her deep feelings toward Alex. She knew it was wrong not informing Alex about her marriage. In the last few years, there had been many changes in her life, and it wasn't easy for her. Her daddy wasn't there to help her make all the right decisions. She felt that life goes on, and Alex would have to accept the changes. He was young with his full life ahead of him. Nancy felt a strong affection for him and believed in her heart they would always be close.

"Hello, Alex, I feel terrible not letting you know. I thought it better if I . . . Never mind. It wasn't right, I'm sorry," Nancy said with deep-felt sorrow. Then she caught herself, reached out and grasped both his hands, and added gently, "Maybe later we can get together, just the two of us, for a little talk?"

Alex was aware the rest of the group was watching closely at the interaction between Nancy and him. "Yes…Nancy. Let me kiss the bride," Alex said loud enough for all to hear as he moved over and kissed her on the cheek. He embraced her tightly, whispering in her ear, "I'd very much like to talk to you later alone."

Nancy smiled at Alex, grabbing both of his hands. She nodded her head slightly while squeezing his hands tightly. Alex knew they would meet later, and his heart started pounding intensely. Life was good again.

Nancy turned gracefully toward the group, showing her trademark warm and friendly smile, and said, "I came in for a few drinks, so let's all sit down, order some drinks, and tell each other about what's happening in our lives."

"Are you still drinking bottle Budweiser?" Phil asked as he moved to the bar for another round.

"Thanks for asking, Phil. But they don't card me anymore, so draft beer will be just fine," Nancy said, waving her hand at Phil. "Before everyone starts asking about me, I know I'm not the only one married in this group. So Johnny, it was no surprise you and Melody got married. How is married life treating you? And why isn't your bride with you tonight?"

"She's home with the chickens," Johnny said matter-of-factly. Everyone stared at Johnny in confusion after his astonishing announcement. Johnny took control of the conversation before anyone could make a comic reply. "Although Melody was raised in the country, her family never had any farm animals. Her dream was to someday have a little farm, and raise some chickens and other animals. She thought it would be neat to gather fresh eggs for breakfast. Right after we got married, we moved into a little farmhouse out near Glenburn. Before she could think of horses or cows, I went out and bought a bunch of heirloom chickens. I figured that a bunch of chickens would require her time and effort. That way we'd see just how much she loves animals, and if she would do the work, I'd buy other animals for the farm. Well, she loves those chickens. So tonight she decided to stay home and make sure there's enough heat in the barn for the young chicks. It's quite amazing that a breed of chicken lays eggs in five different colors: blue, pink, red, green, and brown."

Phil was back from the bar with a couple of pitchers of beer. He had caught the last part of Johnny's description of the chicken farm. As Phil put down the beer, he said almost laughing, "Who's getting laid in how many different colors? I knew if Johnny Thompson had anything to do with it, it would have to be strange."

"Johnny is a chicken plucker," Tommy said very fast.

"A chicken what?" Phil asked just as quickly.

"Very funny, you guys. You may think it's funny. I don't care what you think. Melody and I are having a lot of fun growing these chickens. And they are a good investment," Johnny said proudly.

"Let me see now, Johnny. You said the chickens lay colored eggs; to be a real good investment they should be laying golden eggs," Phil said laughing.

Nancy felt the topic was heating up and wanted to lighten the conversation, so she asked a direct question to Johnny. "Is Melody enjoying herself with her newfound hobby? I can just see her early in the morning choosing fresh eggs for breakfast for her man. It must be nice to fulfill a childhood dream and have a fresh meal."

They all sat silent for a moment; what Nancy said had an unexpected, profound effect on the group. "She is happy with those chickens. And the rest of life is okay too," Johnny said in a mild voice. "I'm working for her father, and he's not the smartest guy in the world. Just because I'm his son-in-law, he thinks he doesn't have to pay me much. Her grandmother owns the farmhouse, so our rent isn't too bad. We save what little money we can and put it in a pickle jar. We're saving up to buy a decent TV. We have an old black-and-white 18-incher. Soon we want to get some furniture. All we have is a bed and a few chairs."

"What do you need more furniture for, Johnny? You only need a kitchen table, a lava lamp, some psychedelic lights, and a bed," Phil said jokingly.

"You don't need to buy a big TV," Tommy said sarcastically. "I don't even watch the six o'clock evening news anymore. It's so contrived. All they broadcast are those antiwar demonstrations and what's wrong in Vietnam. Walter Cronkite with his fatherly, slanted news reports. 'And that's the way it was.' as he ended each news show."

"Tell you the truth; I don't get to watch much TV anyway. Between working for Jeff Brown during the day and taking nightly carpenter classes at Johnson Trade School, my time is pretty well taken up." Johnny paused for a moment and added, "Melody is working full time at the International Salt Company. We are trying to save up enough money to buy our own home. We want to have children; in fact, we are trying now to have a kid."

"If you have a kid, you won't be eligible for the draft. Isn't that right, John?" Tommy asked.

"You're right, Tommy. If you're married with children, you won't be drafted. I know you were over in Vietnam, and you made it back safe and sound. But I'm not sure we should be there in the first place. If I'm drafted I'll go, but I'm not going to volunteer." Johnny took a big swallow of beer. "I go to school with a kid named Bobby Morgan. He works part-time at Western Union delivering telegrams. He told me about delivering a telegram to the parents of Mark Allenwood. Remember Mark was killed in Vietnam about a year ago. Now just imagine Bobby, a nineteen-year-old kid, delivering a message like that. He knew what was in the telegram. When he rang the doorbell, the family was at the kitchen table eating supper. When Mr. Allenwood came to the door, he saw Bobby with the telegram in his hand. Mr. Allenwood started gasping for air and couldn't stop crying. Mark's mother went into hysterics; his younger brother and sister were there, and they started balling too. Neither of the parents would open the telegram, and company policy said Bobby couldn't read it to them. Bobby had to get the neighbors to come over. They took the telegram so Bobby could leave. After that incident Bobby quit his job; he couldn't take delivering telegrams like that any longer. I don't want Melody to be sitting down to dinner some night and have a Bobby young face deliver a message like that. We are just starting out in life, and we're working hard to build a future for ourselves. We're making plans. We just want a chance to be left alone to live our own lives."

"You're right, Johnny. You should be thinking about making a good life for you and Melody," Tommy said in a compassionate voice. "I came home safe and sound, and I wouldn't ask anyone to go Vietnam. If you can beat the draft, fine. There's a lot of kids in college for only one reason: a student deferment. So good luck; it doesn't bother me if you're not drafted, but just don't join the protesters."

"Let's not mention the draft too loud," Alex said jokingly. "I've been out of college for almost a year. They haven't caught up with me yet. But I expect I may soon get a letter with 'Greetings from your friends and neighbors.' So for now the only draft I want to talk about is a draft beer."

Nancy appeared shocked as she stared over at Alex. She never thought of Alex in the army. He wasn't the type. Nancy just realized this military thing, the war in Vietnam, was real and closer than she wanted to believe. These were her dear friends talking about a distant war. Her stomach churned with fear, not for herself but for her friends at the table and the friends she went to college with. An entire generation could be swallowed up in this war. She was raised to love this country, but she was also raised to love peace and goodwill to all mankind. She was against the war morally, but she couldn't be against Tommy and Jerry Weaver who had already served there. The thought of drafting Alex, however, put her on the side of the pacifist, but tonight wasn't the time to disclose her deep feelings.

"So Alex, you have joined the bourgeoisie; you are now what we call a working stiff," Tommy said, half joking. "What type of job do you have?"

"Did everyone see last year's big movie, *The Graduate*? Well I did. We all know what Mrs. Robinson did. But who remembers what Mr. Robinson said?" Alex asked in a loud voice as he looked around the table.

"Leave it to you, Alex, to concentrate on what Mr. Robinson said instead of what Dustin Hoffman was doing to Mrs. Robinson and daughter Robinson," Johnny said, laughing.

"In the movie *Psycho,* Alex was so concerned about the cost of a room at the Bates Motel that he didn't even notice the shower scene," Phil said.

"Very funny. But remember this," Alex said as he raised his hand, pointing his finger to the ceiling. "Plastics! That's what Mr. Robinson said to young Benjamin; the future is in plastics. So I decided to follow Mr. Robinson's advice and have devoted myself to selling polyurethane plastics for the Upjohn

Corporation. From this time on, you can refer to me as the urethane man."

"So you're going to be a salesman? I thought you graduated in engineering? Why would you want to be a salesman with all that education?" Nancy asked.

"Didn't you see *2001: A Space Odyssey*?" Alex said with a chuckle. "In that movie the whole spaceship was made of plastics and computers. Incidentally, do you know how the master computer got the name HAL?" No one answered. "If you take the letters HAL and add the following letter in the alphabet to each one, you will end up with IBM."

"So Alex, you're going to be a plastic pusher," Tommy said, lifting his glass of beer to make a toast. "After the Ice Age, man has lived through the Stone Age, the Bronze Age, and the Golden Age of Hollywood; and now Alex is our guide, leading us into the age of plastics. To Alex."

"Hey, I'm making over nine grand a year with a new company car and expenses," Alex said. He then pulled out his wallet and took out a couple of credit cards. "And thanks to my new Diners card and American Express, I am getting in the habit of using plastic money. So my friends, Mr. Robinson was right! 'The future *is* in plastic, Benjamin.'"

"No more about Mrs. Robinson tonight. But we do have a new Mrs. in our group," Alex said as he looked intently over at Nancy. "So Nancy, how are things in marital bliss? We are all waiting with baited breath to learn the latest developments in your life away from the Abingtons."

Nancy felt a little embarrassed having the spotlight shine on her suddenly. Sitting at a small table in a dark bar late at night with a bunch of guys was not the way she envisioned telling her friends about the distressing changes in her life. She couldn't share openly the radical transition from a naïve, God-loving, young virgin to a hardened social worker married to a political, ambitious, young lawyer. She felt insecure as she searched for the proper way to articulate just how she was betrayed by the love of her life, the perfect student minister she had bragged so much about to them. Nancy had been committed to him; they were to marry and live the life of respectable missionaries. They both vowed not to have sex until their wedding. But unknown to Nancy, he was having sexual encounters with his old girlfriend and ended up fathering a child. Of course the good-living, God-fearing minister married his hometown sweetheart. In doing so he destroyed Nancy's self-esteem, her trust in people, and her faith in God. Her bright future filled with love, hope, and dreams vaporized forever, leaving her devastated, insecure, and ashamed. In her tormented mind, she kept asking herself why she had saved herself for him, and how she could have been so naive, so stupid. If only she had given in to their passionate, backseat desires, perhaps she would be the minister's wife now.

This night Nancy didn't want to discuss all the difficulties she had been through or revisit the emotional graveyard where she tried to bury her hatred and fear. She chose to put on a happy face, revealing enough information to be considered reasonable and plausible. "Let me think, the last time we were together was a about four years ago. Then I was head over heels in love with a young, handsome, student minister. Well, it didn't work out; we had different priorities. It seems it's not proper for a minister's wife to drink Budweiser from the bottle." Nancy laughed; she was enjoying telling her story. She deliberately let her words slur a little. "And there were a few other things we didn't quite see eye to eye on. I think it had something to do with the career he chose. I just couldn't see myself getting up early each Sunday morning; putting on a sweet, happy face; and going to church, kissing up to the hypocrites and sinners—and then paying special homage and adulation to the righteous members who dropped the most money in the collection plate."

"You mean you passed on the minister?" Tommy yelled out. "Just think what you missed out on. Your kids could be singing in tune, 'Yeah, the Reverend Mr. Black was my old man.'"

"How about all those heathens in Africa?" Johnny said with a sarcastic laugh. "Now how will they learn about all those sins they have been committing?"

"So you gave up the minister, a man of the cloth, for a lawyer . . . a man of the bar," Alex said in a serious tone. He picked up his glass of beer, toasting Nancy. "To the man of the bar. I'm sure he is more entertaining, and he doesn't have a collection plate. Attorneys are paid with big handsome retainers."

"Look guys, I married Jim because I love him, not because he's a lawyer. He has a good sense of humor, he's kind and intelligent, and most importantly he loves me madly. I can see you all have achieved your lifelong goals. But Jim and I are just starting out in life," Nancy said. She thought for a moment before speaking again. "Jim is a great guy. He's working as a public defender for the underprivileged and the poor. He's very active in politics, and who knows, maybe he'll run for public office some day."

"He sounds wonderful, Nancy," Phil said coldly. "He's just what our legal system needs, a new attorney in the law firm of Do-we, Cheat-em & How, serving the oppressed and the downtrodden. In the process he can prepare himself for the privileged lifestyle and the unreported bundles of money that find their way to the offices of our chosen elected officials."

"How do you get a lawyer down from a tree?" Johnny yelled out. "You cut the rope." Everyone laughed.

Nancy took a drink of her beer, shaking her head. Alex glanced over at her with a serious look on his face. He asked, "And you, Nancy, what are you doing during this development time?"

Nancy was surprised by the critical reaction of her friends. Was it because they had feelings of protection for her or because she didn't live up to their expectations? It didn't matter what they thought; she felt strongly in what she was doing, and she was up front and proud. "Jim and I both work for Boone County in Missouri. I work in the welfare department as a case worker."

"Then you did become a missionary!" Tommy said. "Instead of showing the poor about how much God loves them, you're giving out government handouts and showing how much the government loves them."

"My job isn't telling them about handouts. This is my first real job since college, and I like it. These people have a tough life. They haven't had many breaks in life, and they do the best they can. Many of them have been born into the welfare system and are happy collecting the monthly payments. Others are trying to get out, and it isn't easy for them. They've been pigeonholed by the locals. They were born in the system, and they are expected to spend their entire life on welfare. Well, not if I can help it. I'm helping some make the leap into independence," Nancy said proudly.

"How did you ever get tied up working for the welfare department?" Tommy asked.

Nancy smiled, looking over her audience. "When I was in college, I took social services courses. One semester I worked on a psych ward. What a trip that was! But it was the most fascinating experience of my life. I came in contact with some real weird people. I remember one patient who was catatonic. He didn't move any part of his body. He remained rigid as a board most of the time. His eyes just stared forward without blinking. Other patients walked in a dreamlike state, bouncing off the walls. Some talked out into the space beyond; others just cried and wailed constantly. Some patients would refuse to wear any clothes at all; they just walked around the ward nude. Most of those patients will spend the rest of their lives in that institution. It is a world apart from what we are used to. But for some odd reason I enjoyed it. When Jim and I moved to his hometown, his father, a judge, had contacts in the county. So I got a job in something I thought would be interesting, and believe me, working for the department of welfare is interesting. It is a different world altogether."

"Do you have to go out and visit these people in their homes?" Phil asked. "That has to be scary out in the country all by yourself."

"I usually don't go alone. But I do go out to check on people to see how they are getting along. I had one client who lived in an old school bus. His dwelling was off the road and up a trail a half-mile from the dirt road. We had to walk up through the woods to find the place." Nancy paused, chuckling as she picked up her beer. "I was just thinking, we could smell the place before we could see it. He had no running water. He peed out the front door and crapped just behind the dump of a bus he lived in. He didn't even dig a trench for his own excrement. It just laid where he dropped it, stinking up the woods. The inside of the dwelling looked as bad as the outside smelled. Then there was another client of mine, a farm worker who lost his leg in an accident. After he got out of the hospital, I helped him as much as I could, getting him some money and food stamps because he couldn't work. Well, even if he had some of his teeth and his eyes weren't crossed, he still wouldn't be my type. But his country girlfriend thought I found him too charming and that I had the hots for him. She told me to keep away from him or she'd beat me up. Just as well, I think Jim was getting a little jealous.

"But with all the craziness of it and all my frustration, there's never a dull moment. I like working with these people with their unique personalities and hats. The fact is they're all messed up, but they keep on living their odd way in the land of the free. And the taxpayers don't mind."

"How is married life treating you?" Alex asked. "Do you like being married to a lawyer and living in a small town in Missouri? Sounds like you married Atticus Finch. You haven't killed any mockingbirds, have you, Nancy?

"Jim is a highly moral attorney, and I like being married. We are renting a small house. I learned to cook. I even made crepes le veau. I have to clean the house by myself, no cleaning lady. I also am quite proficient doing the laundry. No more bleeding of the colors. We do a little entertaining, which is a lot of fun. And you, Alex, how do like the life of a salesman?"

"I have a great job," Alex injected quickly. "I have a new car and a nice expense account. I take customers to the finest restaurants. The work is easy, calling on manufacturers of furniture and selling them urethane foam for seating. Not too much to say about it. It pays the bills, and I have a lot of fun doing it."

Nancy then turned toward Phil. "How about the rest of the gang? Is anyone else coming in this weekend?"

"Jerry Weaver is stationed at Fort Bragg. He called and said he wouldn't be in. Danny Fredrick dropped out of school and is in a band touring somewhere in the Northeast, I think in Massachusetts. So he won't be in," Phil said thoughtfully.

"Tommy, do you see Jerry Weaver at all?" Nancy asked, "Considering you're both stationed at the same military base?"

"We're both stationed at Bragg, but Jerry is a sergeant in the Special Forces—the sneaky Pete's, the Green Berets. They are up on smoke pot hill, as they call it. We've gotten together a few times. But being in different units, we don't get to see each other very often. He loves the army. He's what they call a soldier's solider," Tommy said with a smile.

"I almost forgot," Phil broke in. "I did get a phone call from Ida Freeman. You remember her. She was Danny Fredrick's date the first weekend we went to the breakfast. She graduated from the U and is living in New York City. I think she is working for some kind of fashion magazine. Anyway she said she might be in; she asked if I knew who all was expected."

"Does that mean anything to you, Tommy?" Johnny said with an inquisitive laugh.

Tommy and Ida had dated off and on for almost fifteen months. However, that ended a few years ago. Tommy wasn't enrolled in college, and his future looked somewhat limited. They were in love with each other, but the barrier of economic certainty kept them from a confident bonding. Even though Ida held a deep romantic feeling for him, she had a stronger drive to have the better things in life, including success. Ida believed Tommy had all the right stuff, except for an education and a bright future. Although it was difficult, she decided to end the relationship. She believed if Tommy really loved her, he would make a commitment to use the God-given talents he was blessed with. After they parted company, Ida pursued her education and career. Tommy realized he had to do something to break away from the restricted path that lay ahead. At that point he decided to join the army. With his veteran's benefits, Tommy could afford to go to college when his tour of duty was complete. One positive result of the Vietnam involvement was the passage of the GI Bill.

"I'd like to see her again," Tommy said as he sat upright in his chair. "I always liked Ida and hope to see her if she comes in. And that's all. No more romancing for me for a while. I still have some quality time to spend with my Uncle Sam before I get out. By the way, Phil, did Ida say she was not feeling well and was not coming here tonight but just going to the breakfast tomorrow?"

"Ida didn't say definitely that she was coming at all. She only said that she might fly in for the breakfast. She mentioned she was rather busy, and it had been a while since she'd been to her adopted hometown," Phil said. "So we will just have to see if she shows up."

"I thought she was Danny's girl," Nancy said, smiling over at Tommy.

"She was till Danny went off the deep end. I think he got heavy into drugs, dropped out of school. The last time I saw him he was skin and bones, dressed like a typical hippie. His hair was below his shoulders, and he looked as if he hadn't taken a shower in a long time," Phil said, looking at Tommy. He didn't want to throw salt in any wounds, but he continued, "He got caught up in the antiwar movement. He is traveling all over the country attending different peace demonstrations. Just a few weeks ago, he was in Washington for the big peace rally with over three hundred thousand demonstrators."

"I was there looking for him and the famous baby doctor, Dr. Benjamin Spock," Tommy said, half joking. "I was in one of the battalions from the 82nd that was sent up to Washington in case the demonstration got out of hand. It was very strange to be in full combat gear with an M-16 walking the streets and guarding the nation's capital. It was a scary time; we had machine gun crews set up at the White House. Fortunately nothing much happened."

There was silence among the small group. They all seemed to grasp the serious situation the country was in and how divided the country was. There was no clear solution, only a maze of various national and international solutions. The Paris peace talks were in progress without any significant change in the war. Here they were with a few drinks, trying to understand the world's problems. Perhaps the world's problems had a simpler solution than the problems they each faced.

Phil broke the silence. "The world is getting crazier, but who knows? That rock concert at Woodstock had almost a half million people there without any violence. They ran out of beer, water, food, and almost everything else. But those drugged-up hippies, all wet and muddy, proved some people can get along together. Not only that but this summer Neil Armstrong walked on the moon, and we got to watch it live on TV. Now that's something."

"Yeah, like that Barry McGuire song, 'Eve of Destruction.' Now that's a happy tune to make you feel comfortable," Tommy commented.

"Eddy," Alex yelled out, raising his hand and looking over at the bar. "Bring over a bottle of whiskey, one that Frances hasn't watered down. Make it Southern Comfort. And bring some shot glasses. I'd like to make a toast."

Eddy rarely moved quickly, but when someone offered to buy him a drink, he had wings on his shoes. He was at the table in record time, about three minutes. "Who is paying for these shots?" Eddy asked as he put down the tray of glasses and a bottle of Southern Comfort.

"Here's a twenty, Eddy." Alex handed Eddy a crisp new bill. "And give the hookers at the end of the bar a drink."

"Now wait a minute! We only have nice women that come in here," Eddy said as he took the twenty. He held the bill to the dim light as if inspecting it. "A twenty, hmmm, I didn't know they still printed them that big."

"That's not all, Eddy. Now I hear they have planes that fly without propellers. Can you imagine that?" Johnny said, laughing.

"Another chatterbox!" Eddy said, staring at Johnny with his good eye. "If you're so smart, why aren't you on television?"

"I'd like to make a toast." Alex stood up and poured everyone a shot of whiskey. "To us; we were able to make it back for another historic Thanksgiving Breakfast."

They all downed the toast. Afterward the conversation was lively, reminiscing about the good times and some current topics. There was a lot of drinking and laughing. All too soon the lights flashed, and Frances' voice boomed, "It ain't over till the fat lady sings. And the fat lady is singing, 'Last call for alcohol,' putting an end to the night's festivities.

The bright lights came on suddenly. Everyone was saying their good nights and "see you in the morning at the breakfast."

"Nancy, do you need a ride home?" Alex asked.

"Yes. Thanks, Alex, I do need a ride. My father dropped me off tonight. He said he didn't want me drinking and driving." Nancy's words were slurred. "I told him I don't drink and drive. You may hit a bump in the road and spill your drink." She started laughing at her own joke. "Alex, are you okay to drive?"

Alex was also tipsy. "I'll have to drive; I'm too drunk to walk." They both started laughing. "All I need to do is find the cars to my keys, and we're ready to go. Oh yes, my dear, I'm ready to take you home in my new company-owned chariot." They stood grasping at the moment. "Madam, may I offer you my arm?" Alex said with a large smile. He bowed his head, offering his arm. Mimicking May West, Nancy replied, "I'll take your arm and whatever else you have to offer."

They were in high spirits when they reached Alex's new 1969 Ford Galaxie. "Nice car, Alex," Nancy said as she studied the green car with a black top. "Vinyl roof, looks like a convertible. Does it have air conditioning?"

"It has everything: power windows, electric door locks, cruise control, and even an eight-track tape player, all the newest features available. When you're a top salesman, those are just some of the perks," Alex said as he aimed his key into the door.

"You seem to be on the road to success, Alex," Nancy said as she slid across the front seat. "I mean you have your life all together. You have a great job. Things must look pretty good for you. Are you happy?"

As Alex started the car, he felt Nancy sitting right next to him. She had never sat so close to him before. "Your parents aren't waiting up for you, are they, Nancy?"

"No, Alex, I'm a big girl now. I come and go as I please. What do you have in mind?"

"Would you like to go to the Blue Bird Diner for coffee or take a ride in the country?"

"Let's go for a ride in the country like we used to. Those fun times seem like yesterday and yet in some ways like a lifetime ago," Nancy said, putting her head back on the seat.

They drove up the deserted State Street of Clarks Summit. The streetlights were the only signs of activity, beaming shades of illumination on the deserted facades. All the landscape and buildings were exactly the same as graduation night, and some of the bygone feelings were beginning to surface. "There is a bottle of Southern Comfort in the glove compartment," Alex said as he drove slowly. "I always keep a bottle handy in case of snake bites."

"Well, I think I've just been bitten," Nancy said, laughing as she pulled out the Southern Comfort and taking a gulp directly from the bottle. "Woo, that takes the hair off your chest."

"Should we go over to Doc Stone's to see if the tradition is still carrying on?" Alex asked.

"Yes, let's go to the old stomping grounds and drink to the gods of yesterday. Are you with me, Alex?" Nancy asked in a pleading voice.

"I'm with you, Nancy, and you're always with me," Alex said as they drove to the dirt road that led to the fields surrounding the farm of Dr. Stone. Alex was jerking the brakes as the car came to a slow, rocking stop on the edge of a field. "I think I'm running out of gas," Alex said with a chuckle.

Nancy handed the bottle to him. He took a large gulp without any noticeable reaction. He put his arm around Nancy, squeezing her tightly. Then he said in a kind and loving voice, "Nancy, you know the folk group called The Seekers? They have a song out called 'I'll Never Find Another You.' Each time I hear that song I think of you and the few lines that epitomize my feelings." He whispered the words in her ear, "I could search the whole world over until my life is through, but I know I'll never find another you." He then embraced her, kissing her tenderly.

Nancy wrapped her arms around Alex's neck, squeezing him tightly. Her mouth opened, sucking his tongue into her mouth. She slid her body backward, lying on the seat with her head toward the passenger door, and pulled Alex down on top of her ravishing body. Alex's hands were all over Nancy. His wildest fantasies were becoming real; his emotions were never so high. He kissed her lips and neck excitedly while massaging her breasts. He couldn't control himself. His hands slid up under her skirt with his fumbling fingers tearing off her panties. Nancy was erotically pulsating back and forth, moaning and begging Alex to make love to her. The confines of the front seat made their movements restricted but effective, each tearing the other's clothing off.

Within a few moments, they were both completely nude from the waist down. The excitement of this special encounter was at a fever pitch. Nancy was lying on her back, one leg off the seat and the other extending up on the headrest. Alex mounted her, his heart pounding as he leaned forward. Nancy grabbed his throbbing penis, guiding it into her sacred canal. Alex thrust forth; she screamed in ecstasy as they flexed their bodies in a frenzy of vigorous, passionate sex. Both were gasping for air in this state of high emotional bliss, each pushing and pulling, using all the energy they could muster to achieve a crescendo of sexual satisfaction.

In a few minutes the high-intensity sexual encounter was over. They lay quietly entangled in each other's bodies. He had never dreamed Nancy could be composed of so much passion and unconstrained sexual craving. In comparison he was a novice with little sexual experience. Alex was first to realize the significance of their encounter. She was married to someone else. The feeling of guilt and fear began to take over the intensity of the previous few minutes. Alex started to speak in a low, frightened voice. "I wasn't wearing anything, and I'm afraid I . . ."

"Don't worry, Alex, I'm on the pill and have been for a long time," Nancy said in a shallow voice, holding him tightly. "Please hold me for a few more minutes?" she whispered in his ear.

They lay still together listening to each other breathe, dreaming of distant times, and thinking of nothing at all. Like all wonderful experiences, this time of bliss had to pass. "My leg is cramped; I have to get up and move around," Alex painfully moaned. At that instant the visit to enchantment was over. They rustled together, lightly chuckling as they began dressing themselves. Soon they were sitting upright, staring out into the darkened fields.

Alex picked up the bottle of Southern Comfort, offering it to Nancy. "Would you like another swallow?"

"I think I've earned it," Nancy said, laughing as she grabbed the bottle from Alex's hand. She took a slug from the bottle.

"I don't know what to say, Nancy. I never thought something like this could happen to us. If I had any idea you thought . . . "

"Before you get carried away, Alex," Nancy said with a cool matter-of-fact voice, "let me say a few things to put this in its proper perspective. I'm married, and I expect to remain married. What happened tonight happened tonight. We had sex, that's all. You don't have to be married to have sex; you don't have to make promises to have sex. We are adults; we can do what we want as long as it isn't illegal. Which reminds me, do you have a joint with you?"

Alex was shocked by the sudden change in Nancy. He was confused, but he tried to remain cool. "Nancy, I don't smoke cigarettes or pot. The booze is enough for me."

"Well, Alex, judging by your performance, I think you've been doing a lot more than a little boozing on the weekends," Nancy said in a playful manner.

"I'm a man of the world now. You know what they say about traveling salesmen?" Alex said jokingly.

"Yeah, I know what they say about traveling salesmen. But, Alex, you must know a lot of farmer's daughters." They both started laughing.

"And you, Nancy, did you save yourself until after your marriage vows, waiting for the bliss of your wedding night?" Alex asked humorously.

Nancy lifted the bottle of Southern Comfort to her lips, taking a long gulp. "No, Alex, I didn't save myself for anyone. You see I wouldn't have sex with the one I loved, so he had sex with his old high school girlfriend. And she wasn't on the pill! He knocked her up and married her." Nancy took another sip of whiskey. "That's when things changed for me. My world came crashing down, like in the Skeeter Davis song 'End of the World'." She sang the words breezily, "Don't they know it's the end of the world, it ended when he said good-bye.

"My life or part my of life ended when he married that tramp. You see, Alex, I was head over heels in love with Ron. He represented everything I believed in. He was a good, honest, loving Christian; I had unshakable trust in him. He was my rock, studying to be a minister. We were soul mates; we were spiritually connected. I believe we still are." She started to cry. "Oh God, I still love him." Nancy began to weep.

Alex held her tenderly in his arms. He whispered lightly in her ear. "Nancy, I love you. I have always loved you, and I will always love you. For me tonight wasn't just a romp in the hay. It was an extension of the feelings I have had for you for such a long time. I believe tonight was a bonding of our love. I don't care if you stay married or get remarried ten times; I will always love you."

They sat quiet for a few moments, taking in what was shared between them. Alex stroked Nancy's hair rhythmically and again whispered to her. "There's another popular song that's not a song by Skeeter Davis. There is a verse that goes like, 'You're in my heart, you're in my soul, you are my lover, you're my best friend.' That's how my feelings are for you, Nancy. You're in my soul."

Nancy was still whimpering; she used a Kleenex to wipe her eyes and dry her sniffles. "I'm sorry, Alex. I love you, and you know that. But my feelings for you are not on the same road you are traveling. I appreciate your love for me, and I am so grateful to have someone like you in my life. I wish my feelings toward you were different, but they are not. You deserve the right person to share your love with. We both are adults now; we will be going our separate ways after this weekend. You will be selling Mr. Robinson's plastics, and I will return to my young Perry Mason and my welfare cheats."

"Do you love him?" Alex asked with the voice of an interrogator.

"I'm trying to love him, Alex. Jim is madly in love with me. He came along at a period in my life when I needed somebody to save me. After Ron dumped me, I was devastated. My life was ruined. I was so screwed up and depressed that there was a time I couldn't get out of bed to go to class. I walked around like a zombie in dirty clothes. I realized most people valued me because of my good looks. With my smile I could open a lot of doors and twist people around my finger. I had little to do with my physical design; who I am is not what I look like. I'm a person with intellect and feelings, apart from a smooth complexion and pearly white teeth. I didn't care what happened to me. My grades went to hell; you might say we were going to hell together. That's when I really started drinking heavily. I got into some drugs, mostly pot. There was one guy who took me under his wing or, I should say, under his spell. He was a jerk, but I didn't care. He was just one of the many jerks and one-night stands that were part of my lifestyle for a while. That's when I seriously considered suicide. I remember one night I was drunk and depressed. I sat at my window looking at the small rope on the Venetian blinds, and I wondered if I tied it around my neck, would it hold if I jumped out the window."

Nancy took another slug of whiskey and sat staring out the car window toward the deserted fields. "Alex, I no longer have the core values I grew up with. Everything I believed in is gone. And I won't go back to that old way of life. And I won't ever trust another man. Maybe that's why I searched for love with so many men. I even put out for an economics professor to get a passing grade. He gave me a C+. I guess I did better in bed than I could have in class. I joined a group that lived in something like a commune. We shared a special kind of love that generated energy and commitment to each other and the universe. That was just another of the places I was searching for myself."

"Is that where you met Jim?" Alex asked.

"No, I was working in a bar/restaurant-type place near the campus. Jim and his friends used to come in, and I got to know him. He was the kind of person with a good sense of humor. We became friends. For some reason he took a liking to me just the way I was, crazy and confused. At the time I was lost, still numb with pain, and all my feelings were turned off. Jim was finishing law school. He fell in love with me and wanted to get married and take care of me. I just couldn't stand being alone any longer. I thought marriage to a good person might make me happy again."

"Has marriage made you happy again?" Alex asked.

"Do you think I would be out here lusting it up with you, if marriage made me happy, Alex? I've tried to be happy doing all the wifely things, like cooking good meals, setting up our little home, trying to be interesting with his friends and legal associates. But there's something missing, some connection I'm searching for. I don't understand it myself."

"What are you going to do? Keep living a lie, searching for something out there and you don't even know what it is?" Alex asked in a confused tone.

"I'm going to try to make my life worth living. Jim loves me. He has a bright future in front of him. As lawyers go, he is smart, levelheaded, and gets along well with the right people. He's involved in low-level politics now. But I think he can go pretty far, who knows. For me I'll continue working with my people, as my father used to say, the sick, the lame, and the lazy."

"Don't you find working with people on welfare rather depressing in itself?" he asked.

"It can be depressing, but this kind of work gets me out in the country. I can roam through the farmland, and walk through the fields and the forest. Being alone in nature is kind of a silent blessing for me. When I first got to college, I was introduced to great literature, such as Jane Austen's *Pride and Prejudice,* Tolstoy's *Family Happiness,* Wordsworth's poem, "Influence of Natural Objects," and many more extraordinary works." Nancy was calmer now. She took another sip of whiskey. She rested her head on the back of the car seat. Her eyes were closed. She continued to speak as if thinking at the same time. "Through literature I was exposed to feelings and emotions that I didn't know existed. My mind was opened to how others dealt with love, fear, hate, and various other circumstances of life. I had the latitude to feel deep emotions from those printed words. I was able to explore aspects of life that I had no idea existed. It may sound strange to you, but the affinity I have with these people allows me to experience a vision of life I could not witness any other way. Somehow working with these lowly, outcast, wonderful people, I've been able to dig deeper into my own psyche, searching my feelings to find out who I am and what I will be.

"That's pretty heavy stuff you just laid out," Alex said quietly.

"Yes it is, Alex, and I have to face up to the fact. I'm an adult now, married to a great guy. And I have my own responsibilities that I must attend to. I guess it's time to realize, as Skeeter put to music, 'how life goes on the way it does.' But my life will go on, and I'm going to try to make it worth living."

"You sound better already," Alex said in cheerful voice.

"Thank you, Alex, for being with me tonight, and I'm sorry I dragged you into this den of inequity. You'll never know how much you helped me through my ordeal. For some strange reason, I feel clean and refreshed, like the thick, oppressive fog I've been living in has suddenly vaporized." Her spirit picked up, and with a perky voice, she said, "I was dreading the breakfast tomorrow. But now I'm looking forward to it. For the first time in a long time I'm looking forward to the future. How about you, Mr. Plastic Salesman, are you looking forward to the future?"

"Oh yes, the plastic industry is expected to have a record year. Our sales are going right through the roof. In fact, we are now spraying urethane on roofs. It's the neatest thing you ever saw. We spray a liquid on a roof, and it foams up like shaving cream. In a few seconds, it is as hard as a rock, and you can walk on it."

"Sounds like your business career is off to a good start. Now that I'm married, is there anyone else you could possibly be serious about?" Nancy asked warmly.

"There is no girlfriend to speak of. I just started working a few months ago, and I like my job. My parents were a little disappointed I switched to a business degree and didn't become an engineer. But I couldn't see myself working at a drafting board with a slide rule the rest of my life. With the Vietnam thing going strong, I expect to be drafted soon, so I haven't been dating too seriously. The last thing I want is to leave a weeping, brokenhearted girlfriend behind. Even if I could find one," he said with a chuckle.

"Alex, I'm against the war and the many years we been fighting there. The thought of you and the others going over is frightening to me."

"I'm afraid myself about going to Vietnam. But to tell you the truth, I have my own fears of the future. Right now I have it pretty good. I have a great job and a company car with an expense account. I go to the best restaurants and get free tickets to sporting events. All in all, life looks pretty good. But I am so young in the business world. No matter what I do or what I say, I'm considered a kid. I won't be accepted in the club until I have a puffy face with about ten more inches around my waist and brag about my golf game. I spend a lot of time in the bars at night. In fact, I usually close them. Some nights I don't even want to go to bed. Lying in bed alone, I have a feeling I'm missing something. There's a hollow spot in my gut; I keep searching for something, but I don't know what it is. Whatever it is .

. . it seems so elusive," Alex said as he picked up the bottle of Southern Comfort.

"I thought being a salesman was a great career, a fun job?" Nancy asked.

He took a large gulp and continued his monologue. "Let me tell you some little-known facts about being a good salesman. First you have to be good-looking. I don't mean handsome, but you can't have one arm or a missing ear; you can't have a big scar across your forehead. You must be presentable, dress well, look well. You must like being around people. You can't be a loner. You must instantly establish good relationships with your customers. You call your customers "your friends," but they are not your friends: they are your customers. When you call on them, you may discuss their personal interests like family and sporting events but never politics or religion. The conversation is generally businesslike, friendly, and shallow. The next day you're with a different customer saying and doing the same thing. In some ways a salesman is a kind of business prostitute: good-looking and friendly with good manners and conversational skills. But at the end of the day when the lights go out, he's all alone. There are no bowling leagues or car pools for salesmen; there are no company picnics because as a salesman you're an outsider. The business life of a salesman is contrary to the nature of a salesman. In other words a salesman is a guy who likes being around people in his everyday environment, but in reality he is a loner. And that's where I find myself."

"I never thought of it that way. Like you said earlier, you're new at the job; maybe you will make a lot of friends and a lot of money. Who knows, maybe you could start your own bowling league someday," Nancy said with a smile.

"Yeah, maybe you're right. We'll have to see what the future holds for both of us," Alex said as if in deep thought.

They sat motionless and quiet for a moment. Then Alex looked at his watch and, realizing the late hour, said lightly, "Do you want me to drive you to the breakfast later in the morning?"

"I'll be up and waiting at seven thirty," Nancy said in a comfortable voice.

Alex patted Nancy's hand gently, smiling at her with love and affection in his eyes. "Let's have fun at the breakfast," he said. "I'll pick you up at seven thirty sharp."

Chapter Four

1969

At seven thirty sharp, Alex pulled in the driveway of the Bishop family's home. For Alex this was like old times. Over the past years, Alex acted as chauffeur for Nancy on many occasions. When Alex turned sixteen, he took driving education at school, and he passed his driver's exam on the first try. When he received his driver's license, Nancy was the first person he took for a drive. She was his copilot on many occasions, going to sporting events, after-school events like soliciting ads for the yearbook, and the many parties he drove her to. However, this morning the feeling Alex had was different; last night changed him. He was more comfortable and confident. His sexual encounter had eliminated many of the secret desires he had harbored through the years. He was now happy to have Nancy as a true and equal friend, without emotional attachments or desires. This would be the first day of their honest, adult relationship. At least that's what he wanted to believe.

Nancy was waiting at the side door. As soon as the car stopped, she ran out and jumped in. This time she sat across the car near the door. No cuddling this morning. "Good morning, Alex. How are you feeling on this chilly-willy morning?" she said with a warm smile.

"I'm okay, a little hung over. I have a dry cotton mouth this morning, and I'm so thirsty. I know I should have drank more last night. But when we get to Shadowbrook, I'll have a little nip of the dog that bit me. All I need is a little antifreeze in my veins, and I'll be fine," Alex said quietly.

"My head is a little foggy this morning," Nancy said somewhat casually. "And Alex, I hope what happened last night won't have a drastic effect on our friendship."

"Nancy, we're both adults, and we have to live and act like adults. I've always had special feelings for you, and you've known that. I would do anything for you. I just want you to be happy, and I want you to remember I'll always be there if you need me, for any reason. Now we each have our own lives to live, and maybe the young Perry Mason will make you as happy as you deserve. I really hope so."

"I want you to understand just how much your friendship means to me. I don't want anything to jeopardize our relationship. This is very important to me," Nancy said.

"We do have, shall we call it, a special friendship. We'll stay close, if you know what I mean," Alex said with a chuckle. "So let's party this morning and have a good time at the breakfast." He reached over toward the radio, then added, "Let me put in this new eight-track of Simon and Garfunkel. I just bought it. I hope you don't mind their music." The song "I Am a Rock" started to play. "Sometimes I feel like a rock, cold and all alone," Alex said.

"I would have thought your favorite song would be 'Mrs. Robinson'," Nancy said, laughing.

"Actually my favorite is 'The Sound of Silence'," Alex said as if thinking of the lyrics. "Paul Simon wrote it after President Kennedy was assassinated. It's a very moving song."

"Yes, well, this morning is going to be a fun time; can we put on a little happier tape?" Nancy asked.

"How about Ricky Nelson?" Alex said. "His music is lively. And remember as kids we used to watch the Nelson family."

"That's fine; his songs are lively," Nancy said as they started their early morning journey.

The conversation was light and relaxing as they drove up the twisty Route 611 highway toward Tunkhannock. The rolling hills and rugged, rock-faced mountainsides hadn't changed in the last few years. As they drove through the small village of Dalton, the image of the old Blue Bird Diner seemed to have lost some if its sparkle and charm in the gray, overcast morning. The signature colors of white and bright royal-blue seemed dull, sun bleached, and chalky. But then again it was a late nightspot where the gang would meet after dances and dates. Nancy thought that perhaps the colors, accented by the florescent lighting, just looked brighter on dark nights.

Alex smiled as they drove into the entrance of the white-fenced complex of Shadowbrook Farm. He had a good feeling about returning to this habitat of good times and was pleased with the thought of reacquainting with many separated friends. The two large, fiberglass cow heads were still on the roof, like a symbolic dairy hostess viewing the incoming guests. The setting was picturesque; the barns and all the buildings were all neatly painted white with green trim. Some of the buildings were landscaped with dark green holly bushes, which gave the impression of a clean, efficient dairy farm. Nancy commented on the shiny, new black pavement that replaced the old gravel parking lot. In recent years business had been good to Shadowbrook with its addition of a nine-hole golf course. It was a pretty course, nestled in a farmland valley sprinkled with clusters of pine trees. The edge of the course was bordered on one side by the slow, wandering river and large, shaded sycamore trees.

Nancy and Alex entered the big buffet area together. No one took notice of them as they walked through the large crowd. They were searching the large hall, looking for friendly faces.

"They have really done a nice job on the addition to this place," Nancy commented. "I wonder where the bar is located?"

"If you look straight ahead, the bar is on the far side of room. If you look closely, you can see Tommy and Bean Newman giving it a good workout. Old Carrot Heart is quite a character," Alex said in a jovial tone.

"Is that Bean Newman wearing the raccoon coat? I have only seen a coat like that in an old movie. And how did he ever get that name Carrot Heart?" Nancy asked, laughing and shaking her head.

"First he got the name Bean because he was so tall and skinny. We used to call him Bean Pole. A few years ago he received his draft notice, and he went down for the physical. The army doctors checked him out and said he had an oversized heart. They said it was shaped like a carrot. So we naturally called him Carrot Heart."

"Do you have a nickname for everyone?" Nancy asked. Then she blurted out, "Oh, I see Phil over there."

"You mean Barrow Head? Yeah, I see him," Alex said jokingly.

Nancy looked startled at Alex. Her face was blank. "I hate to think what name you have for me."

"Now what makes you say such a thing? Let's go over to Tommy Talker and Carrot Heart before Barrelhead sees us," Alex said in a humorous tone as he gently nudged Nancy's arm. "Everyone kind of chuckles about their nicknames, except for Johnny Thompson. Whatever you do, don't ever call Johnny 'Wedge Head.' He'll go ballistic."

"I can understand why; it's so cruel to call him that," Nancy said seriously. She then paused for a moment and started to giggle. "You know, when you think of it, his head does look like a wedge."

They all greeted each other; after rounds of drinks were secured, they decided to adjourn to a large table near the center of the banquet hall.

Bean Newman was invited along with Chickie Frazer; both were good friends of Tommy's. The drinks were flowing. The group at the table became loud with laughing as they retold funny stories. It was a festive atmosphere. Chickie and Bean had a reputation of doing a lot of zany things. They also had an exceptional, comical way of describing their misfortunes.

"Tell them about how you sank the Jeep," Tommy yelled across the table to Chickie. There was a loud uproar: "Yeah, how did that happen? Tell us about it."

"My father sent me a newspaper clipping about the story. I showed it around college. Everybody thought it was hilarious. What really happened?" Nancy asked.

The table quieted down so they could hear from the horse's mouth the true facts of the story. Chickie picked up his glass of beer and, glancing over his audience, took a large gulp. "Well, if you really want to know . . . Last January on a bitter cold Friday—in fact, that day it was eleven degrees below zero—I got out of class about two in the afternoon. Bean and I got together for a few brewskies, and we decided to go jeeping on Glenburn Lake. It had been very cold for about a week. Usually we would check to see how thick the ice was. But it was so cold that I didn't need to check the thickness of the ice. I figured it was at least six inches thick or maybe an inch and a half."

The small audience was laughing and nodding their heads as someone yelled out, "Yeah, he knew how thick the ice was all right."

As Chickie continued with his notorious story, everyone's ears perked up, listening to his every word. He started to laugh as he began speaking again. "Now I go to Lackawanna—affectionately known as Lack-of-knowledge—Business College. The dress code required all males to wear a coat and tie to each class. So I was dressed in my leather overcoat, sport jacket, white shirt, and tie. Bean over there was dressed in a sweater and that big raccoon coat." He pointed to Bean who stood six foot five, and everyone burst out in laughter.

"Earlier that momentous day, we met at Dalton's quaint, little watering hole called Dunn's Dump, where the elite meet. After a little liquid courage, we decided to go jeeping out on the frozen lake. We had done it for the past few years. It was cold, and the lake was frozen, so why not?" He paused for a moment, listening to the laughter.

When all was quiet, he continued as if his performance was scripted. "When we got to the lake, it was so cold that I decided just to drive right on out. As we started out onto the lake, Bean yelled out, 'I'm a little scared; we don't know how thick the ice is.'

Chickie's voice increased in pitch, almost yelling. "I said, 'Bean, don't worry, it's plenty thick enough.' We continued driving along without any problem. We were almost halfway across the lake, about two hundred yards from the shoreline. Just then the ice started roaring with strained cracking sounds like a muffled explosion. Bean yelled out, 'The ice is cracking.' He opened his door. 'I'm going to leave my door open just in case.' Again I said, 'Don't worry, the ice always cracks when we drive over it.' Then the ice cracked again, only this time it was a different sound. It was the sound of crushing ice and water splashing as the Jeep pitched in, tilting deeply to the left. The driver's side broke through the ice. I could feel the Jeep floating then sinking. I tried to put it in four-wheel drive, as if that would help."

There was a loud roar of laughing. Chickie didn't miss a beat; he held their attention, picking up with the story. "I could feel the Jeep sinking, and I didn't think it would float for long. I glanced over to the passenger's side. Bean was gone. He'd vaulted like an escaped prisoner. I could see he left his door open, and the water was gushing in like a scene from an old black-and-white, submarine war movie. I tried to get out my side, but the door wouldn't open because it was stuck in the ice. The Jeep was sinking fast, so I jumped across the seats. I tried to get out the passenger's door, but the water was gushing in so fast. All of a sudden, the water was just below my chin. I was caught in the door, and I couldn't move. I yelled out, 'Bean, Bean.' I could see the back of him sprinting across the ice, running for his life. In that big raccoon coat, he looked like a giant muskrat running across the frozen lake."

There was a burst of laughter, but Chickie continued in a serious tone. "But I tell y'all, when he heard my voice, he stopped in his tracks. He turned around and saw me trapped in that sinking Jeep. He stood there for a minute thinking, his eyes as big as headlights, and smiled. Then he gave me the finger, turned around, and kept on running toward shore." There was even more loud laughter. "No, just kidding. In reality Bean turned on a dime, and even though he couldn't swim a stroke, he ran back for me. By the time he got to the Jeep, I was able to get one arm free and was reaching up to him. He looked like a giant standing on the ice, but he grabbed on and pulled me out of that sinking Jeep."

There was a lot of commotion and laughing at the table, many asking what happened next. Chickie continued, "After Bean pulled me out, we both got up just in time to see the top of the Jeep disappear into the cold, black water of Glenburn Lake. We stood there for a minute looking at this giant hole in the ice, wondering what had happened. Bean asked, 'What are we going to do?' I replied that any fool could sink a Jeep, but it would take some brains to get it out."

Chickie picked up his beer, shaking his head and smiling over at Bean Newman. "Now here we are standing on this frozen lake two hundred yards from shore, minus eleven degrees with the wind blowing. I'm standing there soaked to the bones, shivering, and my teeth chattering like a skeleton. All my clothes were soaking wet, including the leather overcoat, sports coat, white shirt and tie, and I had no gloves. We walked over the frozen lake the best we could, the water squirting out of my shoes. My clothes were starting to freeze as we slowly made our way off the lake up to the highway. It was so very cold, and the wind was gusting across the highway. We started hitchhiking, trying to get a ride. The cars just flew by causing more frozen gusts of wind from their high speed. I said to Bean, 'Nobody is going to pick us up. In that ridiculous coat, you look half man and half giant rat.' And there I was with my clothes dripping wet and freezing; I looked like half man and half icicle. Lucky for us Bucky Monroe happened be driving by and picked us up. He couldn't believe it."

"How did you get the Jeep out of the lake?" a voice yelled out.

"I had self-proclaimed expert advisors from all over giving advice," Chickie said, laughing. "Put deflated truck tire tubes under the frame, then inflate the tires, and the Jeep will float to the surface. Another had the idea to have a helicopter lift it out. One idea was to cut a two-hundred-yard trench in the ice and pull it across the lake. There were all kinds of nuts telling me how to do it. But there were even more saying I would never get the Jeep out. I told them I'd get it out if I had to blow up the dam and drain the lake. Then I'd just drive it out." There was more laughter. "It took five days, three skin divers, and two of the largest tow trucks I've ever seen. But we got it out. Within a week I drove it up State Street. I had to chuckle as I watched many shocked faces and people pointing, shaking their heads."

The number of people around the table increased with the volume of laughter. Tommy was laughing so much he was wiping tears from his eyes. Everyone was talking, laughing, and enjoying the homespun stories. Nancy noticed Johnny Thompson and his wife, Melody, walking toward their table. They looked like the perfect couple. They were dressed in similar green ski jackets, both wearing blue jeans.

"Well, I see the comic club of the Abingtons is here, Mutt and Jeff," Johnny said with a sarcastic tone as he looked at Chickie and Bean. "Isn't it a little early to be trying to make people laugh?"

"Well, Johnny, if I really wanted to make people laugh, I'd put up a poster of you in a bathing suit," Chickie said with a laugh.

"Always with a wisecrack, you think you could get people to laugh at a school bus accident," Johnny said right back.

"I probably could if you were lying under the school bus," Chickie replied as others joined in the laughter.

"You're as funny as a screen door in a submarine!" Johnny blasted again; he always had to get in the last word.

Before any more verbal shots were fired, Nancy broke into the conversation. "Melody, please come over here and sit next to me. We can exchange newlywed stories."

Bashful Melody was pleased to get out of the spotlight with her husband, Johnny. She walked toward Nancy. "Hi, Nancy, you look great. I'd like to be over here with you where it is a little quieter. Johnny said your husband couldn't make it in for Thanksgiving; that's a shame. I wanted to meet him."

"You will someday soon, I hope, but he's so busy," Nancy said, then asked, "So how do you like being married? I understand you and Johnny have your own place in the country."

"Yes, we do have a nice little house; it's small but cozy. We are renting it, but some day we hope to buy it. We don't have much, so my parents gave us some old furniture to start off with. Before I got married, I didn't worry about paying bills; that was my parents' concern. John and I don't make too much money. It was so hard for me to learn to write a check to pay the bills. John has always been a take-control type of guy, so he sort of handles the money. Now that John and I have to pay the electric bill, well, to tell you the truth, I go around our little house turning off the lights."

"I know what you mean," Nancy said as she took it all in. "My husband doesn't make much money either. And I feel kind of funny asking him for money. With my father all I said was I needed this or that, and he gave it to me, no problem. But I just can't go to any store and buy whatever I want now. When I was growing up and went to the grocery store, I'd pick the brand-name item. I used to think, what's the difference? It's only a few cents. Now when I go grocery shopping, I compare everything. With my own money, I buy the store-brand ketchup." Both girls laughed.

"How about children, Melody? Are you planning on having some soon, or are you going to wait a while?" Nancy asked.

"John and I have discussed it. But to tell you the truth, Nancy, I am kind of scared to bring a child into this world the way it is now, with the war in Vietnam going on, all those riots in the big cities, and the assassinations of the Kennedys and Martin Luther King. It's a scary time. With all the turmoil we're now living in, I don't think it would be fair to bring an innocent baby into the world right now. I don't think the future looks too bright either."

"I know what you're saying, Melody. All I can say is thank God for the 'pill.' It's been on the market for a few years now, and it seems to be working fine. President Johnson signed a bill giving the 'pill' to the poor. So working for the welfare department, I get mine free," Nancy said lightly.

"Look who just came in!" Melody said with a shocked voice.

Nancy looked toward the entrance. There were about fifteen people milling about. She couldn't make out whom Melody was talking about. Then one person caught her eye; because of the crowd moving about, she could get a clear view. He was tall with long black hair flowing down below his shoulders. At first glance Nancy thought it was a woman. When the person blocking her view stepped aside, Nancy could clearly see that this person wore a full beard. She recognized his posture, and as she strained to identify his eyes, she realized the mystery man was Danny Fredrick, Dressed like a hippie in jeans, sandals, a buckskin jacket, and beads around his neck, Danny spotted the table and started making his way toward his old comrades.

By now everyone at the table noticed the figure walking in their direction. His dress set him apart from the rest of the people. The closer he came to the group, the more people started to recognize him. Danny looked older than his age; his face was thin with mysterious eyes that looked sunken and sad. He raised his right hand with two fingers pointing in Churchill's trademark 'V' for victory. His poker-faced emotion didn't change when he forced a smile and said, "Peace." He stood quietly, waiting for a response to his greeting.

"Peace, Danny," Nancy said as she got up from the table and moved quickly around to give him a warm embrace.

"Yeah, peace, Danny," Alex said as reached out to shake Danny's hand.

"Peace" is all Tommy said in a loud voice.

Johnny picked up his beer from across the table, and he yelled, "Peace. I guess you're an official peacenik now—smoke pot and make love, not war; turn on and tune out. That's you, Danny, and if Uncle Sam wants you, he'll have to track you down. Maybe all the way to Canada?"

Danny looked over at Johnny and replied smoothly, "Hey, man, it may be cold up in Canada, but there ain't no draft."

"The only draft we're talking about this morning is draft beer," Phil said in a stern voice. He knew certain discussions of peace demonstrators would trigger sensitive nerves about Vietnam. "Now let's fill the glasses." And he poured glasses of beer from the pitcher he was holding.

"Come over here and have a seat, you long-haired hippie," Tommy said laughingly as he waved Danny over to an empty chair.

Danny felt comfortable being welcomed by Tommy, a Vietnam veteran. Danny was vehemently against the war in Asia, and he was an earnest advocate for peace throughout the world. The bonds of friendship formed in his childhood were still quite strong with Danny. His political stance was the polar opposite of Tommy, Phil, and other members of the group, but they were still friends who could be persuaded.

Danny picked up a glass of beer and walked unhurriedly over toward Tommy. They sat close together. They wanted a delicate conversation between just the two of them, the peacenik and the warrior. "Thanks, Tommy, I don't mind if I do. It's good to see you again. I really mean it. It is good to see you. I knew you were in 'Nam, and I was very happy to hear you made it back okay."

"Thanks, Danny, I appreciate your concern. I'm glad I made it back okay too. I heard you dropped out of college, and you're now playing in a band somewhere in Massachusetts. How did that all happen?" Tommy asked.

"Well, to tell you the truth, Tommy, I just got fed up with the way things were going. I could see the world was changing rapidly. I wanted to be involved. I just didn't want to stay in college marking time. So I split school to follow everyone's dream and join a rock-and-roll band and be part of the revolution. But we're more than just a band; we're a fraction of a worldwide movement. We're making history, traveling to mammoth peace demonstrations. You should see the crowds there; it's mind-boggling." Danny stared at the ceiling. "Look around you, Tommy. The whole world is freaking crazy. Just think what has happened in the past ten years. The Berlin wall was built; we almost had a nuclear war with Russia over the missiles in Cuba. We had one president assassinated; then his brother, Bobby, was assassinated. The peaceful, nonviolent movement of racial equality has changed to confrontation. Half the cities in America had large areas up in flames with the race riots. Detroit and Baltimore were devastated. Congress finally enacted a civil rights bill. But after that Martin Luther King Jr. was assassinated. The North Koreans captured the spy ship 'Pueblo'—what are we going to do there? Start a war with North Korea? If that happens the Chinese will enter for sure."

He paused for a moment, gathering his thoughts, and then continued as if he were giving a speech on a street corner. "We put a man on the moon and five hundred thousand soldiers in South Vietnam. We're bombing the hell out of Vietnam. We can't go on like this very much longer." Danny paused and drank his beer.

With piercing eyes he looked directly at Tommy. "It's like the song we do on stage, 'Eve of Destruction'." He began to sing the lyrics, "'Take a look around you, boy; it's bound to scare you, boy. Ah, you don't believe we're on the eve of destruction.' That song sends chills up my spine."

"To tell the truth, Danny, I've seen a lot of destruction." Tommy said calmly. "Most of the time, I can't stand people like you. You mimic the flower children of San Francisco who go to college to beat the draft, but even then they still are not content. No, they're out protesting a war that they don't understand or don't know anything about. They listen to some college professor from Berkeley spouting off about peace in the world, and they follow his edict as if it were gospel. And, I admit, sometimes I wonder if you're right. I would like to see peace in the world as much as you do, maybe even more. I'd like to make love not war. But if we don't stop the communist aggression in Vietnam, it could be like the Nazis during the thirties. They will take country after country until they're at our doorstep. Then it's too late."

"Don't tell me you fell for that old domino propaganda Washington puts out," Danny said, shaking his head. He was now being serious. "If Vietnam falls to the Communists, so will Cambodia, Laos, and Thailand. Even if that were true, what business is it of ours? Do you think those peasants working in the rice paddies care what the government does in Saigon? It's a civil war between the Vietnamese. We shouldn't be there."

"Danny, I fought alongside some of those people who used to toil in those rice paddies. They know firsthand what will happen if the Communists get control, and it doesn't mean living happily ever after on Sunnybrook Farm. You and your friends forget about the tens of thousands who fled North Vietnam after the French pulled out. Read Dr. Tom Dooley's book, 'The Night They Burned the Mountain'. You can read firsthand how kind and compassionate the Communists were to the Catholics in North Vietnam and Laos. The South Vietnamese government isn't perfect, but the people in the South have a better chance of living a life of freedom than the Communists in the North. "

Danny shot right back, saying, "What I see is the United States imposing a form of government on a people whether they want it or not. The Pentagon is too happy to flex its military muscles by sending the army and navy over there just to make sure they justify oversized budgets. We are bombing North Vietnam every day, killing innocent civilians for what? The people of Vietnam don't want us there, and I don't want us there either. I think the Tet offensive of last year proved the point. General Westmoreland said everything was under control; we are winning the minds and hearts of the people. Then all hell broke out during the Tet New Year's killing of thousands of people, including a lot of Americans who didn't want to be there either."

"Did you ever see the movie *The Ugly American* with Marlon Brando?" Tommy asked. Danny shook his head. "I think that movie gives a little insight into what this war in Vietnam is about. The story is about a small Asian country caught between the powerful forces of the world, communism and democracy. Brando plays the American ambassador sent to help this country develop into a prosperous, independent country. He is faced with fighting political corruption along with many other problems. But the big political challenge is how to handle the invasion of foreign fighters acting as a local, political, guerrilla force. It's a good movie and shines the light on a lot of aspects of what we are facing."

"I don't need to see a movie. I can watch the six o'clock news each night to see what's happening. It's a war, and it needs to be ended; and I'm going to do whatever I can to help end it," Danny said.

"Tell me, Danny, does it matter to you which side wins?"

Danny sat quietly for a minute, thinking. His eyes drifted around the room as if searching for an acceptable answer. "I want the people to win. I believe the United States should pull out its military force and stop the killing. Then let the people of Vietnam decide for themselves what form of government they want."

"I notice when the news media covers these antiwar demonstrations, your peace-loving, nonmilitary friends jubilantly wave the yellow-starred Vietcong flag. It seems to me that your side is yearning for a Communist victory."

"If that's what the people want, so be it. Let them decide for themselves. The United States should butt out," Danny said.

"What do you think the Communists will do? Make an announcement and say now that the Americans are gone, let's take a vote to see which form of government we should have? Or will they implement communism the old tried-and-true way, with bayonets and machine guns as it's enforced in the other Communist countries?" Tommy asked, waiting for an answer.

"You don't know for sure what will happen, Tommy. Personally I think the people of Vietnam would choose to live peacefully under communism rather than under the constant barrage of bombs and gunfire."

"Tell the truth, Danny. Why do you have so many clean, well-dressed, outstanding, upright citizens at your peace demonstrations? Isn't it really just to get together for boozing, drugging, and free sex? I was in Washington and witnessed one of your peace demonstrations; I saw firsthand what CBS didn't report. It wasn't a peace rally as much as a drug-induced orgy. But sadly while you and your comrades smoke dope, pop acid, and fuck each other, the image you portray for the cameras is as phony as a three-dollar bill. You all look so concerned as young Americans pleading for peace, waving a VC flag. The North Vietnamese show that shit. It's great propaganda and a morale builder for them. In the meantime a lot of brave, young Americans—kids like you and me—will die. You and your friends will help prolong the misery of this war and maybe destroy the hope of a people to live in a free and independent country," Tommy said solemnly.

"Look, Tommy, I know you served over there. You have a right to your opinion, and I have a right to mine. I consider you a friend, but we're going to disagree about this. I know I can't make you change your mind, and you're not going to change mine," Danny said.

"You're right, Danny, we do disagree on this. Fortunately we live in a country where we can disagree. But I'd rather listen to you play the guitar than listen to your political opinions," Tommy said with a chuckle.

"And I'd rather share a beer with you, Tommy, than share your views of the capitalist achievements and joys of democracy," Danny replied and picked up his beer as a toast.

Tommy lifted his beer, almost singing. "All I'm saying is give beer a chance."

"Tommy, it's been a long time since we last hoisted a brew together. To the good times we had and to the good times ahead," Danny said as he toasted his beer.

Both glasses were emptied with the toast. Tommy picked up the pitcher of beer in the center of the table and started refilling their glasses. "It has been a long time, Danny. The last time we were together was just before I went into the army. You weren't quite so politically driven at the time. I thought you and Ida had something very serious going on."

"We were pretty serious, but something happened. I don't know what for sure, but we just kind a drifted apart," Danny said as he was slowly thinking. "I know you had some strong feelings for her; she told me all about how you came on to her. She didn't want to come between you and me. Although she was nice to you, you weren't her type. Ida came from a wealthy family, and they expected her to marry on her social level."

"I liked Ida; she was someone special all right. Beautiful smile, a quick wit. She is a very bright girl, a lot of fun to be with. We were good friends for a while. And you're right, Danny. I wasn't her type," Tommy said quietly. "She knew what she wanted; she was looking for the pick of the litter, of a pedigreed line."

"She was my girl okay; we had something special. I thought we might even get married, but it just fell apart," Danny said again, thinking out loud. "I hope you didn't join the army just because she wouldn't have anything to do with you. I'm sure Ida wouldn't want to hurt your feelings. After all it was me she was in love with, and it was me she wanted to marry."

Tommy stared at his beer for a few seconds, and then slowly picked it up with both hands. He glared into Danny's eyes, asking a question and knowing the impact of the answer. "Tell me, Danny, does she still cry afterward?"

Danny's eyes opened wide; he stared at Tommy as if waiting for more. "You son of a bitch!" is all Danny could say as he sat frozen in thought. He held a posture of intensity as he glared at Tommy for what seemed a long time. "So that's why you went off and joined the army. She wouldn't have you either."

"Like you said, Danny, the man Ida is going to marry would be on her social level. Someone operating a D-8 bulldozer with callused hands and a farmer's tan wouldn't fit in at the country club. As I said we were good friends, even though I was not her type."

The gleam in Danny's eyes seemed to disappear, and his facial expression changed as a somber, melancholy mood came over him. "I guess I wasn't her type either," Danny said. "She dumped me, and that's when I dropped out of college just for one semester to get my head together. That was three years ago. I'm more screwed up now than I was then. I doubt if I'll ever go back for my degree. For now I just go from gig to gig. Someday I'll have to get my act together and get a real job. But God, I hope it's later than sooner."

"I know what you're talking about," Tommy said in a profound manner. "I have to make some major decisions too—whether to stay in the army and go to flight school to learn how to fly helicopters, which includes an all-expenses-paid return visit to Vietnam. Or I can go to college now that congress passed the GI Bill. It's rather ironic but true, because of Ho Chi Minh, who happen to assume room temperature earlier this year when he died, is the one who started the War, and as a result of the war, Senator Yarborough of Texas, was able to get the GI Bill passed. So Danny, with all your demonstrations and bitching about the war, it does have some good points. I was able to see parts of the world I could only read about. Not only that, but I might just get a college education out of it. Then who knows what the future has in store for me."

"Hey, there's Jake the barber," Phil yelled out.

The group at the table was excited to see Jake making his way across the floor. He was carrying a small, leather attaché case. "Hello, everybody," Jake said, smiling and waving to the group. "It's nice to see so many for the breakfast. I've been here every year. Some years the only one of the group I see is Phil. But each time I bring the journal." He smiled, rubbing the top of Phil's head; then he put the case on the table. "Phil, you need a haircut," he said jokingly. Everyone at the table laughed and cheered with the caretaker of the "breakfast journal."

Alex was first to put his hands on the journal. He slowly opened the attaché case, gently taking out the journal. He didn't open it in front of the others; he just held it for a moment, looking at it as if he were trying to visualize the words written on the pages.

"I'll put it over here on the edge of the table. Anyone who wishes to make an entry, feel free to take it," Alex said as he looked around the banquet room for a quiet area with some privacy. He spotted a small table at the far end where the food line was set up. He then pointed and said, "Over on the far corner, there's a table with a little privacy I think we can use." Alex put the journal down and hovered over it, patiently waiting for someone to venture forward to make an entry.

"Hello, everybody." Out of nowhere a deep, feminine voice vibrated across the crowded table. It took a second to register who the voice belonged to. Tommy instantly recognized the voice and, glaring into her eyes, confirmed the tall, distinctly dressed woman was Ida Freeman. Her stature and appearance grabbed the attention of those sitting at the table. She was wearing a calf-length, blue herringbone, Lord Chesterfield-style overcoat accented with a black velvet collar. The coat fit like a designer glove. Her entire wardrobe was in impeccable taste, displaying the cultivated look of sophistication and elegance. The open coat revealed a cream silk blouse under a plum, V-neck cardigan sweater. In her right hand, she carried a handbag with a discreet metal plaque at the center, which bore the name Gucci. She dressed to impress with the sophistication of international fashion. She looked as if she just stepped out of her Park Avenue residence.

It took a few seconds for everyone else to recognize who she was. Danny was out of his seat and instantly by her side. He put his arms around her, hugging her, but when he attempted to kiss her, she turned her head so his lips landed on her cheek. All the guys, except Tommy, ran over to be closer, offering greetings and "welcome back" comments. Nancy and Melody kept their seats, offering their greetings with a wave and forced smiles. Ida was thoroughly enjoying being the center of so much attention.

"What are you doing now, Ida? Whatever it is, keep it up," Phil said jokingly.

"I'm working in the city; I'm working for the New Yorker magazine. Believe it or not, I am now an official reporter of sorts," Ida said confidently.

"I remember many nights you pecking away with that little Smith Corona portable typewriter. You used to go through gallons of whiteout to correct all your typos," Danny said smiling. "But I knew you would be a success at whatever you wanted to do. It looks like all those writing courses you took finally paid off."

"Well, I'm kind of a reporter in training. I did a little of the footwork on a few stories. I did get to write my first story on a new program for kids called *Sesame Street*. It will be aired on the Public Broadcasting Network."

"What is public broadcasting?" Phil asked.

"I'll tell you later," Ida said calmly, then asked loudly, "How do I get a drink?"

Before she realized it, Tommy was at her side, offering her a glass of white wine and speaking in a cool voice. "Chardonnay, I'm afraid it's California. The bartender said he only has domestic white wine in those gallon jugs."

"Merci beaucoup," Ida said carelessly, smiling at Tommy as she took a sip of the wine. Then she added thoughtfully, "With whom I drink the wine is much more important than the vintage."

"Ah, that shows you have discriminating taste. But you've always displayed your preference of a discriminating taste," Tommy said in a shielded tone.

Ida's lips turned up in a smile. For a minute her eyes gazed at Tommy as if in a trance. She leaned forward, putting her hand on Tommy's shoulder and drawing him closer so she could privately whisper in his ear. "I came here to see you. We will talk privately later!"

Tommy slightly nodded his head with a half-smile and made eye contact with Ida, indicating he accepted her invitation.

"Ida, this is the first time I've seen you in a few years," Alex said. "Did you say you're working in New York City as a reporter? And you decided to come back to the Abingtons for our breakfast party. I would have thought the big city would be more fun with Macy's big parade and the Christmas decorations and the bright lights of Times Square."

"You're right, Alex. Some would say it's a lot more exciting in the city. But I've come into Scranton for the fine wine and intellectual chatter." Ida lifted her glass as if toasting, and in a laughing voice, she joked, "And cheap beer. But what I really wanted was that Polish kielbasa and fresh deer venison for breakfast. And of course I longed to see my adopted family here in the Abingtons. And catch up on the gossip."

Phil yelled out, "You chose a good weekend; Steigmeier beer is on sale. And everyone is in but Jerry Weaver. He's stationed at Fort Bragg; I guess you know he is in the Special Forces."

The group settled down, talking about current events and what had happened to them since last they were together. Ida seemed to draw the most attention, considering she was working on a nationally known magazine and she was the most traveled of the group. Tommy was also well traveled at the expense of the military with his visits to Vietnam, Hong Kong, and Okinawa.

"Ida, as a pup reporter have you ever worked on a big story?" Phil asked.

"Yes, I did work on a big story. Some consider it the biggest story of the year," Ida said confidently, waiting for someone to force her to continue.

"Was it about the loud music at Woodstock?" Johnny asked.

"No, Johnny, it was about Senator Edward Kennedy's accident last July at Chappaquiddick. Our magazine sent up a small army to cover the story. The woman I was working for at the time took me along. It was quite an event. You couldn't believe all the reporters there; they were all over that small island. In fact, there were more reporters covering that story than when Neil Armstrong walked on the moon two days later."

"I thought a man walking on the moon was the greatest event in the history of mankind," Nancy said.

"Yeah, I stayed up late to watch that live on TV. I remember Walter Cronkite's voice cracking; he was all choked up when he said in his deep, serious voice, 'The Eagle has landed.' And then a little later, the live pictures of Neil Armstrong hopping off the Eagle and taking the first step on the moon, that was the most amazing thing I've ever seen." Alex spoke as if he was part of the space program.

"The landing on the moon may have been a bigger story, but I can tell you, Ted Kennedy's car at Chappaquiddick sold more ink and paper," Ida said flatly.

"Did you know she was from down the valley near Wilkes-Barre? I think she graduated from Misericordia College," Phil said quietly.

"I didn't know she was from around here, but I do know what happened to her. It was a real tragedy her being with Senator Kennedy," Ida commented.

"It was terrible accident," Phil added quickly. "It was too bad she drowned."

"That's the point," Ida said. All eyes turned toward Ida. "She didn't drown. She died of asphyxiation. Apparently the senator had been drinking at the party. He was speeding, hit the edge of the bridge, and careened off the bridge, flipping the car on its top. It sank into about ten feet of water. Kennedy may have been thrown out and may have tried to rescue Mary Jo. But he had no luck, so he got to the shore and walked past a firehouse and a few homes back to the party to cover his tracks. He didn't even report the accident. A couple of fishermen found the car in the morning and walked to a nearby house. Then the police were notified. When they ran the plates to find out who owned the car, they discovered it was owned by the Kennedys. That's when Ted reported the accident." Ida now had everyone's attention. She continued telling the story like a Girl Scout leader. "Now the story gets interesting. The autopsy reports said she died of asphyxiation. It seems that Mary Jo survived the crash without as much as a bruise, but she was trapped in the car. There apparently was an air pocket in the backseat of the overturned car. That's where firemen found her, in the air pocket without fresh air. They estimated she was alive for about two and half hours after the accident. But Teddy boy didn't even report the accident."

Ida was center stage for a few minutes as she shared her New York experiences with her adopted country cousins. She continued with a few intriguing stories, including the inside scoop on why Jackie Kennedy married billionaire shipping tycoon Aristotle Onassis. After a while the magnetism of Ida and her stories slowly diminished. The spellbound listeners deserted her and went towards the bar for fresh drinks or the buffet table for some scrambled eggs, sausage, and kielbasa. Ida was talking alone with Alex when Tommy appeared, offering her a fresh drink.

"A little Southern Comfort to enhance your New York charm," Tommy said as he handed her the drink.

"This isn't flavored with hemlock, is it?" Ida said, smiling warmly at Tommy as she took the glass.

"I doubt if hemlock would have much effect on you, Ida," Tommy said jokingly. "No, this is just one of your old-time favorites, a Southern Comfort manhattan on the rocks."

"You remembered," Ida said. She took a sip and added, "I'm surprised."

"If you're really surprised, then I would be surprised," Tommy said flatly.

"Now, Tommy, we had some good times together," Ida said freely.

"That is true, we did have some good times. But tell me, how you are doing, living in the big city? For a while I thought you might stay here in the area," Tommy said as if thinking out loud. "Then again it was just for a short while I thought that."

"Let's go over to the bar so we can talk privately," Ida whispered to Tommy.

"What will the others think?" Tommy said as he nodded toward Danny.

"Who the hell cares?" Ida said with a seductive raised eyebrow.

When they arrived at the bar, Ida ordered first and spoke in a loud voice directly to the startled bartender. "I'd like a snowshoe on the rocks."

"A what ma'am? I'm not familiar with that drink," he answered.

"It's made like a manhattan; the difference is you use Southern Comfort instead of whiskey and white crème de menthe instead of vermouth."

"Yes, ma'am, and you, sir?" the bartender said looking over at Tommy.

"She knows how to live the good life. I'd like the same," Tommy said in a cocky tone.

"It's a nice breakfast drink. I discovered it in Anchorage at the Captain Cook Hotel." Ida paused, staring ahead, and then in a low voice, she said, "Sitting at the hotel bar, looking out at the sunset on the placid, reflective waters of Cook's Inlet is a beautiful experience." Again she paused. "But if you're alone, something is missing."

"Ida, remember you chose to be alone, to live in the big, crowded city," Tommy said intently. "You wanted the Broadway shows and the bright city lights, to hobnob with the jet-setters and rub elbows with the shakers and the movers. Your peddling around here in the backwaters was fun for a while, but I guess it wasn't for you, was it?"

The bartender put the drinks on the bar; Ida slapped a twenty-dollar bill down.

"Tell me, Tommy, did you take psychology training in the army?" Ida said coolly.

"I'm buying the drinks!" Tommy said to the bartender, handing him a twenty. "And to answer your question, Ida, no I didn't take psychology. And I don't have a beard like Sigmund Freud. But I understand a little about people. I've noticed they move most radically because of motivation or desperation. In your case it is ambition used as camouflage to conceal your fear of finding yourself. So you go off, traipsing about, searching for the truths of life. You seemed to be on top of the world. So I'm a little curious; why did you come back here at all?" Tommy asked as he picked up his drink.

"Searching for you, Tommy, I came back searching for you," Ida said in a sarcastic voice as she raised her glass as if to toast Tommy.

"Then why did you leave me?" Tommy quickly replied.

Ida stared at the amber-colored liquor in her drink as if looking for the answer. "I wanted something important out of life. I want to be someone of notice. I love this scenic valley with its hardworking, warm, friendly people. They are wonderful folks but they are closed- minded and opinionated. I just couldn't see myself getting married right out of college, having kids, pinching pennies, and saving up to make a down payment on a small rinky-dink house that I'd reluctantly call a home. I don't want to have any children, so living here wasn't for me. I'd go crazy with boredom doing the same thing each day. Talking the small-town talk with no outside stimulation. I wanted a fast-paced, open-minded society like New York, where you can do almost whatever you want and still appear normal. When I walk around New York, my senses are elevated. The noisy streets, the smell of ethnic foods, and considering I don't like to cook, it's a great town for eating out without getting bored. I never liked to drive when I was growing up in downtown Chicago. So I like walking briskly through the city, glancing at the ever-changing faces. When I stroll down the streets of New York, I can feel the energy everywhere. I enjoy the best restaurants, the Broadway shows, and the greatest sporting events. Not to mention that New York is the epicenter of network news and entertainment. Tommy, it's something special to walk down Wall Street, knowing this is the financial center of the world."

"I don't blame you for not staying around here. You've probably done more in a few years than most people here will do in their entire life," Tommy said, looking over at Ida with a sad look on his face. "I know I can't come back here to live, but I don't know where else to go. I too want to do something with my life, or as Marlon Brando said, 'I want to be somebody'."

"I believe Brando said, 'I could have been a contender.'" Ida picked up her drink again, staring at the contents. Her eyes and head drifted toward Tommy.

"I know what you mean, Ida," Tommy replied, increasing the energy in his voice. "I've changed a lot more than I realized. The last few years have been an eye-opener for me. I can see now how protected we were and how little I knew growing up here. I wish I had your guts to go off and do what you did, to carve out your own life, to be strong and independent on your own, living a life others only dream about."

She said, "Making good in your own hometown can be tough. I read somewhere that it's difficult to be a prophet in your own village."

"I know," Tommy said quietly. "We had one guy in our outfit, his name was Kuzneckie. Old Kuz just couldn't wait until he got back home. He wanted out of Vietnam and out of the army in the worst way. All he talked about were his friends in the small town where he grew up. He said that when he got back home, he wouldn't even leave his front porch. He joked that he wouldn't ever wear a green shirt again. There'd be no more standing in line, and he would never get wet in the rain again. He came back to the States before me. When I returned from 'Nam, I was reassigned to Fort Bragg. I was walking across post one day, and to my surprise I spotted old Kuz. I was so dumbfounded you could have knocked me over with feather. I ran over to him and asked what the hell was he doing back in the army?"

Tommy slowly picked up his drink and looked over toward Ida. "Kuz told me after he got home he got a job right away in the basement of a department store, making a dollar seventy-five an hour. He was working in the domestic department, which meant stacking and selling sheets and pillows. His boss had been working there for eleven years and was making two-fifty an hour. Counting sheets, answering questions like is this sheet for a queen-size bed or double? Working this boring job till closing time at 9:00 p.m. Kuz told me he just couldn't take it. He kept thinking of the guys still humping in the jungle. To him working in the basement of a department store with a bunch of nice old ladies was unbearable. He only lasted three days. I take that back; on the morning of the third day, he told his boss he thought he left his car lights on, so he left and never went back. As bad as the army was, he felt more comfortable being back in uniform, and he reenlisted. He told me he couldn't go home again to live. He had changed too much." Tommy paused for a moment and added, "Ida, I'm afraid I am a little like Kuz."

"Maybe we're both a little like Kuz," she said. "We go out into life and are shocked at how the world is away from here. We believe we can always go back to our comfortable little refuge. When I come back here, I feel as if I want to belong. But in my heart I know I'm just a visitor. Perhaps, Tommy, neither one of us was meant to live our lives here in the Abingtons."

Tommy wanted to cry out to Ida. Maybe if we were together, we both could live here. We could be happy for the rest of our lives. But no, not you, Ida; you wouldn't have it that way. No, you just want to visit, observe, have fun, and leave. You're callous about my feeling for you; as a matter-of-fact, you don't care about anyone but yourself. Instead Tommy stared at his drink and said nothing.

"Did you hear what I said, Tommy?" Ida asked.

"Yes, I did, Ida. I'm sorry, I was thinking about something else. Let's have another drink. Bartender, if you please?" Tommy said, waving his hand to get attention.

After they downed the round of drinks, Tommy ordered another round. The liquor was having its effect on the couple as they continued their private conversation.

"Well now, Ida, you're a big success in New York, making the big bucks. Is it everything you expected?" Tommy asked. His words were now beginning to slur.

"I'll tell you, Tommy, living in New York City is kind of like reading a great novel. You can describe the experience in a few sentences, but when you consider the experience, it's really hard to explain the personal impact it has on you. In the first place, New York City is the noisiest place in the world; it's never quiet. The sound of moving traffic, cars, trucks, and busses is constant, with people blowing their horns at all hours of the day, and the sound of fire trucks and ambulances racing up the streets with their sirens screaming. Even when you're walking down the street, there's a constant hum of people talking or yelling about something. Not everyone can live there; it takes a special person with strong desires and beliefs. It's not the friendliest city to live in. If you buy something here in Scranton and you don't like it, you return it. You take it to the store, the salesperson is usually pretty friendly and says fine, okay, no hassle, and you go about your day. If you return something in New York, there's an attitude that you're trying to get something over on the store. Then you have to fight and argue to get a credit. In New York you have to fight for everything. You have to fight for your seat on the subway; you have to fight to keep your place in line. You have to fight just to get a drink in a bar. You're constantly struggling just to claim you own breathing space. You're always in contention with someone to establish you own worth and at the same time not wanting to get hurt."

"Why in hell would you want to live there?" Tommy asked.

Ida was just finishing her drink, and she pointed her glass toward Tommy as if to lecture. "Because New York City is the most fabulous place on earth. It attracts the best and the brightest from around the world. The super smart and most talented people come to New York. They're the ones who stand out with a driving passion to succeed. They want to make their mark in the Big Apple because it's the epicenter of the arts, theater, architecture, writing, international trade, business and finance, and anything else you can think of. And it's filled with young, energetic elitists who want to be around other young, aggressive elitists with a mission to change the world. You know, I've chosen the most exciting lifestyle imaginable. I sometimes feel sorry for those who don't have the opportunities like I've had. It's really great to live in New York."

"Let's have another drinky poo," Ida said with a chuckle. She waved her hand high toward the bartender for another round.

"So you came back here to show us country bumpkins just how successful you really are? I'm sure Melody and Nancy appreciate the latest fashion tips. It all sounds pretty exciting." Tommy paused for a moment, then his voice dropped as he asked in a whisper, "But late at night when you're all alone in your luxurious, tastefully furnished apartment looking out at the bright lights, tell me the truth, Ida, is it always so glamorous?

Ida glared at Tommy for a moment and said in a controlled lower tone, "You can be a bastard sometimes." She picked up her fresh drink, downing half of it in a single gulp. "So Tommy, you really want to know what it's like is to live in the big city? Well, let me tell you, Tommy. There's a certain camaraderie among people who live in the city. It takes guts to live there. It's not for the faint of heart." She slowly took another large sip of her drink. Then turning toward Tommy and staring into his eyes, she said, "For one thing you don't drive; everyone walks and that takes energy. You have to develop an attitude about you. When you walk down the street, you always walk fast with a determined strut, eyes straight ahead, wearing a face without emotion. You create a portrait that says, 'Don't get in my way, and don't screw with me!' At the same time, there's a little voice inside wanting to say, 'Hey there, I'm a really nice person.' It's really difficult to project this tough image and yet have the normal human feelings and desires like everyone else. I'm so busy taking care of myself, I don't let anyone get close to me."

"So there's a human side of the fabulous lifestyle of New York," Tommy said sarcastically.

"Yes, there's a human side of my lifestyle." Ida's head drooped down, staring at the bar. She thought for a moment. "It's funny when I think about the grandiosity of New York coupled with my low self-esteem; it's quite a paradox. In spite of how diverse the lifestyle is in New York, with all the young people, it's hard to meet anyone to care about. I know I have a lot of things going for me, but maybe I've become too tough, and my attitude can turn guys off. It can be so damn lonely. There's no one I can ask casually to help move a heavy box or put up a bookshelf. I don't like to cook, so most nights I order in. But sometimes I have to get out of my four walls just to feel the contact of other people. So I'll go to a restaurant alone and bring my book to read, and I'll sit there looking fine as if I don't care. But really I'm so lonely; I just sit there wishing I were with someone. I like to go to Central Park to take in a little nature, feel the sun on my face, and look at the beautiful big trees. I'll see a young couple holding hands or talking intimately, and that's when I feel the lonely desperation in the pit of my stomach. I often feel ashamed for being out in public all by myself. If I go to a restaurant or a bar and a waitress or waiter remembers my name, I feel wonderful—I'm human, and at least someone knows that I'm alive. There are times when I would give anything just to be normal like the folks around here, but you see, Tommy, normal people don't live in New York City.

"I thought life was so perfect there," Tommy said quietly

"Perfect, hardly," Ida said with a laugh. "The luxury apartment you mentioned I share with an extended family of cockroaches. It's not because my place is a dump. It's because cockroaches are in every apartment in New York. In the higher-rent districts, the lingo is we have them under control. The exterminator is as regular as the meter reader; they both make their rounds once a month. It's true, yellow cabs and cockroaches are found all around the city. The cockroaches disappear when the lights go on, and the cabs disappear when it rains. I guess the really unique thing about New York City is you can get the best hairstyle in the world. And that's what every girl really wants."

"Is that what you want, Ida, a perfect haircut?" Tommy asked sadly.

"I want a lot more, Tommy. I want it all." She laughed out loud. "When I walk down the street, I want people to notice me. And I want Mr. Perfect right alongside of me. The tall, outdoorsy type, who's very smart with a fantastic resume, makes lots of money, and knows how to dress."

Have you found Mr. Perfect?" Tommy asked.

"I came close once; the guy worked on Wall Street for one of the large brokerage firms. He was handsome; oh God, was he handsome. He was a Harvard man with an MBA. He had a big motorcycle; I think it was a Harley-Davidson. We had a fantastic time riding all around the city on that bike. I was a cool bitch, and I dressed for the part in tight jeans, carrying my helmet cocked under my arm. You should have seen the raised eyebrows when we would foray into a restaurant" Ida paused as if daydreaming. "I liked being somebody, and I liked being with this guy; together we made a damn good-looking couple. I really wanted to stay with him even though we really had nothing whatsoever in common"

"So what happened?"

"He was very competitive always looking for something better. That included women. When someone better came along, he chased after the skirt. He disappeared like the sound of the rumbling motorcycle. You've got to remember that competition in the city is fierce; you compete on the job, you compete in the subway, you compete in everything. Guys are always looking for better, prettier, smarter, and newer. I remember standing in line one night, trying to be picked to get into a fashionable club. I was dressed to the tens. My hair was perfect, the makeup was right; I was so confident. I stood there for a couple hours, but I wasn't picked. It was so humiliating. I can't describe the feeling of rejection; it's so tough sometimes. If you're not up for the game each day, well, you get cut from the team. There's always some other girl who's prettier and smarter and might have more to offer, and she's usually an attractive blonde. Then you're left alone again, worse off than before."

"Maybe you should lower your standards a little from Mr. Perfect with his expensive wardrobe and impressive resume to a Mr. Average who's not quite as interested in the stiff competition," Tommy said jokingly.

"I hate to tell you this, Tommy," Ida said as she picked up her drink and looked at Tommy with a smile, "but I have dropped my standards quite a bit. It got so bad I used to buy the New York Magazine, which is the 'in' magazine for young Jewish people in the city. I would go to the back and read the personals. Before you ask, yes, I did get a few dates from there. They were horrible. But I wanted to meet a nice Jewish guy, and there are not many ways to meet Jewish men. This magazine had ads for Jewish singles dance clubs, and so I went to a few. What a nightmare that was. I'd buy a nice outfit for the event and go out with high hopes of finding a nice guy, maybe not to marry but just to have sex with. But secretly I was hoping that I just might meet the right guy, and it could turn into something special. I'd go to the club with a great attitude; I'd stand off to the side making small talk with a few of the girls on the floor. Then some three-hundred-pound nebbish of a guy would come over to ask me to dance with him. My heart would crumble. I never met a nice guy at any of those dances, and the ones I did meet would drive me crazy. They'd called on the phone, and I couldn't stand to listen to their whining Jewish voices. When I'd pick up the phone, I would cringe, my teeth would grind, and I could feel pain shooting up my spine like the sound of fingernails scraping across a chalkboard as I heard, 'Hi, Ida, how are you doing?' I just couldn't take it. So I gave up my quest for the perfect Jewish partner, along with my dreams of going to Fire Island for the summer."

Tommy was chuckling to himself as Ida described her dating dilemma. If she would only realize how much he cared for her. But this wasn't the time for him to make an overture . . .or was it? "Ida, have you ever considered having a lasting relationship with someone who cares about you?"

"Tommy, if you are applying for the job of being my shrink, the position is already filled. That's another thing; you may not know it, but to be a bona fide resident of New York City, you must be in therapy, pay income taxes, and curse more than anyone else. This is the way we carry off the illusion of being independent and enjoying this fabulous lifestyle. So when I come back and visit the common folks living their boring lives, they all can look up at me and say how much they admire me for all I've accomplished." Ida picked up her drink and downed the remaining booze. "I do live a fabulous life, but I pay a high price for it. And yes, there are times when I'm alone in my apartment and I'll open my refrigerator, hoping to find something in there. Then I realize there's no food because I don't cook. I'll just stare into the cold, white, empty interior. That's when I feel what loneliness is, and I wonder why I have to be so dissatisfied with living a normal, comfortable, common way of life. I like to come back here to see these dull people who enjoy being comfortable with each other, doing the things they enjoy doing, and living a quiet, no-hassle, sheltered lifestyle. There are times I wish I could be one of them, but I'd never let them know that." Ida picked up her empty glass and looked over at Tommy. "I've chosen the life I want, and I'm willing to pay the price, whatever it takes."

"I don't know what you want me to tell you, Ida," Tommy said as he looked over at her with eyes of concern. "You're a lot better off than a lot of people here. Look around you. Do you think these people are as happy and content as Carnation cows? They all have their own problems, not the same as you and your friends in New York, but just as real to them." Tommy pointed toward the numerous tables in the ballroom. "At each table you'll find those kind people sharing the secret emotions of frustration, insecurity, fear, loneliness, and jealousy. They may not even know how to express it; they'll probably never tell anyone because they are not in therapy."

"Could we have another round, if you please?" Ida yelled at the bartender. She turned toward Tommy, glaring and with a serious expression, she asked, "Will you come back to New York with me? We could have a great time. I could show you a life you only read about."

"I can't, Ida." Tommy's eyes peered into hers, searching to find a sense of feeling behind what she just said. Was it the booze talking, or was she revealing her true feelings and she did care for him? Or was she just throwing out words as an afterthought without meaning? "Even if I wanted to, I can't. I'm still in the army. Look, you made it clear once before that you didn't think I'd fit in your lifestyle. You were probably right. Let's face it, Ida. What you want out of life and what I want are two different ends of the spectrum. Living in New York City isn't in the cards for me. Hell, I bet you can't even hear the crickets at night."

"Tommy," Ida said with an anxious voice. She didn't have an opportunity to say another word. Tommy happened to glance over his shoulder and saw Danny heading in their direction. Before Tommy could alert Ida, Danny was standing right next to them. "Hey, aren't you two joining our party, or is this a private affair?" Danny said, knowing he was breaking up their quiet rendezvous.

"We're just finishing up our drinks," Tommy said with a voice of authority.

"Well, they've missed you over at the table, and they've started writing in the journal. I'm sure you would want to put in your two cents, Tommy," said Danny with a smirk on his face.

"Yeah, I would Danny; maybe I'll put something about you in it—how much you love the country or how you tried to join the Marines but were turned down. Nah, I don't have enough imagination to even think about it," Tommy said sarcastically as he grabbed Ida's arm and led her back to their table.

"Maybe that's your problem, Tommy," Danny yelled right back, his head cocked back and defiant. "You don't have any imagination."

Tommy walked directly in front of Danny, looking intensely into his eyes and said with a condescending smile, "I don't need any imagination knowing what I'm in for." Tommy glanced at Ida. "Shall we go, Ida?" Arm in arm they walked back to the area where the group was gathered.

Jake was in the center of the group. He was holding the journal in one arm close to his breast. To him it was very important. Over the years some outsiders noticed the strange-looking leather book that Jake always had in his possession at the breakfast. Each year one or two people would ask, "Jake, why is it at every breakfast you have that strange book with you?" Jake would smile, saying, "It's just a notebook. A few of the regulars asked me to keep it for them. It's their way of keeping in touch with each other." He would say no more.

Johnny was standing next to Jake yakking in his ear, apparently telling him some new jokes. Johnny was animated, telling his stories with both arms flopping in the air as he spoke loudly. Jake was politely nodding his head as if he were paying attention to Johnny's conversation, but his eyes were focused elsewhere.

"Alex!" Jake said in a loud voice, waving with one hand.

"Ah, Jake, I guess it's time for our ritual writing," Alex said as he joined the small group. "Who wants to be first?"

"I'll be first!" Johnny said without hesitation. "I'm not afraid to write what I'm thinking. And I don't need fancy words to say it either."

"You're right, Johnny, there are no fancy words for the way you think!" Phil said with a laugh.

Johnny came right back, looking at Phil sarcastically. "Yeah? Well, some people do a lot more work than thinking. And you, Phil, ought to do a little less thinking and a little more working, schoolteacher!"

With that said Johnny grabbed the journal from Jake's arms, walked over to a deserted table, calmly sat down, and started writing.

November '69

One more year of listening to these people who think they have all the answers. They seem to live in a dream world. I know what life is about. It's hard work getting what you want. But you've got to work for it. I'm willing to work for what I want, and we will see if these dreamers ever get what they expect. Melody and I are happy. We are starting out in life on a good note. We have our own place. If things go well, we'll have a nice place in the near future. I love her, and this year could be a good year if I don't get drafted.

Johnny Thompson "69"

When Johnny's brief writing was completed, Melody was quick to go over to the table to make her entry.

November 21, 1969

Hi Diary,

Well, I'm back again this year. This year seems like a good gathering. Other years it's been kind of lonely, but this year is a good turnout. Johnny and I are very happy. He works so hard; I wish we could spend more time together, but we have to work hard to get the things we want. We now have our own place we call home, and I now feel as though I am finally growing up. Soon I hope we will be able to afford to have children. I know God wants us to have children. John is working so hard; I am very proud of him. I am trying to be a good wife and a good Christian. I hope this war in Vietnam doesn't last much longer. There's a possibility Johnny could be drafted. If that happens I don't know what I'll do. I love him so much. Well, we don't have to worry about it now. I hope this year will be good for us all.

Melody Thompson

I hope everyone has a nice Christmas this year, and this war in Vietnam ends soon.

PS: My family is now starting to like Johnny.

As soon as Melody put down her pen, Danny, who was standing alone, bolted over to the table. He sat down without hesitation and began writing quickly.

To whom it may be of interest,

I came in this weekend to see what changes are happening in my old hometown. I don't see any. I wonder why I even came back at all to this phony breakfast with a bunch of shallow, brain-dead morons. The world is radically changing, and no one here even notices. The rest of the world is alive with revolution. People our age now have a voice so powerful we will be changing everything in this reactionary world. It may take a longer time to catch on here, but it will. I don't see much hope here; just a few are using their brains and are being educated. I feel sorry for those that will not see. Most of these people don't have what it takes to get involved. They are so worried about their next drink, a cool car, or buying a cheap house. Our generation is on the cutting edge of a world of change. I am going to be part of the movement. I have a burning energy to make this world a better place, where all people—black, white, and yellow—are treated as equals.

I'll do whatever I can to help the growing protest against this war in Vietnam. And I'll fight against the corrupt government in Washington. I will make a difference. you will probably read my name in the papers. I doubt if I will ever come back here again.

Lots of luck!

Danny Fredrick

Danny stood up quickly and turned to walk away; in his intense state of mind, he brushed along the table and knocked the journal to the floor. He didn't seem to notice for he just kept walking, head held high, right out the main door. He didn't say a word to anyone.

"I know we all march to the beat of a different drummer," Nancy said, staring at Danny with a puzzled look. "But I thought we could at least remain friends."

"You can bet he's not marching to a military drumbeat, that's for sure." Johnny loudly proclaimed.

Phil stood watching for a moment and then in a low voice said, "I think Danny has been marching to his own drumbeat for a long time."

"Don't we all?" Tommy said.

Alex was unaware of the commotion, for he had walked over to the table. He had a concerned look as he genuflected with a motion of reverence and gingerly picked up the journal. Standing for a moment, he glanced at the random page of the opened journal.

November 23, 1967

Dear Journal,

Home is where the heart is!

I'm glad to be home again as a staff sergeant in the United States Army. This will be a short visit, but I hope it will be a fun-filled one. It's nice to be back in the land of the big PX. "you can't really appreciate the good until you have seen the bad." I just completed a tour in the high lands of Vietnam, such a beautiful country. I was with an A-team in the First Special Forces group. It's great to be a real A-team. Our job was to help train and support the mountain tribes or "montagnards" (mountain people) as the French call them, or "yards" as we called them. They're a primitive type, bow-and-arrow people living off the land as they have for centuries, wearing little clothing. They would like to be left alone to hunt and farm the enchanting highlands. But sadly they are caught in a war. Just after I arrived in country, our team went into a village called Pkl Que and rescued over one hundred of these gentle people from the Vietcong. These soft-spoken people, including small children and women, were captured over eight years ago.

The Communists used them as camp slaves. They were tortured and many of them killed. I was proud to be a part of the team that put an end to their nightmare. I really felt sorry for these folks. They are so grateful to us for being there. We now have them at a fortified camp and are teaching them how to secure their own future. They are some of the friendliest people I have ever met, other than those living in the Abingtons. They are an honorable people. They don't lie, cheat, or steal. As small as they are, they would pick up a BAR gun that weighs as much as they do and carry it until they drop. A few weeks ago we had a big celebration, kind of a Thanksgiving. The specialty of the meal was a delicious meat called "roe deer." Of course we have the same animals in America, only we call them "dogs." Later that night the village chief presented me with a Montagnards bracelet. It was quite an honor, something I am very proud of. I will always wear this brass bracelet.

My experience in Vietnam helps me appreciate all we have here even more. It's hard to believe sometimes that many of my friends back here don't understand that a war is going on.

Even as I write in this book today, unfortunately, some American servicemen will die, and tomorrow more will die. I don't know the answer to this. But I expect to do my duty. I love the people here. I love my country. I know I am going a little long, but I don't know when I will be back. I don't want to get teary-eyed and ruin this page.

I hope to be back again. If not, I lived and I loved.

Sgt. Jerry Weaver

Alex read the entry with deep emotional concentration. He didn't notice anyone or anything. For a few moments, he stood like a statue as he read and reread Jerry's words. He was just starting to realize what Jerry and others were doing at this time. Alex was more concerned about what color his new car was or making sure his suits came from the "right" stores. How shallow his life was in comparison to what Jerry and others were doing.

"Hey, what are you reading? How Melody lost her virginity?" Johnny's voice echoed in Alex's ear.

That broke the spell; Alex looked toward those at the bar, smiled, and then sat down to write his thoughts and feelings.

"Johnny! Stop that," Melody said, hitting him on the shoulder. "You're terrible."

"Melody, you mean he was terrible about the virginity thing?" Phil injected quickly with a loud laugh.

Now Johnny's face turned red; he looked over at Phil and said loudly, "Well, Phil, it must have cost you at least five bucks to lose you're virginity!"

"Not really, Johnny," Phil said with a chuckle. "All I had to do was smile, buy her a drink, and tell her I didn't know who you were." Again he laughed

As the joking and badgering went on unnoticed by Alex, he started to write.

Thanksgiving 1969

I have a lot to be thankful for. I have a good job, looks like a nice future ahead. But we'll see about that. Life for me is good. But I do see the pain and horror in the world around me. I hope this war in Vietnam will end soon. We put a man on the moon this summer; maybe we can put peace on earth. I am torn apart with my inner feelings. I believe in what Jerry, Tommy, and others are doing. But I hate the thought that the war will go on and on, yet there seems to be no end to it all. I have a medium-rated draft number; I'm out of college now, so who knows, I may be the next one drafted. I won't go to Canada; if called I will go. The antiwar demonstrations are getting larger and larger, joined by people like Danny. I prefer the courage of people like Jerry and Tommy. But I would like to see no more war . . . like in the Plastic Ono Band's song, "Give Peace a Chance." Let's hope next year will be better.

That's where I'm at now.

Signing off,

Alex

Alex put the pen down slowly and deliberately, staring at the journal as if thinking about writing something more. But he didn't write anything else; he just walked over to the others with a forced smile.

Phil Whitman decided it was his turn, and he stepped forward without saying a word. He walked solemnly over toward the table, sat down, and started writing.

Thanksgiving '69

A good year, and I am happy to be at the breakfast again. One advantage of not leaving town is I get to come to this event each year. I do see the same people year after year, although sometimes I have the feeling I'm missing out on life, being left behind. I'd like to go off to other countries and see what's on the other side of the mountain.

As a teacher, I should mention some of the things that have happened this year. We have a new president, Richard Nixon. He was elected with a plan to end the war. But the big story is Neil Armstrong, the first man to walk on the moon.

The most fascinating part is that we watched it live on TV. We live in a new high-tech era. The British and the French started flying a supersonic jet passenger plane called the Concorde, and our Boeing boys built the giant 747. Back to earth, just over the state border in Woodstock, there was a giant freak show and rock festival that shook the world. On the sports side, in this year's Super Bowl, my favorite team, the New york Jets and Broadway Joe Namath, beat the unbeatable Baltimore Colts.

Last summer I was considering joining the Peace Corps or volunteering to work in the South to help in the segregation battle. But when Martin Luther King Jr. was killed, that put the skids on that. So I guess I will remain at my post as a local high school teacher. There are not many jobs in the area. The only jobs available are ones with family connections, and that means many of my friends and students will find a career and life in other places. It's kind of sad.

I hope next year will be more peaceful; I hope the war ends. I hate to see our young going off to war.

Let me finish on a good note: The Abington Comets had a great football team this year.

Phil

Tommy was next to adding to the journal.

Tommy 1969

Hello again, Journal,

I made it back home for the breakfast. There were times that I didn't know if I would. When I was in Vietnam, Thanksgiving morning and Christmas Eve were the two days I missed the most. My heart was here on both occasions. Since my last writing, the town and many people haven't changed much, but I have. I would like to live here in this area with my family and friends, but I can see my future is pulling me in different directions. I have set some goals in my life: college and being successful in whatever career I choose. Achieving my goals in life in the Abingtons would be difficult. I remember reading in the Bible, Jesus said, "No prophet is welcome on his home turf."

As much as I love this area, I'm afraid my children won't grow up in these hills of Summit. I won't be able to share with them the mountains we tracked through or the fields we played in as children, or swimming and jumping off the ledges at our favorite stream at Little Rocky Glen.

They won't know the comfortable feeling of knowing most of your neighbors and their peculiar habits, or going into any store and knowing there will be someone there who's a friend of yours or a friend of someone in your family. Growing up here was a wonderful experience, but I don't see myself living here or raising my family here, and I'm a little sad about that. But I do enjoy coming back whenever I can.

Until next time,

Tommy

Nancy walked over to the table without any sign of emotion. She sat, quietly writing.

November 27, 1969

Hello Journal,

It's been a few memorable years since I last penned a few words here. Life hasn't been as great as it could have been. I am glad I came in for this breakfast. It's a special weekend. Taking in the old town, spending time with friends and family, visiting some of the old haunts, seeing some friendly faces. It's enjoyable sharing our past experiences with close friends and revisiting the good feelings of our youth. I sometimes wish I could stay here forever. Life would be so much simpler.

But life is tough now with Vietnam on the TV each night, and now my friends are going off to this godforsaken war. I agree with Danny about peace. I can't do much about it. I have a real life to live with a new husband and great hopes for our future. So I will keep my spirit grounded here through this journal. I hope and pray we will have peace soon and a better life for us all.

Nancy

The group stood together talking, laughing loudly. Tommy turned toward Ida and remarked, "Ida, it's your turn to participate in our little ritual. I'm sure as a world traveler you'll have some words of wisdom."

Ida stared into Tommy's eyes for a frozen moment and then said in a cool voice, "Thank you for your consideration, Tommy. I'll be happy to jot a few words for posterity." She then walked toward the table, passing Nancy without comment or notice.

Hello Journal,

It's nice to be back for a festive event such as this breakfast. I do enjoy the warmth of my friends here. So often I think of you all and wish I had more time to spend here. But life is life, and I have other responsibilities. These last few years have been very busy, filled with hard work and fun. So coming to the breakfast is a step back to quiet times and to be with people who accept me for what I am and who I am. I feel comfortable here. Many times, either traveling or in New york when I'm all alone, I often reflect on the kind people who live here and think how nice the world would be if it were populated with these types of people. I'm glad I came back, and we all have good years ahead and keep in touch with each other.

You are my true, deep-seated friends.

Ida

After Ida finished Phil went over to the table, lifting the journal with great respect and taking it over to Jake the barber for good keeping. To those in attendance, this was like a sacred ritual. Jake put the book into his attaché case, said good-bye to all, and left the room.

"Let' have one and done!" Tommy said as he pointed to the bar.

"One more drink at this time of the day won't hurt anyone." Phil said loudly.

""It sure wouldn't hurt anyone if you finally paid for it Phil!" Johnny yelled as they walked toward the bar.

"Johnny, I would pay anything to have you drink yourself into a stupor, but then again who would know the difference?" Phil said with a loud laugh.

They all adjourned to the bar, Tommy ordering the round of drinks. "Beer tender, another bar!" Tommy ordered loudly, adding, "We'll all have a shot of Southern Comfort with the beer chaser!"

"Breakfast of champions, I dare say!" Ida yelled jokingly.

"Alex, you make the toast," Phil said as the bartender set up the round of drinks.

Alex was a little startled at the thought, but he gained his composure and picked up the shot of whiskey. Looking at the group, he spoke in a commanding voice, "To our good times of the past, may they be the pathway to the good times of the future. May we all remain as close as we are." He made the toast as he looked around at the band of merry friends; then he focused in on Nancy, smiling with warm affection, not the intensity of the past.

Tommy and Ida toasted toward each other, staring into each other's eyes, as they gulped down the shot of whiskey. They immediately picked up a couple of glasses of beer from the bar and also doused them quickly.

"Where do we go from here?" Tommy asked smiling over at Ida.

"There's a football game, and there's the Nichols Village Motel," Ida said, cocking her head back, shifting her long hair without using her hands. Then she added whimsically, "Which do you prefer?"

Tommy smiled. Then in a mild but determined voice, he said, "I'd rather play around than walk around."

"So would I, Tommy," Ida said. They were the last to leave.

Chapter Five

1986

Fourteen years had passed since Alex last attended the Thanksgiving breakfast party. Many things had changed in his life. He was now married with two daughters and a son of his own. Alex had developed into a mature adult, a caring husband, and a loving father. He worked very hard to be a good provider for his family. On this cool but sunny Wednesday afternoon, he and his family drove down State Street in Clarks Summit. His eyes searched through the scenery for familiar images of his past. The community didn't seem to change very much. The foliage on the many large maple trees displayed a colorful burst of crimson red and Halloween orange. The scenery felt so familiar; as if frozen in time, much of the natural features appeared unchanged. On the marquee of the Comerford Movie Theater, *Mr. Mom* with Michael Keaton was playing. The small sign of the Holly Lane Dress Shop was still discretely visible on the unique stone building that served as an upscale women's boutique. In the small office building across the street was Jake's Barbershop. A little further down State Street was the focal point of the community, Our Lady of Snows Catholic Church. The Summit Diner maintained its foremost corner position. Although many things were unaltered, there were significant changes in the scenery of Clarks Summit.

In 1970 a fire started in Davis's Five and Dime store, which was located directly across the street from the picturesque fieldstone Catholic Church. The fire spread quickly, engulfing other buildings. The entire community turned out that afternoon to witness this catastrophic event. Within a few hours, this general alarm fire destroyed the entire block of stores and small businesses. Over a period of years, the small retail shops and businesses were replaced with newer facilities. However, the decor of the newer buildings lacked the charm or ambiance of the historic structures they replaced.

There was another change in Clarks Summit that would have a great effect on Alex; the Abingtons most interesting personality and bar owner, Eddy O'Connor, had died a few years before. Alex loved the old character. For Alex, Eddy's death was an emotional veil of separation from the good times of the past. A short time after Eddy's death, his widow, Frances, sold the bar to a young, local entrepreneur. O'Connor's Bar was now called John K's Pub. The new proprietor had high hopes for this business opportunity. After all, it was an excellent location in a growing community.

So many things had changed, yet so much seemed to be the same. Youthful memories of powerful emotions that once dominated Alex's early life were lying just below the surface and were now starting to emerge again. Perhaps for a few hours he could recapture some of the excitement and enjoyment of those carefree days and nights. What he really wanted to do was to hook up with some of his old friends, the A-team. This Wednesday night could be a return to the fun days of yesteryear.

Alex, his wife, Beth, and their children—son Derrick, age eleven, and daughters Courtney, fourteen, and Mandy, eight—were staying with his parents for the Thanksgiving weekend. This would be a rare family holiday spent with Alex's mother and father. Even so it would be party time for Alex and an opportunity to connect with some of the old gang at the newly named establishment, John Kay's Pub. The ownership had changed, but it was still a bar and a good meeting place for old friends to celebrate. And celebrate they would.

The weekend started out fine. Alex was home talking with his dad on their front porch. This was rare that the two spoke man-to-man on any subject. Today's conversation was about Alex and his advancement up the corporate ladder; although his career rise was slow, it was steady. After all, he had been with this food distribution company just a few years, and he had been promoted twice. Mr. Flynn was somewhat confused that Alex had changed jobs three times in the past eight years.

"In my time, you stayed with one company for life. Only shiftless characters changed companies," Mr. Flynn said sternly.

"Things have changed, Dad!" Alex said as if losing patience. "There are no longer cradle-to-grave companies. Guys don't stay with the same company for life. In today's business climate, companies are looking for the best and the brightest. They hire people who are willing to work hard and do whatever it takes to get the job done. And you have to go where the career takes you."

"Does that mean you will never come back here to work?" Mr. Flynn asked.

"What I'm trying to say, Dad, is if you want a successful career, you have to go wherever it takes you. If I wanted to stay here, I'd have to take whatever job I could get. I don't want that," Alex said.

"There are plenty of jobs around here, Alex. I don't understand why you don't want to live here," Mr. Flynn replied in a stern voice.

"Look, Dad, after the mines closed and a few other industries left the valley; there weren't any decent jobs around here. There are no production jobs. The only industries that flourish around here are government and its handout programs. There are lawyers to make sure they run smoothly, social workers, and bankers to supply the money to keep things moving. The other jobs are just service-related, such as gas stations, hospitals, restaurants, all supporting the primary business of this area, which is, social welfare. I want to do something with my life other than collect a paycheck, I want a career creating something." Alex said in a determined voice.

"Alex, if you want to get there early we should be going," Beth said in a determined voice, standing in the hallway.

"You're right, Beth, let's get going," Alex said as he started putting on his jacket.

"We'll see you later, Dad," Alex said.

"You two have fun. Remember, watch your drinking. The cops are starting to clamp down on drunk drivers," Mr. Flynn warned.

A few moments later, they were driving down Grove Street.

"Don't drive so fast," Beth said in a stern tone.

"I know these roads like the back of my hand," Alex said positively as he sped down the familiar street.

"Don't be too overconfident, Alex. That's been one of your biggest problems," Beth said.

"I'm glad you're here, Beth, to remind me of all my problems!" Alex said.

"Let's have a good time tonight, Alex," she said as if trying to change the subject. Then she added as if thinking aloud, "Now tell me all about these wonderful people that we're going to meet?"

"I'd like to surprise you, the way you have surprised me with all your interesting friends," Alex said coolly.

"That's another problem with you, Alex! Whenever we come to Clarks Summit you change, and your whole demeanor changes. It seems as soon as we go through the Leigh Tunnel on the turnpike something comes over you. You change from Dr. Jekyll to Mr. Hyde," Beth said, her voice getting irritated.

"I don't know what you're talking about. All I want to do is have a few drinks with some old friends and have a few laughs. Is that such a big deal?" Alex asked.

"No, it isn't a big deal, Alex. So let's not make it a big deal. All I ask is don't leave me alone like you've done on other occasions. I don't know these people. They're your friends not mine," Beth said unfeelingly.

"When we were dating, all my friends were wonderful. They were all so witty, funny, and very intelligent, and of course you liked them all. That was until we got married. Since our wedding they've all seemed to slip in stature," Alex said.

"There you go again, Alex, blaming me for your bad behavior," Beth shot back.

"Okay, we're in the parking lot now. Let's not start the night out in an argument," Alex said firmly. He sat for a moment gathering his thoughts, then said, "Things have changed. This is the first time I've been in O'Connor's since Eddy died. I don't know who is going to be here tonight. So let's go in and try to have a good time."

As soon as Alex walked into the bar, he realized it wasn't the same old place. O'Connor's quaint little bar was gone forever. The place was now called John Kay's, complete with a new sign along with various other changes. Although the interior was similar, over all it seemed drastically different from the friendly atmosphere he was accustomed to. As he stood at the entrance, his memories returned to carefree, happier times. It was a dreamlike, emotional flash back to his youth. After all, in many aspects this was the place where he entered adulthood. He had his first beer at that very bar. He spent many nights staring through the large picture window onto State Street. This is where he and his friends bonded tightly, discussing the facts of life, both sexual and real. Together they shared so many good stories and laugh-filled nights. This was the meeting site where he and the gang plotted their successful futures.

Standing there for a few moments, Alex realized just how much things had changed. The new overhead lights were bright, illuminating the smoke-filled atmosphere that one could almost cut with a knife. The music was very loud, and yet one could still hear people talking loudly and yelling at each other over the music. The song "Red Red Wine" was being blasted on the jukebox. Alex thought, *how appropriate*. This place was now like a nightclub, complete with a crowded cast of odd characters. This herd was larger than Eddy could have ever imagined would fit in his bar. The patrons appeared to be in the late twenties or early thirties—all drinking, smoking, talking, and having a good time. But Alex didn't recognize anyone on the floor.

Alex stared over the crowd looking for a friendly face with out any luck. He felt alone as if he were in a distant town among strangers. Then over at the far end of the bar, he noticed a large head bobbing back and forth. He smiled to himself knowing at an instant it had to be Phil Whitman.

Alex grabbed Beth's hand. He was now thrilled and wanted to share the excitement. He yelled in her ear, "There's Phil over at the bar. You remember him from our wedding. He's the schoolteacher. He's a lot of fun. Let's go over and say hi."

Alex and Beth made their way through a multitude of people, making a convoluted route toward the end of the bar. Alex was annoyed because, of all these people crowding the floor, he didn't recognize even one face among all those he encountered.

Phil was deeply involved in an animated conversation with a stranger at the bar as Alex and Beth approached him. Alex tapped Phil twice on the shoulder. In an instant Phil spun around on his barstool. His facial expression went from serious to a big, ear-to-ear smile. Phil was off the barstool in an instant, grabbing Alex's hand, shaking it vigorously, and patting him on the shoulder. "Alex, great to see you. I mean it's really great to see you. I'm glad you made it in for the weekend," Phil said in an excited voice.

Alex was a little self-conscious by the warm reception, thinking perhaps Phil was a little inebriated so early in the evening. But it didn't matter; tonight was for partying, and Alex expected to soon be inebriated himself. Alex stared at Phil for a moment, taking in the subtle changes in Phil's appearance. Phil's large clump of hair was now thinner and receding from what looked like a growing forehead. His overall physical appearance had changed too. He had lost some of the once-noticeable muscular definition, and his shoulders seemed to slump a little. A strong leather belt restrained his potbelly.

"Glad to see you, Phil," Alex said in a loud, almost shouting voice. He then turned and extended his hand toward Beth, saying, "You remember Beth, don't you?"

"Of course I do, Alex. Beth, you were one beautiful bride, and I had a great time at your wedding. That's where I was introduced to my favorite after-dinner drink, Drambuie. What a hangover the next day," Phil said jokingly. Then he politely shook her hand.

"Welcome, Beth, to our humble den of perpetual celebration. Is this your first visit to O'Connor's? Or what used to be called O'Connor's or, as we would call it, Eddy's halfway house."

Beth was a little startled at the remark. She then quickly asked, "Eddy's halfway house? Isn't a halfway house a place that helps people with addiction problems to get back into society?"

"Well, yes, in most cases that's what is called a halfway house," Phil said with a puzzled look on his face. As he pointed to the odd-placed window three quarters up the wall that had been the living quarters for Eddy, Frances, and her sister, Liz, he added, "You see that window on the wall over there?"

"Yes," Beth said, looking at the strange window.

"Well, that room behind the window was their kitchen. Frances had the window put in so she could make the family meals and also watch what was happening in the bar. She liked to spy on Eddy. Perched on her kitchen chair, she could keep an eye on how much he was drinking. And if she thought he had too much to drink, she'd come down and raise hell with him," Phil said with a laugh.

"But that's not all Frances did," Phil continued. "In the afternoons she would peek out the window to make sure no one was around, and then she would sneak down to the bar. She would take the whiskey bottles and add a little water to the booze. So even if you drank a lot of whiskey, you'd only get halfway drunk. So we used to call the place Eddy's halfway house."

Alex started laughing, saying, "I remember one night seeing Frances and Liz up there. Both heads were bobbing back and forth, complaining to each other about Eddy. He was down behind the bar sneaking a few drinks. They had enough of him drinking. So Frances and her sister came down to confront him. Boy, did they get into to it that night. Frances threw an ashtray at Eddy. He ducked, and as it flew past him, it broke a bottle of water-downed booze. He was so mad he chased her back up to the kitchen. Oh yes, they were a loving couple."

"Sounds like a story from 'Family Living'," Beth said.

"They were a family all right," Phil said with a smile, adding sadly, "But I do miss them a lot. They were a lot of laughs. We had many a good time here."

"I'm sorry I missed Eddy's funeral. By the time I found out about his death, it was too late to get up here," Alex said quietly bowing his head.

Alex said nothing for a moment. The he stared out the large picture window at the end of the bar and spoke again as if he was talking to someone outside of the building. "When Jerry was killed in Vietnam, I just couldn't go to his funeral. I don't know what it was, but I could not bring myself up here for that. It was just too sad. There's not a day goes by that I don't think of him. But I just couldn't go to his funeral."

"Yeah, it was rough to get through that one. He was on his second tour when he was killed," Phil said, his voice cracking. "Military funerals are always sad, especially at the end of the ceremony when the bugler plays 'Taps' and they hand the burial flag to a family member. It was very hard on his mom."

"I haven't even spoken to Mr. or Mrs. Weaver. I feel terrible about it, but I don't know what to say to them. I keep thinking of Jerry; he was always the one full of life, with an ear-to-ear smile. He'd do anything for anybody. The longer it gets, the worse I feel," Alex said softly.

"Maybe over this weekend I'll stop by for a visit," he added.

"Alex, they moved away a few years ago. I believe they are living in Michigan now. I can get their address if you like," Phil said.

Alex replied. "Yeah Phil, I'd appreciate that . . . if you would."

Phil changed the subject, asking, "How about you two? How is life treating you? I notice you're wearing cheaters now, Alex."

"Oh, you mean the glasses. I've been wearing them for a few years," Alex said.

"I guess when you start wearing glasses it can cause your hair to thin out," Phil said with a chuckle.

"Phil, don't you think Alex looks more distinguished wearing glasses?' Beth asked.

"What distinguishes Alex isn't the glasses. Alex is Alex. He's one of a kind, a true friend," Phil said quickly without thinking. "Remember our old Indian saying, Alex? 'Many summers pass, many buffalo come, three stay'."

Beth turned toward Alex with a confused look on her face.

"Let me explain, Beth," Alex said with a smile. "That was Indiana folklore we used to say as kids. 'Many summers pass,' of course, means many years. 'Many buffalo come' means that to the Indians buffalo were considered a good omen like friends. So the saying 'Many summers pass, many buffalo come, three stay' translated means through the decades of our life, we'll make many friends, but if we're lucky, we will have three true, lifelong friends."

"Well said, Alex," Phil said loudly. "Now let me paleface... buy you and your pretty squaw a drink of fire water. What will it be?" Phil said laughing.

"I guess the fifteen-cent draft beers are gone forever. So I'll have a scotch on the rocks and the same for Beth," Alex said.

Phil stepped back to the bar, raising his hand and yelling to the bartender, "Hey, Rick . . . Rick, could we get a drink here, please?"

"Phil, would you make that Dewar's scotch? Thanks," Alex said to Phil.

Alex peered behind the crowded bar to see what changes had taken place there. He noticed that the old hand-cranked cash register Eddy had used had been replaced with a modern electric one. The once sparsely filled shelves behind the bar were now filled completely. Every space was taken up by different brands of whiskey, vodka, gin, scotch, and other designer bottles of spirits. There now were signs on the walls for pizza and hamburgers. But the most radical change was the large beer refrigerator that could hold hundreds of kinds of beer. All night long the liquid flowed abundantly for the thirsty, partying customers.

The drinks were downed, along with a few more, as the three carried on conversations about all the recent changes in life and the community. Phil, still a teacher, had become somewhat the recorder of the history of the town and the observer of the characters who lived there. He was keenly aware of the changes both in real estate and the conscience of the local townsfolk.

"Alex," Phil said, looking around the bar, "there are new people moving in all the time. But they are a different kind of people than we grew up with. I don't particularly like the newcomers. They have more money than we did, and they live a faster paced life. But I can tell you, these immigrants don't have the same feeling for the community that we have. Sure, they all like our town, that's why they moved here, but somehow they lack the interest in our colorful heritage."

"What colorful heritage?" Alex said, laughing. "Sitting here in the pub drinking?"

"No, the heritage I'm talking about is the people we grew up with, the colorful folks who make this town a town. You know what I mean, people like Chet Miles; he owned a junkyard right here in Clarks Summit, and we all liked him. Physically he's by far the strongest guy in town with the biggest heart. And there's the Nichols family; when you think of it, after World War II, old man Nichols purchased the useless property in Chinchilla. He put in a railcar diner and parlayed it into what we have today, the Nichols Village. And let's not forget old Dr. Carehaw, who is still making house calls and is driven around with his infamous chauffeur, Billy Palumbo."

"And of course there was Eddy O'Connor," Beth said, laughing. "I'll never forget coming in here for the first time. There he was sitting behind the bar, polishing glasses in his white waiter outfit. He paid no attention to me for a few moments. When I ordered my drink, he popped his glass eye out right there on the bar. I almost fainted."

"Now you don't have bartenders in Philadelphia who can pop an eye out for you," Phil said with a laugh.

"You're right, Phil," Alex said, chuckling. "Eddy really meant it when he said, I'll keep an eye out for you."

"That's what I'm talking about, Alex. We're lucky to have grown up here. It's an interesting community with a lot of interesting people," Phil said.

"Let's not forget Mayor Wignal," Alex said sarcastically.

Beth asked, "Who is Mayor Wignal, Alex? I haven't heard you talk of him before."

"Oh, the Mayor as we used to call him; he was quite a character," Phil said, picking up his drink. "He was one of these guys who had been everywhere, done everything . . . why during the big war, Eisenhower used to call him for advice. It was the Mayor who saved General George Patton from being fired. As the mayor would tell the story, 'I said, look, Ike, George is a good man, a good general. Give him one more chance. I'll vouch for him! And Ike said to me, 'Okay, Bill, you haven't steered me wrong so far.' Now that's the kind of guy the Mayor was," Phil said with a serious look with a warm smile.

"He was a character all right," Alex said loudly. "He was a printer by trade and a very good one. Years ago he started our little scandal sheet, the Abington Journal, with all the local news that was boring enough to print. Of course he did enjoy a drink now and then. That's how we got to know him. You might say his thirst for the drink had little effect on his career. He had a small printing shop on Depot Street. The building's still there, just behind this bar on the other side of the street.

It was a one-room printing shop with one room in the basement. He had a little cot, no running water. But the Mayor lived in the shop most of the time because he didn't have any cash. There was no furniture, except for a chair and desk. He would go over to the Summit Diner and shave in the morning and use the bathroom. Bob Parry, who owned the diner, didn't mind as long as the Mayor printed the menus for free. Occasionally during the day, he'd come in here for a drink. When he had money, he would live in the Tenant Hotel up the street. To this day I never figured out how the Mayor lived in that shop. "

"I remember the Mayor," Phil said, laughing. "He used to print the football sheets."

"What were football sheets?" Beth asked.

"They were the point-spread sheets for college and pro football games. The Mayor printed them for the Scranton bookies," Alex said.

"Oh yes, we had our unique social class up here in the Abingtons, Phil said, toasting his drink.

"Some things have changed," Alex said, turning his head to look at the crowd.

"Yes, they have, Alex," Phil said. "They now serve food here at the pub, along with the loud music. And of course the newspaper is forever gone from the floor in the restrooms."

"Speaking of changes," Phil said with a serious tone. "Look who's coming in the front door. It's Mr. and Mrs. Wedge Head."

"Please tell me he's changed," Alex said with a chuckle.

"No, he's the same old Johnny. Although you might say Melody has mellowed a little bit," Phil said.

Making their way slowly through the front entrance were Johnny and Melody Thompson. Both were dressed in the latest fashion: Johnny fitting nicely in tan leather suede jacket and Melody wearing a long, camel-hair overcoat draped with a red silk scarf. By appearance, life seemed to be treating the young couple quite well. They looked happy, both supporting broad smiles, and nodding and waving while talking to many acquaintances. After a few moments, Johnny spotted Alex and Phil at the bar. Johnny, with an added excitement, quickly grabbed Melody by the arm and started to move in their direction.

"Hi, Alex, when did you get in?" Johnny yelled as he approached the bar. He then looked directly at Beth, adding, "Hi, Beth, it's nice to see you. I didn't think you liked bars very much."

"I can tolerate them once in a while," Beth said with a smile.

"Johnny, you and Melody look great. I guess life must be treating you very well," Alex joined in loudly.

Alex reached out to Melody's arms and leaned over, giving her a slight kiss on the cheek. Close up he could see changes; she had aged, not a great deal but enough to notice. Her eyes seemed to have lost some of the gleam. They were no longer crystal clear. Her once smooth complexion appeared rougher with wrinkles sagging slightly. "Nice to see you, Meldoo!" Alex said jokingly.

"Hi, Alex, nice to see you too. It's been a long time," Melody said with a smile and turned toward Beth. "It's nice to see you too, Beth."

"So who are you working for now, Alex?" Johnny quickly asked.

"I'm a regional sales manager for P&G." Alex paused for a moment, then added, "Proctor and Gamble or as we call it, Proctor and God."

"Oh yeah, I remember back in the '60s when P&G built that giant toilet paper plant near Tunkhannock out in the middle of nowhere," Johnny said loudly.

"If it had to do with a toilet, I knew Johnny would have a comment," Phil said jokingly.

"Well, Phil, you should need a lot of toilet paper for all that crap you feed to your students," Johnny replied quickly.

Phil started to turn his large head back and forth as if he was implying no but was smiling as he said, "Now now, Johnny, just because some students like yourself don't learn anything, that doesn't mean all education is a waste."

"Waste! The biggest waste in education is the high pay you teachers get. And even then you're always on strike for more money," Johnny said sarcastically. "Seems to me the teachers have turned their sacred book of learning in for a fat checkbook."

"I can see some things haven't changed much around here," Alex said, grabbing both Johnny and Phil by the shoulders. "So let's have a few drinks to clear the cobwebs from our cluttered minds."

"Johnny, with the size of your mind, a short beer should do the trick," Phil said with a laugh.

"Phil, if brains were made of dynamite, you wouldn't have enough to blow your nose," Johnny replied loudly.

"Enough's enough. You two sound like Abbott and Costello," Alex said. "There's a table over there in the corner. Johnny, grab it while I get us some drinks."

Johnny was sitting alone at the table when Alex joined him.

"The wives are at the bar gabbing, so we've got a few minutes to catch up on old times, Johnny," Alex said as he put down the drinks on the table and took a seat directly across from Johnny. "So tell me how things are going in Chinchilla. I understand you bought your father-in-law's gas station. It looks like you have quite a business there."

Sitting at the table, Johnny's manner seemed to change. He was more calm and composed. Alex was anticipating an instant, quick-witted response to his question.

But Johnny sat for a moment, staring at his drink on the table and thinking. "Life is a nasty experience, Alex. It's a lot of hard work and no appreciation. Your only reward for all your effort is money."

"Well, Johnny, you seem to be doing okay in the money department. I guess you must be working pretty hard," Alex said.

"I do work hard, Alex, on the average of sixteen to eighteen hours a day. When I bought that gas station from my father-in-law, it wasn't making any money although it was in a good location. I was out there day and night pumping gas, cleaning windshields, and checking oil to get it going. A few years ago, I bought a tow truck to earn some extra money, and I made a lot of cash, especially in the winter. When it snowed I just drove around pulling cars out of the ditches at thirty to fifty bucks for a few minutes' work. And that was strictly cash right into my pocket, no taxes on that money. Oh, come to think of it, there are a lot of ways to avoid taxes if you're smart and have your own business."

"I guess there are a lot of ways to avoid taxes, aren't there, Johnny?" Alex asked.

"Sure, we bought a nice farmhouse out in the country. We've got horses, chickens, and a lot of boy toys. Melody and I have new, matching Lincoln Town Cars, charged to the company of course. When we go out for dinner, company expenses cover it. I even bought a big Winnebago; we travel all around in that portable home. We'll go down to the Jersey shore; hell, we've even got our own drivable hotel room." Johnny lifted his drink as if to make a toast and said with a smile, "While I'm down there, I'll run over to Atlantic City to gamble a little. It's all in good fun. And as many hours as I work, I need a little break now and then. After all, I give Melody and the kids all the money they need and plenty more."

"As we drove in today, I stopped to buy some gas. I see your gas station has now grown into a full-scale variety store. You're selling everything . . . bikes, TVs, and all kinds of hardware. I chuckled at your friendly honor system, "Pay in Advance!" But what impressed me the most was your warm greeting poster: 'Attitudes adjusted while you wait'," Alex said with a chuckle.

"Yeah, I know, Alex. Business is tough, and people are funny. I know folks I've grown up with who will buy gas across the street just because it's two cents a gallon cheaper. I'll be at a dollar twenty-five a gallon and the Shell a dollar twenty-three, and for that two cents a gallon, they'll cross a four-lane highway to buy the cheaper gas. Then they'll come into my store when they want to make a deal on buying a TV or something. Like when I had those Cabbage Patch dolls. I bought a whole truck-load of them. I paid sixteen bucks apiece and sold everyone for over eighty dollars each, and I made a ton of money.

"You've done pretty well for yourself, Johnny," Alex said as if admiring Johnny's hard work.

"I've made a lot of money, Alex. I worked hard for it. And remember, Alex, the golden rule of business: he that got the gold makes the rules," Johnny said with a laugh.

"To get your business up and running, did you use the GI Bill? I understand they will help sometimes," Alex asked.

Johnny didn't say a word for a moment; he thought and then he said, "No, the GI Bill didn't help me in any way, Alex. I don't like to even think about it. In fact, Alex, I don't even tell anyone I was in the army or that I served in Vietnam. But I do have my odd way of doing things. We had a video section, but I would not handle anything that had Jane Fonda in it. I used to tell customers that in honor of Vietnam veterans . . . no Jane Fonda in this business establishment. I've seen all the draft dodgers, the college deferment guys that live around here; they come in and get gas. I take good care of them because they're good customers. But occasionally I have one of those peaceniks like Danny Fredrick come in. To me they're not peaceniks if they supported the North Vietnamese. By the way, the last time I saw Danny I told him to get the hell out and don't come back to my place. Yeah, he came into the station; I thought I recognized him. He said, 'Hi, Johnny, how are you doing? I said, 'Fine, it's been a long time. Where have you been?' He said that he'd gone to Canada to beat the draft, but now he was free to come home. I told him I went to Vietnam in his place. So I told him to get the hell out of my store and go back to Canada. I take pride throwing that type of person off my property," Johnny said with a big smile."

"I guess the Vietnam experience still bothers you, John?" Alex asked quietly.

"Every hot day during the summer, each time I see a guy in a uniform . . . or I hear helicopter blades . . .it all brings back feelings of Vietnam," Johnny said as he finished his drink. He sat for a moment and then continued, "Then Jerry was killed on this second tour. It's hard to believe sometimes." He paused for a moment; "Remember, Alex, I didn't join up; I was drafted by my friends and neighbors. I even thought of going to Canada myself. But I couldn't; I had a duty to my country. You see the uncle I was named after died in the Philippines. He was on the Bataan death march. In my military picture, we look like identical twins. I was in the engineers. Our job was blowing things up, and for a while I was a tunnel rat. When I came back, for a while I fought my own verbal war. Alex, not only did I have to argue with peaceniks like Danny Fredrick, but my own father and I fought over the war. He didn't believe in it; he hated Johnson and Nixon. We had terrible fights over Vietnam. I told him his generation voted the politicians in, and our generation had to fight their war. After a while I just stopped talking about it."

"Did you ever throw your father out of the station?" Alex asked with a smile.

"Yeah, on more than one occasion but for different reasons. He was another cheap bastard, always expecting me to give him a deal. Or better yet he wanted it for free just because I was his loving son," Johnny said.

Alex sat looking at his drink; then he asked Johnny, "It's been a long time since Saigon fell. Have you ever figured it out which of you were right . . . you or your father?"

Johnny didn't answer with his usual quick, shoot-from-the-hip style. He thought for a moment and replied, "Ah, a good question, Alex. For a long time I didn't know which of us was correct. But when I saw the boat people bobbing around out in the ocean and hoping someone would pick them up, I knew I was right. And I'll tell you why, Alex. Just think of it, here was a people who loved their land; even their religion taught them that the very land they lived on was to be revered. It was the burial ground of their ancestors who still roamed in spirit form. So to leave their native land was really something. These were not sea-going people who knew anything about ocean currents. They were educated people who packed up their worldly possessions, put their children and families into a little sampan, and ventured out into the ocean, hoping someone would pick them up. Just imagine putting your family in a little boat like that. It must have been so terrible to live under those conditions that they chose the slim odds of survival in the ocean rather than stay and live like that,"

He paused and then went on, "How could we have won? Well, that's a different question for a different time. How about you, Alex? How's life been treating you?"

"Life's been good for me. I guess I was lucky. After college I was drafted; I was sent to Germany instead of Vietnam. Now I have a good job, and we have a nice home in Drexel Hill," Alex said, then looked over at Johnny and added, "But one thing that changed my life the most was when I saw my daughter for the first time in the nursery. I was awed . . . she was so petite with her little fingers and tiny body. As I stared at her, I realized she would depend on me . . . as her father. She would be my daughter, no matter what, for all of our lives. I felt a kind of deep, calm love I have never known. I tell you, Johnny, it was an amazing feeling of love and responsibility. I could never be the same after that."

"That's what being a father is all about, Alex," Johnny said. "But that's only part of the job. You have to be a husband and a father for the other kids too. Plus you have to earn a living."

"I do have a good job that helps on the home front," Alex said.

"So you got the job you always wanted, the wife you always wanted, two pretty little girls, and a son to carry on the family name. Alex, it sounds as if you have the world by the tail," Johnny said.

"Not quite the tail, Johnny," Alex answered quickly. "Don't get me wrong, I am very happy, but there's something I had to face. Just between you and me, Johnny, I'll tell you something very private." Alex paused for a moment as if in deep thought, then continued in a serious manner. "When I started in the business world, I wanted to be the president of a Fortune 500 company. I can see now I'm not on the track to be a corporate officer. Sure I do have a good job as a manager, and if I'm lucky and work hard, I might make product manager or some low-level vice president of something, and I'll make good money. But I realize I'll never get the head job of a large corporation. And at my age, it's kind of discouraging to realize my dream won't come to pass," Alex said as a matter of fact tone.

"You see, Alex, titles never impressed me much," Johnny said in his matter-of-fact voice. "I want to make money, but I don't need a title to do it. I'll work hard and smart. I think even without a college education, I can achieve my goal of being wealthy. And to tell you the truth, I think I'm on the right trail. I even have the two oldest boys working in the station pumping gas. I know it takes a lot of sacrifice, but in the long run, I think it's worth it."

"You're probably right for you, Johnny. But for me it's a little different. I don't want to become a workaholic and put my family second to my job."

"Well for me, Alex, my plan is to work long and hard . . . now. I want to make all the money I can. Melody can raise the kids and take care of the house. When I get enough money set aside, then I can become a devoted father and lovable husband without any financial worries," Johnny said. Then he added as if an afterthought "Sounds to me like you're torn between your job and your family. Is your family life that busy, Alex?"

"Beth and the kids keep me busy. Between teacher conferences, soccer games, band recitals, ballet, and school plays, all my free time is spent going to their events," Alex said.

"I know what you mean, Alex. When we were kids, we'd be lucky if a parent went to a high school football game. These kids today have so many activities, and the parents show up for them all. I mean, go to a little kid's soccer game, and the parking lots are filled with cars. Both parents are there," Johnny said with a look of amazement.

"Working those seventeen-hour days, seven days a week, do you ever get to your kids' events, Johnny?" Alex asked

"We live on our own little world. I go whenever I can, but with three boys and a girl, I can tell you that I can't go to everything. That's Melody's job, and sometimes it's even too much for her," Johnny said coldly.

"Isn't that the way you run your family?" Johnny asked.

"No, not quite the same, Johnny," Alex said with a smile. "Beth is from the main line of Philadelphia. She's a perfectionist with high expectations for the girls and me. I am supposed to be a success in business; a loving, devoted father; and, of course, a sensitive, loving husband. So you can see, Johnny, it's not too easy for me either."

"Yeah . . . I know what you mean," Johnny said quietly. "After working those long hours, I like to come in here for a few beers. But I have a rule: No more than seven beers. No hard liquor; it makes me mean. So I just stay with the beers."

"I remember in high school on the weekends getting a few quarts of Stegmeier beer. That was all we needed to have a good time," Alex said with a chuckle.

"Yeah, I remember drinking that stuff; it tasted like panther piss. But the price was right, three quarts for a dollar . . . what a cheap drunk," Johnny said.

"Our days of a cheap drunk are over," Alex said with a warm smile. "Now when we drink it's not to enhance the pleasures of life, rather it's to escape from the pressures of life. We used to drink a lot, talk a lot, and laugh a lot. Those were the good times when we'd carry on all night discussing each other cars, girls, and futures. Now when we drink we talk about jobs, mortgages, children, and, of course, our happy marriages."

"Yeah, Alex, we used to have a good time back then. But it was a different time too. The kids of today live in a different world. Drugs have replaced the quart of beer. You have to be very careful with your kids. I keep a sharp eye on mine. Even here in the Abingtons, drugs are all around. I know . . . I see kids come in the gas station, dressed well, nice cars, many of them high on something. Some of these kids are from the best families in the area," Johnny said in a somber tone.

"What do you do, Johnny? My girls are a little young for drugs. At least I hope so," Alex said.

"It's Melody's job to make sure our kids stay clean. I earn the money; she watches the kids. I do my job, and she does hers," Johnny said.

Alex was always interested in what Johnny had to say; it was always entertaining even if it were not true. He looked across the bar and noticed that Beth and Melody were engrossed in their own deep conversation.

Melody was quite animated, her hands moving in different directions. She looked intensely into the eyes of Alex's wife, saying, "You have two girls and a boy, and I have three boys and a girl. The three boys are a handful. I was so glad when we had Delaney."

Melody lowered her voice as she spoke privately to Beth, "I was always so scared when I went for my six-week checkup after the babies were born . . . " Melody bowed her head a little closer to Beth, adding, "Twice on my six-week checkup I was pregnant again. I was so embarrassed; I couldn't believe it."

"I know what you mean, Melody," Beth said quietly. "Being Catholic we didn't believe in the pill. So we used the rhythm system; that's how we got Courtney. I was so afraid of getting pregnant again that our sex life was terrible. So I finally went on the pill. That helped a lot although for me sex is always a little fearful."

Melody became a little more assertive as she said, "After Delaney was born, I sent Johnny to see Dr. Snipers for a vasectomy. Now I don't have to worry about getting pregnant each time we're having sex. Now I only worry about when he wants it." Both women laughed.

Almost as an afterthought, Melody said, "I'm glad I have my children; I love them to bits, but I don't want any more."

"I understand what you're talking about Melody, I love my girls too," Beth said and added quickly, "But I tell you, Melody, I have a special bond with Derrick in many ways . . . He's so much like my father."

"Let me tell you, Beth, my three sons are typical boys," Melody said, almost interrupting Beth. "I love them, but I can't relate to them; they drive me crazy most of the time. They're either fighting or yelling or running around the house. All the toys we buy them, all they want to do is shoot them, smash them, or blow them up. Even Delaney's dolls aren't safe with them around." Melody paused for a moment. A smile came over her face as she continued, "I was so thrilled to have a daughter of my own and she is such a typical little girl. It's adorable to see her in her room playing by herself, talking to her dolls, and she's such a good little mother. She takes wonderful care of all her babies. Even before she could walk, she would caress and hug her little dolls. She likes to dress up in my old outfits and wear some of my mother's old hats. I love to watch her try to put on lipstick and makeup. She just seems to be more human than my boys," Melody said with a sigh.

"Beth, I wish you'd come up and stay us for a few days. You and the kids would have a great time. We could let Johnny and Alex do their thing, and we and the kids could have a lot of fun," Melody said.

Beth was the cool type, not into quick, engrossing relationships. "It's very nice of you to invite us up. I'll have to check our calendar though. With the kids in school and all their activities and Alex traveling, I can tell you it's not easy to get away," Beth said in a friendly, polite voice.

"Does Alex travel much?" Melody asked

"Yes, he does, a few days a week. And when he isn't traveling, he's doing paperwork or talking business on the phone," Beth said.

"Johnny works long hours, but at least he sleeps in his own bed at night," Melody said, thinking for a moment and adding, "Although when he gets in about three thirty in the morning and wakes me up—usually with beer on his breath and sex on his mind—it doesn't make for a good night's sleep, if you know what I mean. After my father died a while ago, I started taking sleeping pills. Let me tell you, they help me sleep through the night."

Beth was mildly startled by this revelation from her new friend. "Melody, do you take a sleeping pill every night?"

"I do now, but I don't intend to take them for very long," Melody said as she noticed two barstools being vacated and grabbed them both, signaling Beth to join her. Waving to the bartender, she yelled, "Rick, two more scotches please."

Beth lifted her glass, saying, "I'm fine, Melody; my glass is almost full."

"Don't worry, Beth, it won't go to waste," Melody said jokingly.

"If you don't drink, it I will," Melody said as she emptied her glass and waited for the fresh drinks to arrive. She turned toward Beth as if looking for approval. "I didn't always drink this much or take sleeping pills at night. It's just that I'm going through some tough times now. My father died almost two years ago, and it's very hard on me." Melody's eyes started to fill with tears. "We were very close."

Beth's facial expression showed her concern; in a sincere, compassionate voice she said, "Oh, I'm so sorry to hear that, Melody. Was his death unexpected?"

Melody sniffled, trying to conceal the hurt. "He died on a construction site. He died instantly. But for a while we thought he was crushed to death. It's horrible just to think about it."

The drinks arrived, and Melody took a large sip. "When I was a little girl, my dad seemed so big and strong. He was a tall man . . . broad shoulders with a full head of brown, wavy hair. He'd pick me up with his large callused hands, lifting me high above his head and spinning me around. I was never afraid when he was near. He was a carpenter by trade, and he made my sister and me our own dollhouses. These dollhouses were so beautiful with wallpapered rooms and real glass in the windows. The houses even had little electric lights. He was always there for me . . . all through my life. When we bought the farmhouse, he did more work on it than Johnny. Our kids just adored him; he was always there for them . . . taking them fishing, going to the school events, even taking them to the emergency room on few occasions. I believed he would be around forever . . . that he'd never die."

Beth sat silently mesmerized by the raw emotion Melody was exhibiting. Melody continued to speak, staring off into space, not knowing or caring if anyone was listening. "It's odd, Beth. I don't talk about my father very often; it's too painful. My family just goes on as if nothing much has happened. That's the way life is—here one day, gone the next. But that's not the way it is for me. I think of him every day."

"I remember that cold November afternoon. I was sitting with a friend having lunch at the Gourmet restaurant. Johnny came in, looking for me. I could tell right away that something was wrong. He had a scared look on his face. I thought it was one of the kids or something happened at the store. Anyway he came right over and said to me, 'Come on, your mother called. We have to go to Dalton right away; something happened to your father.' I was so scared. I didn't know what to think. Did he have an accident? Did he get hurt on the job? Was he suddenly ill? Was he suffering? When I got in the car, I didn't know what to think. Johnny started the car; then he looked over at me in a strange way and said . . . Melody . . . your father is dead. The shock of it all, I couldn't breathe, I started to hyperventilate. I remember rocking back and forth crying. My mind was a blank. I remember wailing as we drove through the Summit. I had the most severe pain in my stomach. I just couldn't believe it. It couldn't be true.

"When we got to the job site where he had been working, there were fire trucks, police cars, and an ambulance. I got out of our car and walked slowly up to ditch where he had been working. There were all kinds of people milling around. My mother and sister were already there. Dr. Neumann gave them both a shot of something; they both stood motionless. I looked down at the pit they had been digging and saw that his body was covered with a blanket, except for a lower leg . . . with his work boot showing. I got sick when I saw him lying there in the cold and wet mud. They couldn't move his body until the coroner arrived. I was in a rage. I kept hoping someone would come over say that he was okay. But they just kind of looked at me . . . no one knew what to say. It was all so horrible."

"What happened to your father, Melody?" Beth asked quietly.

"It was very strange. They were digging a foundation for a new house. In the process they had to dig a trench. While they were backfilling the trench, someone spotted my father half buried. At first we thought he fell and was buried alive, but in the autopsy it was revealed he died of a massive heart attack. He was dead as he fell in the ditch. At least he didn't suffer," Melody said as she gained her composure.

"But it's been so hard.' Melody started to whimper again. "At the scene Dr. Neumann gave me a shot of something; after that he gave us pills to get through the funeral. My father had a lot of friends, so it was a big funeral. Our family just went through the motions; we couldn't even talk of him without crying . . ."

"It sounds like a terrible thing to go through Melody. I feel so sorry for you and your family. I wish there was something I could say or do," Beth said as she put her arm around Melody's shoulder.

Melody's head was bowed; with a broken voice, she continued, "I often go over to the cemetery by myself, many times a night, and I sit next to his tombstone with a bottle of vodka. I talk to him . . . I cry for him . . . I miss him . . . and if it weren't for my children . . . I would join him."

Melody sat crying for a few moments. Suddenly she raised her head as if to shake off this morbid mood. She wiped the tears from her eyes. She finished her drink and, without hesitation, picked up Beth's untouched drink and said with a smile, "I told you it wouldn't go to waste."

Beth smiled, saying, "Good, then you feel better now, Melody?"

"Oh yes, Beth, thanks for listening. Sometimes it takes a few drinks now and then . . . a few small pills during the day . . .

and a few big pills at night. I've got everything under control," Melody said in a raised, happy voice.

She took a large gulp of her drink and continued to talk in slurred speech, "Now, when Johnny comes home late at night with booze on his breath and sex on his mind . . .well I can tell you, he may bounce on my body, but he doesn't wake me up from my slumber!"

Beth's eyes grew wider as she listened to Melody's words. Although Beth felt a lot of compassion for Melody, she also had a concern for what Melody was telling her. "Melody, if this medication has that much effect on you, how you handle taking care of the children?"

Melody looked surprised with the question and replied with an optimistic smile. "I don't have any problems with the children. In fact, I feel much more calm dealing with the kids now. There was a time when those kids drove me wild, always fighting, stealing each other's toys, teasing each other . . . and their schoolwork. Oh, forget it. They would drive me crazy. But now I feel as though I can handle them much better. They don't get on my nerves as much as they used to. I don't let things brother me like they did before."

Beth asked in an inquisitive tone, "What does Johnny think of your taking all this medication?"

Melody raised one hand up with a flip as if slowly swatting at a fly. "Johnny has his own worries. He concentrates on earning the money to pay for everything. It's up to me to manage the kids. And let me tell you, raising four kids isn't easy. I do the best I can. I have to be a mother and a father to these kids most of the time," Melody said in a serious manner.

She took a large sip of her drink and then turned her head around, looking to see if anyone was listening. She continued to speak, now in a much lower voice. "I caught John Jr. smoking a joint with a friend in his room. He's only fourteen years old. The drugs around here are getting out of hand."

"I know what you mean," Beth said quickly, also in a low but strong voice. "Last year I found cigarettes in Courtney's purse. I was furious. Then a few nights later, when she came home from a school basketball game, I smelled beer on her breath."

"What did you do?" Melody asked. But before Beth could answer, Melody said loudly, "I'm glad I'm not the only one with problems with my kids. I think there's a lot more happening than we know about.

"Alex was furious. The next day he did some checking around, and we took her down to a drug evaluation program. They told us if she is smoking cigarettes, then she is probably drinking alcohol; and if she's drinking alcohol, then she is most likely doing drugs," Beth said.

"Did she go into a rehab program?" Melody asked.

"They wanted to take her that day," Beth said in a very concerned manner as if she was being misled by these people. "It was almost like a kidnapping. They wanted us to put her in for a twenty-month program. We wouldn't be able to see her for least three months. I think they were most interested to see if we had the money to pay for it all. And it didn't feel right to send her away with such little evidence. If I believed she needed it, I would have sent her, but two years of treatment . . . I don't know. I didn't think she was really into drugs—at least I hoped and prayed she wasn't. And I hope that incident scared her enough to stay away from that stuff."

Beth became rather anxious. She felt perhaps she talked too much about her very personal family matters. She decided to put a positive spin on their discussion about Courtney. Before Melody could say anything, Beth started talking again. "Basically Courtney is a very good kid; we've always been so close. When she was little, she didn't even like spending the night over at her friend's house because, she said, she missed being home with her mother. But now that she's fourteen years old and a typical teenager, she's driving me crazy. I've talked to other parents, and they seem to be going through the same thing with their kids, especially the girls."

Beth took a large swallow of her drink as if to catch her breath and fortify herself. She then continued, "I remember shopping one time with Courtney; she had just turned thirteen. We were in a dress shop, and I was helping her select an outfit for some kind of party she was going to. Out of nowhere she started arguing about me helping her. She started yelling at me, saying she was old enough to make her own decisions. I couldn't believe my ears. This couldn't be my child . . . not my daughter . . . the same loving, little girl who brought drawings home from school, saying how much she loved me. I was dumbfounded at her behavior. I almost lost it there, but I kept my temper, and things calmed down to a heated discussion.

"During this episode there was an older woman in the store shopping by herself. When Courtney went into the dressing room to try on an outfit, this nice woman came over to me and asked in a very sweet voice, 'How old is your daughter?' I told her that Courtney had just turned thirteen. The woman stared at me with deep, penetrating dark eyes and a warm smile. She said, 'All I can tell you is someday she'll return to you.' I quickly asked what she meant. She smiled and said, 'I believe a portion of spirit leaves girls at about the age of thirteen; if you can endure the next nine or ten years, that beautiful, mature spirit of the girl will return as the loving daughter you always wanted. Then she smiled and said, 'In the meantime . . . good luck.'"

Beth then added, "Please, Melody, keep our conversation private, and please don't mention what we talked about. Alex gets very upset about this whole topic."

"I understand, Beth. I am afraid my kids are right at that age where these things begin. And Johnny just doesn't understand what I'm going through," Melody said.

"I guess both our husbands have a lot on their minds. The business world is quite demanding," Beth said as she took a sip of her drink.

"You're right, Beth, the business world is tough. But so is taking care of a family, and after work I can't go out barhopping till all hours of the morning. And I can't take a day off to go down to Atlantic City to gamble when I want," Melody said in a disgusted voice.

While the two women were engrossed in their conversation, neither noticed that a third female had drifted in, listening to their conversation. It was Nancy Bishop. Melody hardly recognized her. Nancy's hair was long and straight. Her skin was pale and drawn close to her bone structure. She was thin, and her overall appearance was not healthy or clean. She was dressed in a bright blue, oversized tunic sweater with many large, different imprints. There were so many different styles of peace symbols all over it that it could pass for a sweater advertisement at a protest rally. The sweater was too large for her frame; it hung loosely from her shoulders to just above her knees. She also wore black clamdigger slacks and leather sandals without any socks on this chilly night.

"Hi, Melody," Nancy said with a large smile.

Melody was stunned at her appearance, but quickly regained her composure and said, "Hi, Nancy, it's nice to see you. I didn't know you were coming in this weekend. How have you been?"

Nancy's eyes were opened wide as if she was on some kind of drug. She kept staring directly at Melody. "I've been fine. Thanks for asking, Melody. Is there any of the old gang here tonight?" Nancy asked.

"Yes, there is, Nancy, but first let me introduce you to Beth." Melody grabbed Beth's arm, pulling her over toward Nancy. "Beth is Alex's wife. Isn't it amazing that Alex is the father of three children? Two girls and a boy."

"Hello, Nancy, it's nice to meet you," Beth said warmly as she extended her hand to Nancy. "I take it you were not born and raised here in Clarks Summit?"

Nancy stared a few moments into Beth's eyes. Nancy then backed away a few steps to get a better view of Beth. Nancy smiled as if searching for the right words to speak. Then in a soft voice, she said, "It's nice to meet you, Beth. You're not quite the image I had in mind . . . I mean the wife of Alex and all. You see Alex and I grew up together; we were very close, and I just couldn't visualize the girl he'd marry. He did very well. I am so happy to meet you. I hope we can be good friends." At that Nancy reached out and hugged a startled Beth.

Beth didn't know what to say; she had never even heard of Nancy Bishop. Her mind was racing to figure out how she fit into Alex's life. She couldn't have been an old girlfriend, perhaps a neighbor who had a girlish crush on Alex. Whatever the case Beth was determined to know more about Nancy Bishop.

"I'm pleased to make your acquaintance, Nancy. Any friend of Alex's is a friend of mine," Beth said in a voice that had the same sincerity as thanking a taxi driver for a ride.

Nancy became more excited. Her movements increased as she looked around the bar saying, "Is Alex here? I don't see him."

"He's sitting with Johnny over at that corner table. Can't you see them?" Melody said, pointing in their direction.

"Oh yes, I see them . . . I would have known him anywhere," Nancy said with a whimsical voice. As if continuing in thought, she turned to Melody and said, "Melody, would you get me a beer? I'll pay you later."

Beth and Melody looked at each other, then Melody ordered a round of drinks for all three, instructing the bartender, Rick, to put the drinks on Johnny's tab. Nancy didn't say a word as she waited for her drink. As soon as the drinks arrived, Nancy grabbed her beer and went directly over to the table to join Alex and Johnny.

Alex had a look of concern on his face as he watched a strange-looking woman approach their table. "That can't be Nancy Bishop, is it Johnny?" Alex said in a low, inquisitive voice.

"You're the one with glasses, Alex. You tell me," Johnny said as he too looked with earnest.

In an instant Nancy was at their table, and Alex was on his feet. He reached out as she extended her arms, kissing him on the lips. "Alex, I hoped you'd be here tonight. It's been such a long time. I've thought of you so often . . . How have you been?"

"I'm here too!" Johnny said loudly, breaking in before Alex could get a word out.

"Of course, Johnny," Nancy said as she turned and slightly hugged him. She added with a chuckle, "How could anyone not notice you, Johnny, with all your good looks . . . warmth and charm?"

Alex was mesmerized by Nancy, but he couldn't believe she had changed so much. The once meticulously dressed preppie girl with every hair in place had changed into a mangy, badly groomed, scruffy-looking hippie. Her calm, facial expression had also been altered; her simple, beautiful complexion had been replaced with a tousled, worn look. Vanished were her striking, crystal-clear eyes that were so exciting; they were now dazed and opened extra-wide as if she was searching for something.

Alex didn't know what to say; he started to gather his thoughts together. He smiled at her for a moment and said, "Nancy . . . it's so good to see you too. How have you been? I mean you've changed so much. Life must be treating you well." He thought to himself, *That's about as positive as I can get.*

"I've been doing okay, Alex. Life's been a roller coaster with a lot of ups and downs," Nancy said in a serious tone.

"It looks as if your life has had a lot . . . of ah . . . uppers in it!" Johnny said mockingly.

Nancy looked toward Johnny, saying with a smile, "Now, Johnny, we all can't be as perfect as you. But we all try our best. But of course you don't need to try, Johnny . . . you're always at your best."

"Let's sit down at the table and talk. How is your husband, the esteemed lawyer Perry Mason, doing?" Alex asked.

They all sat down. Nancy was clearly speaking directly to Alex.

"Oh, we've been divorced for years. In fact, I was remarried and divorced again. So now you can call me a . . . a . . . free spirit, so to speak," Nancy said in a lighthearted way.

"What does 'free spirit, so to speak' mean?" Alex asked.

"Well, Alex, that means I'm no longer tied down although there is someone else in my life. He's quite a character. He's a little different than a lot of the guys I been with before." Nancy paused and thought seriously for a moment to make her next point. "He's been incarcerated for a little while . . . he'll be getting out next week. It seems he bought some speed from an undercover pig, so he got thirty days in a Maryland county jail. So I decided to come home for the weekend bash. My family was thrilled of course." Nancy expressed herself without emotion as if she were telling a story she had heard about someone else.

Even Johnny was at a loss of words. He and Alex stared at Nancy for a moment. Someone had to say something. "You've been divorced twice?" Alex asked with astonishment.

"Yes, twice, Alex," Nancy answered in a matter-of-fact voice. "We all don't live a perfect life in a small house with a white picket fence and a large mortgage. I am living a life of my own choosing. I go where I want to go and when I want to go. I'm living the life of a free spirit. And when Scott gets out next week, we're going out West."

Alex tried to compose himself. A smile returned to his face as he said, "Seems like you've done a lot in the last few years, Nancy. Why don't you fill me in on what's happening?" Alex turned toward Johnny and asked him to go over to the bar to get a round of drinks.

Alex then continued addressing Nancy. "The last time we were together you were newlywed to a young, promising attorney by the name of James Morrow, or as I called him, Perry Mason. You both were off to Washington to help change the world, make it a better place to raise our children. So what happened?"

"Life happened, Alex. I married the wrong guy for the wrong reason. Somewhere along the way I lost respect for him and all his high ideals. Then I married the second guy for other wrong reasons. And now I'm just on my own living a free life, and for me, that's the way it's supposed to be," Nancy said.

"I don't understand, Nancy. You had your whole life planned out. You knew what you wanted to be, what you wanted to do. You had a lot of goals in life. What happened? Why the big change?" Alex asked.

"Oh, Alex, I don't know. Jim and I had a great life, at least for a while," Nancy said as she took a sip of her beer from the bottle. "I thought Jim was ambitious and going places. We were young dreamers with the world on a string. We became very active in Washington politics. In fact, Jim was on the staff of George McGovern when the senator ran for president. What an election that was in '72. We traveled all over the country, endless hours campaigning, days without sleep. Booze and drugs was the lifeline of the entire campaign. But when McGovern lost the election, I think Jim lost something too. Maybe we both did . . . whatever. Anyway, in the process we lost each other. Jim had a close friend who worked with him on the campaign by the name of Robert Sears. We all worked very closely together. He had more ambition than Jim, had better ideas, and actually was better in bed than Jim. He loved me . . . I loved him . . . so I divorced Jim, and I married Robert."

Nancy paused for a moment, looking at Alex. She smiled and continued, "It took four years to find out I didn't love Jim, but it only took eight months to realize I didn't love Bob Sears. I don't know if it was time, the booze, or the drugs but whatever . . . So here I am again, Alex, explaining myself to you. Tell me, Alex . . . do you ever think of me?"

"Of course I do, Nancy," Alex answered quickly. "I often think of you, where you are, what you're doing, how life is treating you."

"Life is just treating me great, Alex." Nancy said. "That reminds me, I met Mrs. Alex over at the bar. She's not quite what I expected you to marry, but then again she does fit the mold you'd want. She's pretty, well dressed, well educated, probably a good mother, and a good wife. She's good for you and . . . actually I kind of like her." Nancy paused for a moment, looking directly into Alex's eyes, and said, "Although I wish I didn't like her."

"Well, I'm glad you do like Beth," Alex said. "You're right about her; she is all those things you mentioned and more. We have three great kids, and I guess I'm very lucky to have her."

"Believe me, Alex, she's the lucky one," Nancy replied, slurring her words a little.

Johnny was back with a few drinks, a scotch on the rocks for Alex and a bottle of Budweiser for Nancy. As he handed the drinks to Alex, Johnny whispered in his ear," I've got you covered. You can talk privately as long as you want. Melody is telling Beth how you and Nancy grew up together like brother and sister."

"Thanks, Johnny," Alex said as he thought to himself, *Old Wedge Head does understand sometimes.*

Alex and Nancy returned to their conversation. "So you were married twice each time to a lawyer? I take it your friend who's a guest of the state of Maryland for the next few days is not a lawyer?"

"No, he's not a lawyer, Alex!" Nancy said sarcastically. "The lawyers that I married broke the law more than anyone I know. Did they ever go to jail? No! They knew how the system worked. When I was married, we and our friends did more drugs in Washington than they do in Berkeley. Drinking and driving . . . no problem, they could get it fixed . . . because we had friends in high places."

"I'm sorry, Nancy. I didn't mean to be rude," Alex said. "I just want the best for you; I always have."

"I know, Alex," Nancy said, her head lowered. "Things are not as I wanted them to be. Two marriages wasted, much of my life wasted . . . I'm almost forty, and here I am not knowing what to do."

Alex felt it was time for some tough love; he looked at Nancy differently now. He tried to reassure her, "Is there anything I can do for you, Nancy? Just say the word, and you know I would do whatever you want," Alex said softly. Then in a stern voice, he added, "But you better get your head together. You've got to straighten your life out. The drugs and booze are taking a toll on you. I can imagine your family isn't too pleased at what has happened to you."

"You're right, Alex. My family is not happy with me right now. And I don't care. I'm leaving as soon as Scott comes and gets me. We're going out West to see what, what we will see," Nancy said without emotion.

"How are you going to live?" Alex asked.

"Scott is very handy. He has converted an old school bus into a mobile home of sorts. He's a talented carpenter. He makes his own furniture, which we sell at craft shows," Nancy said proudly.

"How did you meet . . . Scott?" Alex asked with a bewildered look on his face.

"We met at a party a few years ago. He has a lot of exciting ideas, and he's full of energy. Although he is a few years younger than I am, he's done so much—working the carnival circuit for a few years, traveling through South America." Nancy looked and smiled at Alex, saying warmly, "He's not a capitalist like you, Alex. Scott is a dedicated environmentalist; he believes in recycling everything and living off the land as much as possible."

"So you're going to travel around the country in the school bus . . . mobile home?" Alex asked quietly, as if he was hoping to be corrected by his question.

Nancy cocked her head, raising her chin as she spoke in a condescending tone, "I can see, Alex, you don't approve of Scott!"

Alex was angry and frustrated. "If you were my sister, I'd . . . ah," Alex started to say.

"But I'm not your sister, Alex," Nancy cut him off. She looked toward him with a hurt look on her face. "I thought you'd be the one person I could talk to . . . who would understand . . . who wouldn't be so quick to judge me." Nancy took a slug of beer from the bottle. "Life's been tough, Alex. I always tried to do the right thing in life. I trusted in God. I believed he had a plan for me . . . that He would guide me. But it didn't work out the way I thought it would. Let's face it, I went to college to be a servant of God's . . . a missionary of all things! I fell in love with the perfect guy—a minister, but he goes off and knocks up his tramp girlfriend . . . and marries her."

Neither said a word for a moment. Nancy sat staring at the floor, saddened, remorseful- looking, emotionally drained. In a low, shallow voice, she started speaking. "That's when my life started to fall apart, Alex. I ran around with any guy in pants. One-night stands or afternoon stands, it didn't matter . . . as long as they could screw. Then I married my ambitious, drinking, drugging husband who was just as bad as I was. We had a marriage of understanding . . . so we both screwed around. I got tired of all that and married another loser who was going to change my life and make things better. He made it worse. He was a control freak who was going to restore me to being a worthy person. In doing so I'd have sacrificed me and my freedom, and be his servant . . . and I do mean servant! I met Scott at a party one night. He's different . . . he was kind to me . . . he took an interest in me. He liked me the way I am with all my hang-ups and my dysfunctional, emotional baggage. I left husband number two without hesitation. Will Scott be number three? I don't know. Will Scott and I be together forever? I don't know. I know he helped me get away for the control of evil men. We'll just have to see what the future has in store, Alex . . . I hope it's better than the past."

"I hope the future is kind to you, Nancy," Alex said as he reached over the table and put his arm on her shoulder. "You deserve it."

Nancy peered into Alex's eyes, and hers started to fill with tears. She sensed the invisible bond between them was still there, deep and strong. She felt warm in her soul. She was grateful for his friendship, love, and understanding. A silent voice sounded in her head, why couldn't it be you, Alex?

"I hope you'll always be here for me, Alex," Nancy said with a voice of concern.

"I will be, Nancy," Alex replied in a determined manner patting her hand to comfort her.

Perfect timing, Alex looked up to see Beth, Melody, Johnny, and Phil all standing near the table. "We left you two alone long enough," Johnny said loudly. "Yeah, we came over here, Alex, because it's your turn to buy a round of drinks."

"Johnny's already spent his kids' Halloween money on the one beer he bought for himself," Phil said, joking.

"If we were waiting for you to buy a drink, Phil, we'd die of thirst," Johnny shot right back.

"All I have to say Johnny is it's a good thing air is free, or you'd be the first one dead," Phil said as everyone laughed, joining in at the table.

The group's conversations were lighthearted and witty, their voices competing for the floor, talking about what had happened over the years. However, Beth's attention was zeroed in on Nancy. She didn't quite understand the relationship between her husband and this strange, disheveled woman. Melody had filled her in on the fact that Alex and Nancy were buddies all through school, and there never was any hint of a romantic relationship between the two. But considering that Alex had never even mentioned her name raised suspicion in Beth's mind. It was apparent to everyone that Nancy and Alex did have some kind of close connection; Beth wanted to know more about it.

They all sat around the table talking with each other; Beth sat next to Alex. Nancy was on his other side. So when Alex got up to go to the men's room, it was Beth's opportunity to find out what she could in a tactful way. Beth learned over so she could talk directly to Nancy. "Someone mentioned that you and Alex used to date when you younger?" Beth hoped that this simple, direct query would tell a lot, and she waited to see Nancy's reaction to her loaded question.

Nancy had a puzzled look on her face as she tried to answer Beth's question. It could have been because the subject matter was so sensitive or because Nancy had too much to drink and was trying to think of an answer.

"We never dated," Nancy said in a slurred voice. "I don't know why . . . we just never dated."

"You seem so close," Beth said, hoping for a response.

"We are close," Nancy said, her head weaving slightly. "Very close in a strange way. It's been years since we last spoke, but time hasn't seemed to have changed our friendship very much."

Nancy had a large smile as she again looked toward Beth and said, "Beth, Alex and I are good friends, nothing more than that. You don't have to worry about me stealing any husbands. I've been there . . . and had it done to me."

"Oh, I didn't mean anything like that, Nancy," Beth said quickly. "It's just I've been meeting some of Alex's friends for the first time, and I want to get to know them. That's all."

"I understand, Beth," Nancy said, slurring again. "Alex and I were good buddies growing up. We still are . . . at least I think we are. You know we went to grade school together. As little kids we attended each other's birthday parties. We learned how to ride bikes together. He's been like a brother to me. You've got to understand; there are few people in the world like Alex. You never have to worry about him. You are very lucky to have married him. Just ask anyone who knows him. He's as straight as a laser beam; you'll always know where you stand with Alex."

"Look who I found at the bar," Alex yelled as he returned to the table. All eyes were focused on the two men standing in front of them: Alex and Tom Wilkinson. Both had their arms around each other as if they were posing for a picture. Alex stood a little taller than Tommy, although Tommy was clearly the most impressive-looking of the duo. Tom was dressed like a male model in a tan suede blazer with a button-down, blue denim work shirt. His dark hair was styled to accent his weathered complexion and sculptured face. The boyhood scar above his right eye was more pronounced, adding to his mystique.

"Well, look who the cat's dragged in!" Johnny yelled.

"It's too bad the cat can't drag you out, Johnny," Phil said quickly.

Nancy and Melody were on their feet in an instant, rushing over to hug Tommy. Beth sat for a moment taking it all in. She didn't say a word. She just stared at him, thinking, Now this friend I'd really like to know more about.

After reacquainting himself with the gang, Tommy and Alex made their way over to where Beth was seated. Now all of Tommy's attention was directed toward Beth as he greeted her. His warm smile and large, clear blue eyes seemed to melt into her soul. Without saying a word, she was smitten.

Alex stood next to Tommy with his hand on his shoulder to present his dear friend to his wife. "Beth, I'd like you to meet one of my best friends . . . ever! Tommy Wilkinson."

Tommy bent over slightly, offering his right hand, and said, "Hi, Beth. I'm Tom. It's."

Before he could finish his introduction, Beth was on her feet with a warm embrace, kissing Tom tenderly on his right cheek. She then reeled back, placing both hands on his shoulders to get a better look. "Tom, it's so nice to finally meet you," she said with affection. "Alex has told me so much about you. Didn't you used to jump out of planes and stuff? And weren't you in Vietnam?"

Tom was a little startled by Beth's warm reception, remembering others had told him that she was like a cold fish. "In my younger years, I did some crazy things. Then again no one was crazier than your husband," Tommy said jokingly.

Beth was pleased with Tom's warmth, but he didn't answer her question. When Beth asked a question, she expected an honest answer. She asked again, "Were you in Vietnam?"

The smile left Tom's face; he now had a serious but pleasant expression. "Yes, Beth, I served in Vietnam. I was a paratrooper, and I did jump out of perfectly good airplanes," Tom said in a polite, amusing way. He now wanted to change the subject. He didn't like to talk about Vietnam, especially in a bar. He recalled from his Dale Carnegie course, "How to Win Friends and Influence People," have people talk about what they enjoy the most. "I understand you have three beautiful children. Are the girls as pretty as their mother?"

"We have three kids who sometimes drive me crazy. But they are basically good kids," Beth answered. "We like to think the girls, Courtney, fourteen, and Mandy, eight, are beautiful, but I must admit they have a lot of Alex's features."

"We all know Alex has brains, but looks aren't his strong suit. These beautiful girls must have more of your features, Beth," Tom said, knowing he was going a little overboard with compliments. But as he often said, he'd never been slapped for being over-complimentary.

"Tommy, come on over and sit with us; tell me about yourself," Beth said in a very interested way; it was her turn to hand out compliments. "Are you married? Do you have children? Where do you live? Alex has told me about you; now I'd like to hear your version." Beth surprised herself with this sudden, keen interest in Tommy's life.

Tommy sat next to Beth. At first he was a little uncomfortable, then he relaxed as he began to speak, "I was married once; we have a son, Sean. He's ten years old now. He lives with his mother who is now remarried, and they live in Oklahoma. I don't get to see him much because I travel a lot. I work in the oil industry on pipeline projects throughout the world. They usually take years to complete, so I'm out of the country a lot of the time."

"Did you work on the Alaska pipeline?" Beth asked almost without thinking.

"Yes, I worked on the Alyeska pipe line in the seventies. I worked up in the northern section near Prudhoe Bay. That was quite a project," Tommy said with an air of confidence.

"Did you work in the wintertime?" Beth continued in her inquiry. "That must have been horrible."

"We had to work in the winter months. That's the only time we could work on the tundra. In the summer the tundra melts; it becomes a giant swamp. We couldn't hurt the ecosystem with all of our heavy equipment, so during the coldest time of the year when the ground is frozen, that's when we worked on the pipeline." Tommy said.

"How could you work in such cold temperatures?" Beth continued her questioning.

"You have to dress for the climate even though we rode in school busses that drove us from our camp to the work site. In the coldest months, we could only work outside twenty minutes out of an hour; the rest of the time, we would be huddled in the busses just trying to keep warm," Tommy said. He started looking around the table as if looking to change the subject from himself.

"You must have worked on these pipelines all over the world, haven't you, Tommy?" Johnny asked.

" A lot of different places, Johnny," Alex said.

"It's been a long time since I've seen you, Tommy," Phil yelled out.

"When was the last time you were in the Abingtons, Tommy?" Nancy asked.

Tommy quickly responded, "The last time I was in . . ." He paused for a moment, and his emotion started to show. He then said sadly, "The last time I was in Clarks Summit . . . it was for Jerry Weaver' funeral."

The group was shocked and got quiet for a moment. Tommy sensed the sudden somber mood. He knew he had made them sad, so he would try to make them happy again. He picked up his drink and said, "I'd like to make to toast." He looked around as each one picked up their drinks. Tommy waited a moment till all was quiet, then he said in a clear, distinctive voice, "To Jerry Weaver . . . who in spirit is still with us." Tommy lifted his glass above his head. Beaming, he said in a loud, lighthearted way, "To you, Jerry . . . this is the first one today!" He laughed as he downed his drink, as did everyone else.

The conversations returned to where have you been, what have you been doing, and kid stories. Melody noticed some people gawking out the front windows. She dispatched Johnny to go over and find out what the commotion was. He was back in a minute.

"Well, Johnny, what's everyone looking at? Was there an accident out front?" Melody asked.

Phil said, "If there's an accident, Johnny, you better go and get your tow truck."

Then he yelled, "Yeah, you can rip off the customer and rip off the bumper at the same time!" Everyone laughed.

Johnny didn't take it; he reeled right back, saying, "If anybody got ripped off, it was you, Phil . . . when you bought those elevated shoes! They're as phony as the shoe polish you dabble in your hair."

"Now, Johnny, let's not talk about hairdos." As soon as Phil said that, there was silence for a moment.

"Go ahead, Phil, how about the latest Wedge Head joke!" Johnny said sarcastically. Everyone shuttered for a moment, hoping this verbal bashing would end.

"You know I'm only kidding with you, Johnny," Phil said warmly. "If I didn't love ya, I wouldn't kid ya." Phil then grabbed Johnny around the shoulder, hugging him and laughing. Even Johnny laughed.

The waitress appeared with a tray full of drinks, and as she was setting the glasses on the table, she commented, "There's a big limo parking out front; over at the window they're trying to see who is getting out."

"If two big guys with long overcoats get out with a violin case, they're probably looking for Johnny," Phil said jokingly.

"I'll bet it isn't one of your former students, Phil," Johnny said with a laugh. "Unless he's being buried tomorrow." This time Johnny's repartee received a laugh.

Alex leaned over and whispered to Nancy, "Maybe it's Scott."

Nancy wasn't amused.

Just whose limo was it? There was no doubt about it. That question was answered as she entered the pub. She was tall and sleek, with the air of a woman who deserved to be chauffeured around in a limousine. By her hairstyle alone, it was apparent she spent a lot of time at chic, cosmopolitan salons. The hairdo was stunning and specifically designed for her full mane of glossy, auburn-colored hair. It was brushed straight back from her forehead with the sides draping her shoulders, accenting her beautiful facial structure.

She wore a long, glamorous, herringbone coat with a large mink lapel and matching mink cuffs. At a glance one could tell that this dramatic tailored coat along with the spiked boots would be considered all the rage in New York City. She carried herself in a manner that reflected the excellent taste of her elegant wardrobe. As she entered she held her head high and erect; she carried herself in a carefree but determined mode. She walked through the bar as if she owned the place, not acknowledging anyone until she saw her friends sitting at a table.

"Over here, Ida," Melody yelled.

About the same time Ida heard Melody's voice, she spotted the friendly group at the table. Ida's entire face came to life; her eyes opened as if suddenly surprised, and instantly an ear-to-ear smile developed across her radiant face.

"How's everyone doing?" Ida yelled as she moved toward the group.

Ida moved around the table like a newly elected politician, laughing, talking, hugging, and kissing everybody, until she got to Beth. They both froze for an instant, staring at each other. Alex stepped in, grabbing the hands of both women as if he were holding the gloves of two prizefighters.

"Ida Freeman, I'd like to introduce you to my wife and the mother of our three children, Beth Flynn," Alex said with a little pride in his voice. "I hope you two can be good friends."

Ida and Beth smiled at each other. They hugged and kissed each other on the cheeks. Both were showing genuine signs of admiration for each other, and both said kind words to each other. On the surface these two appeared as two strong women who would have a lot in common. But behind the eyes and between the ears, they didn't exactly like each other. Both felt it didn't matter much as this would be a short encounter for the both of them.

Ida continued to traverse the table greeting everyone. Tom watched Ida with keen interest as she made her joyous small talk with all the others. He stood there motionless without any facial expression, patiently waiting for his opportunity to reconnect. As she approached Tom, her eyes narrowed into a focused gaze. Her large smile was replaced with a serious look of wonderment. All those standing there felt the intensity of their encounter.

"Tommy, it's been too long," Ida said warmly.

"Yeah . . . since we last met, I've torn a lot of pages out of a lot of calendars," Tommy said with a forced smile.

"It seems as though time has been very good to you, Tommy," Ida said as she looked deeply into his eyes. "I think you are even more handsome than I remembered."

"And you, Ida, you've only gotten better," Tommy said jokingly. He cocked his head, smiled, and then added, "And of course . . . much more beautiful."

Ida reached out and embraced Tommy with much more enthusiasm than anyone previously. They then shared a passionate kiss that lasted what seemed like a long time. Beth was surprised by the vigorous reunion of the two. She looked into the faces of the other members of the group; all had smiles of approval.

Except for Johnny who said loudly, "Hey! This is a public place . . . save that stuff for the parking lot."

With Johnny's proclamation the couple quickly regained their composure, although Ida seemed somewhat embarrassed, like a young schoolgirl being kissed for the first time. Tommy, on the other hand, was pleased with the overall reception, and his facial expression couldn't conceal it. His eyes were gleaming, and his complexion appeared to have a blushed radiance.

Ida's attention heightened. She glanced around at her friends, as if seeking a reaction, as she said loudly, "I would like to buy a round of drinks. Is anyone thirsty?"

A loud roar of approval burst in from the table of partiers. More drinks were served, and the group was bubbly with laughter and storytelling.

While Johnny was telling one of his interesting stories on how he won a lot of money in Atlantic City, Tommy whispered into Ida's ear, "Is the limo going to wait all night for you?"

Ida looked directly at Tom with an innocent smile and said, "I told him to wait out front for twenty-two minutes. If I didn't come out, he was to leave."

"Did you think it would take you twenty-two minutes to find out if anyone was here?" Tommy asked.

"Oh, I knew someone would be here," Ida said, smiling. "I thought it may take twenty minutes to say hi to everyone. And it would take just two minutes to decide if I was going to leave with you or not."

Tommy looked at his watch as he said, "Your twenty-two minutes are almost up."

Ida smiled, picked up her drink taking a long slow sip, and said meekly, "Really? I'm not worried." She paused for a minute, looking at her watch. "Thomas, you do have a car? If not I have one minute to hold the limo for us."

Tommy took a serious look at Ida saying, "I have a car, Ida."

"Good," Ida said with a lighthearted, girlish tone. "We're both in luck. You have a car, and I have a room at Nichols Village."

Tommy studied Ida's expression for a minute, then asked, "I thought you're marred?"

"I'm also Jewish, but I don't go to temple," Ida said in a wisecrack way.

"What does that mean?" Tom asked.

"It means I'm here because you're here. And I want spend the night with you," Ida said in a matter-of-fact way.

"No argument from me. I'm yours tonight, babe." Tom said.

The lively conversations continued through the night, along with the laughter, joking, and storytelling until management flashed the lights at 1:45 a.m. The pub would close in fifteen minutes, so the bartender announced, "Last call for alcohol!"

"Is anyone interested in going to the Blue Bird for breakfast?" Melody asked in a slurred voice.

"We'll have one and be done!" Phil yelled out.

"Another round of drinks for me and my merry followers," Tommy said as he ordered the drinks.

An independent observer would describe the group as being "half-pasted." They were all legally drunk, but that didn't stop them from having one more round of drinks.

"You shouldn't drink and drive," said Phil in a loud, slurry voice, "Yeah, you could hit a bump and spill the whole thing." Everyone laughed noisily.

Tommy thought it was a good time for one of his jokes, so he jumped right in. "A few weeks ago, I was out drinking all night. While I was driving myself home, a cop pulls me over. He gives me a sobriety test, and then he asks me why was I driving in such a condition?" Tommy stopped, looking at his small audience. "I said I had to drive . . . I was too drunk to walk." Again there was loud laughter from the group.

The drinks arrived for the final toasts. Everyone picked up their glasses as best they could. Nancy yelled out, "Alex!" She sounded as if she were nominating him for office. "Let Alex make the toasts."

Alex was caught off balance, physically and figuratively, and he was somewhat happily nervous, or put in other words, he was half-pasted. As he started standing up, he also began to lift his glass, preparing to make a toast. Alex was happy but had a serious look about him as he glanced in to each of their faces. He tried to keep a sober decorum about him, although he swayed like a pine tree in a windstorm. Beth was not amused at the specter of her husband taking center stage with the spotlight shining on him . . . being a little tipsy. It was a good thing she was under the influence, or there may have been words spoken in anger.

Alex stood tall and erect, his head lifted as high as it could reach. He paused for a moment, awaiting their attention. When the clamor died down, he cleared the throat and said, "I'd like to make a toast."

"Well, make it a short one; the bar closes in fifteen minutes," Johnny said, laughing loudly.

Alex looked directly at Johnny as if was the guest of honor and said with light emotion, "To Johnny, whose words of wisdom are always appreciated by all." Everyone laughed but Johnny.

After things quieted down, Alex again raised his glass to make a toast. "Again to Jerry Weaver and other friends no longer with us, and to our friendship, may it grow in time and strength! And remember, friends, we will drink again in the morning."

They all chugged their drinks down. "Is anyone interested in going to the Blue Bird for breakfast?" Melody asked again in a slurred voice.

"Alex, are you okay to drive?" Beth asked in a harsh tone.

"I'm fine . . . we'll be home in a few minutes. I've made it home in a lot worse condition than this," Alex said calmly.

"Yeah, tonight you shouldn't have to stick you head out the window to stay awake while you're driving home," Phil said laughing.

Beth said in a motherly way, "I know that group called Mothers Against Drunk Driving is really putting the pressure on the police to crack down on drunk drivers."

"Well, I hope they don't make the law retroactive, or we'd all be in big trouble," Johnny said.

The night was ending, and everyone was putting on their jackets and coats. Alex wanted to talk privately with Nancy. As he approached her, she was in a heated discussion with Phil about his teaching career. "Excuse me, Nancy; do you need a ride to the breakfast in the morning?" Alex asked.

"Thanks, Alex, but I'm not going tomorrow. Tonight I've seen everyone I wanted to," she said.

"Do you need a ride home?" Alex asked in a polite manner.

Nancy was clearly drunk but apparently in control of her own life. She looked directly at Alex and said, "No thanks, Alex. Jim Mooney is going to give me a ride home. You remember him from high school, don't you?" Nancy then abruptly walked toward the bar. Suddenly she stopped, turned around, and now supporting a big smile, said, "He always wanted me, ever since tenth grade." With that said she continued toward her rendezvous.

"Your friend Nancy is quite an interesting woman," Beth said coolly.

"She is living an interesting life but sadly not a happy one," Alex said in a glum voice.

"Who would have thought Nancy Bishop would turn out this way?" Phil said quietly.

Room 301

Nichols Village Motel

Ida lay comfortably on the king-sized bed; she had just lit up a cigarette and sighed. With a whimsical voice, she said, "Hmmm . . . you haven't lost it." She turned on her side facing Tommy. She looked directly into to his eyes, saying, "In fact, I believe you've gotten better."

Tommy smiled back and said, "It's not only wine that gets better with age, Speaking of which, may I freshen your glass with fresh wine, Madame?"

"Merci beaucoup, monsieur," Ida said in a light French accent.

Tommy reached over to the end table, retrieved a bottle of red wine, and filled Ida's glass and his own.

"I love it when you talk dirty to me in the 'language of love,'" Tommy said with warm affection.

"We do have a good time together . . . don't we?" Ida asked as if thinking out loud.

"That we do," Tommy said.

"We should spend more time together, don't you think, Tommy?" Ida said as she took a sip of her wine.

"I do, but I doubt if your husband would agree with me," Tommy said seriously.

"Why do you bring him up? We're having a good time. Let's not ruin it," Ida said in a stern voice.

"You're right, Ida. Let's not ruin our good time with the obvious. After all we can stay in this room for what . . . a day or two, and then what? We'll have to face reality," Tommy said as he rolled over to grab his own glass of wine.

Ida rose to a sitting position in bed. She was in a sober mood. "Our reality, Tommy, is the result of our decisions. And we both made our own decisions independently. You did what you wanted to do, just as I've chosen to do what I wanted to do."

Tommy also was now in a serious mood. "You're right, Ida, but you have the sequence of events wrong. You made your own decision on what was good for you. And then I made my own decisions on what was good for me."

"Here we go again, Tommy," Ida said in a frustrated voice. "If you remember correctly, after you got out of the army, I already had a career. And I was willing to help you start yours. But you preferred to live a crazy lifestyle with no goals and no future plan. I knew it wouldn't work out."

"Yeah, you're probably right, Ida," Tommy said, his voice dropping lower as if accepting fate. He took a large drink of wine. He continued as if reminiscing about old times. "There were some crazy times back then. Wild, all-night drinking parties, decadence with carefree carousing that ended with smashing up cars along with a notorious reputation. That's what I called my 'turbulent' years. I'm glad they didn't last forever."

"They lasted long enough, Tommy!" Ida said with a light tone to her voice.

"It wasn't all debauchery; after all I did go to college," Tommy said with some pride.

"You barely made it through school. You had to drag yourself in each morning, you had hangovers most days, and you slept through most of your classes," Ida said scornfully. "That was not a formula for a lifestyle of success."

"I wasn't your typical college student. I was older than those teenagers. And I wasn't prepared for college. My family didn't have the money to send me to college, I didn't know if I would ever get a degree," Tommy commented. He thought for a minute and added, "I didn't have a rich father to pay my expenses for college."

Tommy stared for a moment at the blank TV set hanging on the wall. "I have two men to thank for my college education. One was Senator Yarbrough from Texas who introduced the GI Bill, and the other was Ho Chi Minh for starting the Vietnam War. Without the Vietnam War, there would no GI Bill, and without the GI Bill, I wouldn't have been able to go to college."

"You could have gotten student loans if you really wanted to go college," Ida said.

"Look I had terrible grades in high school. I couldn't get into a good college." Tommy took a large swallow of his wine. His mood changed a little. He smiled, looking over at Ida as he readied for an amusing story. "I remember when I applied to Lackawanna Junior College. I was pleasantly surprised when I was invited in for a personal interview with the president of the college." Tommy took another drink of wine. He was now wearing a large smile, breathing deeply, as if very pleased with himself. "I thought the head of the college had read something about me in the newspapers when I was in Vietnam. I had been awarded a few medals that made the papers back home. So I figured he wanted to meet a genuine war hero. So I showed up for my appointment right on time, nicely dressed in a coat and tie. I introduced myself to his secretary. After a few minutes, she escorted me into his big office. I saw him sitting behind his large desk, which was covered with a bunch of folders. He was reading what appeared to be my file. I could see he was a busy man, but he was taking time out of his hectic schedule just to meet me."

Tommy paused, took another sip of wine, and sat erect in the bed. He then continued talking. "After he finished reading the folder in hand, he looked up at me and said, 'Tom, I'm glad you came in. I wanted to meet you personally.' Well, my little chest was all puffed out, and I said, 'I'm glad to meet you, sir.' And then he peered at me through his thick glasses and looking over the top them, said, 'The reason I wanted you to come in for an interview is because I wanted to meet a guy with enough guts to apply to a college! With grades like these! I can't believe this . . . you had Fs and even double Fs!'" Tommy began to chuckle at himself, shaking his head and reaching out his hands to emphasize the humorous point he was making. He continued, "My big ego, the size of Montana, was reduced to an ego the size of a banana seed."

Ida was laughing. "What did you say then?" she asked.

"After I picked up my jaw, I told him the grades were a reflection of an immature high school student. Since high school I had served honorably in the service of our country and, if given an opportunity, I would bring honor to his school. He went on tell me that he had spoken to Mrs. Jewett, my high school counselor, and she thought I deserved a chance. So I was allowed in for one semester on probation. Not what you'd call being welcomed with open arms, but I did get in."

"But you did get in, you had your chance," Ida said coolly.

"Yes, I did, Ida. I did have my chance, and I took it and completed college. But you didn't want to wait. You had your chance, and you took it. You lived the good life in New York; you slept with the best. Then you married the divorced news executive and lived happily ever after."

"That was cruel thing to say, Tommy," Ida said flatly.

"Yes, it was," Tommy said. "And I'm sorry; it's just that you meant so much to me. And sometimes I feel as though I was just a plaything for you to enjoy."

"Tommy, I loved you. I still love you for some unknown reason. And you've been the love of my life. But I needed someone who loved me that I could depend on. I wanted to be married to someone who would make me happy and I could be proud of." Ida spoke in an intense tone as she searched Tommy eyes for reaction. She continued, "Maybe it's my upbringing in Chicago or living in New York, whatever. I wanted someone to fit into my world. I wanted my husband to be my partner in my career. Is that so bad?"

"No, it's not bad, Ida," Tommy said somberly. "But it's pathetic. All the requirements and ideals you set for your husband were fine, except one. You didn't even talk about the one outstanding prerequisite most brides look for in a groom: you never mention the word love. What did you do? Have your fiancé fill out a job application? Then you married him on the third interview?"

"If I did love Charles, do you think I would be here tonight with you, Tommy?" Ida asked.

Tommy seemed to have a puzzled look about him as he said, "I don't know, Ida. You say you love me, but I don't think you love me as a person. I think there's something about me that you relish. Maybe it's my background, my unpredictability, or my wild streak. Whatever it is, you seem to enjoy it for a while, and after you've had your fix, it's back to the real world of New York."

"You think I come to the Abingtons just to be with you?" Ida yelled in a sarcastic tone. "Get real. In the past ten years, I've been here more than you have. I have friends here; Clarks Summit is my adopted hometown, and I love it."

Tommy seemed to be getting a little agitated. "You may claim this is your adopted hometown; you even know some people you call friends. And of course you want everyone to know who you are. And I'm just one of the casts of characters you seem to enjoy here. But when your limo gets back on the interstate, you won't look back or think back about us. You're a taker, Ida, not a giver."

"Tommy, I'm sorry you think so little of me. I do care about the people here, and I do love you a great deal. And yes, I can be a hard-ass at times. And I know my New York attitude can be offensive, but that's me. I'm not perfect."

"No, you're not perfect, Ida," Tommy said in a matter-of-fact tone. "But sometimes I think you're a tad on the selfish side. You remind of an opera singer warming up." He then cleared his throat. In a low voice, Tommy started to sing, "Me-me-me-me." Then in a slightly higher voice, he sang, "Me-me-me-me." And then in his highest voice, he sang, "Me-me-me . . . it's all about . . . meee!"

"That's very funny!" Ida said with a laugh. "Performed brilliantly by our own Tommy Wilkinson, this year's recipient of the Dr. Livingston Award for his unselfish dedication to betterment of all mankind. We are so proud of all your achievements, Tommy." She then started to applaud.

Tommy seemed worn out; he exhaled deeply and asked, "What are we fighting about, Ida? It doesn't matter much. We both are going to be in town for a short time. Then it's back to our own worlds. So let's enjoy ourselves during this fun-filled respite."

"I'll drink to that. So let's have a few laughs," Ida said as she reached across the bed with her empty wine glass. She continued to talk as Tommy filled her glass. "So tell me, Tommy, what all happened after we said our good-byes?

"Let's put it another way, after you left me with a broken heart. I did what you expected me to do." Tommy was very animated as he told his story, "I tried to hang myself from a big old tree right out front of the pub. But the rope I used turned out to be a bungee cord. How humiliating it was bouncing up and down while the drunks cheered."

"Seriously, Tommy," Ida asked.

"Well, I continued to go to Lackawanna or as you called it 'lack-of-knowledge.' Although I was in school, I did make time to squeeze in some fun . . . drinking at Rudy's Bar in Scranton, running around with a bunch of Marywood girls. And when the weather was right, I'd take the girls from Keystone jeeping on the power-line trails," Tommy said lightly.

"You were living at home, weren't you?" Ida asked.

"Yeah, I lived at home. Except for the time my mother threw me out the house for being thrown in jail," Tommy lamented as he reflected on the story.

"I never heard that story," She asked with an astonished voice. "Go on I'd like to hear about it."

"Well, Charlie Frazer and I were out drinking all night, and we ended up in some after-hours bar down in Scranton. We got into a brief fight, but we made our way outside okay. When the police paddy wagon pulled up, two large Irish cops got out and asked us a few questions. Charlie mouthed off to them. So they threw him in the paddy wagon and took him to the city hall to the drunk tank. And they told me to go home."

Tommy smiled as he continued to sip his wine and tell his story. "I couldn't leave a friend in need. So I went down to the police station to bail him out. After all, this is America, and we have rights. I had a few words with the sergeant in charge. I believe he took offense to my thoughtful words of wisdom. He then threw me in the drunk tank along with Charlie. This all occurred early on a Sunday morning, which happened to be Mother's Day, a slow news day. I still remember the headline: 'Man chastises police and lands in city lockup.' The fact that I stayed out all night, not calling or anything made my parents pretty mad. So when they saw my name in the Sunday paper, that's when they threw me out. I moved in with Billy Reese for a while. He had his own little farm near Dalton."

"Yes, I remember when you lived on that little bachelor farm. I was in one weekend, and on Sunday afternoon I saw your mom and dad over at Palumbo's Bar. I remember talking to your parents when Billy Reese came up to talk to your mother. He was very serious as he told her how well you were doing. He told her that you got up each morning with the chickens."

"And your mother said . . ." Ida could hardly keep from laughing. "Your mother said, 'Yeah, Tommy may get up early with the chickens, but at night he sleeps with pigs.' I crack up laughing every time I think of that story," Ida said as they both started laughing.

"Tommy, you must have driven your parents crazy, Ida said as she had another taste of wine. She then looked rather serious and asked, "Do you think Vietnam had anything to do with your wild behavior?"

"No! Being in Vietnam didn't have anything to do with my behavior!" Tommy said in an irritated, strong voice. He then calmed down and said mildly. "I just did a lot of things other people didn't do . . . like a lot of drinking and a lot of partying . . . and I wrecked twelve cars in just over two years, and I did a few other things that were considered . . .a little on the wild side. So perhaps I got on my parents' nerves a little—not to mention the rest of our quiet little community."

Ida cocked her head and put one hand up to her chin, portraying the image of someone thinking a great deal. She looked over at Tommy and said, "And you wanted me to give up my career in New York . . .to share in your lifestyle of fine living, partying, and wrecking cars . . .just to be with you?"

Tommy gazed into her eyes, smiled, and said, "Ida, you weren't going to give up anything for me . . . or for anyone else. You live for Ida."

Ida smiled and lifted her glass to make a toast: "To us, Tommy. We're a matched set."

Chapter Six

1986

Seven thirty on the dot, Alex was walking out the front door of his father's home. Beth was a step behind. She wasn't in a happy mood as she walked briskly across the driveway.

"I can't understand you, Alex. Any other occasion I'm trying to make sure you're on time for your appointments. But when it comes to your friends, you make damn sure you're ahead of schedule," Beth said as she walked out, buttoning her coat.

"Come on, Beth, I just want to be there on time. Why is it such a big deal? If you don't want to come along, just say so! You could have stayed in bed and gotten some of that much-needed sleep you're always complaining about," Alex said as he walked over to his new company car.

"I still don't understand why anyone wants to get up this early in the morning to go drinking. Only in Clarks Summit would this be considered normal behavior. After last night you'd think you might want to give up drinking for a while," Beth said in a disgusted voice as she buckled herself in her seat. "You better buckle up yourself; you're a family man now and get used to it; they're going to make the seat belt law mandatory."

"I drive with a seat belt when I think I need one. It's not the law yet." Although he was angry, he buckled up anyway just to avoid another argument. Alex started driving the car with hyper attention; he seemed to be getting agitated. "We're hardly out of the driveway, and you're already complaining. This is the first time you've ever been to the breakfast. If you don't want to drink, you don't have to. The reason we are going is to have a good time and see some of my old friends," Alex said calmly.

They drove in silence through the familiar streets of Clarks Summit, turning north onto Route 6/11, which followed an ancient Indian path named the Lackawanna Trail. They quietly traveled up through Glenburn past the now-closed Holiday Inn Coffee Shop that was the high school hangout for Alex and his friends. They descended into the small valley where the Glenburn Dam was built many years ago, creating the Glenburn Pond—the same pond where Alex's notorious friend's Jeep crashed through the ice on that cold January afternoon.

"Isn't that where your friends sank the Jeep?" Beth said in a cool but warming voice, attempting to literarily break the ice herself.

"Yeah, that's the place, all right," Alex said, trying to keep a low verbal profile.

They continued to drive quietly through Dalton past the Blue Bird Diner, and then turned onto Route 6 into the picturesque valley toward Tunkhannock. Alex thought it might be a good time to start a conversation again before they arrived at the breakfast.

"Driving across a frozen pond is not as crazy as it may seem. We used to drive our cars on the frozen pond without any problem. I guess they just hit a soft spot. When we were young, we did a lot of crazy things. It's kind of fun to have old friends like that."

"Yes, Alex! Your old friends . . . that's the problem. This whole weekend is about your old friends!" Beth continued to argue.

"You're right, Beth. These are my old friends! They played a part in forming who I am and what I am. When you and I first met, I was already an adult. I was pretty well set in my ways as an adult. For good or bad, these people helped develop that person," Alex said with frustration.

"I think they had more to do with forming your drinking habits than anything else," she said briskly.

Alex drew in a deep breath. He searched for words that shared his confused feelings. "Beth, I grew up with these people; we explored our world together. As a kid growing up, some of the most important things I learned were not from books at school. They were lessons I learned by dealing with the people that I knew. I learned at an early age that there are good and bad in people . . . who to trust and why. I loved growing up here. We climbed some of these mountains. We hunted in a lot of these fields and had beer parties in them too. I used to swim in the river down the road a little." Alex pointed down into the distant valley. "That over there is Little Rocky Glen; one summer I pulled a kid from that river after he dove in and fractured his skull and broke his neck. It was a horrible experience . . ." He paused, thinking for a moment, and then added as if thinking aloud, "You can see my character, good or bad, was developed around here with these people. You might say who I am . . . is the result of where I came from."

Beth listened patiently but not without strong feelings. She had her own opinion of Alex and his youthful fantasies. "Alex, you grew up here, and I understand you loving it here. But you're married now with your own family and living in Drexel Hill. It's fun to come up here for a while, but let's not get carried away with how wonderful it is." Beth paused for a moment to gather more thoughts. "Remember, Alex, if it was so wonderful here, why did you leave this paradise filled with all your wonderful friends?"

Alex's facial expression changed to a forced smile that was more like a frown. He was angry but wanted to keep his temper. It was too early in the day to continue this argument. He had just one more thing to say before changing the subject. He took in a deep breath and said calmly, "When we were dating, you had a great time around here. You loved all my friends. They all were such great people . . . until we were married. It's such a shame they all changed so much."

"We've all changed since we were married, Alex. Let me think how you've changed. Hmmm . . . oh yes, you are now a husband and a father of three children for starters," Beth said, feeling the last words were spoken on the subject.

"You're right, Beth." Alex said meekly. "But when I come up here, I just like to have a good time and reminisce about some of the fun things we did in the past."

Beth didn't say anything for a few moments; she just stared out the window as they drove up Route 6/11. "Alex," she said, "perhaps the reason I don't like it up here as much as you do is because of the way you behave. You are like a different person to me, not at all like the guy I met in Philadelphia who was thoughtful, funny, and wanted to be with me all the time. Here you seem to be more interested in who you used to be . . . rather than who you are now. Up here you're more concerned about living in the past with these people than being with me and the children."

Alex put on his serious face. "I know I'm a little different, but you've got to understand, these are the people I am most comfortable with. We grew up together, and they know me a certain way . . . like before we were married. And they kind of expect me to fit a certain pattern. And I do get sucked back into being my old self, laughing at the same old stories as if I was hearing them for the first time. But that's the way they see me—as the same old Alex."

"I don't know that person who existed before we were married. I'd like to see more of the person that I did marry. He's a good, likable person who's married to me. I know these are your friends and the people you grew up with. But I want to ask you, Alex . . ." Beth said in a sober tone. "And I want you to think for a minute before you answer. Of all these friends you know, do any of them bring you as much happiness as your children? Do any of them love you as much as we do?"

Alex didn't say a word for a few minutes as he drove quietly through the roaming farm country. He started to smile a little as he listened to the song "Jack and Diane" by John Cougar on the radio. "I guess we're not Jack and Diane, but we do have a nice family. And I do love you and the kids. So I'll try a little harder to be the guy you married – although I must warn you: I may slip back to my good old Alex from time to time."

Beth breathed a sigh of relief, saying, "That's all I ask, Alex, is a little consideration. And please don't drink much this morning; we have a long day."

"Yes, we do have a long day, so let's enjoy it." Alex turned up the radio a little, then said, "And I'll try to be on my best behavior." "Wasted on the Way" by Crosby, Stills and Nash was playing on the radio station. "This song reminds me of my life a little. 'Did you envy all the dancers . . . Who had all the nerve . . . look at all my friends who did and got what they deserved?' I was a shy kid, always kind of afraid to do things. I didn't have a serious girlfriend until I was in college."

"What about Nancy Bishop?" Beth asked quickly. "She seems quite interested in you. You've been just friends all these years?"

"Yes, Beth, Nancy and I have been good friends all these years. And that's all."

Beth paused for a moment. "Tell me more about Tommy Wilkinson; he seemed to be an interesting guy."

"Tommy and I were always good friends. He was a smart kid but never applied himself in school. After high school he joined the paratroopers and was one of the first to go to Vietnam. When he came home, he had changed a lot. He became a real hell-raiser, drinking a lot, wrecking cars, and getting into trouble. He's a good-natured guy. He and Ida had a thing going for a while. They broke up; Ida married some big shot in New York. He took it pretty hard, and then he buckled down and finished at Lackawanna Junior College; then he went to Florida to finish college. After college he tried to come home but couldn't get a decent job. He had a buddy from the army who lived in Oklahoma. He went out there to work and met some girl; she became pregnant, and he married her. But it didn't last long. I understand he works on pipelines all over the world. He's been just about everywhere . . . Alaska, South America, Singapore, Saudi Arabia. You might say he's had an interesting life."

"I think there's still something between him and Ida," Beth said.

"You're probably right. From the first time they met, there was a strong bond between those two. I guess there still is," Alex said.

Alex paused for a moment as they were driving through the village of Factoryville, the home of Keystone Junior College. "Charlie and I used to go to dances over there at Keystone. We had a lot of fun then." The drive continued as they approached the Blue Bird Diner. "We spent a lot of late nights at the old Blue Bird Diner. It looks pretty much the same. The parking lot still not paved."

"It's nice to drive down memory lane with you, Alex," Beth said in a half-sarcastic way. She was looking off toward the distant mountains as they drove through the valley on the way to Tunkhannock. "But I must say this is beautiful country here, with the endless mountains off in the distance. I can almost visualize the Indians who once roamed the area."

Alex was pleased that Beth was starting to relax. He thought she would be interested in the rich, historical significance of the area. "There was a big military campaign during the Revolutionary War that came right through Tunkhannock." Alex pointed to the mountains that lay ahead. He got more excited as he continued to thrill Beth with his knowledge. "It was called Sullivan's March. It seems that the British along with their allies, the Iroquois Indians, came down the Susquehanna River to Wyoming just north of Wilkes-Barre. There they killed about three hundred American settlers. General Washington and the Continental Army were fighting the British in New

Jersey; he could have the British to his rear. So he sent General Sullivan to chase the Indians back up the river to New York and destroy all the Indian villages along the way. There are a lot of roadside markers that tell about it."

Beth seemed mildly impressed; in a whimsical manner of speaking, she said, "Being raised in Philadelphia, I do know a little about the Revolutionary War, Alex. In fact, I think they signed a document there, the declaration of something or other, and of course our neighbors over at Valley Forge remember the guys camping out during the winter."

"You know, I forgot you were from Philadelphia; you seldom mention it unless we're with other people," Alex replied quickly. There was silence for a moment as they listened to the radio; then the song "Eye of the Tiger" came on. "I like those Rocky movies. I think I'm going to get an eight-track put in my car so I can listen to the music I like," Alex said.

"Yes, Alex, anything you want to entertain yourself." Beth said.

"I do spend a lot of time in my car. I need some distraction when I drive. I'm even thinking of getting a CB radio so I'll be able to talk to the truckers. They know about traffic problems and where 'Smokey the bear' is hiding with his picture taker." Alex was exerting some personal power.

"That will impress your friends at the breakfast," Beth said with some sarcasm.

"We are almost there. So remember, Beth, we are here to have a good time," Alex said with a hopeful smile.

Their drive continued through the farmlands of rolling fields and wooded hillsides along the Tunkhannock Creek. Beth was relaxing a little, listening to the soft music on the radio, taking in the countryside she rarely visited.

"There it is," Alex said with a rare show of excitement on his behalf. He drove into the entrance and down the long driveway. He handled his car with the confidence of a pilot about to land his plane on Fantasy Island. "Shadowbrook... Well, it looks pretty much the same. The golf course looks great for this time of year. Still has those two giant cow heads on the roof.

As kids we'd drive all the way out here for ice cream. It's made right here with their own milk from their own cows. Ahhh . . . my favorite was cherry vanilla; it was the best ice cream I've ever had!"

Beth was impressed with the country complex, taking in all the scenery, and the bright-colored ice cream parlor on top of the hill. She liked the clean white barn in the valley with the evergreen shrubbery and the manicured lawn stretching through the golf course. "It is beautiful up here, Alex. But the thought of drinking this early in the morning takes away much of the charm of the picturesque setting."

Alex pulled into the parking lot; he was in his own little world oblivious to any outside distraction, including Beth. "The parking lot is pretty full, looks like a good turnout. I see one of Johnny's new Lincoln Town Cars. I knew he'd be early."

Beth drew in a deep breath as she opened her door and with gritted teeth she said, "Let's go in and have a good time. I know this means a lot to you, Alex. You must impress your friends. But please remember this is going to be a long day, so please don't drink too much this morning."

"Yes, dear," Alex said with a smile in a subservient, humorous tone as he got out of the car.

Alex and Beth entered the banquet area located next to the golf pro shop. The large room looked like a wedding reception that was in full session. The multitude of tables was almost full of joyful guests. The bar at the far end was crowded with drinking revelers. Alex looked over at the large number of people . . . he recognized some of his old teachers, classmates, friends and family of friends. It was like old home week. There was such a warm feeling, seeing all these people that he knew so much about. These were the people who knew him as a little kid, who saw him riding his bicycle, working part-time jobs, driving his father's car too fast, selling ads for the high school yearbook and many other things he did when he was young. And now, as an adult, they would learn more about him. Surely they'd be impressed. At least he hoped so. After all he was now married to a beautiful woman. He was successful in business and a good father. Alex felt very happy in these surroundings and wanted a drink to enhance his good feelings.

There were some friendly faces that recognized Alex, and some came over to greet both him and Beth. Of course Alex didn't recognize all of them but was able through courteous manners to introduce everyone to Beth. Carroll Coleman, an old girlfriend of Alex's, proudly introduced her airline pilot husband. There was Bobby Graig, a distant friend of Alex, who acted like his best friend, bragging all about his athletic son. But all in all everyone was pleasant and seemed pleased to see so many old comrades in attendance.

"Over here, Alex! We're over here!" Johnny Thompson was yelling as he stood beside one of the large tables toward the far end of the large banquet area.

As they drew closer, they could hear Johnny loudly talking to an acquaintance or customer of his. "Thanksgiving is my favorite holiday. I don't have to work, don't have to buy any presents, and don't have to grill any hot dogs or hamburgers. I get to sit down to a big meal and watch football, and we start out with this reunion, which means I can drink in the morning."

When Alex and Beth arrived at the table, they introduced themselves, and they were welcomed instantly. Phil introduced his wife, Molly Whitman. She too was a schoolteacher like her husband. Molly was born and raised in Scranton. She was a newcomer to the Abingtons, having lived there for over fifteen years. Phil and Molly met in college. She was an attractive blonde, slightly smaller than Phil. She was overly friendly with a keen sense of humor. Molly was well liked and respected by all who knew her, and she knew everyone. She had a strong-willed Irish wit about her that would flare up occasionally.

The table was a buzz of who was at the breakfast and who was married to who, who was running around with who, and was divorced by who. There was also talk of who looked good, who put on weight, whose kids were going to what schools, and who would have thought that so and so would be so successful. And there was the typical "I never liked so and so anyway." Beth was a little uncomfortable because she didn't know any of the people everyone was talking about. She felt like an outsider listening to small-town gossip.

Melody leaned over, yet her voice was loud enough for all at the table to hear. "There's Linda Strong over at the far table near the door; she's been married four times, and now she's with her latest beau, Larry Burke. And I hear she's going to marry Larry in the spring," Melody said in a snippy voice. "I'll say one thing about her, she's not a quitter."

Phil chimed in, saying in a sad tone, "Poor Linda Strong . . . always a bride but never a bridesmaid." Everyone giggled.

"Alex, let's go over to the bar," Johnny said loudly "I'll let you buy me a drink."

"Now I know how you can buy the two new cars, Johnny," Phil said laughingly. "You resell all the free drinks you get people to buy you."

"I'd be an old man with a hump back waiting for you to buy me a drink," Johnny shot back at Phil.

"You'll be a lot older than that before Phil would buy you a drink, Johnny," said surprisingly by Phil's normally quiet wife, Molly.

Alex looked sheepishly at Beth. He smiled and asked, "Would you like a glass of wine or something else?"

Beth didn't want to act like a prude and was trying to be considerate of the atmosphere. "I'd like to get something to eat first, Alex, but you can bring me back a glass of chardonnay if you would."

"There's plenty of food over on the buffet table," Johnny said to Beth. He then emptied the beer mug he was drinking and said proudly, "Ahhh! The breakfast of champions!"

Johnny bent over toward his chair and picked up a small canvas bag. There appeared to be a wire protruding from it. "Here, Melody, make sure no one walks off with this."

"What's that, Johnny?" Alex asked.

"That's my car phone. It also has a battery in the bag so I can carry it with me if I leave the car," Johnny said as he handed the bulky bag to Melody.

"You have a car phone, Johnny?" Alex was perplexed.

"Oh yeah, Alex, it comes in handy. I bought it for business to keep in touch. Every time I go somewhere, something happens. With the car phone, I'm just a phone call away."

"How much did it cost for that portable phone?" Alex inquired as they walked toward the bar.

"I got good deal on it; I paid twenty eight hundred. They usually go for about four grand," Johnny said.

"How much does it cost to make calls?" Alex asked.

"About three fifty a minute, but I use it for business mostly. It's expensive, but for me it pays for itself," Johnny said.

Beth and Melody sat next to each other, exchanging niceties. In a few minutes Alex returned with two glasses of chardonnay for the girls. Beth was a little embarrassed drinking so early in the morning. She waited for Melody to pick up her glass first. Melody did so, taking a large gulp of wine in the process.

Melody then smiled at Beth and said, "Oh well, while in Rome do as the Romans do . . ." She held up her glass, looking around the room, and continued in a serious voice. "While in the Abingtons, do as we do: pretend."

Beth lifted her drink, not knowing what else to do as she sipped a taste of the wine.

She then put on a forced smile, toasting to Melody, and said, "Let's have a good Thanksgiving day breakfast."

"One to remember," Melody said, lifting her glass high as she took another drink.

Beth liked Melody but sensed there was something troubling her. "Is everything okay, Melody?" Beth asked softly.

Melody looked at Beth with a startled look on her face. "Life is great. Johnny is quite successful and works very hard. A lot of long hours . . . sixteen-, eighteen-hour days. We have expanded the gas station into a small department store, and we are doing quite well. The kids drive us crazy occasionally, but that's to be expected I guess."

Beth thought for a moment, and then spoke softly, "Alex is working hard and traveling, leaving me to raise the kids by myself."

Melody seemed not to listen to what Beth was saying. But as soon as Beth stopped talking, Melody spoke in a light, serious manner. Melody's eyes were sad with signs of pain as she stared at Beth and said tenderly, "Beth, I want to thank you for letting me spill some of my feelings last night. There's no one around here I can share my true feelings with." Pausing for a moment, she then picked up her glass and took another sip, adding, "so I have to confide in an out-of-towner. It's kind of sad, isn't it?"

"Melody," Beth said, patting her hand gently on Melody's arm "What we tell each other is just between us. I don't even tell Alex about our private conversations." This was not completely true for she told Alex everything.

Melody continued to speak in a more positive mode. "Actually we have a pretty good life. Johnny bought a new Lincoln Town Car. I liked it, so he went out and bought me one just like his. He works hard and makes a lot of money; and we spend a lot of money, and we do have a lot of fun. We travel a lot in our Winnebago, going out west and, of course, our frequent trips to Atlantic City."

She paused, taking a sip of her drink. Then she added, "Of course the Atlantic City trips are so Johnny can visit the casinos."

Beth was determined to have as good a time as possible, so she raised her head erect and said briskly, "We're here to have some fun this morning. So let's go mingle with the crowd and have some fun." With that both women got up and started to walk about.

Alex walked slowly toward the bar. He was looking at the floor, thinking and speaking loud enough for Johnny to hear him. "You know, Johnny, I could use one of those car phones. I spend so much time on pay phones, and finding one isn't always easy. Some pay phones along the road have long, six-foot cords that you can use in your car if you can get close enough. But most times I have to go into a noisy gas station, a bar, or a restaurant. But I could never get the company to spring three or four grand for a car phone, although my phone credit card is over three hundred bucks a month."

Johnny spoke quickly, "I think the price will come down a little. Some rich people may buy some, but the car phone is going to be used for business only. It's just too expensive for family use."

"I don't know, Johnny," Alex said. "Take computers for example. They used to cost millions of dollars; now you can get an IBM home version computer for about three grand. They say computers may become as common as a home TV. Someday every home is going to have one," Alex said.

"I think home computers are a fad. Like that Walkman. Who is going to walk around with a headset to listen to the radio?" Johnny said with his usual voice of authority. "What can you do with a computer . . . hardly anything? You can play a few games and type letters with them. Big deal. They are just so difficult to learn how to use. The average American is too lazy to spend all that time on a thing that makes you so mad to use in the first place."

"I think you're wrong about computers, but you weren't wrong about me buying you a drink, Johnny," Alex said as he ordered a drink at the bar.

Beth and Molly Whitman made friends instantly. They had a lot in common. Both were educated at Catholic colleges—Beth at St. Joseph's in Philadelphia and Molly graduated from Marywood, until recently a women's college in Scranton. Molly was a teacher at Abington Heights High School. Beth was a scientist with a master's degree in microbiology. Although she worked a short time for a pharmaceutical company, her first dream was to be a science teacher. And what really brought them together was that they both married guys from Clarks Summit—a treat not always appreciated all the time.

Both women chatted lightly about their children, schools, sports, and other activities. Beth finally got up her nerve to ask Molly, "After living in Philadelphia, how do you like living in the Abingtons?"

Molly thought for a moment before she answered. "Phil has a lot of guy friends . . . no problem making friends with the guys; they fall all over you. But making friends with women is a big challenge, and it takes a lot of work and skillfulness to make good women friends. For me to live comfortably here, I wanted to have my own girlfriends . . . ya know what I mean. Women who would accept me the way I am. And it took some time to develop those friendships. For an outsider it's not easy to make close friends in the Abingtons. You almost have to be born here. It took me a while, but once I made the nucleus of good friends, I felt that I belonged here . . . and now I really enjoy living here."

"We live in Drexel Hill," Beth said in a perplexed manner, "and I've had a hard time making friends there too. People are polite, but it seems rather difficult to have close women friends like I had in school."

"I know exactly what you're talking about, Beth," Molly said with enthusiasm; the subject apparently grabbed her attention. "Making new friends is very difficult for women. Guys don't seem have the same problem we do. They're competitive with each other, and they seem to tolerate little white lies about fishing, golf, sports, or some other minor topic. But they have a couple beers, tell a few stories, laugh at a few jokes, and they seem to get along okay. But with women it's entirely different. How many times have you asked one of your so-called good friends for one of their recipes, only to find out later that she left out an important step or ingredient?"

Molly quickly stood up, turned around, and asked Beth, "How does my ass look?"

Beth was startled. Her expression was the 'deer eyes staring in the headlight look'. She was at a loss for words.

"Well, how does my ass look?" Molly repeated the question as she turned around. She then sat down, leaned forward toward Beth, and smiled saying in a low voice. "I don't just ask anyone that question. That's my little test to see what kind of friend I have. Remember, women as a rule don't tell other women they look good. I know what my ass looks like. I want to hear what they say; then I know if I can trust them or not."

"Oh, I see," Beth said, although she was still bewildered by Molly's method.

"Let me tell you, Beth, to find real friends takes a lot more than just spinning around and asking someone, what do you think of my butt? It took me a long time to figure out how to make good friends. First you've got to start with the basics. Women don't trust other women, and there's no one more catty than a jealous woman. We like to think that we dress up to impress the men, but the truth is we dress up to impress other women. Just think for a minute . . . men don't notice your fingernails or how well your dress fits or if it's the right color for you. Do you think they even notice if your heels match your outfit? Let's face it, women are very critical; they judge you from the first time they lay eyes on you. Not only your clothes but the way you carry yourself, your hairstyle, your makeup, fingernails, weight, even the whiteness of your teeth are evaluated. Women are very competitive, and the better you look the more resentment! And even close friends still don't trust any woman around their man. You must always be on guard with women friends because you are always the competition. Even if you give an innocent kiss or suddenly pat the hand of a friend's husband, it's noticed. If you have a joking conversation that's a little is too long or too private, all the alarms go off in her head. And men don't help the situation. When some guys get drinking too much, they may kid around, sometimes even make innocent flirtations with you; they may be playful in their antics, but the wife is usually not in a joking mood by the end of the evening."

Beth was aghast with all this insight Molly expressed on the theory of women relationships. She started warming up to Molly. She liked the fact that Molly spoke frankly and openly without any fear. Beth shook her head with a smile. She had a thirst for more information so she asked, "Molly, where did you learn so much about the ins and outs of modern women?"

"My mother had a dress shop. Now that's like graduate school to learn how women really interact. She worked with a lot of nurses, and nurses are the hardest group to break into; they just don't like newcomers. So mother and I had a unique view into the subterfuge of some women, and we observed some of their malevolent activities." Molly paused and lowered her voice as she continued, "Women don't like to be outdone by other women. I have seen some women steer a friend away from a beautiful dress that looks great on her, because woman number one didn't want to be shown up by woman number two, her best friend. And they are much more jealous and cunning than men. The warfare of womanhood is very calculated and cleverly disguised. The real vamps are skilled at making snide remarks and critical comments behind another woman's back. Many times the victim is completely unaware of what's happening. Women in conflict are kind of like submarine warfare: little is seen on the surface; all the real battles are under sea, unseen, silent, nasty, and lethal. They may whisper their cruel, insulting comments, which can be deadly and effective like silent torpedoes, and once launched, they are rarely ever detected until they strike the intended target. Then after the wound is inflicted, there is always a warm smile with words of concern and expression of how difficult it must be."

Molly spoke as if she were telling a ghost story. She lifted her glass of white wine slowly, taking a long, slow sip. Then she continued in her mesmerizing manner. "And the prettier you are the more trouble you'll have. Being attractive can be a curse in itself. A lot of women don't like to be around attractive women. They don't want to be friends with them. They don't want them at parties, and most of all they don't want attractive women near their husbands."

Beth injected quickly into the conversation, "I've noticed some of that myself. Not that I'm beautiful, but some women I have met seemed not to like me. I couldn't understand why. I'm beginning to understand a little more clearly what you mean, Molly."

"As I was saying," Molly continued without missing a beat, "good-looking women have a lot more problems than most women. Men fall all over them, acting stupid, paying more attention to them, listening more to what they say, and laughing at their jokes. But to other women, they are not so cute. And if anything goes wrong for an attractive woman, if she gets dumped or cheated on, there is a lot less sympathy. Instead there's a certain sad, joyous look women give to you. 'Oh, I'm so sorry to hear that, dear' they say as they try to suppress the glee in their eyes. And all the time they're thinking, 'Well your good looks won't help you now, dearie . . . now you're just like the rest of us, and I hope you're just a little bit miserable."

Molly took another sip of her white wine, looking around the table as if she were holding court. In her position of woman headmaster, she continued on, "So to make women friends, you have to get over the looks department . . . the worldly goods department like . . . the size of her house . . . the cars and the clothes thing. And remember the basics: To have a good friend, you must be a good friend. And for women it's different than it is for men. When a new guy comes into a group, he's generally accepted, but we must earn our friendships. One way to do that is by privately sharing secrets with someone you want to befriend. And by secrets I don't mean that your husband drinks too much or that you once had financial trouble. I mean positive secrets like a really good makeup that you may use for skin care, or perhaps you have a unique perfume that's hard to get. You may want to share your favorite dress shop even though it may be one of your personal secrets, and of course, the secrets to your guarded, favorite recipe, which includes all the crucial steps and ingredients!"

Molly paused for a moment as she finished drinking from her plastic cup of wine. After returning the cup to the table, she seemed rather pleased with the lecture. "One more thing, children," she said as she looked around the table with a large smile on her flushed face. "Now this is very important. My aunt Frances used to tell us, 'Listening without comment or judgment may be difficult, but it's the building block of true friendship.' So be a good listener, and you'll always have a good friend."

Susan Carr joined the few women at the table as Molly was finishing her homily. A native of Clarks Summit, class of '68, she was a somewhat aggressive insurance saleswoman. She was attractive and had been divorced for a few years. She was also a good friend of Molly's. "I've been listening to you talk, Molly, and I know one area where women can really surprise you. Let me tell you, if you ever get divorced, you'll see another shocking version of womanhood. And take it from me, it isn't pretty."

"Susan, sit down and drink up," Molly said in a friendly, warm way. "I've been talking about how difficult it is making lasting friendships with women."

Susan sat next to Molly, holding a mug of beer in her right hand and using the mug as an emotional pointer as she began to talk. "I know what you're talking about, Molly. I thought Jim and I had a lot of friends while we were married. We were invited everywhere together—sporting events, cocktail parties, dinner parties, and holiday parties, whatever. But once we split up, I had to change and become a different person. In my gut I had to change. A lot of my women friends came down with the Debbie Reynolds syndrome, which ended a few of my friendships." With that said Susan took a mouthful of beer, paused for a moment, and then continued to tell her story. "We all remember what happened there. Debbie and Eddie Fisher were good friends with Liz Taylor and Mike Todd. When Mike was killed in a plane crash, Eddie went over to comfort Liz . . . and he never came back. He ended up dumping Debbie for her best friend, Liz Taylor. It's the old, 'it could happen to me' syndrome. There are a lot of women who have a fear of their husband being sucked in by a recent divorcee."

Susan took another large drink of beer; her words were starting to slur as she began talking again. "Some people try to be really nice, but after a while I hated to see that big cow-eyed look of distress some women gave me as they asked in a low, concerned voice, 'How are you doing, Sue?' 'Are you doing okay?' 'You'll get over it.'" Susan paused to take a sip of beer as everyone waited for her next comments.

Susan continued in a sad tone. "But it's hard to tell them what it is really like . . . as an example, watching the evening news every night with no one to talk to. Or drinking alone every night, forcing yourself to go to bed alone, waking up alone. And not having anyone to take out the trash, check the oil in my car, see if there's air in the tires, or put in washer fluid for the windshield. I miss going out as a couple; now if I go into a bar, guys around here think I'm on the make. As a single woman, I don't even get invited to many of the parties that my married friends have. During this nightmare comes a complete loss of self-esteem and red puffy eyes from constant crying. I had to make new friends, and that's not easy. Between crying and babbling, I had a hard time carrying on normal conversations with my friends. Many of them couldn't take it, and I lost some friends as a result. But some people surfaced unexpectedly as real friends and troopers. But I've changed a lot, as much as I could. In fact, I bought all new dishes, silverware, pot and pans, new pillows, sheets, towels, even got a new key chain." She started to whimper a little…"But there's no way around it, I still feel so alone."

"You're dating Michael Sullivan. He seems like a nice guy. And you did get a nice settlement, Susan," Molly said to cheer her up. "Remember the old saying, the divorced wife is always happy if she gets more money than she expected." They all laughed at the table.

"I put up a good front for a long time for everyone to see, but inside I was a complete train wreck. But I was determined, and I fought. And it's true I did get a lot more than I expected. But all the head games he put me through, it wasn't worth it," Susan said as she finished her beer. She had abandoned sadness about her. One could see the pain in her eyes as she said, "Sometimes I feel I have so much, and yet I have nothing. There's a unique pain for the person who feels rejected and left behind in a relationship. You ask yourself over and over what you could have done differently. Was I that bad of a person that he couldn't stand to be with me? And I don't know if you ever get over it."

The table was quiet. Susan took another sip of her drink then continued in a low, painful voice. "Jim was the love of my life, but life goes on and so will I. Right now it's very difficult. I can tell you, the hardest part of my day is in the evening between five and eight, which was our dinnertime when we used to talk. Now it's so lonely I hate that part of the day. I think of other people, eating with their families, talking, and laughing. It's so hard to cook a meal for one person. Many nights I don't even eat. I have a few drinks and go to bed alone."

"You have to move on, Susan!" Molly said in a motherly tone. "There's a whole new world out there for you. You have a new life and new friends. It'll take a little time, but you'll get there. Remember the B & B effect of life... After a bad event in our lives, we can choose to come away either bitter or better. Always choose the better."

Susan sat up straight, picking up her drink, and in a defiant voice said, "I can tell you one thing, living through this hell time has made me become a much stronger independent person than I ever thought possible, and yes, I'm a little bitter, but a lot better."

One women's voice rang out, "Honey, just turn it over to the L and Ls . . ." There was silence for a moment. Then the anonymous voice added, "Oh, what that means, honey, is turn it over to the Lord and the lawyers. The Lord has the all power, and the lawyer won't have any mercy on the no-good, cheating son of a bitch." There was muffled laughter from those at the table.

Melody continued with a positive outlook and a joyful, loud voice. "When we were kids, divorce was almost unheard of except for movie stars. Nowadays, a lot of people get divorced and marry someone else. And they have better luck because they have the experience of what to look out for."

Molly raised both hands shoulder high to add motion to the humorous point she was about to make. "I asked my mother a few years ago if she ever considered divorcing my father because of all the problems his drinking had caused." Molly began laughing and waving her arms around as she told her story. "'Well, Molly,' my mother said to me in a serious tone, 'Remember we are Catholics, and we don't believe in divorce. So I put up with a lot of your father's drinking and other carrying on. As a good Catholic, I never considered divorcing him . .

. but murdering him? Yes, many times! But never divorce!" The mood was lightened with the laughter.

Tommy and Ida arrived together, and they strolled around the reception like a couple completely at ease with each other. She was dressed like a New York model in her winter ensemble. Although she was married to someone else and he was an eligible bachelor, they presented an image of a close couple immersed in meeting old friends, and sharing laughs and stories with whomever they met. They were greeted warmly as the ideal couple as they mingled through the crowd. Tommy noticed Bobby Parry standing off to the side with a drink in his hand, talking with a few old friends. At once Bobby waved Tommy over to join in his group.

Bobby Parry was a well-known local character. When he was growing up, his father owned the Summit Diner located in the center of town. For many years it was the social center of the Abingtons. In the sixties Bobby was a high school football star, drove a new car while in high school, and was always popular with just about everyone, especially the girls. Bobby was medium height with brown hair, and he wore turtle-rimmed glasses. He always had a warm smile for everyone he met. He was a real people person with an uncanny ability for remembering names and faces, and he seemed to enjoy the individual characteristics of whomever he came in contact with. Some thought it was because of the many years he worked in the diner, but for whatever reason, everybody knew Bobby Parry.

Times had changed for Bobby. His family had sold the diner, and Bobby was in the trucking business, owning a large fleet of semis. Life seemed just to get better for Bobby as the years went by.

"Tommy, come on over and say hi to a few old friends," Bobby said in a loud, joyful voice. "You know the guys here, Jimmy Millet and Johnny Connell."

Tommy's eyes lit up as he walked toward the group, all talking together. These were his basic boyhood friends. Seeing them brought back memories of when they all first met back in the first grade. They did everything together—they joined the Cub Scouts, the Boy Scouts, the Little League baseball team, and even had a bicycle club for a short time.

This group had a very close relationship that developed into a strong bond throughout the school years. But after high school they drifted apart, because of girlfriends, jobs, and education. Each had taken a separate path leading to different stations in life. Now here they were, standing together and talking and laughing. They appeared older but had retained many of the childish characteristics they always had. Tommy could have picked each of them out in crowded stadium. They hadn't changed too much. He recognized their familiar appearance, but time had added a physical maturity to them. Tommy observed corporal changes because of their age; their hair was lighter in color and much thinner. Interestingly they all had receding hairlines; Jim Millet's was the most outstanding. Their faces had also changed somewhat. Tommy suddenly realized something startling; this was the first time he had seen them looking this way. He noticed that they all had a universal badge of manhood; they had typified signs of a five o'clock shadow. They were adult men now. They all appeared to be living and dressing well, portraying the classic middle-age image: the protruding stomach area and the round face with added flesh that concealed their once youthful facial bone structure. There was one outstanding feature that remained constant: their eyes hadn't changed at all. Their eyes were as unique as their personalities. Tommy noticed right off that each one still possessed a twinkle of mischief.

"Tommy, I haven't seen you since high school!" Someone yelled out as he approached the group.

""It's been a while since I've seen you guys," Tommy said as he shook hands and patted their backs with a great deal of enthusiasm. He was very happy to see them all and wanted to show it.

"The last I heard, Tommy, you were a lifeguard in Ft. Lauderdale," John Connell said in a loud voice.

"That was a long time ago," Tommy answered quickly.

"Did you ever save anybody?" John quickly asked.

Tommy paused for a moment, putting on a serious look, and said in a sober tone, "Well, the water is pretty calm in Ft Lauderdale, so I never went into the water to save anyone . . . but I once saved a girl from being raped!"

The group went quiet until Jimmy Millet asked in a serious tone, "You did? How'd you do that, Tommy?"

Tommy cocked his head to the side as if he was reliving the experience and then said, "Well . . . I just stopped chasing her!" He then began to laugh along with everyone else.

Further down the bar, Phil was talking with a few of his colleagues; they too were teachers at the continually growing Abington High School. Phil waved Alex over to meet some of his old teachers and the principal of the school, Mr. Ziak. Mike Ziak was a rather short, stout man only about five foot two. His hair was coal black and slicked down with oil; the long sides were combed to the back of his head in a style known as DA or "Duck's Ass." This style was common with rebellious youths of the fifties like James Dean. He started teaching in the early 1950s. He wasn't married and was always well dressed and flashier than any other member of the faculty. Every two years he would buy a new blue and white Mercury convertible. Many of the high school girls and some of the women faculty had crushes on him. But he remained above the trials of everyday life. He had a persona that established a guise not to get in his way. Although small in stature, like Napoleon, he had an air about him. Wherever he went he had a stride of determination. When he walked down the halls of the school, the students would part away as if he had an invisible barrier around him. He demanded and received respect from all who knew him.

He was tough but fair, with a dry sense of humor that came in handy as the principal of a large school.

Mr. Ziak worked hard while supporting all the extra school activities. When he first started teaching, teachers did a lot more than just teach a class. The school had only one maintenance man (janitor), and his responsibility was to clean the classrooms and the hallways, cut the grass, and shovel the sidewalks when it snowed. One of Mr. Ziak's responsibilities as a young teacher was to lime the football field before the Saturday football game, even selling hot dogs and sodas at the refreshment stand.

Phil started waving at Alex. "Come over here, Alex! Mr. Ziak wants to talk to you about missing school!" Phil said in a loud, drinking voice.

Alex had a boyish smile as he slowly walked toward the group gathered at the bar. In a shy, timid voice, he said, "Hello, Mr. Ziak." At the same time Alex reached out his hand toward him.

"Alex Flynn . . . yeah, I remember you being in my office a few times," Mr. Ziak said with a chuckle. Then adding as an afterthought, "Weren't you involved in some mischief at the school grounds up at Trail High School the night before a big game back in the '60s?"

"I was innocent!" Alex said as if humorously protesting. "At least I said so at the time. But we did go up and burn CSA into the front lawn. That's when gas was cheap . . . twenty-eight cents a gallon."

"A lot of things were cheaper and different then. I remember we had a rifle club back then. Can you imagine today walking down the halls and passing a dozen or so other students going to class carrying their rifles with them? And we never had a problem with any of those guys," the principal said as the smile left his face.

Phil handed Alex a drink as the three shared the bar and the conversation continued. "High school has changed a lot since the 'Happy Days' we enjoyed back in the sixties and seventies. No more hitchhiking to school dances or late nights down in Scranton," Phil said as he raised his drink.

"The sixties were the golden years of teaching for me," Mr. Ziak said with a joy in his voice. "The school was much smaller then, maybe a hundred students in a graduation class. I knew everybody then. I remember the parades before the games and the bonfires in the school parking lot the night before the big games. It was a community event. The school was the focal point in the town. The kids back then dressed like high school students not fashion models, and the teachers dressed like faculty. The students seemed to get along better. They were more fun-loving. There were some fights, but the students settled them. And we had our share of pranksters who caused some problems, but half the time I laughed under my breath at the things they did. Sometimes when I caught them doing one of their funny cranks, I had a hard time keeping a straight face as I was yelling at them. We had stern teachers then, and they would come down hard on the students, but in the faculty lounge, we would swap funny stories about what some of these crazy kids were doing. The biggest thing I had to worry about was catching cigarette smokers in restrooms and maybe some squirt guns in the springtime."

"It's not like that now, Mike," Phil said with a sad tone to his voice. "Remember a few years ago that Tylenol poisoning in Chicago that killed eight people? They still haven't found who did it, but we have to pay for sealed, tamperproof containers that are now childproof. Try to open one . . . it's not only childproof but old people-proof as well. When my girls were little, they loved to lie in the back window of our car. Now we have put our kids in car seats. And don't ever spank your child in public; I wish someone told my parents that when I was growing up."

Johnny yelled out, "I don't think your parents spanked you, Phil. I think they beat you in the head, and the swelling just never went down."

"If you got the beatings you deserved, Johnny...you'd have worn out your parents' arms." Phil said in a loud, laughing voice.

After listening to the banter, Mr. Ziak started to laugh. "This is the type of stuff I had to put up with when you guys were sent to my office . . . after you were thrown out of class!" There was laughter for a few moments.

"Things were a lot different then. Some of the teachers still had paddles in their desks, and they knew how to use them," Ziak said, looking over at Johnny and saying in a lighthearted way, "Isn't that right, Johnny Thompson?"

Mr. Ziak paused for a moment. He lifted his head in a serious tone and said, "Back then I knew the faces of almost all our students. And, yes, I knew there were some weekend beer parties around graduation, but no one really got into big trouble. We had the respect of the kids and their parents. If I called a parent about their kid, I didn't need to worry too much about disciplining him. When he got home that night, he'd get an additional dose of justice."

"That was before the era of overprotecting parents," Phil added.

"That was before Kennedy was assassinated and the drug scene with all the Vietnam protesting," Ziak said in a matter-of-fact voice.

"I think the kids resented their parents, thus it was reflected in the school," Mr. Ziak said sternly.

Mr. Ziak continued, "I think the problem started in the eighties when we had a big influx of newcomers to the Abingtons. They seemed to lack the feeling of our community. As we expanded our school and faculty, I think we lost our identity, so to speak. The new breed of teachers we hired didn't have the same feeling for our school or our students. They had a different attitude . . . teaching was just a job. They were not as involved as we used to be. A lot of them didn't even dress like teachers. I can tell you . . . back when I started teaching, we did a lot more than just stand in front of a class. The school had only a few cleaning women and and limited staff, for a couple years I collected tickets at the stadium."

Mr. Ziak started to chuckle to himself as he picked up his glass and took a large sip. He started to mildly shake his head as he started to laugh and tell a story. "I remember back in 1948, the school board scheduled a home football game against

Duryea at night down in the 'rock pit.' The only problem was we didn't have any stadium lights. So the school board decided to rent portable lights for the big event. It turned out the generators didn't work very well, so we could only light half the area. So we played the game using the lower half of the field. We lost the embarrassing game. The frustrated coaches blamed the school board for the loss. To this day the school board doesn't want to take the blame for losing another game. So all our home games are still played on our traditional Saturday afternoon."

He wasn't finished yet. He enjoyed his audience, and they enjoyed his stories. "After teaching all day, we all worked on school plays, including making the sets, painting the scenery, writing the scripts, directing, and even playing a few bit parts now and then. And I remember being the chaperone at the many dances, and of course, all of us did a lot for the big event of the year: the senior prom. Back then we did a lot with the students and had a lot of fun doing it."

"Yeah, I remember we couldn't even wear blue jeans to school," someone spoke from the crowd.

"Unless you lived on a farm," Mr. Ziak said firmly.

"Now we have our teachers union," Phil said. "We must be paid for every little thing we do, and I guess we should. But we can't even volunteer our time even if we wanted to. I agree with you, Mr. Ziak. Neither the students nor the faculty have the same camaraderie we had years ago. We had problems, but we had a lot of fun too."

"It was a different time then," the principal said as he took a sip of his drink. Then he continued as if lecturing in class. "Of course that was before 1970 when the perfect kids and their self-righteous parents would bring their lawyers in with them when there was a simple problem. I remember one lawsuit we had over some girl who didn't make the cheerleading squad; another time we were sued because some kid didn't make the National Honor Society. I remember we used to expel a student for smoking cigarettes on school property. Now the students have their own smoking lounge in the school!"

"Another thing that gets on my nerves," Mike continued as his words began to slur somewhat. "Our graduates now all have to go to these big-name schools as if there is a tinker's difference in the real education. Let's face it, the laws of physics and electricity and many other subjects are taught the same in state schools as in Ivy League universities. But so many in our enlightened community think it's better to spend a hell of a lot more money sending their precious offspring to a far-away, bumper sticker-named college." He paused for a moment, gathering his thoughts, and then added, "From what I've seen in life, it's not the sheepskin hanging on the wall but an inquisitive mind and first-rate work ethics that are the key ingredients in a successful life.

"The sad part is unless their family owns a business or is politically connected, the best and brightest of these young people don't come back here after they finish their expensive education. There are no jobs for them here." He paused again, looking around at his listening audience, then carried on with his comments. "Sometimes I think this region is like a large missionary training area. We raise and educate wonderful young people who go to the far ends of the world, being quite successful wherever they go. The only time we see many of them is at these reunions.

"Well, it's the eighties now; I don't have to worry about such things, and I'm glad I'm not involved in the school district anymore," Mr. Ziak said as he took another sip of his drink. "Except once a month when I cash my check!" The friendly listeners warmly cheered, lifting their drinks in support.

Tommy walked over to the bar to get a drink. As he stood there waiting for the bartender, he noticed Bucky Manson standing next to him. Although there was a few years' difference in age, they had been friends in earlier times. Bucky hadn't changed a bit; he looked the same as in high school. He still had a small frame and neatly trimmed brown hair; and he dressed in his traditional preppy look, wearing a green crewneck sweater, a white oxford shirt and khaki slacks. Tommy and Bucky had been drinking buddies and hell-raisers back in the late '60s. Tommy always admired the style of Bucky's wardrobe.

Tommy recalled when Bucky was going to college at the U in Scranton. They would meet up on Wednesday afternoons to drink fifteen-cent beers and play shuffleboard at a little bar in Dalton called Dunn's Dump. Bucky would come in dressed to the 'nines' and neat as a pin, wearing a three-piece business suit, a classic striped tie, and an oxford shirt, with black wing-tip dress shoes. He looked like he had just finished a photo session. Then he would start his ritual of playing shuffleboard and drinking. He would finish up his week on Sunday afternoon at Palumbo's still drinking and wearing the same outfit. His stunning Fifth Avenue appearance had warped into warped into a disheveled mess. His hair would be messed up, along with a four-day beard and still wearing the dirty, wrinkled ensemble that showed the results of four days of bar-room drinking. But in spite of his notorious college lifestyle, he completed college and was promptly drafted into the Army and sent to Vietnam.

Bucky was talking and laughing with someone at the bar as Tommy put his arm around Bucky's shoulder, giving him a slight hug.

"How the hell have you been, Buckster?" Tommy said in a loud voice while squeezing and rocking Bucky.

Bucky turned quickly, his eyes opened widely, and he flashed an ear-to-ear smile. While holding a drink in one hand, he put his other arm around Tommy and hugged him tightly. "Tommy, where the hell have you been? I haven't seen you in years," Bucky said in a loud, intoxicated voice.

"Oh, I've been around here and there. How about you, Buckster? What have you been up to?' Tommy asked.

"I've had a few jobs with big companies. But I started working for myself. I started my own construction company a few years ago, and I'm doing okay," Bucky continued. "I even got married. And have a daughter. Beautiful little girl," he said in a slurry voice.

"Is you wife here?" Tommy asked. "I'd like to meet her."

Bucky laughed, raising his hand above his head and pointing one extended finger in the air as to make a point.

"Lips that taste wine will not taste mine," Bucky said with the accent of a poet. "She doesn't believe it's proper to imbibe in 'the nectar of the gods.'"

"I bet when you imbibe, Bucky, she uses the names of the gods," Tommy said, laughing.

"Yeah, she does, Tommy," Bucky said, lifting his glass of beer as if toasting a drink.

Then he yelled out, "Beer tender, how's about a bar for my friend here!"

The two continued to laugh and talk about some of their earlier escapades. Then suddenly Bucky happened to see someone he recognized and said in a low voice, "Hey, look over there, Tommy. I think that's Jeanie Simmons. You remember her."

Tommy's eyes searched through the crowd for a few moments, then nodding his head, he said softly, "Yeah, I see her. She is still beautiful."

Tommy stared at her without saying a word for a few moments. Then as if in deep thought, he spoke to Bucky in a serious manner. "She taught me a very important lesson in life."

Bucky was a little startled and asked, "What lesson did she teach you?"

"Look at her, Bucky. She's still beautiful, just the same as she was years ago when I wanted to go out with her. But she wouldn't have anything to do with me back then. But one night at a party, we got together. And after some drinks that beautiful girl and I ended up in the back of my car."

Tommy paused for a moment as if reminiscing about the episode. "It was a very dark night in the backseat of my car. We both had a good time. But during this experience, I recognized something weird. The awesome power of her physical beauty diminished in the dark, and she lost that distinct advantage of her good looks. I realized then that darkness was a great leveling field as far as women are concerned. She was just like any other girl in the dark. " Tommy took a sip of his beer, and then added jokingly, "Bucky, there ain't no tens in the dark."

"I don't know about any tens in the dark. But the women I ran around with . . . well, we sure had a lot of fun in the dark," Bucky said, laughing.

"Speaking of dark nights, I heard all about that dark night you should have gone to jail," Bucky said, laughing.

"What time was that?" Tommy asked with a chuckle.

"Joe Bachlor told me the story," Bucky said as he picked up his beer. "From back in the sixties, just after you got back from Vietnam, during your crazy times. Joe was driving back from Scranton about two thirty in the morning when he saw you driving that old station wagon of yours... and you were Pasted!'

"Oh yeah! I remember that night," Tommy said, shaking his head with a big smile on his face. He Picked up his drink and continued, "Joe Bachlor and I were in the same shop class in high school, and I hadn't seen him in years. How he recognized me that night I don't know. But he told me later what all had happened. It was kind of interesting, all right."

A few people gathered around to hear the story, and those who knew Tommy knew the stories were true.

"Anyway Joe told me about the incident. It happened late one night about twenty years ago. He was driving up Route 6/11 through Chinchilla about two thirty in the morning. There was hardly any traffic at that time. That's when he noticed my car in front of him, swerving at a slow speed. He flashed his lights, trying to get my attention. As I started to drive up the Summit Hill, I drifted to the far left all the way over, my car glancing off the curb on the far side. Now remember Summit Hill is four lanes wide, with two lanes north up the hill; at the top is a signal light at the corner of Grove Street where the left lane is for turning only. After hitting the curb, I woke up and headed back to the far right-hand lane going up the Summit Hill. When I got to the top of the hill, I stopped at the red light. Then I realized I was in the right lane, but that was the wrong lane because I wanted to turn left onto Grove Street. I sat there for a moment, and when the light turned green, I turned left not realizing I was cutting off the car in the left lane. Now remember he is sitting there in the left lane ready to turn left. When the light changed to green, I cut in front of him going west on Grove Street. And that car I cut off was a state police car. You could imagine what that cop was thinking as I pulled in front of him." Tommy took a sip of his drink as he was laughing to himself and continued the story.

"Well, the cop's jaw must have been on the floor as he sat there, as I drove in front of him. But before he could react, another car passed him on his left side while he was turning left to go after me. That other car pulled in between the cop and me. I was unaware of any of this, as I drove over Grove Street. We drove a few blocks, and turned right on to Bedford Street, and I then ran over the stop sign. I was so drunk. Again I woke up and backed up, and that's when I saw the flashing red lights of the police car. I didn't think it had anything to do with me, so I was startled when the state trooper came up to my window and started yelling at me. 'Do you know what you just did?' he screamed. 'Hey,' I said, 'I just was going home. My house is right up the street.' I noticed another car that the cop had pulled over, but I thought it had nothing to do with me. The cop was so mad he couldn't even talk straight. 'I never saw anything like this in my life.' He then went over to the other guy, who happened to be Joe Bachlor, and started yelling at him. 'And what the hell were you doing cutting me off?'

Then Joe told him that he was a friend of mine, and he hadn't seen me since I came back from Vietnam. He knew what he did, but he didn't want to see me get in any trouble and just wanted to make sure I got home safely that night."

Tommy continued to shake his head as if he was telling a story that was too hard to believe. "The cop was frustrated, but he thought about this crazy, courageous deed that one guy was doing for a friend . . . it just kind of melted the cop's heart. After considering everything for a few minutes, he turned to Joe and said, 'Okay, you take care of your friend. You and your buddy drive him up the street to his home and make sure he gets into his house all right. And don't every let me catch any of you doing anything like this again.' The cop then got into his car and left."

Tommy's face became somber as he looked directly into Bucky's eyes and said in a serious voice, "I was amazed at what happened, and I said to Joe, 'I haven't seen you since our high school days almost ten years ago. Why did you put yourself between that cop and me?' Joe smiled and said, 'Tommy, I didn't want to see you get in trouble. You're a friend of mine.'"

All was quiet for a moment. Tommy was thinking, considering all of what was said, and then he added, "You know, Bucky, if it were the other way around, I'd probably drive by and say 'Isn't that Joe Bachlor in trouble with a cop?'"

Tommy again paused, staring across the bar as if talking to himself, and said, "And I haven't seen Joe Bachlor since that night. I don't know anyone else who would do anything like that."

Tommy emptied his glass, and then said, "But you know, Bucky, I've seen Joe Bachlor's face many times in Vietnam. He was the real GI I served with. Without any fanfare or bragging, he was the soft-spoken guy you could count on. He would hump the jungle without complaining, would share anything with you. He'd work like a mule and fight a lion. At the end of the day, he could always smile and would kind of shrug his shoulders as if it were all in a day's work."

Tommy and Bucky turned toward the bar so they could talk privately with each other. Bucky yelled to the bartender, "Could we get a few drinks here?" Then looking directly at Tommy, he said, "I know what you're talking about." Bucky said in a thoughtful manner thinking of his own life experiences, "I saw that kind of behavior all over in Vietnam, where some guy would risk his life to help another guy."

"You're right, Bucky, it was amazing to see. What would be considered courageous behavior here was an everyday event over there. GI's risked their lives just to help or do a favor for someone, like switch weapons or take his place on a patrol," Tommy said in a serious tone.

Tommy went on to say, "You know, Bucky, I don't even tell people I served in Vietnam."

Bucky bowed his head and said in a somber tone, " After the treatment we got when we came home, letting everyone know you were a veteran wasn't the smartest thing to do."

"It wasn't the average guy on the street that bothered me. But it was the guy in the bar who claimed he was a Vietnam veteran," Tommy said as he took a sip of his drink.

"They would tell the same old stories," he said as his voice gained energy the more he spoke. "Every one of these barroom warriors was in Special Forces or a Recon Marine. Their best buddy died in their arms. Out of two hundred, there were only eight of them left who survived a brutal, jungle fight. And they all were sprayed with Agent Orange. Then when they came home, they were all spat on and called baby killers in the airport."

"That's the one reason I don't talk about it either," Bucky said meekly.

Tommy continued, "I remember years ago I was in a bar, and some guy was bragging about his exploits in Vietnam. So I asked him what unit he was with. His voice stammered while he blinked his eyes, and he said proudly he was in the Green Berets. So I asked him what altitude he jumped from. 'What . . . what do you mean?' Again I asked from what altitude he had jumped out of an airplane. All Green Berets are airborne qualified. He looked at me and said, 'I think it was eight thousand feet or maybe ten thousand . . . they really didn't tell us'. Well, the standard altitude to exit an aircraft in the military is twelve hundred and fifty feet. Like so many other barroom warriors, this guy had no idea what the truth was . . . but was so convincing while lying about being in Vietnam."

"I think we're better off not even talking about it," Bucky said. "I'll be back in a few minutes. I'm going to drain my bladder. Remember you don't buy booze, you only rent it."

Alex was positioned at the bar to order a few drinks. Suddenly he felt a hug of his shoulder. It was Tommy standing next to him. "Beer tender how about a bar?" Tommy yelled at the bartender, and they both laughed.

"It's been a while since I heard a drink order placed like that," Alex said as he looked over at Tommy, both guys smiling at each other. "I can still see Eddy with his white waiter jacket on, his glass eye looking in one direction, and his good eye looking directly at you."

"Those were some fun times we spent at that old bar," Tommy lamented for a minute as they both kind of stared off into space. "So many things have changed around here. And yet a few things seem to be the same."

"I know what you mean, Tom. I guess we've changed a lot more than the Abingtons . . . with our jobs, family and stuff," Alex said quietly.

"Yeah, I think you're right, Alex. We now have what is commonly referred to as our responsibilities."

"Well, Tom, at least your responsibilities are interesting . . . working on those pipelines around the world. You've been to so many interesting places and have done so many things. Coming back here must be a bore to you," Alex said in an envious tone of voice.

"We'll I've been a lot of places . . . been in a lot of airports around the world, but I must say flying into the Avoca airport is quite a treat. I came in yesterday afternoon," Tommy said with a chuckle. "When the stewardess announced the landing procedures, she said, 'We'll soon be landing at the greater Scranton, Wilkes-Barre Airport. Please fasten your seat belts. You may now set your watches back twenty-five years." Again they both laughed out loud.

"It's the only airport in the country with an 'A1' car rental agency that only has 'A' car to rent," Alex said with a laugh.

"Do you get in town much, Alex?" Tommy asked.

"No, not as much as I would like to. I come up to visit my parents a few times a year. But between the job and the kids' activities, I don't get up here as often as I'd like." Alex then added almost as an afterthought, "Beth doesn't like it up here, so we don't come up very often. How about you, Tom? I guess with all your travel, you don't get in very often."

"No, I don't get in very much." Tommy paused for a moment; then he started to talk again in a thoughtful manner. "You know, Alex, when I do come back home, I get some mixed feelings. It's kind of strange. I feel out of place for some reason. I remember when we used to live around here. It seemed as if we knew everybody, and they knew us or one of our family members. Even the cops knew our cars on sight. Now it's as if no one ever knew me or that I ever existed. I feel like a stranger in my own town."

Tommy emptied his drink. He was feeling somewhat mellow. He stared through the large window toward the distant mountains. He said speaking in a mild tone saying, "Sometimes when I come back here I feel like an outsider—like an old Indian who, after many years away, revisits the beloved land of his birth. As a young Indian brave he knew the area so well, every trail, stream, and rock. As he returns to his beloved valley, he finds the sacred hunting land is no longer covered with large forests, but now it's a farm with plowed fields owned by the white man. It's all changed so much. He tries to see the area as it used to be, but now many of his reference points are gone . . .it's vanished forever, this land of his youth. He is no longer part of the environment; there is no place to relive his youthful triumphs or plan his future conquests. Alex, sometimes I feel like that Indian who has no homeland sanctuary to return to."

Alex finished his drink and ordered another round. After thinking for a few moments, he looked directly at Tommy and said in a supportive way, "I know what you're talking about, Tommy. When I come back, I'm always looking for the friendly faces that might remember me. I look around and see many of our friends making a living here. They all go the same restaurants and shop at the same stores we did as kids. They seem to be happy, but they haven't experienced the outside world as we have. I enjoy my life with my family. I like the challenges of the world that exist on the other side of the Pocono Mountains."

Alex paused for another moment. He was looking straight ahead as he said with deep feeling, "But sometimes I wonder if I should have stayed here. I could have gotten some kind of job. I might be driving an older car, living in a smaller house . . . But I don't know if I could be content living here. I'd always be remembered as good old Alex. I know I wouldn't be married to Beth and have the family I have. I guess my life's question is: did I give up my contented soul for that of an ambitious seeker of some allusion I don't know?"

"Life's funny, Alex. This world is full of interesting people. Some of them love living on a farm, growing the same crops year after year. They work very hard, and they're perfectly happy. Their main concern is whether there will be enough rain and sun to produce a decent harvest, and then hopefully they can sell the crops and make some money. That's their main concern in life. And it's great for them; it's what they do, not knowing anything about the world on the other side of the Poconos. But I know guys who have an inner drive to find oil reserves. They will travel the world . . . at times living under terrible conditions, often producing only a dry hole for all their efforts, a complete sacrifice of time and money. But they continue searching, and it's not only for the money.

"And if and when they make a find, they are so proud of their achievement. It's what they do. You'll find the same drive in many careers in life—being a good teacher, salesman, or fireman—it's what they do that is important. It's their personal contribution to mankind. I believe we all have this inner drive to do what we think is important, our own personal contribution to mankind. And I believe we have to follow that inner drive, and for you and me, it takes us away from here."

"You're lucky, Tommy, you have an interesting job. What you do really does change the world. You can see the results working on something like the Alaskan pipeline. That's pretty exciting," Alex said.

"Oh yeah, it can be exciting—riding a D-9 bulldozer as it's trying to scramble up the side of a frozen mountain in the Brooks Range in Alaska, or laying a pipe through a swamp in the jungles of Brazil, no civilization for a hundred miles. Not to mention working in the desert of Saudi Arabia with temperatures of 126 degrees in the shade. I don't know if I'd call it exciting, but it was different. And it had its own pitfalls. I won't go into the loneliness or the hardships of living in some of those isolated sites, but it was a job for a while."

"That's what I'm talking about, Tommy, doing something that has a meaning to it. Not just selling soap products," Alex said in a disheartened manner.

"Selling soap may not mean much to you. But it sure does to the people who have invested billions of dollars in the manufacturing of that soap—and the store employees who sell it, and needless to say, the customers who use it. Oh, that soap's important to a lot of people."

Tommy took another sip of his drink and added, "I didn't get my job because I was looking for an exciting career. I got it because I had a friend in Oklahoma who worked in the pipeline business. I was out of work . . . no job at the time. And that was one of the hardest times of my life. Not knowing what to do next."

The fresh drinks were put on the bar. Tommy picked his up, downing a large portion. Then he continued, "I remember the first job I had after college. It was selling copying machines in Philadelphia. It was a very competitive business, and I did okay for a while. Then they had a cut back. I lost my job. It was a very tough time for me. I tried and tried to get a job without any luck. So I had to go down to the state offices and sign up for unemployment pay. It was so humiliating, standing in line . . . answering all those stupid questions. Deep down inside I felt like something was wrong with me, that God was mad at me for some reason. It seemed everyone had a job but me. I'd drive down the highway and see the road crew standing there, looking at each other, hardly working. But I would think to myself, they were better off than I was… they had a job. They would get a paycheck at the end of the week. When I'd go into a bar or to a party, someone would ask, 'What do you do for a living?' I'd tell them I was out of work. I could have gotten the same reaction if I told them I just got out of jail. I could read their minds; 'Wow, what did you do to get sent to jail?' Or 'Hmmm, what did you ever do wrong to lose your job? You must not have been a good worker, or maybe you were just lazy. Then people would kind of shy away from me altogether. I felt they believed unemployment is contagious. Believe me it was very difficult time."

Tommy looked around the room, his hand waving and finger pointing like a wand in all directions. In a cool voice, he said, "Look around here, Alex. I bet half the people here at one time or another lost a job. But only a few would admit to it. It's a terrible shame for some people to be fired or to lose a job. To be out of work . . . for a guy it's a lot worse. It seems if a man doesn't have a job, he doesn't get respect. In fact, it can even get worse. I met a guy in Atlanta who had been out of work for over a year. I asked him what it was like to be out of work that long. His reply was kind of strange; he said it was the nearest thing to being dead or a ghost. He went on to tell me that at first people would ask how he was doing; they'd tell him that things would work out okay. But after a few months, they stopped asking about job opportunities, and then they wouldn't talk about their jobs in front of him. After a while that changed; at parties or family gatherings, he was more like an observer. He would listen to people who would talk about their jobs, especially the men, but he was not invited into the conversations; he had nothing to contribute. He didn't work. So he would stand a short distance away and listen to them talk about what they were doing with their careers. He was like the invisible man. He'd hover about and listen, but he could not join in because he didn't have a job and wasn't considered a part of the working community. That's why he said it was like being a ghost. Not having a job was like not being completely alive."

"I know what you're talking about, Tommy," Alex said, "In many ways our jobs define us, they're who we are—our character, our worth. With our job we kind of sketch our own silhouette. In many ways what we do is who we are, and when you think about it, we'll be remembered mostly not for what we did in our life but by what job we had in our life."

"Men aren't the only ones who have a fixation on their jobs," Tommy said rather abruptly. "Ida is one of those women who is so dedicated to her own career. That's why we could never have a lasting relationship. She wanted her career more than she wanted me."

"Remember when we were kids, our moms didn't work," Alex said, then paused. "Although there were a few mothers who worked, but they needed the money. But nowadays it seems every woman wants to have a happy marriage, a nice home with a backyard, a couple kids, and a career. Beth wants to go to work. Her friends have jobs outside the home, and she wants to be like all the rest of them."

"So what are you going do?" Tommy asked. "Beer tender, another bar. I say drink over it!"

The two continued discussing the various business aspects and foolish life experiences. Tommy regaled Alex with some of his construction antics. "Alex, there was so much money made by the guys I work with—a hundred fifty thousand a year for a dozer operator with no living expenses. The company paid for everything: transportation, food, housing, everything but your personal clothes. And some guys spent the money as quickly as they got it; others saved enough to buy their future. I remember being in the Anchorage airport, when the crews from the slope were going home. Guys would be drinking at the airport bar, buying rounds of drinks for everybody, anyone who came into the bar. Those were some crazy times."

"It sounds as if you had some crazy times, Tommy. And I would imagine you had some crazy women too?" Alex asked with a smile.

"Oh yeah, I had some fun with the women throughout the years," Tommy said with a smile on his reddish-colored face. "And some of them I didn't have to pay for!" He laughed.

"With your job you can have a lot of women, and you can love 'em and leave 'em," Alex commented.

Tommy stopped talking for a moment and lifted his drink. As if he were talking to the glass, he said, "Alex, I'm giving up my job in the pipeline business. I've been thinking about it for a long time. I've saved up a decent amount of money, and now I want to start my own business. I'd like to start a construction company and see if I can make a go of it."

Alex had a confused look on his face as he glanced over at Tommy. "Why do you want to go in to the construction business? You don't have any experience at it."

"Alex, one thing I've learned over the years is that I can do a lot of things. I've done more than just lay pipelines. You know I've worked in construction projects in desolate parts of the world. We had to do everything, so taking on construction projects in North Carolina shouldn't be that tough. Over the years I've saved up a lot of money, and I believe I have enough to get started." Tommy paused for a moment, then added, "Away from here people accept me for what I've done in life. They trust me and believe in what I am capable of doing. They don't care about what I did as a kid. And let's face it; around here they're still talking about some of the crazy things I did twenty years ago. You could just imagine someone trusting me to take on a big construction project. No, I don't think I could be a success here."

Alex thought for a moment, reflecting on his own business experience, and said in a cautious tone, "Tommy, do you realize that most businesses fail in the first two years? In fact, statistics show that 95 percent of all businesses don't make it five years. With those odds even Johnny Thomson wouldn't bet on it."

"I've always worked against the odds, Alex. What I've been through and lived through are against all the odds," Tommy said in a strong voice. With a warm smile, he added, "I remember during my turbulent years, when I was crashing up cars, after I had one of my car wrecks, people would say, 'I see you smashed up another car; you're going to kill yourself.' I'd smile and say, 'The graveyard is full of people who only had one accident.'"

"Throughout the years I've experienced a few things and learned a little. And I've thought about doing this for a long time, Alex. And I'm willing to take the chance to build something that I am solely responsible for. It's the American dream to create your own business, and you know I have always been a dreamer."

Alex paused for a moment, saying, "I remember reading something a while ago that went something like, 'At the end of our lives, it's not what we do that we regret, but rather it's what we didn't do that is what we regret.'

Alex stood erect, looking Tommy in the eyes in an admiring way. "I'm happy for you Tommy, going out and starting your own business. That takes a lot of guts. Being your own boss, doing things the way they should be done instead of someone telling you every detail of what to do and how to do it. It's a gamble, but somehow I think you will make it."

"Thanks, Alex," Tommy said in somber tone. "Sometimes I think life is like a poker game. It all depends on the cards we're dealt and how we play them. Look at you, Alex. You've done pretty well for yourself. You're a sales manager; that's a great job. You get paid well, you've got a company car, an expense account, and all you do is schmooze customers all day. It doesn't sound bad to me," Tommy said as he took a sip of his drink.

"Being in sales isn't what it's all cracked up to be," Alex said as he lowered his head. "It's kind of like being a business prostitute. Just think of it for a minute. You have to be decent-looking, free of any physical defects. As an example, have you ever seen a one-armed salesman? Or one with rotten teeth? The answer is no. Because a corporate salesperson has to be good-looking with a good sense of humor, and be a first-rate dresser, well mannered, and versed in most topics well enough to carry on a decent conversation, but not allowed to voice a strong opinion on most subjects. He always has to be in a good mood and be able to make friends easily."

Alex picked up his drink, taking a large gulp. Looking seriously at Tommy, he said, "Ya know, Tommy, the interesting thing about salespeople is they're a breed of people who enjoy being around people. But the frustrating part is that we don't get to build personal friendships on the job. We are always calling on different people each day, or calling on new customers and forgetting whom we called on yesterday. We don't have good friends at work because we are travelers. People who work in factories or offices develop camaraderie. They may go out for a few drinks after work or go to parties together. But there's no Wednesday night bowling league for salespeople. When you think of it, being in sales is a pretty lonely profession."

"I never thought of it that way," Tommy said quietly. "But we all got to do what we all got to do, right?"

"You're right, Tommy," Alex said, while his mind was quietly drifting off, thinking about his own future. Then Alex perked up a little, asking, "We all got to do what we all got to do. How about you and Ida?"

"I don't know, Alex. I guess we're going to do what we always do. We say hello . . . and then we say good-bye."

"Hello, boys." A distinct, low male voice startled Alex and Tommy.

As they turned around to see the mysterious voice, both broke out with wide smiles. Alex recognized Jake the barber. Alex spoke first as if he just found a long-lost friend. "Jake . . . it's great to see you!" He reached out, using both hands to grab on to Jake's hand and shook it vigorously. Jake hadn't changed much, except his once slick, telephone-black hair was a memory; he was now bald as a cue ball. Other than the loss of hair, Jake looked the same. He stood erect like a soldier, although his shoulder seemed to slump a little. He looked well groomed and healthy, and his facial features had aged well. He maintained his warm, positive image, bobbing his head with his signature big smile and loud, warm voice. He looked around to see who was listening as he said, "I'm dating a good-looking Protestant girl now. Yeah, she's a real left-footer!"

"What happened, did you run out of Catholic girls? Or did the bishop warn them about you?" Tommy said with a laugh.

"No, what happened is . . ." Jake said as he looked around again to see if anyone was listening. "When I started charging the priests the regular price for a haircut, they stopped giving me tips on which girls to take out. So I had to take my chances on the non-Catholic girls," he said with a chuckle.

Tommy smiled and asked, "Tell me, Jake, are you still giving Johnny his signature 'wedge head' hairstyle?

"I'm not the only one giving Johnny a haircut," Jake said in a serious tone. "Once Atlantic City opened the casinos, Johnny was getting scalped there on a regular basis."

"Is your barbershop still on State Street?" Alex asked as if he were going to make an appointment.

"Yes, I am, Alex. I'm still located in my home office on State Street. I call it my home office because it used to be someone's home before we put my shop in there," Jake explained with a little smile.

"It's been a long time since I've seen you, Alex. How long has it been, fifteen, twenty years? Jake looked deeply at Alex, noticing the changes in him. He took on a cheerful expression as he said, "By the way, after all these years, I still have the breakfast diary. I bring it each year. There's usually someone here to write in it. I have it in the car. I'll bring it in a little later for you."

"Thanks, Jake. I look forward to seeing it again," Alex said calmly. Although Alex was a little startled, he had forgotten all about the diary. All of a sudden his memories rushed to the surface; he had a flashback recalling the excitement of buying the journal so many years ago. What a treasure this journal was. He thought of what was written and by whom. He would be able to read some of their old entries about what they were thinking of in their younger years.

From some distance away, Johnny Thompson's voice was heard yelling, "Let me tell you, Jake, if you could move your scissors as fast as you move your jaw, you'd be a rich man." Johnny was laughing as he walked up to join the group.

"I could be even richer if I could patent your hairstyle, Johnny." Everyone laughed. "But come to think of it, there are not too many heads like yours, which is a good thing. So you can keep your one-of-a-kind haircut."

"Well, as they say, Jake," Johnny said quickly. "In your barbershop you have one chair, and you cut everyone's hair one way."

Jake walked away slowly toward the bar, smiled and said, "You're a legend, Johnny."

"How've you been, Alex?" Johnny asked serious troubling tone.

"Oh, I've been doing fine. How about you, Johnny? How are things going for you?" Alex put the burden on Johnny.

"Life's been pretty good to me, Alex. Business is good, and I'm making a lot of money now. But those kids of mine are spending it as fast as I make it," Johnny said with a frustrated voice.

"I know what you mean, Johnny. Those kids of mine are expensive; all their clothes have to have an alligator emblem or some other marking to show it cost more," Alex said.

"That's not what's costing me so much, Alex," Johnny said in a strong, quiet voice. He looked around to ensure that no one could hear their conversation. Johnny continued, "What's costing me so much is paying off the cops and judges around here. I'm not kidding. I've spent a small fortune keeping my kids out of jail. Drugs are rampant around this area, and a lot of adults and kids are involved. But my kids seem to get caught a lot." Johnny started shaking his head. He continued speaking in a low voice. "Alex, you wouldn't believe it. I mean hard drugs like cocaine and heroin are being used by high school kids."

"Johnny, I find that hard to believe . . . cocaine and heroin around here," Alex said in a disbelieving tone.

"Believe me, Alex, it isn't just my kids who are having problems. There are doctors' and lawyers' kids on heroin right here in the lily-white Abingtons."

Alex was stunned at what Johnny was saying, however Alex also knew Johnny embellished many of his stories. So Alex didn't put much credence in what he was saying.

"I don't know what to say, Johnny. I never thought something like that could happen here. When we were in high school, the biggest thing was a beer party. And that was a big deal," Alex said.

"Things have changed around here, Alex. I bought a big Winnebago just to get out of here, so I can take Melody and the kids on vacations whenever possible. He paused and then added in a somewhat lighter tone, "Of course I take the Winnebago to Atlantic City, so the kids can be near the ocean . . . and I can be near the casinos."

"Do you gamble much, Johnny?" Alex asked.

"We go down for fun weekends occasionally. The shows are great, and we stay in the best of casinos. It doesn't cost hardly anything. They comp me rooms, food, and shows," Johnny said proudly.

"To have rooms and shows comped, you must be a player?" Alex said.

"It's how you play, Alex. You let the management think you're a real player, and they'll treat you like a king," Johnny said as if speaking to a younger person, letting him in on how the adults do things. "Sometimes I will spend a lot of money on chips, then walk around for a while, gamble a few bucks on different tables, and then cash in the unused chips. They think I gambled a lot, so I get free rooms and free shows."

"When you do play, Johnny, are you ahead of the game?" Alex asked.

"To tell you the truth, Alex, a few years ago I was broke, didn't have enough money for payroll," Johnny said in a low, serious tone as he looked around to make sure no one could hear him, "I was at my wit's end, so I went down to Atlantic City and won fifty-three thousand dollars. That paid off all my debts plus payroll."

"Now, Johnny, you don't win like that all the time," Alex said, recalling his father telling him stories about his uncle Al who was a gambler and all the money he had lost, and all the lies he would tell. 'He would never tell you about his losses, only about when he won.' It sounded like a tape playing in Alex's head.

"No, I don't win all of the time," Johnny was quick to respond. "But I can tell one thing. I've taken more money out of the casinos than I left."

"Tell me, Johnny, do you ever think maybe you gamble too much?" Alex asked.

"I only gamble with what I can afford to lose. And I will tell you right now, Alex, I won't lose enough money ever to hurt my family. That will never happen! The juice man will never knock on my door. I tell you, Alex, sometimes we go down to the AC just to get away from this rat race around here and to have some fun." He paused for a moment, adding, "You've got to remember I work seven days a week, sixteen to eighteen hours a day. If I can slip away for a few hours of relaxation, I take it. And I am pretty good at the blackjack table. You've got to know how to play. If you do, you can win." He paused again and said, "And I win a lot of the time. The key is knowing when to quit."

Alex was quiet, taking in what Johnny was saying. He knew how narrow-minded, stubborn, and sensitive Johnny was to any criticism. Alex asked himself if it were right to address Johnny on the evils of gambling, not knowing how he would react. Johnny was thin-skinned and had a history of insulting customers and friends. He was known to end relationships, cutting people off and never speaking to them again.

Alex had a concerned look on his face as he looked directly at Johnny, saying in a very serious tone, "Johnny, you and I have been close friends since third grade. I don't want to jeopardize our friendship, but I have to tell you my little story, and then I'll shut up.

Johnny had a look of impatience as he took in a deep breath, and with his sarcastic smile, he said in a matter-of-fact tone, "I've probably heard it all before, but if it makes you feel better, go ahead, Alex. I'm all ears."

"With those big ears you should be able to fly," Alex said jokingly. He then continued in a serious manner. "Years ago I was talking with my dad about gambling. I said that I didn't think it was that bad. So what if a guy gambles—betting on football games, playing a little cards, or going to the casinos. My dad told me that gambling was the worst thing a guy could do to his family. I asked, 'How about an alcoholic or drug addict, aren't they worse?' He looked at me and said, 'They will all lie and steal, but what's an alcoholic going to spend on drinking

. . . twenty dollars a day or even fifty dollars a day. If he's real bad, his wife can get control of the family money and throw him out before they lose everything. She and the kids can usually survive on their own if need be. The drug addict, the same. The family can intercede, casting him out and taking control of the money before all is lost. But for a compulsive gambler, there is no limit to the money he can drop in a short time. I've seen successful people lose businesses, beautiful houses, and life savings; end up penniless; and run up debts without the family having any idea of what was happening. And I mean doctors, lawyers, business owners and members of the country club. I've seen those families completely destroyed without any idea of what was happening. There are no limits on how much you can lose. A gambler can lose generations of wealth overnight, depriving the family of even a place to live."

"That can happen," Johnny said quickly, after listening patiently for Alex to finish. "I've known people with a real gambling problem. You remember Dr. Quillem Evans, Alex; he lived in Lands Down. Now he had a real problem. He would gamble on everything and seemed to lose all the time. You've got to know what to gamble on, how to play the game, and when to quit."

Alex took a sip of his drink, then said, "Johnny, do whatever you want to do. I just wanted to tell you what my dad told me."

"I understand what you said, Alex, and I appreciate your opinion, but you've got to remember there are some people who do win and make a lot of money gambling. And keep in mind, if nobody won, no one would gamble."

Before Alex could speak, Johnny continued talking. "I work hard, and my family is well taken care of. I earn the money, and I choose the way I want to spend it."

"Okay, Johnny, no more criticism, but between you and me, I'm trying to understand . . . what's the real lure of gambling?" Alex asked in a sympatric tone. He continued quickly before Johnny could get angry. "I understand the alcoholic craving a drink to get drunk or settle his nerves, or the drug addict getting high, or even a sex addict craving physical satisfaction, which I think you may be guilty of too," Alex said with a chuckle. "But what do you think it is that causes some people to take up gambling? Some of these people seem to gamble not for the money, because if they win they go right back and lose, and if they lose they go out to find more money to go back gambling. I'm not saying you are like them, but you like to gamble. Why do you like it so much?"

Johnny stared at Alex for a moment as if thinking what to say. He picked up his beer, took a sip, and slowly started to talk. "First of all a lot of those people you describe have a mental problem or addiction of one kind or another. As I said before, I gamble to take my mind off work and relax." Johnny paused again for a moment, gathering his thoughts, and with carefully chosen words, he continued, "Like I said before, Alex, I work very hard in my store, sometimes under the hood fixing engines or out towing cars late at night. But when I am at a blackjack table or a roulette table, and especially if I'm winning, it's quite a feeling. Even though I may lose later on, for a while the dealer and the other players are looking at me. If I have enough chips in front of me, the pit boss and the floor manager will come over to watch me. No one knows who I am, but for a while they know I'm a big player . . . I'm a winner . . . I know how to win. Standing there and watching those people looking at me is quite a feeling that's hard to describe." Johnny spoke as if he were a preacher giving a moving sermon.

Tommy was still at the bar nursing his drink and waiting for Ida to finish her greetings tour with her girlfriends, when a distant but familiar voice said, "Hi, Tommy." Tommy turned around, searching for the face that went with the voice. Standing in the midst of other people, he noticed a thin-faced, long-haired, aging hippie with an inquisitive look on his face. He was dressed in old jeans and a well-worn, blue oxford shirt with a leather suede blazer. "Danny Fredrick, how are you?" Tommy said as he extended his hand.

The two exchanged warm greetings and pleasantries for a few moments. Danny told Tommy of his recent almost fame with a folk album he released. It was popular in the Northeast but fizzled everywhere else. The group he was with split up, and now most of the group had real jobs or at least were working for a living. He went on to say the he had opened a waterbed store in Worchester, Connecticut.

"Tell me about your waterbed business. How did you get into that business?" Tommy asked.

"I was out on the West Coast a while ago and ended up in San Francisco. Waterbeds were the newest craze out there, and it seemed like everyone was buying one. When we came back East, our band broke up so I had to do something. I decided to open a store to catch the wave of the waterbed boom, so to speak," Danny said proudly.

Tommy was interested in the fact that Danny had started his business without any experience in retail sales. "So tell me, Danny, what was it like starting up a new business?" Tommy asked.

"It was slow for a while. There were many days I would ask myself what had I gotten into. It was a new product. Most people never even heard of a waterbed. Our customers are young people who live in older homes, so the weight of these waterbeds is something to consider. Then New England is cold in the winter, so we have to make sure they have the right water heaters. It seems as though our customers are mostly under thirty-five, so the idea of better sex in a waterbed trumps the few downsides. So over time we started to sell more and more."

"Let's go over to the bar and get a drink," Tommy said.

"I usually don't drink this early in the morning," Danny said sheepishly.

Tommy looked at him with a cold stare, with a forced smile said, "I am sure there are a lot of things you don't do early in the morning. But there's a football game this morning, and we have our little reunion. That is reason enough for a drink."

"Oh yeah, I forgot about the game," Danny said as he followed Tommy to the bar.

Phil Whitman strolled over, joining in the conversation as they walked toward the bar. "Hi, Danny. I see you made it to the breakfast. It's been a long time since I've seen you at one of these events," Phil said.

"It has been a while. My wife, Mary Ellen, wanted to come in for the weekend. Her mother lives alone and is not doing well. This could be her last Thanksgiving, so we decided to come in," Danny said.

"It could be your last Thanksgiving . . . if Johnny Thompson has too many drinks," Phil said in a sarcastic manner.

"Old Wedge Head . . . he'll never change. But life goes on and so have I," Danny said confidently.

"Danny has his own business now. He has a store selling waterbeds in Connecticut," Tommy said as if to support Danny.

"I heard about all the interest in waterbeds; they say they are great to get laid in," Phil said. Then with a chuckle in his voice, he added, "Do you give demonstrations on the art of making love . . . not war?"

"How did you find out about waterbeds, Phil? I know you have never seen one because you have never left the Abingtons," Danny shot back.

"Well, if the waterbed thing doesn't float, maybe you could sell mood rings. I hear they are a new West Coast craze too," Phil said.

"If my business doesn't work out, I could always become a teacher and do very little for nine months out of a year and have my summers off," Danny said.

"But first you have to get a college education, Danny. In other words you've got to finish something you start," Phil said boldly.

Danny stared at Phil for a moment, saying without any emotion, "Yeah, Phil, whatever you say."

"Come on, guys, let's have a drink," Tommy inserted quickly.

"I'll catch you later," Phil said as he walked away.

"Some people can't get out of the rut they live in," Danny said as he watched Phil walk away.

"Some people haven't forgotten that you went to Canada back in the sixties," Tommy said.

"I did go to Canada, Tommy, because for me it was the right thing to do. You went to Vietnam, and I respect you for you doing it. But you did it because you thought you were doing the right thing. And so did I!" Danny said.

Tommy looked directly into Danny's eyes for a moment. It was as if he was searching for the proper words to say. He then smiled and said warmly, "Let's have a drink; I'm buying."

Both men stood at the bar staring at the beers in front of them, each waiting for the other to speak first. Tommy picked up his glass of beer, took a small sip, and then started to speak. "You're right, Danny, I did do what I thought was the right thing to do. Some guys joined, some were drafted, and some had deferments of one kind or another. There was another category, the ones who went to Canada. Was your motivation hatred of war or fear of fighting in a war? Only you know your true feelings of why you left the country. I put on a uniform and served my country, I mean our country. Johnny Thompson did, Bucky did, and so did a lot of other guys around here, and Jerry Weaver was buried in his uniform. One thing is for sure, the ones who served never forget."

"Do you hate me too?" Danny asked in a sad, low voice.

"No, Danny, I don't hate you. I want to believe you're against all wars, and you did what you thought was right. I'm against war; I've seen the face of war and the terrible high cost of life, energy, and treasure. There are a lot of people that love our way of life and the freedoms it offers. There are a lot of people in the world who resent our way of life. We could eliminate war; all we need do is to choose which dictator to live under, and there are evil men who want just that. Hitler and Stalin were examples, but they couldn't agree on who would rule the world and eliminate war. It's hard to believe, Danny, but there are some things worse than war. Slavery is just one of them. We have a military to ensure we keep our freedom. In spite of what you may think, freedom isn't free," Tommy said.

"That freedom allows me to express my opinion even if you or your friends don't like it," Danny said in a vigorous tone.

"You are right, Danny. You do have the right to express your political viewpoint. Again we donned our military uniforms to ensure you have that right. And we have the right to disagree with your opinions and you."

"Tommy, I didn't come here today to argue about the Vietnam War. We both have strong opinions about that, and neither will convince the other," Danny said.

"This is not the time or the place to argue politics, Danny. We're here to have a good time. So let's enjoy the morning without heavy discussions of how to solve the world's problems," Tommy said in a conciliatory tone.

Danny didn't say anything for a few moments as he was sipping his beer. He slowly turned toward Tommy and said, "Tommy, I've got to tell you the truth. When I first started going to those antiwar demonstrations back in the sixties, it was mostly for the free sex, drugs, and rock and roll. Vietnam gave us a reason for the gigantic parties. Hell, half the people didn't know what was going on. But it was party central, and I loved it. We were righteous in our beliefs, and we were going to be forever young."

Tommy listened calmly until Danny finished. Tommy lifted his head, smiled and said in a light, whimsical voice, "While you were at party central protesting the war, out drugging, screwing, and burning the American flag, I was out in a jungle playing hide and seek with Charlie and friends. But that was a long time ago, Danny, and I have kind of moved on."

Danny looked at Tommy with a warm sign of affection. "Tommy, after all this time, do you know which of us was right?"

Tommy looked at his beer for a moment, without taking his eyes off the glass, and said in a low, sober voice, "I believed I was right, but I wasn't sure for some time. But the fighting and dying continued for years, and I wished it would all just stop. Then I didn't know which one of us was right for a long time. I was torn up inside.

Tommy picked up his beer, taking a large gulp; he then turned, staring into Danny's eyes. "You've got to understand the Vietnamese boat people were not fishermen. The people on those boats were well-educated, cultured people. They had a high standard of living with TVs, cars, and air conditioning, living in a beautiful country. Could you imagine leaving everything—everything you own, your home—and putting your family, your parents, and your young children in a small boat and going out in the ocean, hoping someone would pick you up? Millions of Vietnamese people made that dreadful decision to escape. Because the way of life they would live under was so terrifying, they chose the horrors of survival on the open sea rather than the known horrors of living under that tyrannical, North Vietnamese Communist. When I saw that sign of courage and determination, I knew we were right. We tried to prevent the atrocities that happened after we left, which led to the killings of millions of innocent people in Vietnam, Laos, and Cambodia. "

Neither spoke for a moment, and then Tommy continued, "So Danny, I think I was right."

Danny gazed admirably at Tommy, saying in a sober tone, "I'll drink to your health, Tommy . . . someone I can truly respect." He lifted his drink, took a sip, and then added, "I'm going to find my wife. She's around here somewhere. I'll see you later, Tommy."

Tommy remained sitting at the bar, deep in his thoughts, when a pleasant, sexy voice whispered in his ear, "Tommy Wilkinson, is that you?"

Tommy's ears perked up as he turned to see an attractive, middle-aged woman looking directly into his eyes. He scanned her face, hoping to recognize this sweet voice from his past. She was a beauty with blonde-streaked hair, a smooth complexion, and expensive, skin-tone makeup. Her deep blue eyes seemed to peer directly into his soul. He felt uncomfortable, for when he looked at her, he recognized her face but didn't know how he knew her. He jumped up from the barstool as nervous as an eighth-grader meeting a high school cheerleader.

"Yes, I'mmm . . . ah, Tommy Wilkinson," he said in a sheepish voice as he tried to gather his composure. He couldn't get over the way she looked at him as if she knew all about him

"Hi, I'm Lessie Parker, a friend of your sister, Barbara," she said in a deep, sensuous voice that matched everything about her. She extended her hand toward his. "We met a long time ago. You probably don't remember me. It's been so many years now. Your sister and I were good friends, and we happened to meet at a football game. Barbara and I were only about thirteen at the time, and you were in deep conversation with one of your girlfriends. As I remember you didn't have much time for your little sister or her friend. My maiden name was Lessie Williams."

"Oh yes, now I remember you," Tommy said, realizing he was telling a little white lie. He was searching his mind to figure how he could have forgotten such a beautiful face. Although he tried to be cool, he couldn't take his eyes off her. But it suddenly dawned on him that she was Mrs. Parker. And he could sense right off that she was not the kind of woman who would entertain any kind of out-of-marriage activity. She was a friend of Barbara's, and she was just being polite.

"Do you live in the area?" Tommy asked as he returned to the real world.

"Yes, my husband, Dave, and I live in Waverly. We have three children, two girls and a little boy," she said in a very pleasant manner. "I just wanted to say hello, and it's nice to see you again . . . even if you don't remember me," Lessie said with a light laugh.

"I never forget a pretty face," Tommy said in a convincing way.

She maintained her classic, warm smile and nodded her head as she turned away. "And tell your sister I said hello," she said as she departed.

Tommy stood alone, staring at Lessie as she walked down to the end of the large room. He started thinking to himself. *She was something else . . . kinda wished I would have noticed her a long time ago. She was a life changer of a woman.*

"Who was that you were talking to?" Ida asked.

Tommy was startled by Ida's voice. "Oh, ah, her . . . She's a friend of my sister, Barbara's. Lessie Parker is her name. I guess they have been lifelong friends. She said we met many years ago when they were just kids. She just wanted to say hi."

"She's no kid now," Ida said in a matter-of-fact manner.

"No, she isn't . . . She's married to Dave Parker, and they have three children," Tommy said flatly as he was trying to change the subject.

"I was just talking to an old friend of yours . . . Danny Fredrick," Tommy said.

"And what did my old friend Danny have to say?" Ida asked as she took a sip of the drink she was holding.

"Danny is Danny. He can't understand why everybody doesn't like him. He just did what he thought was right by running off to Canada," Tommy said.

"You didn't get into an argument about Vietnam again, did you?" Ida asked.

"No, we didn't argue about Vietnam. We had a civil conversation, and we both expressed our opinions without yelling at each other." Tommy then cocked his head and added, "I know you hold him in high esteem, so I didn't tell him what I really thought about him."

"That's what makes you so special, Tommy," Ida said as she kissed him on his cheek. Then she added with a little girl accent, "It's your compassion for your fellow man."

"The compassion I have for my fellow man is not wasted on Danny Fredrick," Tommy said abruptly.

"Now, Tommy, both you and Danny have strong opinions on things. We discussed this before; you did what you thought was right, and he did what he thought was right," Ida said as if she was a moderator.

"We both had lofty goals, and we each traveled different paths and made our separate sacrifices. I went to Vietnam, and Danny went to Canada. I won't go into the obvious differences we had. And it's not the effect he has on me that's so upsetting . . . it's how he affects the other guys who have served," Tommy said.

After a minute or two, Tommy picked up his glass of beer, taking a large swallow. Ida sat motionless next to him not saying a word, waiting for him to finish what he had to say. Ida could sense that Tommy was quite emotional at times, and this was one of those times.

Tommy put down his drink hard on the bar and said, "What a sacrifice he made! He went to Canada, played in a band, and protested! I wonder how many flashbacks or nightmares he's had!"

Tommy paused for a moment as if to gather up steam, but then he spoke with growing emotion saying, "I look at Johnny Thomson, Jimmy Hess, Jim Waldner, Bucky, and the others, knowing each time a helicopter goes overhead, they hear a loud bang, or see rice on a plate, their minds flash back to the days that scared their lives. Not to mention the fears and frightful, unanswerable questions, the sleepless nights and physical nightmares . . . haunted by young faces . . . that will never grow old. No Danny Fredrick and his kind didn't pay the same price we did."

"I understand, Tommy." Ida said softly.

"You think you do, but you don't understand, Ida. You put Danny and the rest of us on the same level. In your mind we both did what we believed was right, and we should be respected for standing up for our beliefs. My friends and I were good warmongers, and Danny and his friends were honorable peaceniks," Tommy said coolly.

The drinking was starting to show on Tommy as he continued to speak, "There is something you don't understand, my dear Ida. You see we warmongers have Jerry Weaver on our team. You remember Jerry; he was that fun-loving guy we went through school with . . .the same Jerry Weaver who was killed in Vietnam. In Washington there are statues of all kinds of great Americans. They are all part of America's heritage. Well now, Jerry Weaver's name along with fifty-eight thousand others are etched forever in black granite on the Vietnam Memorial. Their names are part of America's heritage. Long after we're dead and buried, including Danny and his friends, history may forget about us. But Jerry Weaver and the other names of the heroes etched in stone on that wall will be noted and honored.

As long as there is a United States of America, those names will be evidence of the dues we pay for our freedom."

Looking over at Ida, Tommy picked up his glass and, making a toast, said, "Yes, President Kennedy, let every nation know . . . we bore the burden, we endured the hardship, we supported a friend, and we paid the price, trying to assure the success of liberty. We were true to our beliefs."

Ida wiped tears from her eyes, something she wasn't used to doing. She put her arm on Tommy's shoulder, pulling him close to whisper quietly in his ear, "I guess I don't really understand much at all, but I'm trying to learn, Tommy."

They both sat silently for a moment, and then Ida spoke. "Oh, I almost forgot; Alex was looking for you. I guess he wants to talk to you."

Tommy quickly glanced over at Ida as if he had just woken up; his mood had changed. With a warm smile, holding his head high, he said, "Oh, Alex. Yeah, I'll go track him down."

As he was getting up from the barstool, he looked at Ida in an awkward way, saying softly, "Ida, I apologize for the little outburst; I didn't mean to upset you. Sometimes I just kind of lose it."

"That I do understand!" She said with a chuckle and they both laughed.

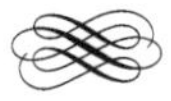

The hour of the kickoff was nearing, and some of the guests started to drift out. Phil Whitman was standing at the bar, talking to Bob Parry about the traditional Thanksgiving Day football rivalry between Abington and Tunkhannock. No matter the record of either team, this was the most important game of the year. For most seniors it would be their final time in uniform, the last time they'd be playing before a large crowd. To some it might be the highlight of their life. All their life through, they would remember that final game. And when they came back for their Thanksgiving Day breakfast, they would have special, cherished memories.

Alex was down the bar, talking to Jake the barber who was holding the diary at his side. To a casual bystander, it looked like any other common book.

"I guess it's time for the sign-in. It looks like you have a good showing, Alex," Jake said as he stood calmly looking around.

"Yeah, I guess I should order a drink for our toast, Jake. What can I get for you, Jake?" Alex asked.

"Oh, I've had too much to drink already, Alex. I have to be careful if, I get caught drinking and driving, it will mean a lot of free haircuts for the local cops," Jake said jokingly.

"Well, let's have one and done!" Alex proclaimed.

Alex ordered the drinks, and after a few minutes of additional conversation, Jake seemed to loosen up a little. "I tell you, Alex, being a barber is a lot more than you might think. You know, most people think I just stand there telling a few jokes and listen a little. My shop is a one-man shop . . . you know why, Alex?" Jake was starting to slur his words a little. "Because my customers come in for me to cut their hair. Oh, I hired other barbers, but whenever they worked, it would be a slow day, and my customers would wait for me anyway. It's an amazing place if you think about it. The barbershop is one place where a guy can come in to relax and really be treated special . . . kind of letting his hair down. For some guys I'm the only one who touches them at all. My hands are on their neck and their heads. And I'm up close and very observant. I can tell how my customers feel about money, how long it's been between haircuts, and if he'll leave a tip. I can see the car he drives; his jewelry, dress, and shoes; if he's wearing a clean shirt or a highly starched one, or even if it's old and frayed. I usually cut his neighbor's hair, so I get additional info about the guy. I have the boozers with liquor on their breath at nine thirty in the morning. It may be a little shop, but it's a beehive of gossip and some honesty. I tell you, Alex, quietly relaxing in a barber's chair with a razor at their neck, they sometimes tell me more than they realize. I've made a lot of money on some insider stock tips from a few of my wealthy customers. I usually find out who's cheating on who . . . even before the divorce lawyers do. I know because I cut the lawyers' hair too.

Alex was startled at the openness of Jake's insights. "I never thought of all the things a barber was aware of," Alex said with an astonished look on his face.

"It's true, Alex," Jake said in a loud, slightly intoxicated voice. "Don't get me started on politics. That's a whole different show. One other thing I like about my profession: if I want to find out something, I have customers who are experts in just about everything—finance, medicine, the law, carpentry, electricity, plumbing, or any other thing you could think of. While relaxing in my chair, they will tell me anything I want to know."

"I hope you don't tell them what's in the diary you keep, "Alex said with a chuckle.

"I may learn a lot of things, but I don't tell a lot of things I know," Jake said seriously.

Ida and Tommy, both with drinks in hand, came walking slowly from the far side of the room, approaching Alex and Jake. They kept stopping and speaking to each other in an intense, confidential manner.

As Ida was walking, she seemed to be slightly pleading with Tommy as she was saying in a frustrated voice, "I can stay a little while longer, Tommy, but you've got to remember I promised Steven I would be back for Thanksgiving dinner."

"Have the limo pick you up at Nichols Village about four. We can skip the football game and go back to the room for a little breakfast dessert," Tommy whispered in her ear as he put his arm over her shoulder.

"That would get me back in the city about six thirty." She paused for a moment, her head looking down staring at the floor as they walked. "Is there any wine left?" Ida asked.

Tommy smiled and, with a phony French accent inflection, he said, "Madame, wine is the lubricant of making love, my little chickadee. As long as you are near, the wine will flow."

"Where will you go after four?" Ida asked in a serious tone.

"To my sister Barbara's. She's having the family get-together. Dinner will be over by then, but sometimes I like having the leftovers."

Ida's eyes flared up with a defiant stare. She again turned toward Tommy, saying in a hurtful voice, "What do you mean by that? You don't need to have leftovers on Thanksgiving or any other time."

"I didn't mean anything by saying sometimes I like leftovers. I'm just saying my sister understands that I kind of float in and out. I've always been that way, even as a kid," Tommy said.

"Yes, you float in and out of people's lives, Tommy. Do you think that's fair?" Ida asked scornfully.

"Life isn't fair, Ida, but I try to live the best way I can. You chose to live the best way you can." Tommy was quick in his response, but so was Ida.

"I would change my life tomorrow if you'd ask me to," she said. "I've already told you I would give up everything for you."

"And I already told you I won't have people think that I am after you for your money. I love you, but we must be on an even plane," Tommy said.

"So you think it's more honorable sneaking away on weekends, having an open affair with no commitment. Yet you're concerned about what some people may think about our financial relationship?" she asked.

Before he could say a word, she continued, "That's the same as telling someone you love that you can't have anything to do with them because they're poor."

"I know what I think, Ida. And I do love you, and I am going to change my life and try to achieve the necessary things that can make our being together possible," Tommy said.

"What the hell does that mean? It sounds like the beginning of a vague business plan," Ida said.

"I've made plans to start up my own construction company in North Carolina, and if I'm successful, which I plan to be, it will change a lot of things . . . like us being together," Tommy said with a shaky voice.

Ida now had a look of a pleasant surprise on her face; as she started to smile, tears started to well up in her eyes. She turned to him and kissed him openly to the astonishment of the remaining few guests who noticed.

In a short time the small group had gathered near the end of the bar. They were all there: Johnny and Melody, Phil and Molly, Alex and Beth, Tommy, Ida, and Danny, without his wife.

Alex looked around, smiling at everyone, and with an elevated voice, he said, "It's great to see you all here today and now it's time to pry our journal from the grasping hands of the Abingtons most skilled and trustworthy barber."

With that announcement Jake turned over the journal to Alex with a warm handshake.

"Okay, before we start writing our thoughts of the day, I'm going to order a round of drinks for our Thanksgiving toast," Alex said.

"I'll order the drinks. Who wants to go first?" Alex said as he held up the journal.

Johnny proudly walked forward, saying, "I'm always first at everything around here."

"You were first all right, Johnny," Phil yelled out, laughing. "First to let someone else buy the drinks."

Johnny took the journal from Alex, thinking for a moment, and said, "Remember, Phil, what the Bible says, the first shall be last and the last shall be first, but in your case . . . the least shall be last."

Johnny walked over to a nearby table, taking pen in hand, and started writing into the journal:

Hello again,

I am here again; this year has been a good one. Business is good. The family life is good. I still love Melody and the kids, and things are getting better. We traveled a lot in the last few years in the Winnebago, making a lot of fun memories. These are what I like to call "the magic years." And I hope Melody enjoys life again.

I do hope everyone else has a good time here, and I wish them a lot of luck in the future. I hope luck stays with me in the future too.

Johnny Thompson '86

Johnny got up from the table, offering the pen to whoever wanted to be next. Melody spoke up as if it were her wifely duty and said in an upbeat mood, "I'll follow my husband. This can't be as bad as some of the places he's led me to over the years. Doing this, I don't mind."

November 27, 1986

Dear Diary,

How nice to be here with our old friends. I feel so blessed to have grown up and raised our children here .We still have our little farm with the farm animals, still have the chickens and now we have Clydesdale horses. It's been a good couple of years.

It's going to be difficult this year without my father. Johnny's mother died a few years ago. He hardly ever talks about her. But each day I think of my father. I miss him so much. Thanksgiving was his favorite time of the year. He loved the big turkey dinner, watching football games afterward, and playing with his grandchildren. I miss him so much, especially on holidays, which now are filled with tears. But we are slowly creating a new family holiday tradition, and we will get by.

Johnny is working very hard and long hours. Sometimes I think it's too much. I pray my children overcome some of the childhood difficulties we are now experiencing. It all is becoming a real burden. I hope it's just the times we're in and that it will clear up soon. We need to start keeping an eye on the friends they are running with. And I have to get off all the medicine my doctor has me on.

Hoping this next year will be filled with happiness and love.

Love,

Melody Thompson

Phil asked his wife, Molly, if she wanted to write in the journal. She declined because she said, "This tradition started a long time ago, and it's best if the original people sign it." She just didn't feel comfortable writing anything at this time.

Phil walked over to the table. "Hey, Phil, don't steal the pen," Johnny Thompson yelled out.

"Johnny I'm surprised you remembered how to use a pen," Phil said as he sat down.

Thanksgiving 1986

Well, I am back as usual. I try to be here each year, and it's good to live in this area year after year. However, there are times when I wish I could travel to some of the places I read about and teach about. Many of my friends have traveled and experienced a life away from here. I wonder what it's like to go on a large cruise ship, perhaps to the Caribbean or better yet to the Mediterranean, or travel to a foreign country like China or the Soviet Union. As much as I may dream about such an adventure, I guess I will be here next year writing the same thing.

But in spite of what I have written about, I am very happy teaching school. It really is a great profession. As time goes by, it is more and more difficult to keep enthused about what I am doing.

I am very happy with my family life; I love Molly and the girls with all my heart. I try to be a good father and husband, and I am blessed with good friends . . . except Johnny Thompson. Just kidding. He is an outstanding character of our community, and I love him.

Hope everybody has a good weekend and a wonderful year, and I hope we are all together again soon.

Phil

Danny was talking nonchalantly with the old gang although he seemed to have that air of self-importance, which reflected his true feeling of low self-esteem. Danny's old, playful humor and warmth seemed to be in hibernation during his strained visit this holiday. Alex seemed the only one who Danny could relate to; even that revolved around business discussions. But he did go over to sign in the journal.

As Phil got up, before anyone else could say anything, Danny spoke in a cold, matter-of-fact way, "I'll be next." He promptly walked over to the table and started writing.

Greetings! To whom it may concern:

I am back here again. I was hoping the people here had changed a little, but I see they are the same close-minded, backward goofs I left many years ago. After living the life I have lived and seeing what I've seen, I could never live back here. Everything and almost everybody is the same as when I left. I am glad for one thing: Now I know why I left, because of the way they live here.

I know I shouldn't be that harsh. I do have some fun memories of my youth, and Alex, Tommy, Phil, and even Johnny were good friends growing up. It's kind of sad to see the way they have changed.

My wife is waiting for me so I am out of here!

Daniel S. Fredrick

Daniel got up and walked boldly toward the bar for the drink Alex had ordered.

Tommy, Ida, and Alex were talking together. Tommy spoke to Ida in a warm, suggestive voice, "Ida, why don't you go next and add your script to the journal?"

She just smiled at him and said, "You want me to go first so you can read what I have written." She then lowered her voice to a whisper so that just the three of them could hear. "You just want to see if I'm going to write anything about Danny," she said with a large, affectionate smile.

"I was thinking more on the lines of women before men," Tommy said.

"Okay, I'll add my thoughts of the day," Ida said as she strolled over to the table.

November 27, 1986

Journal entry

Thanksgiving and here I am back in the Abingtons with some of my dearest friends. For some reason this place seems like my hometown. Just to get away from the hustled lifestyle I'm used to living, sometimes I just can't wait to come up. I look forward to it with so much enthusiasm and joy, especially this time of the year with the football tradition and the reunion. I love coming here with the mountains, the valleys, and the small towns; and I love the way I feel when I am here. But most of all, I love the people. They are real, and I love the way they make me feel so welcome. Although I didn't grow up here, I am so grateful to have found this community, which I consider my adopted home. While I'm here I don't want to leave.

I don't know when I'll be back, but I am going to strive to come in more often and enjoy this lifestyle and strengthen my relationships with my friends here. Hopefully there will be many changes coming in my life. The next time I make an entry into this journal, I hope I can be half as happy as I am this morning.

Life with love is wonderful!

Ida!

Ida got up from the table and turned toward the bar, her eyes searching intensely for Tommy. In an instant their eyes met, and she walked directly toward him, carrying herself erectly as if she were entering center stage in a theater play and presenting him with the pen as if it were a king's scepter.

They smiled warmly at each other without saying a word. Tommy accepted the pen, clenching it tightly in his hand as if it had a hidden value, as he walked toward the table.

Thanksgiving 1986

It is great to be home for the holidays and to see my old friends. It would have been great if Jerry Weaver was here, but he is not forgotten. It has been a long time. Now at least it's for a happy occasion this time. It was difficult to come back for the funerals of both my parents. They died within six months of each other. I do miss them so; now it's Barbara and me. I regret all the problems and heartache I caused them, and there are times when I wish I could have been here for them.

But my wandering way of life leads me away, and someday I hope to return to live.

On the positive side, the old gang seems to be doing okay. Nancy seems a little rough, but she will pull through. Alex, Johnny, and Phil are doing great, and I have hopes for our friend from Chicago. What's her name? Oh yeah, Ida.

That's about all for now. I do look forward to a bright future.

Tommy '86

Tommy got up from the table and walked directly toward Ida, although he was smiling at everyone as he strolled toward the gathering at the bar. "Your turn, Alex," Tommy said quietly, handing the pen to Alex.

Hello, Diary,

It's great to come to these reunions, to travel the old roads, visit the old haunts, and be with old friends is a great experience. I hope to spend more time up here as time goes by. This is the area of my childhood, and I would like to share some of it with my daughters, even though Beth may not love it as much as I do.

I was glad we made it in this weekend; much of the old town seems the same. We are lucky to have such long-lasting friendships. I hope Nancy finds happiness and contentment; she deserves it for all she has gone through. And I wish Johnny good luck in the casinos. He is a hard worker, and everyone in the area likes and respects him; well, at least they respect him. Phil and his wife seem to be doing quite well; he is an asset to any community. It was great to see Tommy again. He's changed somewhat for the better. I believe he is going to do quite well in his new life (with Ida, who knows). Then there's Danny Boy, still carrying that little chip on his shoulder.

If this were a perfect reunion, Jerry Weaver would be here. I think we all miss him not being here. However, I do believe he is here.

That's about all for now.

Alex, 1986

Alex closed the journal, picked it up, and carried it with reverence over to Jake the barber, entrusting it to his care till next year. He then walked over to the bar, joining Beth and the others. They all stood silently, waiting for Alex to make the toast.

To you dear friends,
May love always surround you
May good fortune always be with you
May the angels always protect you
May heaven be rejoicing to welcome you.
Till me meet again, dear friends!

They all drank with a cheer. The couples each kissed each other, some more affectionately than others. Beth kissed Alex softly, saying, "That was a beautiful toast. I know why I love you." She kissed him again.

Tommy and Ida kissed and embraced for what seemed like a long time. "Where do we go from here?" Ida asked lovingly.

Tommy smiled, saying tenderly, "First to the football game, then back to Nichols Village; afterward, who knows?"

Chapter Seven

2009

Driving up the Pennsylvania turnpike was something Alex Flynn had done many times over the past fifty years. Mozart's Piano Concerto was playing softly on the wraparound stereo system in his new Lexus. It was a nice, relaxing drive. His mind was drifting from one subject to another when he glanced at a highway sign that read, "Lehigh Tunnel one mile." Alex smiled to himself, reflecting on the many times Beth had commented on them driving through the tunnel. She believed it was some kind of time tunnel, and when they drove through it, she felt Alex reverted to the behavior of his carefree single life, hanging with his old friends and ignoring his wife and children.

This trip was a pilgrimage of sorts back to his hometown in the Abingtons. It had been many years since he traveled the route alone. His wife, Beth, had died of cancer a few years prior to this venture back to his hometown reunion. Their children were now grown with children of their own. To Alex's way of thinking, the memories of the past held more pleasure than the prospects of the future. He was going to his native land as he left it many years ago; this time he was traveling alone.

He switched the CD from peaceful, classical music to the new CD set he recently purchased, *The Folk Music of the '60s*. "This Land Is Your Land," by The New Christy Minstrels was playing loudly as the car entered the mile-long tunnel through one of the mountains of the Blue Ridge range. Alex was singing along as his car exited the tunnel heading north. His spirit changed, and his senses heightened as he took in the scenery that was all about him.

It was a beautiful fall day for a drive through the country. The air was crisp and clear. He could see for miles on this bright autumn afternoon. The sky was bright blue with scattered, large, white puffy clouds, the kind seen in classic paintings. In the distant countryside, bright beige bundles of cornstalks as silhouettes dotted the golden fields. The pastures were palmetto tan with tinges of faded green. The leaves in the large maple trees were majestically touched with bright colors of orange and crimson. He was feeling comfortable now as his memories shifted back to a time when burdens were light and close friends were plentiful.

However, he was determined to make the next few days a special time. His sister, Barbara, was pleased to have him staying at her home. She and her husband were empty nesters living in a large, four-bedroom home; their children were grown and lived outside the area. Alex would have ample time to visit the old haunts and meet with those remaining of the gang of old friends.

Many things had changed since his last visit. For Alex an abundance of gray hair had started appearing some time ago. For him it was a sign, a harbinger of changing times, the limited future, and the little happiness he had left. He felt the gray hair was an omen as natural as the autumn leaves changing color in the fall, a warning of the coming of winter. It was like reevaluating the life cycle of birth, maturity, and death. Alex felt this trip was symbolic and emotional, like the salmon's return to its birthplace in the headwaters after living in the cold, northern ocean. As a young person, he knew leaving the nesting area was inevitable; it was part of his life cycle. Traveling down the river of life was exciting, pursuing all that life and the world had to offer and searching for the opportunity to discover life's treasures in seeking achievement, success, and happiness. But when all these objectives manifested, it all seemed too elusive to retain or possess.

Now he was returning with only his experiences, composed of many emotional scars, assorted memories, and some hard-earned wisdom. He was filled with a new perspective as he made the return journey alone, swimming up the sentimental stream to the headwaters where it all began, his hometown. He asked himself if Thomas Wolfe was right, "You can't go home again."

As Alex was driving up the Pennsylvania Turnpike, he had a feeling that nothing had changed on this highway in over fifty years. The four-lane highway itself was the same, except for the new-style guardrails and the renaming of the John E. Fitzgerald Memorial turnpike bridge that spanned Clarks Summit.

After getting off the turnpike, he started traveling along Route 6/11 into the Abingtons. Alex noticed an uptick in development in the area. New franchise restaurants seemed to be everywhere, and gone were the locally owned gas stations, which had been replaced with the large gas and food stores. However, Alex was pleased as he drove down State Street. Although many of the storefronts were under new ownership, the community seemed to retain some of its charm.

Slowly motoring down State Street, Alex had mixed feelings about what he saw. After all these years, the Sunoco Gas Station still held its status position at the top of Summit Hill on the corner of State and Grove. The Old Grove House hotel and bar across the street was now a bank with a large parking lot. The Comerford Movie Theater has been converted into a modern-designed office complex. The picturesque stone building that housed the Holly Lane Dress Shop retained its charm and was now an upscale office building. The fieldstone Catholic Church remained the anchor of the community. Across from the church, State Street had a new health store along with other village shops. Bunnell Hardware was still serving with doors open for all needs of the handyman. The unchanging Summit Diner remained a beacon of the town on the corner next to O'Connor's Bar, which was now the State Street Grill.

After driving down State Street, Alex decided to drive through the Abingtons up past the old high school on Grove Street, which was now a junior high school. He then drove up and down the shaded streets of his youth, Electric Street, Powell Avenue, Midway Avenue, and Center Street, slowly coasting by the homes of his boyhood friends. The large maple trees still lined the streets as they did in his childhood. Alex was amazed to see that most of the homes hadn't changed in over fifty years. Even the colors of the homes and the landscaping seemed the same.

As he looked out his car, the memories came rushing back. Looking at the childhood-era homes, Alex could almost feel the anticipation of Tommy Wilkinson or Johnny Thompson running out of the house, carrying a bat and ball, ready for some excitement on the play field. He asked himself, was it so long ago we ran in these streets and played in these yards?

Alex glanced at his watch; it was nearly 4:00 p.m. In a few hours, he was to meet his friends at the State Street Grill. He had made all the calls earlier in the month to ensure that all who could be there would be there. Johnny Thompson and Melody each promised to attend, although they were no longer married. Tommy Wilkinson, Ida Freeman, Danny Fredrick, and Phil Whitman all assured Alex that they would make it Wednesday night at the State Street Grill. But the one Alex was keenly interested in seeing again was Nancy Bishop.

Again looking at his watch, Alex realized he still had about two hours to kill before the evening rendezvous. It was an unusually warm afternoon for this time of the year, and Alex was feeling a little melancholy, so he decided to take a ride out to Lake Winola. This was another sector of his youth where a lot of summertime memories were made. Many sunny afternoons and evenings there were full of laughter and high school romance. Even though this was a long drive out and back, Alex was confident he could make in the allotted time frame. After all he had driven this highway many times. He remembered it to be a beautiful ride out past the state mental hospital into the scenic mountains, driving through local farmland and small villages. It had been over thirty years since Alex had driven this lengthy, winding highway.

In less than twenty minutes Alex arrived at Lake Winola. Two things shocked him. One, the ride was so short; Alex thought it should take at least forty-five minutes; it took less than half the time. The other oddity was the ride was precisely how Alex remembered it. It seemed as if nothing had changed in over forty years. The homes, villages, and farmland were almost exactly like they were when he last drove it as a teenager. In forty years nothing had changed on this highway; there were no new shopping centers, schools, housing developments, or industrial parks. It was as if time had stood still. As Alex drove around Lake Winola, one other element stuck out in his mind. The lake seemed much smaller than he remembered it. In his youth Lake Winola seemed as if it was the sixth Great Lake. But driving around it now, the lake seemed so small. The large beautiful lake homes were just small, common, lake cottages. Many of the old cottages were in need of repair.

On the return ride back to Clarks Summit, Alex reflected on how he blew out of proportion the distance, size, and reality of his childhood. His flawed memories that he assumed were true had little to do with actuality. He believed the drive to the lake would have taken a lot longer, but it didn't. Drawing from his childhood memories, he was certain Lake Winola was much larger than the small lake he now surveyed. There was a big difference in what he thought was true and what turned out to be real. He was shocked to learn how wrong he had been about something so basic, the short time it took to drive out and the smaller scale of the lake. As he drove back towards Clarks

Summit, he asked himself what other distorted beliefs he stored in his memory that were now contradicted by reality.

In a short time, Alex was back in Clarks Summit driving up State Street. He parked behind a new BMW directly in front of the State Street Grill. Alex was a little early and wanted to go in alone and see for himself just what changes had been made to their hallowed shrine. As he slowly got out of his car, Alex took a careful look around the entire frontage of the bar. He wanted to take in everything, and he wanted to prepare himself for any other emotional surprises that lay ahead. Alex stood for a few moments outside taking in all the changes that had been made to the pub over the years. Gone were the big, beautiful, maple trees out front replaced by stylish outdoor couches, a table, and chairs that took up the entire front lawn. For cool evenings gas heaters were placed conveniently throughout the outside area for the comfort of the pampered customers.

Alex walked slowly into the bar, taking in the interior changes. And there were some. But the core elements of the bar area remained pretty much the same as when Eddie owned the place. The interior walls were still the original knotty pine, although refinished to reflect a more affluent image. Gone were the pictures of old-time boxers, replaced by framed, modern-style works of art. The restrooms no longer had newspapers on the floor as in the O'Connor's Bar were now equipped with soft lighting and Italian tiles, complete with no-touch, warm water sinks and automatic towel dispensers. The interior furniture was also modern, dark wood tables and chairs. The same style could be found in New York and San Francisco's best restaurants. The bar and the barstools were still in the same place, facing the northern wall. The large window on the far right side of the bar remained, preserving the splendid view of State Street.

Alex smiled as he looked over to the back of the restaurant and, to his surprise, he noticed the 'Frances window' was still intact—the window Frances O'Connor had put in so she and her sister, Liz, could watch Eddy while he worked. Alex took it all in and was pleased at what he saw, realizing that many things had changed but a few items remained to be appreciated.

The new owner was a master at what his customers wanted and strived to ensure their expensive needs were met. It appeared as an elite watering hole, and the menu confirmed the image with a nine-dollar glass of house wine and a twelve-dollar hamburger. The newest drink rage was the house special, an apple martini, only eight dollars during happy hour. The food menu was also exquisite and tastefully pricey. Customers could enjoy one of the evening's favorites, sesame-seared ahi tuna or cheese sacchetti with some sweet potato fries.

The afternoon was warm, so Alex decided to have a drink on the patio on the front lawn. He sat on one of the couches, basking in the setting sun, daydreaming, and watching the traffic on State Street. He hoped to recognize someone he knew as they drove by, but the only thing he noticed were the many trucks going by; one out of five vehicles was a large rig. They were hauling equipment to the recently discovered gas and oil fields known as the Marcellus Shale. Alex recalled reading an article about it. Northeastern Pennsylvania sat on one of the largest gas reserves in the world. The gas and oil companies had leased much of the farmland in the area. With this development many of the poor farmers in the area became instant millionaires. How this wealth would change the area was anyone's guess. However Alex had other things to daydream about, seeing his old comrades and taking notice of the local, beautiful people who were frequent guests of the State Street Grill.

Alex was titillated as he pleasantly evaluated the young shapely women who entered the chic, stylish establishment. Their attire was voguish, expensive, and tasteful; their hair was cut in the latest style; and the profiles of their frames were evidence of the many hours spent at the health club. They seemed to be pleased with themselves, conversing joyfully at a nearby table, thus confirming the impression that they deserved the luxuries of the good life, because of who they were or whom they married.

Alex noticed during their lively conversation that they gazed intently at each other as if vehemently interested in the topic, slightly glancing off to see if anyone was noticing them.

Alex smiled to himself, thinking it was too bad there were no mirrors installed so they could enhance their pleasure.

He sensed they were just trying to capture the fleeting elegant way of life they were experiencing. As he watched the hustle and bustle of those enjoying the evening, he remembered that, not so long ago, this place was his domain for good times. Now O'Connor's or the State Street Grill belonged to a new generation of fun seekers who were creating their own memories. They were blissful and enjoying the moment, not aware of the history or the characters that haunted this captivating place. Then he thought of an old Japanese expression and how true it was: "The water flows by, but the river stays."

Relaxing with his mind drifting off on different levels, Alex spotted an old friend slowly walking in from the side entrance; he immediately recognized Tommy Miles right off. Alex thought to himself how little Tommy had changed over the years, even though he was near seventy years old. He still had blond curly hair, his handsome face, and boyish, mischievous broad smile. However, Tommy's outstanding feature was his glass eye that seemed to tear often. He had been a gifted football athlete in college. One weekend as they were flying home, he was the copilot with his father when their small plane ran out of fuel. During the crash Tommy's face smashed into the joystick with horrible results.

Tommy and his father survived the crash. Although this accident altered Tommy's life, he never let it interfere with whatever he wanted to do. He was still strong as an ox with a reputation for his bone-crushing handshake. His family owned a junkyard that became a salvage yard then a parts store that Tommy managed.

"Tommy, how are you?" Alex asked

Tommy was a little startled at first, then turned toward Alex and said with a loud voice, "Hey, Alex, how are you doing? Did you come in for one of their famous apple martinis or are you a cosmopolitan man?"

Alex stood up, extending his hand carefully so as not to get caught in Tommy Miles' famous, crushing grip. "I just came for a snack, Tommy. I was looking at the menu but just can't make up my mind between the grilled Kobe sirloin with a port wine-vanilla reduction in bleu cheese or the duck confit with creamy sweet potato polenta and a sage-cranberry demi-glace," Alex said with a perplexed smile.

They both paused for a moment, smiling at each other. Tommy cocked his head and said laughingly, "I think Eddy liked the duck the best . . . at least he had to duck a lot when Frances was throwing pots and pans at him."

They both laughed about a few things, enjoying their brief conversation. Tommy started to turn away when he spoke again. "How long are you in town for?"

"I don't know for sure yet, Tommy," Alex said.

"Well, you've got to have breakfast with us over at the Sunrise Café. A lot of the old high school guys meet there every morning. Your old buddy Phil Whitman is like a fixture there. You'll have a great time," Tommy said as he slowly walked away.

"Is that the little restaurant over on Depot Street?" Alex asked. Then he continued, "Yeah, maybe I'll stop in on Saturday morning."

The afternoon sun disappeared, and Alex decided to move inside and wait for the group to show up. He sat at a corner table taking in the new ambiance. Gone were the days of Eddy bantering or arguing with his customers; now young, well-groomed bartenders were pleasant, efficient, and polite but not warm or friendly. Absent was the face of Frances spying through the side window, checking on Eddy. The tone of the chatter had also changed; in Eddy's day there was loud laughter and outspoken opinions of all kinds. Now the conversations were soft-spoken, more private and intense, without the awareness of others in the room. After a few moments, Alex went to the men's room. He entered smiling, reminiscing of long ago when newspapers were spread on the floor for sanitary reasons. Now the men's room had Italian marble-tiled floors and linen towels next to the granite sink with a modern pewter fixture.

Alex returned to the table and relaxed for a while. He causally looked up from his drink and glanced over to the activity at the front door. Often he would look over, waiting for someone he might recognize as many entered the bar, but these were different times. Gone were the days when he knew everyone who entered this treasured bar. The new breed of customers cared little about the history of the place. They all seemed to be preoccupied with their own self-importance.

There were now so many unknown patrons that it seemed useless to inspect each customer as he or she strolled in at different intervals. After what seemed like a long time, a female entered who sparked his attention.

Alex focused in on the woman's hair; it was as dark and shiny as anthracite coal, accented with a red ribbon. Peering through the crowd, he could just make out her blurred image. She had a smooth, blushed complexion, but the unique way she held her head and her posture intensified his interest. As she took a few steps, he knew in an instant. It was Nancy Bishop. She was attired in a light camel-hair jacket with a green sweater over a black turtleneck jersey. She still dressed in that preppie style and was still appealing enough to draw attention in a crowded room.

Alex stood up waving over to Nancy. He yelled out her name in an excited voice, "Nancy, Nancy . . . over here!" but she didn't hear him. She seemed confused and startled by the unfamiliar faces. Nancy walked slowly, her head turning from left to right as if searching for someone she knew. From a distance she looked as if she was a lost soul in a foreign bus station or train terminal, trying to find a friendly stranger.

Alex made his way through the noisy crowd, yelling and waving, trying to get Nancy's attention. Finally their eyes met, although many people separated them, and she stood halfway across the room. In an instant both faces lit up with excitement and joy. Even though many years had passed since Alex and Nancy were in each other's company, in an instant they recognized the enduring bond that existed between them. They were together again; it was blissful just to look at each other.

They gazed into each other eyes; 'the window of their souls' hadn't altered a bit. Although their outer appearances had changed radically, they were the same basic souls who grew up together . . . loving each other. They could feel it; they could see it reflected in each other's stare.

Alex wrapped his arms around Nancy with a strong bear hug. He closed his eyes and whispered in a strong sweet voice, "It's been a long time."

Nancy hugged Alex tightly with all of her strength as if to squeeze his love into her own spirit. Gently, but with a great deal of emotion and strength, she said, "Oh, Alex, I've thought of you so many times. You'll never know how much I've missed you."

The couple stood in the middle of the bar area, no one taking notice of two old friends embracing after a long separation. After all it was the Wednesday night before Thanksgiving, and there would be a lot of reunions at the place.

"I have a table over near the corner," Alex said as he gathered his composure. "I'm the first one here, so let's go over and talk before the rest of the gang shows up."

Nancy followed Alex as they made their way across the room to the table he had claimed for the evening. The small table had a half-consumed drink placed neatly on the center of a napkin. As they sat down, Nancy spoke in a nervous, kind voice. "Alex, I don't drink anymore." She then anxiously looked around the bar as if she was embarrassed to be there. She then added quickly, "I usually don't come into places like this. But today is special, and I want to see my old friends."

Nancy stared into Alex's eyes and continued to speak in a calm but determined voice, saying, "Alex, I stopped drinking a long time ago. I go to AA; I'm an alcoholic." She paused, staring at Alex and waiting for his reaction.

His reaction was not one of surprise but of understanding. Alex smiled, speaking in a warm, kindly voice. "Whatever makes you comfortable, Nancy? I'm glad you came tonight. If it bothers you too much, we can go somewhere else. Of course we may be alone because everyone else we know will be here drinking," Alex said in a light, joking voice.

"I'm okay, Alex. This place is fine," Nancy said in a sheepish way, as if seeking his approval. "It's just . . . I don't like having to explain myself in front of people I know or I don't care about. And it's none of their business anyway. I just wanted you to know!"

"Nancy, in the last twenty or so years, I've had a lot of friends, relatives and acquaintances who have given up drinking. Many of them have gone to AA, some not." Alex then added as if asking a question, "And if you think about it, almost every family I can think of has someone who has a drinking problem. And very few ever do anything about it."

"You're right, Alex, and I appreciate it; you've always been kind to me," Nancy said as she seemed to gather her composure.

"There's a friend of mine in AA, or as I call it, 'The Club.' Anyway he tells of a friend of his who had a real drinking problem. In fact, his friend died. So my friend went to the funeral home to console the widow of his friend. The grieving wife said she was pleased that he came to show his respect. She then went on to say that drinking killed her husband. My friend asked if he ever went to AA for help. She said, Oh no, he wasn't that bad." Nancy and Alex both shared a warm chuckle together.

"Will it bother you tonight being here with all the drinking going on?" Alex asked in a sensitive manner.

They both sat down at the table in the corner. Nancy seemed comfortable as she sat erect with an air of ease and self-confidence," Oh no, I'm fine, Alex. I learned a long time ago that the world wasn't going to change because I changed. My family still drinks and I have a lot of friends who drink. I kind of think I'm like a diabetic. They can't eat candy, and I can't drink alcohol. I will have a tonic with a twist of lime, and I'll be fine." Nancy paused for a moment and then added, "I used to drink soda, and then everyone would ask, 'You don't drink?' So I drink tonic with a twist of lime, and no one ever comments."

Alex was excited and wanted to reestablish their close relationship. "It's been a long time since we had a talk together. Tell me all about yourself if you'd like to. What are you doing now?

"It's a long story, Alex; are you sure you want to hear it?" Nancy said as if she wanted to make certain he was truly interested and caring.

"Of course I'm interested, Nancy. We're a lot more than just acquaintances; our friendship, or I should say our relationship, goes back to when we were just small kids," Alex said in a convincing voice. "Feel free to tell me anything you wish, and if there is anything that's not my business, just simply say, 'That's none of your business, Alex.'"

Nancy smiled and relaxed.

"Would you like to order a drink ma'am?" the uneven, cold voice of the waitress asked.

Nancy was a little startled but gathered her composure quickly. Without hesitation she said, "Yes, thanks. I would like a glass of tonic with a twist of lime, thank you."

Alex looked at Nancy as she nodded, smiling with approval. "I will have a Johnny Walker Red with a splash of water, thank you," Alex said quietly.

Alex watched the young waitress maneuvering toward the bar. He noticed her healthy, groomed hair and the chic uniform of the day, which consisted of black dress slacks and a white shirt with a black cummerbund. One could tell at a glance she was skilled, carrying herself with determination and representing the urban symbolism of the place. Alex chuckled to himself, thinking, *if Eddy could only see the place now.*

"I see you still have an eye for the ladies," Nancy said jokingly.

"I was just thinking how much things have changed in the old bar," Alex said with a smile.

"I never noticed you looking at Frances that way. I think Eddy might have been jealous," Nancy said.

"If Frances ever looked like that, Eddy would have a right to be jealous," Alex said, then paused for a moment and added, "It's amazing how some things have changed, and yet things haven't changed. Take this place, for example; it's a modern-day bar and restaurant with the latest menus and style. It's a lot different from when Eddy had the place, yet the building's foundation is still intact. The basic layout is the same: the entrance, floor layout, and the bar is still near the window. But there is a big difference in the look of the place: new windows, curtains, lighting fixtures, even the changes outside; however, the heart of the place is basically the same. It kind of reminds me of the people. I know we've all changed, some more than others, but I believe our core seems be the same."

"Now that's something to think about," Nancy said with an inquisitive voice. "You must have been thinking a lot to come up with that conclusion."

"I've had a lot of time to think about a lot of things since Beth died," Alex said quietly as he lowered his head after a quiet moment.

He then raised his head, smiling and saying, "Oh, I'm sorry, Nancy. I didn't mean to sound so maudlin, but over the years life has changed so much . . . for us all. When I remember how we used come in here and party all night. We were young and carefree but determined to venture out to experience a fascinating life. Now we're here looking back at what that life experience has been and where we are at now. Or I should say I'm looking back on my life's journey. I feel the past is the best part of my life. There's not much to look forward to at our age."

"Alex, your life's journey isn't over yet," Nancy said abruptly in a kind, stern voice. She went on, "In this life's journey, as you call it . . . it's kind of like driving a car, and you must look ahead. It's good to look in the rearview mirror to see what's behind you and where you've been, and reflect on your memories. But don't concentrate your attention on where you've already been. Life is still in front you. Just like in a car we need that large, clear windshield to see what life has in store for us and a little, rearview mirror to remember what's in our past. Who knows what the road ahead has in store for us. It could be a lot of fun."

Alex sat back a little startled, smiling and looking at Nancy with pleasant admiration. "It's funny, Nancy. I thought I would have to be perking you up, but instead you are uplifting me. You appear so happy and contented. You seem to gotten a positive grasp on life."

"Well, the last time we met, Alex, I think I was in one of the lower pits of life. I'm glad to say those days are over for me, and they have been for some time now," Nancy said.

The waitress delivered the drinks with napkins neatly placed under the glasses, ladies first. Alex and Nancy both stared at the drinks for a moment, Alex was a little nervous and embarrassed about picking up his drink as if he needed it. Nancy smiled; she was amused at his boyish predicament.

Nancy picked up her drink with a firm hand and with the masculinity of a woman pirate, speaking in a humorous, solid voice, "To life and what may lie ahead!"

Again Alex was startled by her spirit and charm, and he too lifted his drink, proclaiming, "To life and what may lie ahead!"

After taking a sip of his drink Alex leaned forward and in a sincere, intense voice said, "Nancy, it is so good to see you. Although it's been such a long time since we've been together, in some aspects it seems like only yesterday when we were here laughing and joking."

"Well, Alex, it has been a long time, and I'd like to know more about you and your life," Nancy said.

Now Alex put on a serious face. He took another sip of his drink. "All right, Nancy, where would you like me to start, when we were little kids?" he asked.

"I have fond memories as us kids growing up together right up to college. I'm more interested in the adult Alex Flynn. Tell me about the years in between then and now. I'd like to know about how your life changed from the days of drinking Budweiser out of a bottle to sipping Johnny Walker Red on the rocks," Nancy said with an inquisitive, perky, humorous voice. Then she added in the tone of an old teacher, "And I don't mean how your taste buds have changed your desire from beer to scotch."

"It's funny you ask about my adult life, Nancy," Alex said with a light, humorous tone as if she had brought up the very topic on his mind.

"That's something I've been reflecting on for some time. I physically feel pretty good. I am of sound mind most of the time. And I keep asking myself, where did all the time go? Earlier today I drove out to Lake Winola; it was a trip. Except for the Schultzville Airport, almost nothing had changed on that highway in over forty years. As I was driving, I was listening to The Byrds sing, 'Turn, Turn, Turn.'"

Alex sat back, relaxing a bit, and took a sip of his drink; then he continued speaking in his most convincing manner. "Now I'm driving along looking out over the hood of my car like it was forty years ago. It was as if nothing had changed; the road was the same, the music was exactly the same, and my feelings were the same. I was driving out to Lake Winola to have some fun. I felt like I was seventeen, happy, and carefree . . . life was good, I was happy. I had to look in the rearview mirror to see the old guy with gray hair. It was like something out of the *Twilight Zone*. I mean I knew who I was, but I shared both feelings of the seventeen-year-old and the guy with gray hair. Many times I had to catch myself; I have the spirit of that young person but the body of the old guy. When I looked in the mirror, I saw the guy who had been married many years with grown children who had families of their own—my beautiful grandchildren. But when I turned my head forward, as I was driving a little too fast with the music blaring, I felt young, energetic, and carefree. And the years in-between were a foggy part of my memory. I asked myself, is this for real? Did time really go by that fast? Then why don't I feel old?"

Alex again sat back to relax, looking directly into Nancy's eyes, and said, "sometimes I think . . .I think too much."

"Oh, Alex, stop thinking and start talking," Nancy said. She paused for a moment and then added, "I'm listening."

Alex continued talking about his life and opened up his heart and his adult history, sharing with Nancy as much detail as he could recall. He dove deeply into his own emotional past to areas that even Beth was not exposed to. He confessed how much he had partied through college, even struggling to keep his grades just above average. He laughed as he talked about some of the wild parties he attended and the large fictional lists of his love conquests. Alex discussed some of his dreams of life . . . some he achieved; yet others eluded his capture. He expressed some frustration and real maturity in analyzing his twisted path of life. He told Nancy that although he had high expectations in life, he felt he lacked the competitiveness and the resilient, energetic drive to achieve great success. Yes, to his peers he was a success; after all he was a vice president at Proctor & Gamble. But as time went by, there was a mantra in his soul that told him he could be much more.

Alex spoke of how he met Beth. While he was in college, he was a waiter in an upscale restaurant outside of Philadelphia. Beth and her family came in for dinner one night, and Alex was the waiter. He would often jokingly say, "She came in for dinner one night, and I was her waiter; and I have been waiting on her ever since." He went on to discuss his early marriage, the intense love he felt, and yet the uncertainly of a committed relationship and all it entailed. Alex was very open about some of his early doubts and fears of marriage and parenthood. Could he live up to what was expected of him? In their early marriage, Beth had had her doubts about him being a good husband, and even more importantly, would he be a good father?

Alex sat erect at the table, then staring out the distant window as if daydreaming, he said in a thoughtful tone, "I remember being at Fitzgerald Hospital outside of Philadelphia. I sat patiently for hours in a sparse, dimly lit waiting room. There was no TV, just a couple of out-of-date magazines. I was there about two or three hours, waiting for our child to be born. I didn't know what to think; I was all alone. Then all of a sudden, a little nun came in about 3:00 a.m. 'Mr. Flynn, your child is born; would you follow me please?' We walked down the hall to Beth's room. I was nervous and scared as any time in my life when I entered that room.

"Beth looked pale and exhausted, lying in her hospital bed. Her hair, which was always so neat and perfect, was flat, oily, and messed up. I gently grabbed Beth's hand and kissed her. With a beaming, brilliant smile, she looked deeply into my eyes and whispered to me, 'You have a daughter.' I was overcome with a rush of feelings of love and all kinds of emotions. I didn't know what to say. I think I fumbled around and said something." Alex relaxed for a moment.

He continued to speak in an enthusiastic, loving manner. "Then they brought in our little girl and put her in Beth's arms. I stood in awe, looking at her as she lay sleeping in Beth's tender cuddle. I instantly loved her more than I thought possible, totally without condition. As I looked down at her . . . her tiny little fingers, she was so beautiful, so fragile, so dependent, and so dainty. I knew then . . . my life had changed forever. From this point on, she would be my daughter, and I would be her father. I had the responsibility to love her, take care of her, make this a better place for her. She would depend on me for so many things in her life. I couldn't let her down in any way. I loved her, and I would take care of her no matter what. There was a new kind of bond between us, and I had changed forever. At that moment we became a family."

"How beautifully put, Alex," Nancy said calmly.

"Beth told me later that it was during this hospital encounter that she really was confident that I would be a good husband and father. Until then she had serious doubts," Alex said as he took a sip of his drink.

"It looks like you overcame her doubts," Nancy said.

"We did have a good marriage—not a perfect one, but we did get along very well, except when I came back to the Abingtons. She would tell me I changed as we drove up the turnpike. When we drove through the Leigh Tunnel, Beth claimed it was like watching the Dr. Jekyll and Mr. Hyde transition," Alex said with a smile.

"My transition of Dr. Jekyll and Mr. Hyde took place in my own home," Nancy said jokingly. She paused for a moment, picking up her tonic for a sip. "But what changed me into a Mrs. Hyde was booze and drugs, and I'm glad that part of my life is over."

"I'd like to hear about your life, Nancy. I've been talking about mine for a while," Alex said. "Not yet, Alex. I want to hear more about your life. Don't worry, I'll tell you about

myself . . . but later on," Nancy said softly but firmly.

Alex went on discussing the normal events of a young couple with small children who were trying to make it in today's society. Alex referred to this time as the fun years. They were just starting out, and they had little money, watching every penny, looking for bargains, sales, and the other usual things struggling couples did. Then out of nowhere a windfall would happen; maybe because Alex would win some little sales contest at work or an income tax refund would come in unexpectedly or at the end of the month, they just ended up with a few extra bucks in their pockets. It was time to celebrate. Forget spaghetti and meatballs at home. They'd take the family and go out for cheap dinner to have fun.

Alex went on to speak about many of the close friends they made as a young couple. He expected those friendships to develop into deep, long-lasting relationships like the ones he developed as a kid in the Abingtons. But as he looked back on it now, they seemed to be more of surface acquaintances rather than the lifelong friendships of his youth. Perhaps it was because the adult friends he met didn't share the open bonding experience of growing up together.

He discussed his children with the stress and aggravation of guiding two daughters through the teenage years. The girls required ten times the energy and attention as his son. It seemed generally raising boys was a lot easier than girls. However, he jokingly commented that the three of them were so different "sometimes I feel the only thing they had in common was their last name." He told Nancy there was some truth to the old saying, "A son is a son until he takes him a wife. A daughter is a daughter the rest of her life."

Alex paused for a moment, long enough to take another sip of his drink. Then he continued revealing to Nancy some feelings he hadn't put into words until this time. "It's funny; my daughters and I are very close. And I love my son very much, and as father-son we're close. I've come to believe that daughters and sons show their love of their parents in different ways. To me it seems my daughters love me in their own way. Their love is appreciative, easygoing, warm, and forgiving. Sons on the other hand are dissimilar. Although Derrick's love is genuine, it's different. His love seems to be somewhat distant, competitive, and judgmental. Now he wasn't that way with his mother. He adored her."

Nancy sat staring at Alex for a moment and asked in a solid, firm, warm voice, "Alex, you talked about a lot of topics today. Would you like to talk about Beth?"

Alex paused for a short time. He then took a small sip of the Johnny Walker Red. He then looked directly into Nancy's eyes as if searching to make sure she was the one who he could confide in. In a low voice, he started to talk. "I guess we have a little time before anyone else arrives. I assume you're more interested in the end time."

"I don't want to pry into an area that you aren't comfortable discussing. But I am interested in knowing about your life, and I'd like to know how you endured losing someone you loved so much . . . your wife, Beth," Nancy said.

Alex picked up his drink and emptied the glass. He then stared at the floor for a moment and started talking in a low tone, "Beth seemed to be losing energy, being tired all the time. She also had a persistent cough for a while, but she was taking some high blood pressure medicine that had a dry cough as a side effect, and that's what we thought it was. I was working at home that Monday morning, plugging away on my computer, when Beth yelled from the hallway that she had an X-ray at eleven thirty and it should only take a few minutes and afterward perhaps we could have lunch together. I said, 'Sounds fine to me.' So I drove her to the hospital for the X-ray."

Alex noticed the waitress walking by and raised his hand as she looked at him. "Could you bring me a bottle of Budweiser, please?' He then glanced over at Nancy and said with a smile as he returned his attention to the waitress, "in a frozen glass, please."

Alex again looked directly at Nancy as he started to talk again. "I want to keep my mind sharp. This is the first time I've gone into many of the details with anyone." He sat back as if to regain his composure, and then started speaking again. "Now where was I? Oh yes, we went to the hospital for the X-ray. Beth checked into the radiology department and disappeared behind closed doors. I read a magazine for a while, and then I began to think this was taking a long time. After a while a nurse came out and told me my wife was in another part of the hospital and she would take me to my wife. I was a little nervous, but there was nothing to be scared of, so I followed the nurse. We ended up at the emergency room. At first I thought Beth had fallen, fainted, or something. I suddenly entered into a sectioned-off area for newly admitted patients. Beth was in a bed with an oxygen mask on. I still couldn't understand what was wrong. When I looked into Beth's eyes, I knew it was very serious.

"I reached out for Beth's hand and asked what happened. She couldn't talk. Just about that time my cell phone rang. It was our family doctor. The doc told me the hospital had called a little while ago and told me that x-rays showed both of Beth's lungs had massive black areas. They checked Beth's oxygen level, and it was at eighty-four, so they admitted her to the hospital for additional testing. I then walked out in the hallway away from Beth and asked the doc what he thought it could be. There was silence on the phone for a minute. Then he said matter-of-factly, 'It looks like lung cancer.' Another pause. 'We will have to see. You should let the rest of the family know. This is very serious'."

The waitress arrived with the beer, placing it neatly on the table along with the iced glass. "Is there anything else, sir? She asked.

"That's fine, thank you," Alex said as he poured the bottle of Budweiser into the frozen glass.

Nancy stared at Alex as he slowly performed the ceremony of pouring the beer into the glass, thinking how it reminded her of a classic beer commercial.

Alex then picked up the glass of cold beer, taking a sip as if to sample the taste. "After talking to the family doctor, I called the kids just to tell them that Beth was in the hospital, and they should come when they could. They were all upset and confused when they got to the hospital. Because Beth was the picture of health—she taught yoga, never smoked, and was a health advocate—she wasn't one to go to the hospital on a whim.

"The three of them arrived separately and were shocked with the fact that Beth was in such bad shape. A staff doctor, a pulmonologist, came by to talk to us. He said, 'Let's not jump to conclusions; let's do the tests first. Then we will see.' He went on to say it could be a moss or fungus that can grow in the lungs. But we wouldn't know until they did a biopsy in the morning. Beth was going to be moved from the emergency area to a room on the second floor. We all decided to spend the night with Beth. Mandy was single at the time; Derrick had two little girls; and Courtney had three young children. Both Derrick and Courtney didn't want their children there that night."

Alex picked up his beer for another sip. "Beth and I had some private time for a little while before she was moved to her room. And that's when she drew upon her inner, deep, stoic character. As we sat there together, I could tell she was afraid; she had tears in her eyes and trembling hands, but she exhibited a smooth inner strength that flowed from her. And when she grasped my hand, she spoke softly but very effectively. 'Alex, no matter what the outcome, you have to be strong for the children. They will need you. And I will need you. We are depending on you."

Alex paused and said, "I was scared and confused. My emotions were all over the place. I didn't know what to do or how to handle anything like what I was facing. I was caught up in the fact that I might be losing my life's partner; we were like a pair of harnessed horses. How could I go through life without her? What about the plans we made? I felt so badly that I hadn't made her life as happy as I could have; I still had a lot to prove to her. I knew I did things wrong, but I wanted to please her and wanted her to be proud of me. How was I to handle this bleak, unknown future? How could I be strong enough to know how to guide our children and grandchildren through this ordeal that lay ahead? I was in shock, devastated, and broke down and cried. I wasn't prepared. I didn't know if I could do it."

Alex had tears in his eyes as he stared at the table. He picked up a napkin, wiping the tears, and continued talking. "Beth again held my hand and said gently, reassuring me, 'Alex, I'm not afraid. I know where I'm going. I know this will be hard on you, but we will be together again. You can still talk to me. I won't be able to talk back, but I will hear you. And I will be near you to help you.' I then fell apart, crying like a baby. Beth consoled me during this terrible time. She was the strong one. We both cried in each other's arms for a while, and then gradually I got emotionally strong enough to start thinking about doing the right things."

Alex sat erect in his chair as he gathered his composure. He looked over at Nancy to see her reaction to his story. Without waiting for her to say a word, Alex continued as if he was confiding with a shrink these unspoken feelings for the first time. "I was glad we were leaving the busy ER area with all the hustle and bustle, bright lights, and that equipment. We went to a quiet room with just the family. It was getting late by the time Beth got settled into her room. After a while I suggested that the kids make arrangements with their own families. They wanted to stay.

"The three kids and I spent the night together in Beth's room, talking, crying, and laughing. We all wanted to be together with her and were determined to make the best of the situation until we knew more. We took turns lying in the bed with her, trying to comfort her and ourselves. Beth was very brave and loving, embracing and comforting her grown children as if they were toddlers who needed their mother. We were desperately trying to show our love and affection for her. At times that night, we alternately participated in a unique party atmosphere right there in that hospital room, telling many old family stories, some incidents for the first time, and we laughed right out loud. The kids shared with us some of the antics they pulled off in their youth, shedding some light on unsolved family mysteries such as why the bottle of vodka turned bad like stagnant water. And there were late-night coded phone calls and vacation parties while Beth and I were away. We talked, laughed, cried, and napped throughout the night. It truly was a night to remember. Beth was so happy having us around, smothering her with love. If she hadn't been so sick, it would have been one of the best nights of her life."

Alex sat back, taking a few deep breaths and a sip of beer. Although everything he was sharing was deeply serious, he seemed to relax a little. He then continued to tell Nancy his story. "In the early morning, they came in and took Beth to the operating room for the biopsy. It was hours before the results came back, and the kids happened to be in the cafeteria having a snack."

Again Alex stopped talking for a moment as if he was trying get up his nerve to actually describe the next phase of the narrative. He took in a deep breath and continued, "The doc came into Beth's room in a serious mood with a folder in hand, and in a matter-of-fact way, he told us, 'The biopsy confirmed it was the cancer.' He spoke all about the procedure and how it was done, which was too complicated to remember. He went on to say it just didn't seem right, looking at Beth with her wonderful color and appearing to be in perfectly good health, except for her lungs. He then said sadly, 'There is no doubt about it. It's stage four lung cancer. I don't believe there is much we can do about it.'

"Beth was stunned, lying quietly in her bed with tears in her eyes. Even though we expected bad news, it was still a shock when it came. I followed the doctor from the room and asked if I could speak to him. I said to him, 'Doctor, I have children I have to talk to. What can I tell them?' He just looked at me and said to me flatly, 'You can see for yourself, your wife is on oxygen because her lungs are full of cancer, and that cancer is racing throughout her body. There's nothing that can be done—no operation, no chemo. All I can suggest is take her home and make her as comfortable as possible.' I then asked, 'How long?' He looked me straight in the eyes and said coolly, 'You're looking at weeks not months.' I stood there motionless as he walked away; I couldn't think or talk for a few minutes."

Alex paused for a moment, but he didn't wait long before he picked up right where he left off. "Everything was happening so fast; our entire life was crashing down. What was I going to do? And how was I going to do it? I had to notify family and friends of our peril, and how was I going to handle this entire nightmare that lay ahead? About this time the kids were returning from the cafeteria after taking a snack break. I had to inform them of the heartbreaking report I had just received from the doctor. I led them down the hall to a sitting area where I had to explain to them the terrible situation we were facing . . . that their mother would be dying soon. I started by telling them the indication from the pulmonologist was very bad; there was a limited time we had left with Beth. Their eyes filled with tears, and they started sobbing. Courtney started crying hysterically, shrieking that she couldn't face the future without her mom. Mandy said that she wanted to take Beth to a Dave Matthews concert in six weeks. Beth and Mandy were big fans of Dave and had attended a few concerts together. With tears in my eyes, I said there may not be enough time for that. I said to them, 'As difficult as this is—and believe me, it's horrible—in a way we have been blessed too. We know that Mother won't be with us long, but if we look in the newspaper tomorrow, we will see many names of people who died unexpectedly. They were in a car accident or hit by a bus or just died suddenly. And their loved ones didn't have an opportunity to say good-bye to them. So as bad as it is, we are blessed in a way . . .each precious day we have left is an opportunity to tell and show Mom just how much we love her. We may not have a lot of time, but we have valuable time to fill with deeds of loving, kindness, joy, and dedication. Whatever time Mom has left, we can use to our advantage.' They gathered up their composure and agreed to be as positive as possible. Before we left the sitting area, I told them, 'And there's one more thing. I'm going to put a note on Mom's door that says, 'If you can't smile, you can't come in!' And then we headed back to Beth's room."

Alex took another break. He smiled over at Nancy to see her reaction. Nancy didn't say a word. She sat unchanged in her posture, retaining a quiet, warm smile and kept staring at Alex. Nancy seemed to appreciate his sharing of these deep, emotional revelations.

"Alex, I can only imagine how terrible it was for you and your family," Nancy said with indication of deep emotion.

Alex picked up his beer, taking a small sip, and said, "It was very difficult, and that was just the beginning."

Alex casually looked around the bar; he noticed a crowd was starting to come in. But it didn't seem to bother him or Nancy as he continued, "As soon as we entered Beth's room, there seemed to be a change in attitude; we all became more positive. Courtney spoke first, saying, 'Okay, we know the worst; now let's make the best of it.' As a family we decided to leave the hospital that day. We would go home to make Beth as comfortable as possible, making the best of a bad situation.

"We made the accommodations for oxygen and other medical items that would be needed at home. I drove Beth home with a portable oxygen tank in the car. On the way home, Beth made a strange request. She said to me, 'Our children now have homes of their own, and Courtney even has a lake house now. I want you to sell our home and keep the money but divide our household items, all the furniture, TVs, and the antiques among our children. I was puzzled at this request and said, 'Well okay, but why?' She said to me, 'Look, Alex, we have already discussed downsizing and selling the house anyway. The kids will get all of our stuff someday anyway. This way it speeds up the process, and by doing so, Alex, you will be forced to live with one of them. You see, after I'm gone, I don't want you to live alone. I don't think it would be good for you."

Alex stopped speaking for a moment as if he was coming out of a daze. He glanced over at Nancy and continued talking as if on an complete different subject. "At the time I was in a fog and didn't much care about anything but making Beth happy. So I agreed without question. As I look back at it, I think Beth was right.

"At any rate where was I?" Alex was back, focused on his topic, as he continued with his narrative. "When we got home, Beth said right off with a big smile, 'If I have little time left, I'm going to enjoy myself. I want a big Whopper and large fries.' We wanted her days to be as happy as possible, so we put on the happiest front for her and went all out, even popped a bottle of Dom Perignon Champagne for the occasion. We decided to have as much fun as we could. We sent out for what sounded like good exotic food items to make this time special; we even enjoyed some Russian Beluga caviar," Alex said as he shook his head and smiled.

"It turned out to be a whole new phase in our lives—having the hospital apparatus shipped in, learning how to monitor the oxygen system, and making household changes that needed to be made. But the main task was to make Beth as comfortable as possible. I had the difficult task of calling friends and relatives, informing them of Beth's condition, and each call was a tough one. Friends were in shock, then disbelief. Everyone would ask, 'Is there anything we can do?' I would simply say, 'Beth loves flowers, so instead of sending them to a funeral home, we are arranging delivery dates to choose from. In this way Beth can enjoy a constant flow of flowers from her friends and her loved ones.'"

Alex then took on a serious tone, saying, "Then we settled down for Beth's strenuous, disheartening, long good-bye. The kids took time off work to be with her, and the grandchildren were over a lot of the time. Beth loved to have the grandchildren in bed with her as often as possible. At first it was almost fun; we made special holistic meals for her. We had every kind of berry and natural juice you could think of. The neighbors were wonderful and kind, delivering great meals each night. Beth's friends came by often, but as time went by, it seemed to get sadder and gloomier as Beth got weaker and weaker. After a while her friends stopped coming around, relatives stopped calling. It was a difficult situation, and I guess some people just felt emotionally worn-out. Beth's family was devastated but slowly accepted the inevitable and started preparing for life afterward."

Alex picked up his beer, taking a small sip as if he was doing so just to break up his thought pattern. He then continued speaking in a low voice. "We believed in miracles, and we tried everything including chemo, hoping we could extend Beth's life some. Chemo drains energy and kills all growth cells in the body, and cancer is a growth cell. So are hair cells; that's why the patient loses hair. Additional medicines such as steroids are part of the treatment system, and they too have side effects that can alter the mind as well. The patient can become paranoid and aggressive, and Beth exhibited many of the expected side effects, which changed her personality completely. At times Beth hated me and carried on, yelling at me and complaining about everything I did. She told friends that I was mean and treated her terribly. She even contacted her sister, who lived in St. Louis, and told her that our daughter Courtney and I were slipping her poison and trying to kill her. I knew it was the medicine causing theses delusional problems for Beth. But it became quite difficult, and I started going to the gym whenever I could to work off the stress of it all.

"I remember looking into her eyes, trying to avoid her bald head, and forcing myself to smile with her whenever I could. She no longer had enough strength to dress herself or put on her own shoes. We were still forcing ourselves to use uplifting words, even though we no longer believed them. The treatments and the medicine drained all of her energy. I recall that during this phase it seemed the only pleasure we shared was having coffee and doughnuts each morning, and we enjoyed watching reruns of *Frasier*."

Alex paused again. He seemed deep in thought as he was reflecting on his memories and feelings. Nancy could sense that he was experiencing some pain as he was sharing this intimate revelation. "Alex, if this is difficult to talk about . . ." Nancy said in a concerned tone.

"Oh no, I'm fine," Alex said. "I was just thinking how hard it was on Beth. She refused to believe the cancer would kill her. She was always hoping and expecting a miracle. But lying in that bed day after day, losing her battle, had to be so crushing for her spirit. I went into her room one day, and Beth was crying, 'I don't know what's happening to me. I want to make jewelry; I want to go to the Jersey shore. I want to be normal again.'

"And taking care of Beth became more and more challenging for me. I didn't mind; in fact, I was kind of awed by the tremendous responsibility it placed on me. I had told Beth over the years that I loved her, and now I was proving it to her . . . and more importantly I was proving it to myself.

"Watching Beth's energy slip away slowly each day was so disheartening. Walking into our bedroom became more and more straining. Even though we had room fresheners and flowers, there was still that stagnant odor of dying. And seeing her lying in the bed, not looking like my beautiful wife but like an old aunt or elderly person one might visit who was sick, it was hard to believe this disfigured being, who used to be so striking, was now too weak to even smile. Her clear, bright blue eyes were now glossy with a faraway look and sometimes filled with fear or pain. She drifted into being helpless, not even caring about her appearance, and her dignity depleted.

"Soon she couldn't even walk anymore and was reduced to watching TV and sleeping. We had to put her in a wheelchair when we changed the linen. I moved the potty into the room when she couldn't make it to the bathroom. Beth had to wear adult diapers, and I would have her stand up, holding on to the bed, as I put the diapers on her. She was embarrassed to be in such a circumstance; it was so sad. Even as bad as it was, I knew how important it was for me to be there for her, making sure her medicine was taken properly and her meals were served on time. We tried to make her as comfortable as possible, making sure she had a fresh glass of water, a room that wasn't too hot or too cold, and so many other little essential things that were important to her. It was a family commitment, and it was also very hard on the kids.

"I remember a time when Beth insisted that she could walk to the bathroom. She didn't take three steps and then pointed toward the potty. I helped her over to it, taking off the bottom of her pajamas and the Depends. Then suddenly there was a kind of explosion, and the excrement went all over the potty, the floor, her pajamas, and herself. It was a smelly, awful mess. I think that was the low point for me, and I didn't want the girls to see their mother in this condition. It was quite a task getting things back to normal, changing an adult diaper, cleaning up the excrement. Thank God for carpet cleaner and room fresheners. It was then we decided to have a nursing agency come in.

"We decided to have the hospice home care program started. The tough part of using hospice was the fact that Beth could no longer take treatment medicines. The hospice program was designed to help the patient pass over as peacefully and comfortably as possible."

Alex drew in a deep breath and stared at the floor; he then took a sip of beer as he gathered his thoughts. He started speaking again as if he were testifying at a trial or exposing this private secret no one else knew of. "It was a very difficult morning that day. I had to tell Beth that she wasn't getting any better and that her disease was fatal; nothing more could be done. Although she was weak, Beth glared at me with hatred in her eyes as she spoke in a heated temper that I was lying, that I was just trying to kill her. She said she was getting better! What made me think she was dying? I asked her, 'Please . . . look around you, Beth. You're in a hospital bed on oxygen.' She yelled back that it was not her choice. 'I liked my old bed,' she said. I said, 'Okay, but you need a hospital bed, the portable potty in your room, the oxygen, and all these other things because of your condition. The cancer is growing in you, and you're not getting any better.' Beth pleaded with me that she was getting better and wanted to prove it. She struggled to get out of bed but couldn't even get her legs to move. I held her hand, and we both broke down and cried.

"It wasn't long until we had to move Beth to a hospice facility. I remember how sad it was that morning as we shared our last fresh coffee and doughnuts and watched *Frasier* for the final time. Later that morning an ambulance arrived to take Beth to hospice. She still insisted she was doing okay. As they helped her on the gurney, she told the medics she was in fine shape and walked each day. At first I didn't want to move her, but Jo Ann, the hospice nurse, convinced my daughters of the need to move her. 'Look at your father's face, and you can see how the strain is taking a toll on him.' Watching them lifting Beth into the ambulance was a heartbreaking event, knowing she was departing her personal sanctuary with the beautiful rock gardens she designed and the variety of incredible, bright flowers she loved planting each season. She would never return to our home she lovingly furnished and where she spent so many happy years cooking our meals, celebrating our holidays, and comforting us from the outside world."

Alex was quiet for a moment. "As I look back at it now, in a strange way it seemed like the first part of her funeral.

"When we arrived at hospice, everything was handled so smoothly. Beth was convinced she was there just to regain her strength and get better. The next day they helped Beth into a wheelchair, and we went out and toured the elegant grounds around the facility. Beth was still mad at me. She said I abandoned her here to die. I explained that she was there because of her illness. She objected and said the only reason she was there was because she wet her pants. I asked if it were reversed, what would she do with me. She said she would put me in an old folk's home . . . and never visit me."

Alex smiled as he glimpsed over at Nancy and reflected on what he said. "She was a tough one all right. But as she got so weak, I even had to brush her teeth for her. We had to feed her most of her meals, but she still insisted on Haagen-Dazs ice cream and knew the taste difference.

"The end was tough on everyone—Beth, the kids, and the grandchildren. At times I felt like a prisoner; I could leave the building and go to the store like a trustee or maybe sneak out for something to eat, but I couldn't be gone for long. In a sense I was sharing her illness, and I felt as though we were being punished by God for something I did.

"Gone was the loving, happy person we loved all these years. She was a shell of herself. She was so unhappy. The illness had made her disfigured and ill tempered, with no hope for the future. It was difficult to witness. Then Beth started to drift in and out of a coma, and the nurses indicated that it wouldn't be long. We as a family said our good-byes, telling Beth that we loved her . . . and we would miss her. We each told her it was okay to leave. We were on a deathwatch, not wanting it to happen but wishing it was over. I remember walking down the hall, and when I entered her room, I had a sickening feeling . . . I was hoping Beth was gone. But she was still hanging on, and I felt terrible for the thought of hoping she was gone. We knew she would be leaving soon. We knew her pain would be over, and she would be happy rejoining her mom and dad. But she seemed to stubbornly cling onto life.

"The last night I told the kids to go home and get some sleep. The nurses said her vitals were still pretty strong, so she should make it through the night. Beth was taking very deep, curdling breaths, commonly known as a death rattle. I settled in for the night in the chair next to her bed. At the two o'clock injection of OxyContin, I woke up as the nurse was leaving the room. I followed her down the hall to ask a question. When I reentered Beth's room, everything was quiet. Her deep curdling had stopped. In silence I stood there in shock. I picked up her warm lifeless hand and held it for a moment. I could feel the tears running down my face as I kissed her cheek, then her forehead, telling her that I loved her and I would always love her and I didn't know what I would do without her. I stood there staring at her, asking what had happened to our wonderful life. Beth was gone forever.

"I didn't want to leave her, and I didn't want to call the nurses' station because I didn't want her body disturbed. But I knew I had to. So I notified the front desk. They came right away and confirmed Beth was gone."

"I then called Courtney and Mandy. I told them Mom's pain was over. She was with God now. I remember Courtney yelling over the phone, 'What happened? She was fine when we left,' as if I had done something wrong. I could hear her and Mandy both crying loudly. They said they were on their way now and not to touch a thing. I then called Derrick. He answered the phone, and I said, 'Derrick, Mom's pain is over; now she's with God.' He said in a very sad, broken voice, 'I knew it, I'm on my way.' The nurses arranged so we could be with Beth until the funeral director arrived."

Alex started talking again, as if he were thinking out loud. "I must say although we expected Beth's death for some time, when she actually died, we were in such shock. No matter how well we thought we were prepared or might even welcome the end of her suffering, when the end came, we were deeply grief-ridden. The fact of her actual death had the same impact as if she were hit by a bus or died suddenly at home, falling down the steps or something. We were all in shock and heartbroken."

Alex bent his head toward the floor, with his right hand rubbing his forehead, as if he were hiding his face or his pain. "It was the happiest and saddest funeral I have ever attended," Alex said softly. "She was loved and respected by so many people. It was interesting as they came up and told me their personal stories of how she helped them in her special way. But when I saw the five grandchildren at the casket, touching her shoulder and holding her hand, I believed Beth was happy and would be pleased with them hovering around her."

Alex perked up a little and, with some pride, briskly added, "The experience with Beth was the most difficult thing I ever did in my life, and I'm grateful I had the opportunity. I think it's kind of like basic training in the Army. It's a great experience, but you don't want to do it twice."

Nancy looked over at Alex with a newfound admiration for him. She thought she knew him well, and his sharing this part of his life confirmed how highly she felt about him. This was the Alex she grew up with. He was so different from any other guy she had ever met. To Nancy he represented all the good there was in a man. He was a dedicated, loving father and a devoted, loving husband right to the end. As in death do we part.

Alex…That was a beautiful and moving story. And thank you for sharing it with me. I know it must be very difficult for you to relive those memories," Nancy said in a convincing manner. She then continued, "I am proud to know you, Alex. You are one of the most remarkable people I have ever known. And I've known that for all these years."

Alex was startled by Nancy's compliment. He cocked his head with a half smile and said, "Thank you, Nancy." Alex wiggled in his chair uncomfortably for a moment, again looking down at the floor; he then lifted his head and said, "Nancy, before you nominate me for the man of the year, I should tell you there is a little more to the story that's not for publication because I'm not proud of it."

It was Nancy's turn to be startled as she sat with an expression of disbelief. In a concerned voice she asked, "What is it, Alex?"

Alex paused again, searching for the words to express what he was about to say. "Nancy, I told you about the hospice nurse who helped us in our home. Her name was Jo Ann Burke. She was very supportive with Beth and our family while we were going through our terrible ordeal. And while we were going through our ordeal, Jo Ann was going through one herself . . . her husband of twenty-five years had left her and her two children. I was losing my wife because of cancer, and she was losing her husband because of another woman."

Alex again gathered all his diplomatic skills as he tried to explain to Nancy this delicate revelation. He cleared his throat as he tried to speak clearly in a low, convincing voice. "We developed a special relationship that's difficult to describe and even harder to understand."

Nancy went from startled to shock. She sat frozen, staring at Alex. Nancy couldn't believe it was the same man of just a few moments ago who was so honorable. It was like a Jekyll and Hyde exposure. Alex seemed like two different characters, telling two different sides of his life at a critical time. The stories seemed contradictory. One account was of love and dedication to his wife and family right up to the very end, and the other tale was of a cheater on his wife's deathbed with the attending hospice nurse as the paramour.

It was apparent Alex was uncomfortable as he struggled to find the proper words to address this touchy subject. He glanced over toward the front entrance nervously as if he were looking for someone. He leaned forward toward Nancy, trying to be closer to her as he wished to confide a deep secret. "It started out innocently enough. We were both members of the same gym near where I lived. We ran into each other one night when we were both working out. She was a professional nurse and was very close to our family. I didn't think there was anything wrong with having a drink with this new friend of the family. I suggested we meet for a drink afterward at a nearby Applebee's."

The waitress suddenly appeared, bending over the table to pick up Alex's empty beer bottle and asked, "Would you like another Budweiser, sir?"

Alex looked puzzled for a moment, being in deep thought, then replied as if the answer just popped into his head, "Yes, I would like to have a Johnny Walker with water in a tall glass, please."

The waitress smiled, turning toward Nancy, and asked with a warm smile, "Would you like anything else, ma'am?"

Nancy glanced down at her half-empty glass of tonic seemingly to make a judgment. She replied quickly in a matter-of-fact tone. "No, I'm fine, thank you."

Alex paused as the waitress picked up his glass and napkin, then departed. He turned his attention toward Nancy. Before he could say a word, Nancy spoke. Her voice escalated in tone and sarcasm as she said, "Tell me more about this Jo Ann Burke,

Alex. How old is she? Is she attractive? Had her husband ever left her before, while she was working for a potential, grieving widower?"

Alex was startled by Nancy's comments. Before he could answer, Nancy spoke again, this time in an emotional, apologetic, warm voice, pleading, "Oh, I'm sorry, Alex. I didn't mean to be so judgmental. Please forgive me. It's just with my experiences in life, having had three husbands and a bunch of lovers and boyfriends; I've listened to so many lies and excuses. And to tell you the truth, Alex, I've made up just as many lies and excuses myself. Living in the foggy world of lies almost destroyed me. I've found it necessary to be skeptical of everyone. I know that's not fair to you, Alex, and I'm sorry."

Alex smiled at Nancy, saying, "You have a right to your opinion, Nancy. I know the cheaters' mantra: they are misunderstood, their spouse just doesn't understand them, and the marriage has been over for a long time anyway. And I'm not trying to make excuses for my behavior. You see I loved Beth. I wasn't misunderstood and, although not perfect, we had a good marriage. I was immersed in taking care of Beth. I wasn't out looking for love in all the wrong places, and I had no intention of betraying Beth."

The waitress returned with Alex's drink, bending slightly forward as she quietly placed a white napkin; then in the center of the napkin she placed the tall glass of Johnny Walker Red and water. She smiled at Alex and Nancy and quickly left the table.

Alex picked up the drink without looking at Nancy and took an unemotional sip. He stared directly at the glass he held in his hand. "She was ten years younger than me. Jo Ann would be considered attractive, not beautiful, but she would draw a certain amount of attention as she entered a room. She worked out at a gym a few times a week, so she had a nice body. And she was very easy to talk to," Alex said as he tried to describe Jo Ann in a low-key kind of way.

Alex put down the glass again and focused all his attention toward Nancy. "I had no intention of any extramarital affair. I don't think Jo Ann did either. We met by chance at the gym. I invited her to join me at Applebee's restaurant for a bite and a few drinks afterward. It was very innocent, and we talked about Beth most of the time. She knew and understood the intense circumstance my family and I were in. We knew her to be professional, kind, and considerate. She told me of her personal life and how devastated she was because her husband had just left her and her children for another woman. We'd see each other at the gym and went out for a few drinks. Off duty we shared our agony together. Everything was above board; I even told my daughters that I happened to see Jo Ann at the gym.

"One evening I went to the gym. We didn't have a date or anything like that, but Jo Ann was there, and we talked for a few minutes. I could tell something was wrong, and I asked her what it was. She said that one of her favorite patients had died that afternoon. She told me that usually death didn't have much effect on her, but this case was different. I asked if she would like to go to Applebee's for a drink. She said she couldn't because she had put something in the oven at home. She asked if I would I like to come to her house for a drink.

"I agreed, and we went to her home, which was just a few miles from the gym. She made me a scotch on the rocks, and it was a lot stronger than the drinks they serve at Applebee's. We sat and talked for a long time. She understood everything I was going through, and I listened to everything she had to say. We didn't tell each other what to do or how to feel. We both just listened."

Alex took a small sip of his drink, then smiled at Nancy and said, "We laughed at lot that night. I knew I was developing strong feelings toward Jo Ann, but she was our nurse, and I thought she was just being nice to me because I was her patient of sorts. Well, after we poured a few more drinks, we . . . we kind of poured our hearts out to each other. A simple, slow dance in the living room led to a complex tango in the bedroom," Alex said, half joking, using his almost forgotten boyish charm.

For Nancy, listening to Alex relate this event was like reliving one of his high school escapades, only now he had gray hair and a mature, weathered complexion, but he still retained his warm smile and those inviting, bright blue eyes.

"You were always a good dancer, Alex. It sounds like you added a few new steps to your dance repertoire," Nancy said with a chuckle.

Alex relaxed a little as he changed his composure and entered a somewhat serious mood. "It seemed like a terrible situation I was in. How could I be so disloyal to my dying wife? I was ashamed and seeking pleasure at the same time? I was living two lives. My daughters noticed a positive change in me and were very happy for me. I told them that going to the gym helped me feel a lot better, and that was partially true.

"I knew what I was doing was wrong, but at the same time it gave me something to look forward to. I became a better caregiver knowing I could escape from the constant, draining responsibilities for a little while and have my emotional batteries charged. I felt guilty and talked to Jo Ann about it. She told me it was quite common to have these feelings of detachment. It's called therapeutic transference; it often happens when one party in a strong relationship is dying. The pattern appears automatically, and the survivor unconsciously latches onto someone to replace the dying partner. It was quite common, like a patient falling in love with the therapist. In the old days, widowers would often marry their sister-in-law. Or like when Liz Taylor's husband was killed, she latched onto Eddie Fisher. The survivor naturally needs to go on, and this is nature's way of helping the living process."

Nancy listened patiently, then lifted her glass and took a sip of her tonic. She seemed relaxed as she spoke again this time, softly saying, "I understand about emotional transference. As a nurse I've seen a lot of it. I see men married for fifty years fall all over some unscrupulous nurse, and she takes him for a bundle."

"It wasn't like that with us, Nancy," Alex said quickly. "We were both honest and mature about our relationship. We were helping each other through our difficult times. She told me of some of her experiences dealing with bereaved families. She realized how delicate the relationship was. Jo Ann explained how a special bond develops while helping a family during the dying process—hearing the many personal stories and dealing with the emotional ups and downs during the final time together. If it weren't for the gym, I don't think anything would have happened."

"Are you still seeing her?" Nancy asked.

"No, we split up a long time ago," Alex said. "I believe it was good for me at the time, and it was good for her at the time. She helped me through a very difficult time of my life. And I think I helped her through a very difficult divorce. Her husband was a very successful contractor in the Philadelphia area and at one time made a lot of money. When he filed for divorce, he claimed he was broke. I helped direct her to a good lawyer who secured her marital rights with the children. And I helped secure a forensic accountant who audited him into a hefty financial settlement for her. With her new wealth and freedom, she wanted to do certain things in her life, and I wanted to do certain things in my life."

Alex paused for a moment, reflecting for a time, then added, "I heard this a long time ago: Some friends are here for life, some friends are here for a reason, and some friends are here for a season. I think Jo Ann was here for a reason."

Alex then perked up, saying, "Enough about me; let's hear about your life. How are you doing?"

At that point a distant, loud voice was heard. "Hey, what's going on here? Just like in high school, you two are squirreled up together talking to yourselves," Phil Whitman said as he walked toward their table with a big smile on his face.

Alex was up in a second as he briskly moved toward Phil. Alex reached out to shake Phil's hand, but Phil ignored the handshake and grabbed him in a large bear hug. "It's been a while. How have you been? Molly and I talk about you all the time. How have you been? Okay?" Phil said as he held Alex in a powerful embrace.

"I've been fine, Phil. Thanks for asking, and thanks for being a real friend. Especially these last few years your friendship has been so important to me. I'll never forget it," Alex said with deep conviction in his voice.

"Nancy, you're looking fine. It's so good to see you again," Phil said as he embraced her. She too was in for a big hug.

"It's nice to see you again, Phil." Nancy said in a jovial voice. "Of course I see you all around town. You're like the mayor. You seem to know everyone."

"Being a teacher here after all these years, I should know a lot of people," Phil said with a lively tone.

The trio sat at the table in a good mood, all smiling and enjoying the prospects of a fun weekend. Quickly and silently the three were taking notice of the changes in each other, even though no words were spoken. Alex and Nancy had already gone through the ritual, and now it was Phil's turn to be visually evaluated. They noticed Phil had lost much of his dark, curly hair; it retreated to a long, exposed, widow's peak style. His youthful physique and muscular upper body had seemed to drop and settle at his beltline.

The waitress arrived quickly on the scene with a friendly smile, placing a napkin in front of Phil. Then in a pleasant, uplifting voice, she asked, "Would anyone like a drink?"

Nancy and Alex both answered they were fine. Phil thought for a moment, saying with a laugh, "I'm almost retired, so I guess it's okay to drink in public. I'll have a Coors Light. Thank you."

Phil sat back in his chair, looking around the bar area. He lifted his right hand, waving at a few people he recognized. "Hi, how you doing?" he said with a large, animated smile as they returned the welcoming jester with equally friendly acknowledgments. He seemed to be in his element, enjoying the ambiance of the place and the harmony of the people.

The waitress was back with Phil's drink and placed the napkin neatly on the table. Alex signaled at the waitress and said, "You can put that on my tab." He then smiled at Phil, saying, "I know you teachers don't like to give out high grades or pay for drinks."

"Why, thank you, Alex. Your appreciation of my public service is greatly appreciated," Phil said jokingly as he lifted his glass of beer in a humorous sign of respect toward Alex.

Phil took in a deep breath as he surveyed the surroundings, remarking in a happy, inquisitive voice, "Just think over the years how many people came in and out of this place, how many friendships were developed here. And I guess a few friendships probably ended here. But if these walls could only talk, they could tell some funny stories. We could hear a lot of laughs and maybe hear some sad stories as well. We've had our share of good times here . . . so tonight let's make it a good time like we used to do!"

"Hear, hear!" both Nancy and Alex said as they lifted their drinks to Phil.

Nancy then added, "Phil, a popular fellow around here."

"Living here all my life, I guess I do know them." Phil said.

"Being a teacher here all of these years, you've probably had most of them in class," Alex said.

"I've taught a lot of them. And I've been teaching for a long time, maybe too long," Phil said.

"When do you plan to retire, Phil?" Nancy asked.

"I will become a 'used to be' in a few years," Phil said as he picked up his drink in a triumphal manner.

Alex had a puzzled look on his face as he asked Phil, "A 'used to be'? What's that?"

"You're a 'used to be,' Alex," Phil said, smiling and looking directly over at Alex.

Alex was startled by the comment but acknowledged the familiar smirk on Phil's face. It was an image Alex recognized that went way back to their younger days when Phil was trying to be funny and sarcastic at the same time.

"A 'used to be' is someone who's retired. He used to be a truck driver. He used to be a brain surgeon or a housepainter. He used to be . . . Now when someone asks what you do for a living, he merely says, 'I used to be a . . . they are no longer a housepainter, a brain surgeon or a truck driver. They are no longer players in the arena of their expertise. They are members of the biggest club in the world, the 'used to be' club, where everyone is on the same level. They now are used to be's."

"So Phil, you're going to join the club of the 'used to be' in a few years? Any regrets?" Alex asked as if returning the verbal barb.

Phil sat silently, contemplating his answer for a moment, and then said, "I'm glad I chose to be a teacher. But there are a few things I would have done differently if I had it to do over. For one, I would have joined the military. I would have liked the experience of serving with diverse people of assorted backgrounds. I grew up here, went to college near here, and I taught school here all these years. When you think about it, I've been in school here all my life. I've not experienced what it is to live anywhere but here, never had the unpredictably of living and working in a different community. I live in the McDermott's old house three streets over from my parent's home. Everyone here seems to live in someone else's old home. Everywhere you go or everything you do, you see the same people day after day, year after year, family after family. In this area we grew up together knowing everyone we came in contact with—and their brothers and sisters, their parents, and sometimes even aunts and uncles. Now I see their extended, married families with grown kids and grandkids. Everyone seems to be related to someone. It's like living in a small pond, seeing fish making other fish, making other fish."

Phil's posture stiffened, and his eyes opened wide in a distant stare as he gazed around the bar, viewing the crowd that seemed to be slowly growing in numbers and noise. "Wednesday evening before Thanksgiving was the biggest night of the year for me, and it was a thrill just to go to the bars to see who was in town," Phil said in an entrancing, dramatic voice. "That's the night everyone would come home for the holiday. This was the only time I would get to see so many people who had left here. They came back from all over the country. They would tell me what they were doing in their careers and what it was like living places I'd only read about or saw on TV. I was so happy to see my friends and later students who were out in the world doing exciting things."

Phil paused for a moment, picking up his drink and staring at it just before he took a sip. Then he added, "It feels as though I lived all my life in the shadow of a big tree. It was comfortable and secure, but I would always be near the shadow of that tree. Sometimes I think I missed out on some of the excitement in life that existed far away. And now it's too late to venture away from the security and comfort of living here."

Phil hesitated for a moment, taking another sip of his beer. He seemed to be in deep thought as he continued—as if he were trying to remember a forgotten story. He said, "But there was a time when I almost got out of here, and I sometimes wonder about . . . I had just started teaching. That winter Carl Lohman and I went up to Newbury, Massachusetts, skiing. We had a great time; I loved it there. I went back a few times that winter, making friends with the locals. I was offered a job selling Jostens class rings to area schools. I was all set to take the job and move up to Massachusetts, to live in a distant state and work in a different career. But back here in the excitement of getting my plan working, I celebrated a little too much. Molly became pregnant, and we got married, and I've been here ever since. I don't regret it. I've had a great life here, but sometimes . . . not often . . . but sometimes I wonder."

Nancy asked Phil, "I always thought it was great to stay in the area. You certainly have many friends here."

Phil replied quickly, "Living here does have its advantages; there's no traffic jams. The area is beautiful with the surrounding mountains and rivers. But the winters are tough, especially January and February. And living all these years with the locals can drive you buggy too."

It was Alex's turn to ask, "What do you mean living here with the locals?" Phil picked up his drink, smiling and taking a sip, he said, "Some of the people around here have such a negative attitude, and they are the nosiest, most gossipy people you ever want to meet. They are narrow-minded, misinformed bigots, and they don't listen to reason. They vote for the most corrupt politicians in the country. Nothing is good enough around here. If you want to really ski, you have to go to Vermont. If you need medical treatment, you must go to Philadelphia. If you want to dress properly, don't buy locally; no, go to New York. Your kids have to go out of town to college. The only thing you can get locally . . . is a haircut!"

"I can see why you didn't leave teaching and open a business," Alex said jokingly.

"Oh, don't get me started on the constant complaining they do about buying something," Phil said as he continued his tirade. "We always are being screwed by somebody or some company. If you say you're going to buy a new set of tires, they'll say, 'Don't buy them at Summit Tire, they'll screw you.' Or if you want to buy a new TV, you will hear the same thing; 'Don't buy it at Sears; they'll screw you," or don't buy it at such and such, they'll screw you. Just remember around here, every business is out to screw you."

Phil laughed as he said in a mocking manner, "Those companies are in business just to make money!" He paused, then laughed and said, "What other reason is there to be in business except to make money!"

"Well, Phil, your job as a teacher is to 'learn them how' to live a better life," Alex said jokingly.

"I am glad that career is coming to the end, not too soon either," Phil said in a serious tone. "Times have changed so much since I started teaching. The qualification for teaching is becoming so highly specialized you can't teach any subject you are not certified in, and you need a master's degree in that particular subject. And you must be politically correct at all times and be so legally mindful of everything you say and do in and out of school. Many parents treat us like adversaries. Nowadays you have to be especially careful about what you say or do in a classroom. No joking or zany comments. Some kid, without you knowing it, can video you with his cell phone, and he has all the evidence."

Alex happened to glance over toward the front entrance and noticed a familiar silhouette entering the front entrance. He stared over at it for a moment before he realized who it was. It was Danny Fredrick. Alex recognized him immediately as he stood at the bar, gawking as if he was looking for someone in particular. He stood for a moment, tall, rigid and aloof with that perpetual chip on his shoulder, thus adding to his image. He was dressed quite fashionable in a double-breasted, camel-hair overcoat, with a black, woven cashmere scarf. His long hair was brushed back, styled with the Wall Street look. Judging by his demeanor, he was looking about for someone who must be important. It didn't take Danny long to spot the table where Alex and the trio were seated. He walked briskly across the floor.

"Hello, everybody," Danny said as he walked up smartly, addressing the table. He reached out to shake the hands of Alex and Phil as they rose to greet him. Nancy was on her feet with her arms open to give Danny a warm embrace. After the greetings were exchanged the four sat at the table to continue the night's festivities.

After they were comfortably seated, Alex spoke first. "Danny, it's been a long time since I've seen you. Tell us what you have been doing all these years."

Phil belted out, "Please, the Reader's Digest version."

Looking directly at Phil, Danny said mockingly, "Condensed versions for condensed minds."

Nancy injected her calm, humorous voice, saying, "Now, boys, we are here to have a fun night. Let's not pick up where we left off."

At that time the waitress was at the table, and Alex ordered a round of drinks as he said, "I'll have the same. Phil, do you want the same?"

Phil nodded his head, and Nancy's glass still had a lot of tonic in it. The waitress took a quick look toward Danny.

"I will have a Chivas Regal on the rocks." Danny said in a cool manner.

Nancy spoke up quickly and asked, "Danny, do you still play the guitar or play in a band anymore?"

"I gave up my dream of a musical career a long time ago," Danny said with a whimsical tone. "But I still play the guitar a little, and on the weekends I sometimes play with a little group where I live."

"Where's that?" Alex asked.

"Sanford, a little town in Maine," Danny said off the cuff and then added matter-of-factly, "I've lived there about fifteen years now. It's a nice little town."

"The last time we talked, you were in the water bed business; you had a store in Connecticut. Are you still doing that?" Alex asked.

"No, I sold that business a long time ago. I've been in furniture sales for over ten years now. It's a great business, very profitable. I've been very lucky if you know what I mean," Danny said very confidently.

"So Danny, you kind of liquidated your water bed store, did you?" Phil said, half laughing. Alex and Nancy joined the chuckle.

"Yeah, I sold the store, Phil!" Danny replied quickly and scornfully. He continued in a rough manner, "You see, Phil, I was what you call an 'entrepreneur,' which means one who takes a risk in business. I went out in the world and worked for a living. I didn't work in a school building all my life where job security is the number one objective."

"They almost had to burn the schoolhouse down to get you out." Phil said, laughing again.

Nancy jumped in again, trying to referee the sarcastic bantering. "Now boys, or I should say you two old coots, tonight we're here for a good time." To break up the tension, Nancy asked quickly, "What does 'LSMFT' mean?"

"Lucky Strikes Means Fine Tobacco," Alex said quickly and proudly.

"Here all these years I thought it meant Lord save me from Truman," Phil said jokingly. He then added as he got up, "Even the lord can't save me from bodily functions. I have to go to the men's room. I'll be right back after I check the newspapers on the floor." They chuckled again.

As soon as Phil was out of sight, Danny said, "I like Phil, but sometimes he gets on my nerves. He can be funny, but he can also be kind of sarcastic." In a perceptive tone Alex replied, "You may have hit a nerve when you said Phil spent all his life in a school.' You see, Phil may have some regrets in life about living here all his life."

The cute waitress delivered the drinks. Alex told her to put the drinks on his tab as he continued talking to Danny. "So you can see, Danny, Phil may be a little sensitive, especially tonight. He sees people coming in from all over the country. He has never left the area, and sometimes he feels as if he's missing out in life."

"Yeah, I hear what you're saying, Alex." Danny said as he picked up his Chivas Regal, taking a long sip. "Phil's like a hot dog on a bun; he hasn't changed a bit in all these years."

Danny took another large sip of his scotch. "To me, Phil had it pretty easy in life. He's had a job all these years and has never missed a paycheck. He's never been laid off or fired from a job. He's never stood in an unemployment line. He didn't have to go on job interviews that were a waste of time. His mother worked for the school district, and he didn't get his job on his ability; he got it because of his connections. The only way anyone gets a job around here is because of family or political connections. Just think for a minute about all the kids we went to school with. If their family had a business or a profession like a doctor or lawyer, after their education they would come back here and work for them. But the other kids without connections, who were some of the best and brightest, had to go off and build their careers, growing companies in other parts of the country. The ones who remained here didn't need to be that good because their family connections got them their jobs. People around here don't have a competitive business attitude; they have an inherited business attitude. That's why businesses here are second rate. Their motto is 'We don't have to be that good . . . because we are here!'"

Danny was upset as he spoke. He took another long sip of his drink and continued talking, "You know a few years ago when I had my band, we traveled all over the country in all the major cities doing the hotel-motel circuit. During the show we would announce we were from Scranton, Pennsylvania. You would be amazed how many people would come up to the bandstand to tell us what part of the Scranton area they were from. They would ask if we knew so and so. And then they would tell us where they were born and raised, or tell us about their careers or the key positions they held with large companies. They're working other parts of the world because there are no jobs here."

"Danny, that's not Phil's fault," Nancy said.

"I know," Danny said in a remorseful tone. "I guess it's the crooked politicians, the unions, or the heavy snowfall, but something is keeping this area from developing. And that's my gripe about this area. Nothing seems to be happening around here."

"There are changes, Danny," Alex said. "I agree that around here things seem to go a lot slower. I remember as a small child we didn't have a phone. We would go to our neighbor across the street to use their big, old, crank phone. Now I have a smartphone that does everything but cook my breakfast."

Nancy said jokingly, "Now, Alex, you're really dating yourself."

"I'm just saying things have changed a lot in fifty years, even here," Alex said.

Danny relaxed and said, "I'm just saying, look at the three of us. We had to go and live in other places, only coming back home for visits. And I must say living and trying to raise a family in a faraway town can be lonely at times."

Danny's head turned right and left, looking over both shoulders, to ensure no one could hear as he leaned forward and in a low voice said, "I trust you both, so please don't say anything to anyone else." He again looked around before he continued. "Twelve years ago I went broke in the water bed business. It was a terrible time; I lost everything I had. There was no one to turn to. For a long time, I couldn't get a job anywhere. I was so embarrassed. You can imagine what it's like to see your name in a newspaper filing for bankruptcy—seeing in print that you're a failure and realizing other people you know are reading that same newspaper, then trying to avoid your neighbors and friends and business people you know. I felt so low and worthless; I had no real friends to turn to. Oh, I had some surface-level friends but no true, deep-rooted friends like those who exist in a small town—the kind of friend who accepts you the way you are, because they know how you really are on the inside, not the image with an expensive hairstyle, the jewelry, expensive clothes, and the other trappings that create a façade of the person the outside world thinks you are. I learned the hard way. There are no friends like school friends. It was a rough, lonely couple of years before I got back on my feet again. It was the worst time in my life. And please, I don't want anyone to know. It hurts just to think about it." Danny lowered his head, staring at the table.

Nancy reached across the table, gently grasping Danny's hand. With a tender smile and a warm, comforting voice, she said, "Danny, in everyone's life there are secrets. It's best if we keep them hidden under the spare tire in the trunk of our car. No one cares to look there."

Nancy's mood lifted, and with a light, jovial voice, she said warmly, "Danny, you're like a big old salmon with a few scars that has returned to the little pond you swam away from many years ago. In our little pond, there are other big old salmon with their own scars or glory ribbons swimming around. No one notices nor cares. We are just happy to see the familiar salmon we grew up with back in the pond and enjoying the swim."

One look into her eyes and Danny knew she understood pain, indignity, heartbreak, and redemption. Danny was pleasantly surprised with the concerned kindness and wisdom Nancy had extended to him. At that moment Danny had an epiphany of what true friends do.

"Now this is a sight for sore eyes," a familiar voice rang out. The trio at the table was startled and quickly glanced at the sudden intruder. It was Tommy Wilkinson, standing with his arm around Phil Whitman. Tommy stood tall, full of life. He still had the bright, clear, sparkling eyes; a big, radiant smile; and a flock of bushy, sandy-colored hair. Wearing a buckskin jacket, he resembled an old cowboy without the ten-gallon hat.

The five were all on their feet, exchanging greetings and exchanging short stories about each other and other friends and relatives. After a few moments, they all sat down as the waitress reappeared. "Would anyone like a drink?"

"I would like another drink, please." Danny said politely.

"Was that Chivas Regal, sir?" the waitress asked.

Danny nodded his head slightly as if not trying to draw attention. He then said in a low, polite voice, "Please put this round on my tab. Thank you."

Nancy passed on a refresher, but Alex and Phil ordered their drinks. Next the waitress, with pen in hand, glanced toward Tommy for his order, saying, "Sir, what would you like?"

A hush came over the table as Tommy placed his drink order. "I would like a club soda with a twist of lemon, please."

"Straight club soda!" Phil asked.

"Yes, straight club soda, Phil," Tommy said without emotion. But he continued speaking in an uplifting way, "Today I'm not drinking any alcohol, but that shouldn't stop any of the festivities of the night. So let's party on. It's kind of quiet around here. Where are the honeymooners, Meldew and Johnny?"

Phil was somewhat reluctant to speak, but he broke the silence, saying, "Melody and Johnny divorced about seven years ago."

"That's shocking," Tommy said in a serious but humorous tone. He then added, "That's shocking she stayed with him that long." All laughed for a moment.

"Unfortunately Melody had some kind of medical problem," Phil said as he lowered his voice and his head as he looked down at the floor. Phil cleared his throat and continued speaking in a sensitive tone that seemed foreign and difficult for him, "Apparently she developed a blood clot in her leg. A short time later, she had to have her left leg amputated. This just added to the pile of problems they already had."

Then Tommy said in a more somber voice, "Actually I'm sorry to hear that they split up. I didn't know of all these tribulations they were going through."

Phil again spoke in a serious tone, "About nine years ago his oldest son, George, died of a drug overdose. After that they both changed a lot. He continued to gamble and lost everything, and she became more reclusive. She found someone new, and he is now back to being the same old Johnny."

"Tell us about what you've been doing, Tommy!" Alex blurted out.

Nancy's voice broke the mood when she asked, "Tommy, did you ever get remarried?"

"No, never did. I was kind of holding out for you, Nancy," Tommy said, glancing over at Nancy with a big smile.

"I'm ready if you're ready," she said jokingly.

"Never mind about romancing Nancy. That can wait till later. Go on with your story; what have you been doing with your life?" Alex said.

"Where do I begin?" Tommy said. He sat motionless for a moment; then he began speaking like a fine storyteller. "The last pipeline project I worked on was a hundred ten miles of twenty-four-inch pipe for Shell Oil in Nigeria. In case you didn't know, Phil, Nigeria is in Africa," Tommy said jokingly as he looked over at Phil with an inquisitive smile.

"I know where Nigeria is, Tommy," Phil shot right back with his quick wit. "I have a friend who lives in Nigeria, and his family is entitled to a large sum of money. And I'm helping him get it out of the country. In fact, I just sent him my banking information that he needed to complete the deal."

All at the table sat still for a moment until Phil started to chuckle.

Tommy continued with his story. "This was before cell phones, and out there in the boondocks, we had no landline phones. Our only means of communication was by radio. You could not get through to the States on radio, so we had to drive almost forty miles just to use a phone. On a trip like that, we had to hide money in various parts of the vehicle, because there were so many roadblocks by the military and bandits; if you didn't have any money to bribe them, they might shoot you. I worked in a lot of places and conditions, the winters of the north slope of Alaska in minus-seventy degrees and the deserts of Saudi Arabia in one hundred forty degrees. I worked in the mountains of Chile, and the jungles of Brazil and Malaysia, but I never worked in a more frightening place than Nigeria. After that project I quit and went to South Carolina to start my own business. We used a spray on polyurethane insulation on some of the pipelines I worked on. So I started a plastic company using that technology for other applications."

"Is that what you are doing now?" Alex asked.

"I'm kind of semiretired. My son is running the company now. And I thought I would like to travel around a little," Tommy said.

"I hope your kids are better than mine," Phil said, shaking his head. Then he continued in a lighthearted way, almost chuckling. "My kids are like alligators; they have bulging eyes that see everything I do. Little ears, that are used selectively and big mouths to let me know how smart they are, and they have very thin skin, seems they are very sensitive about any advice, and they have short arms that come in mighty handy, when the check comes at a restaurant."

"Tommy, I would have thought you traveled enough in your lifetime," Nancy said.

"Well, I just returned from a trip out in Montana, Wyoming, and the Dakotas. I had a great time out there. I got to see what I believe is some of the most beautiful scenery in the world. It was spectacular, and it's right here in the U. S. of A."

"So you liked traveling out West better than traveling in all those exotic places you've been?" Alex asked

"Yeah, I sure do," Tommy said as he sipped his club soda. "Out west everyone speaks English . . ."

There seemed to be a slight commotion at the front entrance. It was Johnny Thompson. As he entered he seemed to be talking to almost everyone in the place. He was like a local folk hero of sorts. But the real reason people acknowledged and greeted Johnny was due to the fact that so many people had dealt with him at one time or another. Not everyone liked Johnny's strong personality, but almost everyone had a personal story they could tell about dealing with him. They may have bought fuel at his gas station, utilized his towing or road service, or had their vehicle repaired at his garage. Or they may have shopped in his general store, which sold just about everything including fireworks, life jackets, TVs, appliances, and Cabbage Patch Kids.

Johnny could usually be found at his store morning, noon, or night with his unique personality. He still had that sign over the cash register proclaiming, "Attitudes adjusted while you wait." This sign, along with a few other proprietary symbols, seemed to capture the core of Johnny's business sentiment. Not all of Johnny's customers were happy customers, but he did maintain a steady flow of business throughout the years. There was an unspoken belief in town that if you ever dealt with Johnny, you'd never forgot him.

Over the years Johnny had built up his business. In fact, he had developed two distinct businesses: one, the small, country-type department store with gas pumps; the other, auto repair and towing. The towing business was operated in an unusual manner. All his tow trucks had the appropriate large booms with flashing lights. They were distinctly painted bright red and white (his business colors) with large company logos. Johnny made a lot of money with these towing trucks. He got people out of ditches and other places where they were not supposed to be. He helped other customers in very delicate incidences. Sometimes he was the first one at a vehicle accident rendering service that proved to be helpful and discretionarily valuable, such as providing a cup of coffee or other items that could freshen up one's breath. Johnny developed many loyal customers and a number of grateful, mysterious ones as well. It seems the towing business had a off the record element that could be quite profitable if one remained discreet and confidential. To some around town, Johnny was a combination of the Godfather and the Fonz. Johnny and his business were well-known in the area. Not everyone liked him, but everyone had a humorous, personal story they could tell about their dealings with Johnny.

Johnny spoke to almost everyone as he slowly made his way to the table. He hadn't changed much over the years. His piercing, catlike eyes with a slight twinkle were the same as in his senior picture as was his signature, condescending smile. And he still had his prominent unique hairstyle—a partial flattop with the sides brushed up toward the back, thus exhibiting his infamous "wedge head" look. He carried himself like an agile athlete. His tapered waist and broad shoulders indicated he was in good shape for a man his age. He was dressed like he was going to a high school dance, wearing khaki slacks, a blue blazer, and a blue, button-down oxford shirt.

"I'm glad you came out to see me," Johnny said in a loud, joking voice as he got close to the table.

"We could hardly wait," Phil said loudly. "That's why I'm considering leaving!" "If you're leaving, Phil, it's because it's your turn to buy!" Johnny said in his loud, sarcastic, jovial voice.

"Not everyone has your wealth, Johnny," Phil replied.

"Well, Phil if you can't play a sport . . . at least be a sport!" Johnny said.

Everyone extended handshakes, hugs, and good greetings. After the commotion settled down, Alex and Johnny were standing together. Alex leaned over toward Johnny lowering his voice in a serious manner saying, "I was sorry to hear about you and Melody breaking up."

By this time Johnny had a drink in his hand and used it like a prop as he looked directly into Alex's eyes. Johnny said coolly, "We didn't just break up, Alex. We used to break up when we were in high school. As adults we got married, had children, and stayed married for a long time. And now we are divorced. And life goes on." Johnny took a long sip of his drink, then said in a lighter, joyful voice. "And you know me, Alex . . . I'll make the best of it."

"Knowing you, Johnny, you have already been making the best of it," Alex said lightly.

Now it was Johnny's turn to inquire. He put on his serious face, asking, "How are you doing, Alex? I know it must be tough for you and your kids after losing Beth. How are you holding up? It's been a few years now; have you dated or met anyone yet?"

"I've had a few dates, but nothing seems to interest me much," Alex replied and asked, "How about you, Johnny? Are you dating?"

Johnny looked around the bar to make sure no one was listening to their conversation, as if anyone would care anyway. Johnny started talking as if he were lecturing, "The dating scene is an altogether new thing nowadays. And at our age, there are family considerations you have to deal with. When we were younger, we had to impress the girl's parents, being pleasant, considerate, and well mannered, at least in front of them. Now you have to play that scene all over again, only now you have her kids and grandkids that you have to please and make a good impression on. But in all honesty, the children are happy just to have Mom going out with anyone. With mature women you can ask, if we have a good time tonight, should I call you in the morning for breakfast or nudge you?"

"I don't know, Johnny; I don't seem to have the same charm you have. I've gone out a few times, and I haven't found anyone who interests me," Alex said with a disheartened tone. "I guess I'm pretty well set in my ways, and the women I've met were pretty well set in their ways. Let's face it, people our age aren't looking for someone to build a life with. They're looking more for companionship, which means someone who is practical. And I'm not at the practical level yet. I am still a dreamer when it comes to women."

"Have you tried the Internet?" Johnny quickly asked. Then he added, "I've heard that's a good way to meet someone. I've known a few people who have success doing that."

Alex picked up his drink, taking a taste, and reflected for a moment. Then as if searching for the correct words, he said, "I've tried the Internet and found some very nice women. But they are in Philadelphia, Harrisburg, or some other town. If I were to get serious with one of these women, it would mean being introduced to this lady's lifestyle in her town with her friends, children, and family. It is too confusing and time-consuming to figure all this out. Johnny, I'm at a time in my life when I want to enjoy as much as possible. I've lost a lot of my desire for adventure and excitement. I want to explore life in a comfortable, joyful way in familiar surroundings. So if I were to select anyone, I would like her to be from around here so we could talk about the people we grew up with. We could enjoy a full life in the community we live in. As I said, Johnny, I'm still a dreamer, and if I'm to meet someone, it will happen. In the meantime I'm enjoying a great life."

Alex picked up his drink, offering it to Johnny to clink glasses in a toast. They both enjoyed a large swallow. Alex then turned to Johnny and asked, "and how are you doing? It must have been difficult after being married all those years."

Johnny emptied his drink and signaled over to the waitress to bring them two more drinks. He stared briefly into a far-off space and then said thoughtfully, "Alex, Melody and I had a lot of what I called the 'magic years.' You could say they were too magic. Business was very good, and I was making a lot of money. Melody and the kids had everything they wanted—new cars, a nice house in the country, swimming pool, horses, and all the toys the kids wanted. We traveled around the country in a large Winnebago. We had a good life. Then the kids got involved in drugs, and the magic of the good years seemed to disappear." Johnny hesitated for a moment, looking directly at Alex, then added, "Sometimes we cause the very thing we're trying to prevent."

The waitress was back with the drinks and placed them neatly on the table. Alex and Johnny both picked up their glasses and took a sip, waiting for Johnny to continue.

"Alex, I spent a fortune on those kids, in and out of rehab centers, and that money was the least of it. I spent hundreds of thousands of dollars on bribes to police and judges up and down the valley. I wanted to draw a line and try to put an end to it. But Melody insisted we do everything possible to protect our kids. It caused a rift in our marriage and ended up when our oldest son, George, died of a drug overdose."

Johnny eyes welled up as he continued, "I know a part of each of us died with George. When a tragedy like that happens in a marriage, each one needs the help and support from the other. But if there is a rift in the marriage, and the gap is too large to breach, it can have a devastating effect. We were like a high-flying trapeze act. We needed and trusted each other all throughout our married life, but when George died we weren't there for each other. We faltered and crashed. Our high-flying routine was over. Our marriage cord became so twisted and tied up in knots, it became unbearable for the kids, Melody, and me. The stress of it all caused us to grip harder and harder on this twisted marriage cord, straining it with so much tension, pulling so tightly that the knots could never be untangled."

Johnny paused, took another drink, and continued, "We could not untie what had happened. Therefore, for the kids' sake, divorce was the right thing to do. They wanted the money, so I gave it to them. I tried to be fair about it. But I'm sure Melody would have a different view. She and I are on a kind of friendly cord now, but the knots are still there and twisted very tightly, so we avoid them."

Johnny paused for a moment, taking another sip of his drink. He then continued. "It was a tough, lonely couple of years. There were many times I wished we could return to those magic years. But as they say, 'You can't paddle up the river of life,' especially after Melody went off with some guy she met through the horsy set. He has a farm up near Hallstead." Johnny paused again, taking another sip of his drink. He took in a large breath, and then in a deep low voice, he said, "To tell you the truth, Alex, I never thought I would ever fall in love again. But one thing is for certain, we don't know what the future is . . . and that's for certain."

"You thought you'd never fall in love again?" Alex asked, surprised.

Johnny's spirit lifted as he replied, "There I was all alone after thirty years of marriage, a broken man facing a bleak, lonely future. There was this woman I had known over the years on a casual basis. She became a close friend, and then as sudden as a heart attack, I was in love. She's a beautiful woman. I tell you, Alex, I felt like a prisoner out on good behavior. I didn't think it was possible at my age, but I was like a teenager in love, complete with all the desire and excitement of the young and foolish. And our sex life was better than my teenage years, and that's saying something. I felt like a salmon swimming in the fresh headwaters, regenerating not only my youthful spirit but a new love interest beyond anything I could have dreamed of."

Johnny paused for a moment, taking another sip of his drink and readying his mind to continue his saga. "And to tell you the truth, Alex, the sexual part was only a part of the attraction. Just to go out with her, I'd get all dressed up like I was going to a high school dance. I wanted to make sure wherever we went it was a first-class restaurant, and she appreciated every little thing I did for her. We're having a great time. We laugh together about silly things. Sometimes we just break out in sporadic laughter because of a gesture or what someone else says. We seem to talk for hours about everything. Some of our conversations are deep; others are simply fun and just about anything we care to talk about. And we don't end up in an argument if we disagree about something. We get along so well and have so much fun. I sometimes wonder what my life could have been if I had met her years ago. It's so refreshing to have someone in my life who enjoys being around me. And when we are not together, we're like teenagers on the cell phone all hours of the day or night. And now we're even texting. Would you believe it? I remember when you would never go anywhere without cigarettes. Now you won't go anywhere without your cell phone."

"It seems like you are very happy with this woman," Alex said.

"Her name is Sandy Lewis. You remember her; she had red hair. She was a few years behind us in high school. She lived on Electric Street. She's divorced with two grown daughters," Johnny said.

He continued, "We're very happy together; even my kids say they haven't seen me this happy in years. When you think about it, Alex, I've been lucky in life. I've passionately loved two women, and they both have loved me. Melody's chosen another, and that was sad; but Sandy has chosen me, and that's very good. We are at a comfortable time in life, no real pressure; our kids are grown, and we don't have to scrimp and save for the future. We are in good health, and we both have a few bucks to do whatever we want. Sandy loves and accepts me the way I am . . . she even chuckles at my irritating, little 'quink a kinks' and tolerates my shortcomings, if any, and she knows I'm too old to change. And she's okay with everything we do."

"I bought a nice convertible, and I tell you, Alex, it's taken twenty years off my life. Sandy and I go driving whenever we can up to Towanda or the Poconos. It doesn't matter as long as we're together. We have so much fun together, more than I thought possible. Like they say, Alex, life isn't over till it's over."

"Are you going to marry her, Johnny?" Alex asked.

"Love is blind, but the sight returns soon after the marriage ceremony," Johnny said, chuckling. He thought for a moment, then answered, "I used to tell my kids, 'Don't get married unless you have to.' Now I don't mean that the girl has to be pregnant. The point is don't get married if you're comfortable being away from the other person. But if you're miserable without each other, and you can't stand to be separated, then you have to get married. So Alex, I am nearing the have-to-get-married point of our relationship. But for now we're at a nice stage. I tell her, 'I don't have to lie to you because we're not married,' and we're having so much fun, I don't want to ruin a good thing."

Tommy smiled at Nancy and asked, "Nancy, are you a friend of Bill W.?"

Nancy returned an equally friendly smile and replied, "Yes, I am, Tommy. I've been in the program for almost fifteen years now, and I noticed you don't drink either."

Alex was a little confused, and it showed by the expression on his face. "Who's Bill W., and what program are you in, Nancy?" Alex asked.

Both Nancy and Tommy chuckled as Nancy cleared her throat and spoke in a light, whimsical manner, saying, "Bill W. is short for Bill Wilson, the founder of Alcoholics Anonymous, which is what some folks call the 'program' so now you know our little secret Alex."

Alex seemed a little embarrassed or uncomfortable as he said, "I didn't mean to pry or anything."

Tommy was quick to set Alex at ease. He went on to explain, "There are times when I am at a cocktail party or social gathering and someone isn't drinking, perhaps is a little nervous. Instead of going up and asking, 'Are you in AA?,' I merely ask politely, 'Are you a friend of Bill W's?' If they don't know who Bill W is, I just carry on with some small talk. But many delighted eyes have replied positively with a warm smile, which means they have just made an instant friend who shares a mutual bond. You know I've met a lot of nice people that way."

"How about you, Tommy? How long have you been a friend of Bill W's?" Nancy asked.

"This sounds like it may be a little personal; maybe you two would like some private time," Alex said.

Nancy and Tommy answered in unison, saying, "We're fine, Alex. Yeah, we're okay."

"Hang around, Alex, you may learn something; we certainly have," Tommy said.

"Oh well, I promised Alex I would tell him all about my in-between years and what has happened since our last reunion." Nancy seemed comfortable and relaxed as she sat back, readying herself to tell her story. She smiled over at her two listeners as she began to speak, "As I look back over my life, I think of how high my expectations were on the highway to happiness, but I didn't stay on that road long; I think I got off at the first exit."

Tommy sat quietly, taking it all in. He drew in a deep breath as an indication that he was going to speak. "I started drinking in my senior year in high school. Although it was illegal, we would get a couple of quarts of beer and drink them in my dad's car. In the beginning it was fun, filled with a lot of laughs and good times. We were young and enjoying ourselves; we drank occasionally just to have a good time," Tommy said in an uplifting manner.

He became serious when the continued talking. "When I joined the Army and then was stationed overseas, I went into high gear drinking; after all I was an adult and drinking was what everybody did whenever we could. When I came home, I drank every day, every night, and in-between. Those first few years after I came home were the wild ones, or as I call them, my turbulent years. When I think back about the trouble I caused, how many cars I wrecked, how many people I upset because of my drinking . . ."

Tommy paused for a moment, shaking his head. "In two years I wrecked eleven cars, was thrown in jail, embarrassed my family, and ended a few friendships. But it didn't matter; I was having a good time—at least I thought I was. But I didn't need a drink in the morning . . .only alcoholics did that. I sobered up enough to go to college, although I drank and partied all through college and most of my young adult life. When I started my business career, drinking was part of the everyday working ritual. And I thought everything was all right with me and boozing . . . well, almost all right. Sometimes I would wake up in the morning with a hangover, feeling lousy, and say to myself, 'I hope I had a good time last night, because it cost me a lot of money.' Like a lot of people, I considered myself a social drinker. So if someone said they'd like to have a drink, I would pipe up and say, so shall I.

"My drinking went from wanting a few drinks just to have a good time to needing a few drinks just to get along. I noticed I required more drinks to get to my comfortable level of feeling good. With a few extra drinks, I was funnier and much more intelligent and, I believed, even more charming. I befriended people who drank and avoided those who didn't drink.

"Having a few drinks at the end of every day became an unbreakable routine. And I didn't want to go to any function, whether it was a baptism, graduation, or funeral, where there was not any booze. I remember one time a coworker commented to me that, perhaps, sometimes I drank a little too much and suggested that I be careful because, he said, 'You don't want to end up with a drinking problem.' I told him I was aware of alcohol and the potential problems it could cause, and I told him I was keeping my drinking under control. And of course that was a complete lie. I felt that this was my life, and I could live it the way I wanted. After all I wasn't hurting anyone but myself. But don't ask my wife or my boss; they may have a different viewpoint. They saw the effects, you might say, up close and personal."

Tommy smiled, shaking his head and lifting his right hand as if to emphasize a point. "Now this is when I started to smarten up. In front of other people, I pretended that booze wasn't that important. I'd put ice in my beer, or I'd switch to wine to sip on. But when I got home, I would make a real drink the way I liked them: strong! Then late one night I was leaving a restaurant. I pulled out onto the highway and had a little fender bender. The other driver insisted we call the police. When the cop showed up, he did a few tests and off to the police station for a blood test. Now I'm not usually good at taking tests, but on that one I scored pretty high with an alcohol level of 3.2. Fortunately for me it was a small town in Oklahoma, so I got a good lawyer and worked around it."

Tommy sat back, and a serious look took shape on his face. "I was drinking quite heavily, but so what; if you only knew the problems I had, you'd drink too. I was lying to myself and everyone else about my drinking. It was about this time that my marriage started to fall apart. I remember driving somewhere while listening to the radio, and I heard a song by Johnny Cash titled 'Sunday Morning Coming Down.' The opening lines resonated deep in my soul as I felt those lonely words, 'Well I woke up Sunday morning with no way to hold my head that didn't hurt and the beer I had for breakfast wasn't bad, so I had one more for dessert.' After hearing that song, I remember looking in the mirror and seeing a sad, puffy-faced, red-eyed character looking back at me. I was frustrated because I had tried so hard to control my drinking but it only got worse. I thought I was so clever at hiding bottles in my luggage, the trunk of my car and the basement. I started avoiding people in general, especially those who didn't drink. I lived on breath fresheners with my hand over my mouth, so no one could detect I had been drinking. My carousing got worse and worse; I remember driving home in the middle of the winter with my head out the window, singing with the music blasting so I could stay awake."

Tommy paused for a few moments with his eyes fixed on something on the floor. He turned his head slowly and continued speaking in a low, painful manner. "This was the lowest part of my life; I had tried to stop drinking, but I couldn't. My wife, Kathy, was leaving me with our son, Bobby. At that time I knew I couldn't continue to drink; my life was falling apart. But I couldn't make it through a day without a drink. I was barely functioning with a few drinks, and I couldn't function at all without a drink. Alcohol was my god, and I was its slave. About that time I remember sitting in a plane, flying back to Oklahoma from somewhere. I sat there so depressed and frightened, looking out the window of the plane and daydreaming; I was hoping this plane just might crash, and all my pain and shame would be over. Kathy would be set for life, and Bobby would remember me as being a good father who was killed tragically. My life was so low, I was looking up for the bottom."

Tommy took a Kleenex from his pocket, and blew his nose lightly. He continued, "You know, the definition of an addict is someone who is compelled to do something they don't want to do. I knew I was addicted to alcohol; I didn't want to drink, but I had to."

Tommy's demeanor changed somewhat; he picked up his head, looking directly at Alex, and then in a persuasive tone, he said, "Alex, the best analogy I can use to help explain what an alcoholic goes through is, think of this way: To an alcoholic booze becomes his food. If you notice real alcoholics don't eat much; they push food all over the plate. Well, how long can you go without any food? Nothing to snack on, you know how irritable you can get. To an alcoholic going without booze is like going without food."

"What happened, what changed, Tommy?" Alex asked.

"I was staying in Kalamazoo, Michigan, in the downtown Sheraton. I was drinking Southern Comfort Manhattans at the bar. When I left the bar, going down the hall toward the elevator a young waitress approached me and asked if I was all right. I was surprised at her interest in me and said I was fine. Did she think there was anything wrong with me? She had a concerned look on her sweet, young face, like that of a loving daughter. Then she said to me, 'I noticed you at the bar drinking by yourself; you drank a lot. You looked so sad and lonely. Your only interest seemed to be the Manhattans you were drinking.' She paused for a moment. She seemed unsure of herself; maybe she didn't want to step out of line. But she continued, saying, 'You seem like a nice person who's troubled and maybe could use some help.' I was astonished at her and what she was saying. She continued speaking in a loving, kind way. 'Please don't be offended, but I've seen the heartbreak of alcohol, and you don't need to suffer. You may want to try AA. I know it works. I hope I haven't offended you. I just would like to see you happy.' She smiled and walked away. Was she an angel? I doubt it, but she was a messenger."

"When I got back home, I called AA and went to a meeting," Tommy paused for a moment and smiled over at Alex and said, "You know, Alex, I've done a lot of things in my life—jumped out of airplanes, rode helicopters into battle, smashed up cars, got in a lot of fights, and faced a lot of fears of the unknown. But the hardest thing I ever did was stand up in front of a few people I didn't know and admit I was an alcoholic."

Tommy then chuckled to himself, saying, "For a long time, other people were calling me an alcoholic . . . I guess I was the last one to admit it."

"So you can never drink again, Tommy?" Alex asked

"I don't say I will never drink again, Alex, but I won't drink today. And today is the only day that counts." Tommy pointed a finger at Alex and jokingly said with a smile, "You have to remember, Alex, it's alcoholism, not alcohol-*was*im."

"What are those AA meetings like?" Alex asked.

"It's the darnedest thing," Tommy said in a puzzled way. "Like I said, I tried everything I could think of to control my drinking—praying, pleading, going for periods of time with not drinking—but nothing worked. I went to those meetings, sat there, listened to others talk, and spoke myself; and it worked. I've gone to church all my life and read about miracles, but I never saw one nor did I ever talk to anyone who'd had a miracle. And today I have no desire to drink, and to me that's a miracle. In my club meetings, I've seen the miracles working in other people's lives. It's the screwiest thing in the world, but it works. Just go to meetings, listen, maybe talk a little, follow the advice, and you'll live a good life."

Tommy smiled at Alex and said, "Life is life with all its difficulties, but for me, I feel like I am living in the Garden of Eden, and all I have to do is not eat the apples—or in my case, don't drink alcohol—and I can have a great life."

"So Tommy, once you stopped drinking the gates of heaven opened up?" Alex asked.

Tommy responded in a thoughtful manner, saying in a determined voice, "I don't know if the gates of heaven were opened up . . . But I know the gates of my living hell were opened up, and I got out."

"The gates of hell have opened. Is that where've you been, Tommy?" the familiar voice of Ida Freeman asked. Her sudden presence shocked the trio.

Ida seemed to appear out of nowhere, standing next to their table, head held high. Her short-styled, signature black hair was now invaded with strands of gray; her complexion was tan and worn. The fashionable glasses she now wore added to her worldly mystique. She was still remarkably beautiful, and her wardrobe was the latest New York had to offer. She was dressed to the tens down to her black, red-soled, Christian Louboutin shoes. She wore a woolen, dark green plaid, double-breasted Edwardian overcoat by Ralph Lauren, draped with a chic, black silk scarf. It was a visual delight witnessing her distinctive style and the way she was making a significant fashion statement that was complemented by the way she carried herself, as if posturing for a camera. Her distinctive beauty was matched by her dynamic personality and the intensity of her inquisitive, piercing eyes and her warm, embracing smile.

"Hi, everyone. It's nice to see you all," Ida said to the stunned group.

In an instant the group was on their feet, hugging and greeting Ida with compliments and chitchat about her and the community. Nancy and Ida gravitated to each other and drifted into a one-on-one conversation. They both had a lot to catch up on, for it had been years since they were together. Tommy and Alex drifted toward the bar, talking to a few peripheral friends.

Nancy Bishop and Ida Freeman had just sat down at the table when the pleasant, neatly dressed waitress reappeared, and that seemed to annoy Nancy a little. However, a thirsty and grateful Ida greeted the server enthusiastically.

The waitress neatly placed the napkins on the table, asking the two women, "May I take your order please?"

Nancy replied quickly looking around for her glass. "I know I had a drink around here somewhere or . . . well, someone must have picked up my glass. I'll have another glass of tonic without ice and with a twist of lime, thank you."

Ida took a deep breath as she contemplated what to order. "I'd like a Stoli Orange Vodka with a splash of diet tonic, if you please."

Ida, with the enthusiasm of a tabloid reporter, turned toward Nancy, asking her questions as if she had a deadline to meet. "Now, Nancy, tell me all about yourself. How are you doing? You look just great. I understand you are living back in town now. Do you like it?

Nancy was a little taken aback by the sudden blast of the questions. Slowly Nancy gathered her composure, thinking how to properly answer the sudden inquiries. "Well, Ida, let me answer your last question first. I thoroughly enjoy living here. When I came back after being away for such long time, it was like nothing had changed. Wherever I go, to shop or go to church or the library, someone recognizes me; they may have known my mother, father, or a friend of mine. It's hard to be nameless around here. There's nothing like living in a small town; you may know not what you're doing but everyone else sure does. But all in all, I like living here, I have a job I enjoy, and I'm pretty happy."

"Where are you working, Nancy?" Ida asked.

Nancy answered with a somber voice; I'm a nurse at Allied Services. We provide health care for people with disabling injuries because of accidents and illnesses and also care for the elderly." Nancy paused for a moment, and then spoke casually, "And I also do hospice care."

The waitress was back at the table, breaking in with the drinks. "Please put the drinks on my tab, thank you," Ida said without even looking at the waitress. She stared at Nancy as if trying figure out something.

"You work in hospice," Ida asked, sitting motionless as if in a daze, not even noticing the drinks on the table.

"I've worked in the hospice area for quite some time now," Nancy said.

"Forgive me for staring, Nancy, but I'm just surprised to hear you're a hospice nurse," Ida said as she picked up her drink, taking in some refreshment. "The first one today," Ida said with a chuckle, trying to break the tension.

"Are you familiar with the work that hospice does?" Nancy asked.

"Yes, I am, Nancy. My mother passed away a few years ago, and her final days were in a hospice right in the center of New York City. I would go over every day before work, and when I could, I'd go over at lunchtime. It was a beautiful place, and the people were so kind and loving."

Ida picked up her drink for another sip and continued speaking in a soft, sensitive voice. "I go by that building every day. Each time I look at it, I think of my mother's final days. Sometimes I feel so sad because I miss her so much, and then I feel so grateful the way she was taken care of there. Whenever they have fund-raising events, I visit her room and leave a little flag and say a little prayer. But how did you get involved in helping people die?"

Now it was Nancy's turn to pick up her drink as she thought of what to say. Nancy took a sip, then stared at the glass in her hand, and began speaking thoughtfully. "I believe we are called to our chosen careers like a veterinarian, fireman, teacher, fisherman or whatever. Some people are called to minister on the final days. As a young nurse, I loved working in the delivery room of the maternity section, welcoming newborns into this world. There's nothing like being in the delivery room helping a newborn to enter the world. It's so exciting and moving, like witnessing a miracle. At the other end of the spectrum, we have a unique bond with our patients as we help them depart this world, and that too is miracle to witness. A nurse working in hospice requires certain skills and a different mindset. You are no longer trying to improve the health or the life of your patients; you're mission becomes helping to control pain and making the final days and hours as comfortable as possible."

"I've never heard it put that way before, Nancy. But isn't it difficult working with the terminally ill?" Ida asked emotionally.

"It takes a special calling and attitude. You have to be open and honest about what we do. Most of us look at it as a privilege. Just think of it for a minute, Ida." Nancy became more animated as she spoke. "I've been there with the bright, loving faces of the families seeing a newborn for the first time, anticipating the joy and happiness this newest member will be bringing to the family. And I've been there assisting a heartbroken, grieving family saying goodbye to a loved one, who will be leaving a large void in their family. It's such a paradox of my nursing career. For the newborn you look at your tiny patients in awe, realizing they came in this world with nothing, and you wonder what amazing life experiences are in store for the little ones. Then you have the hospice patients who are departing this world, taking with them nothing but their unique, life experiences. It can be an intense relationship during this time. We get to spend the final days and hours of some fascinating people. At the end of their lives, sometimes they will tell stories their families didn't even know. I remember talking to a World War II bomber pilot who crashed in Iceland. He spent six months half frozen and lost both legs. He told me of that ordeal, and he told me in detail about the men on the plane who didn't come back. I had one patient who was a gold prospector in Alaska, who lived in a one-room cabin six hundred miles from nowhere. He told me how his two other partners died of a fever in the winter—he couldn't even bury them—and how he made it out alive. And I even had a circus elephant trainer; now his stories would melt the paint on the wall. It can be a beautiful experience bringing whatever pleasure you can to a patient who is so dependent on you. And many times I'm the last person this patient will see on this earth."

"Nancy, you make it sound so fascinating; you are quite lucky to find a career you enjoy so much," Ida said in a voice of admiration.

"It does have a few drawbacks," Nancy said. "It can be so lonely at times, and occasionally we do get too attached to our patients and their families. So when death comes, it is still painful. We feel the grief and loss along with the loved ones. But the good outweighs the 'not so good.' The families are always so appreciative of what we do. I can't tell you how many times family members have said to me, 'Thank you so much; we don't know what we would have done without you.' Knowing you helped a family during this difficult time is quite rewarding. Just being there in the final hours, doing kind little things no one will ever see or know about, and adding whatever pleasure you can for a patient who depends on you so much and has so little time left. Being a hospice nurse is so satisfying. At the end of the day, many times I am dead tired, but I feel as though I accomplished something good, and I earned my pay. And when driving home, I feel contented, joyful, and happy knowing I'm being helpful to so many."

Ida sat listening intently to every word Nancy was saying. When Nancy was finished talking, Ida smiled, shaking her head approvingly as a sign of high esteem and admiration.

"I must tell you, Nancy, how much I respect you and what you do. When I think back to when we first met, I remember you being so young and idealistic that you wanted to go off and spread the word of God throughout the world," Ida was saying but was suddenly interrupted by Nancy.

"I may not be spreading the word of God through the world," Nancy said matter-of-factly. "But I believe I am doing the work of God in this part of the world."

"And right you are, Nancy," Ida said in a supportive voice. "I apologize if I sounded rude; I didn't mean to imply anything but admiration for the work you do. It's just we all have changed so much in these years, and I'm so happy you are doing so well."

Nancy smiled warmly at Ida, taking notice of her apparel, and said with a chuckle, "You look like you are doing quite well yourself, Ida."

Ida was taken aback for a moment as she glanced over her outfit, looking down to her expensive heels with the red sole. Her voice picked up, and she sounded like a Southern belle when she said, "You mean this old outfit. I just grabbed something out of the closet before I came over here." The both laughed out loud.

"Seriously, how is life treating you, Ida?" Nancy asked.

"Well, Nancy, life is kind of what I expected . . . in a way," Ida said in a confused sort of way as she picked up her drink, taking a sip, and continued. "I wanted to be a part of the Big Apple and have a big career. I did both, but it's funny. Neither one turned out to be quite as I had hoped. At first I enjoyed all the energy and vitality of New York with the best of everything a big city has to offer: Broadway Theater, opera, the sport teams of all sorts, and so many great restaurants. Living in that atmosphere is intense and challenging. When you're young, it's fun fighting for a seat on the subway, walking on the busy streets, making your way through the crowds, and hearing the constant noise on the street. But with age comes maturity and calmness, and the hustle and bustle of the everyday crowds and traffic loses its charm somewhat. But I do still love going to the city."

"How do you like coming back here, Ida?" Nancy asked.

"When I come back, I feel so comfortable. Seeing old friends is so much fun," Ida said.

"I know what you're talking about, Ida. I noticed that when I came back and saw my old friends." Nancy paused for a few seconds as if searching for words and continued, "It was like when we were in high school; in June we got out for summer vacation, and we all went our separate ways, getting summer jobs. When we got back to school in September, our friendships picked up where we left off in June. Oh, we asked each other what we did during the summer, but no one really cared. We were back in school and having fun. And that's the way it was when I came back home after being away for thirty years. When I met some of my old friends, it was like September in high school. No one cared what I did in my summer job or what I did for thirty years. We just picked up where we left off."

"It is nice to grow up with and keep in contact with your school friends," Ida said as if she was trying to convince Nancy. "The friends I had in New York were good people. Although I may have liked them, I only knew the individual person. I didn't know any real history, the little stories of their life or what made them who they were. I hardly knew anything about the family they came from. As a result I didn't develop any deep feelings for them. They were like a tree standing alone in an open field. The friends we grew up with are like trees in a forest; we can see where they came from, how they grew up, and how they fit in. In addition to our friends, we know their families as well. When I look at Alex, I see him and think of his sister and his mother and father. I knew them all. And we remember everything about the family when his mother died, when his sister got married. In a small town, you know not only your friends but their entire family, including aunts, uncles, children, and now grandchildren. When you look at your school friends, you see the roots and the extended branches of the person."

"Ida, do you ever regret leaving the small-town life you got to know?" Nancy asked.

Ida perked up, saying, "I'm happy with my life, and I'm glad I went out and did what I did. It was tough and very competitive, but I would not have changed a thing. I worked in the broadcasting industry right in the heart of New York City. That was a feat in itself. In the skyscraper where I worked, I was a big deal. I helped choose the shows and the people who would make it on network television. And I saw firsthand how 'chance is the catalyst of destiny.' But in New York, no matter what you do, whatever your job is . . . you're just another worker. You may have a big job with a lot of responsibility great expense account and a big paycheck, but outside the office on the street, you don't get any recognition, and no one cares as they pass you on the street."

Ida picked up her drink and emptied it. She then looked around for the waitress; after catching the eye of the waitress, Ida lifted her glass to signal for a refill.

Ida then continued talking. "That's one of the reasons I love to come back here and visit this old town. People still remember me and notice me. I enjoy myself here. It used to be difficult to keep in contact with long-distance phone bills, but now with e-mails and Facebook, I've been able to renew some old friendships."

"Do you ever think of moving back here, Ida?" Nancy asked.

Ida thought for a moment. "I'm kind of like a little bird that flies over this beautiful little village," she said. "Well, this bird doesn't want to fly too close to get caught up in the problems of everyday life here. You see, I know a lot about the forest of people around here. And there's a lot of scrub oak and bushes this little bird doesn't want to get tangled up in."

The waitress returned, handing Ida a fresh glass. Ida quickly lifted the glass toward the waitress, a sign of her appreciation. Ida took a sip, and then said in a loud, joking voice, "Yes, this old town looks mighty pretty . . . especially from a distance."

Ida then nervously looked around the bar and became a little fidgety. "I could use a cigarette about now. Will you excuse me for a minute, Nancy, while I run outside to breathe in some fresh smoke?"

Standing alone outside the Grill near the front entrance, Ida looked out at the traffic move slowly up State Street; she was mesmerized, watching the combination of the moisture of her breathe and the smoke of her cigarette that condensed into a small, visible, disappearing cloud. She was enjoying the night air and the solitude of the moment.

"Are you waiting for a limousine?" the affectionate voice of Tommy Wilkinson asked.

Ida turned toward Tommy without any emotion, saying, "I drove myself in this weekend."

"Where is Charles this weekend?" Tommy asked.

"Charles is being taken care of this weekend by caregivers; he has progressed into a deeper lever of Alzheimer's," Ida said sorrowfully.

"I'm sorry to hear that. I understand Charles was always a nice person," Tommy said in an uneasy voice.

"Thank you for your kind consideration, Tommy. However, I'm here to have a good time," Nancy said.

"Where are you staying?" Tommy asked.

"With all this gas drilling going on around here, there's not a motel room available. I was able get a room at the Radisson in Scranton," Ida said.

"The Radisson Hotel, that's the old Lackawanna Railroad Station. I've been there. It has one of the most beautiful dining rooms in the world." Tommy thought for a moment. "Perhaps you would like to have breakfast there." Tommy paused again and then said, "Would you like me to call you in the morning . . . or nudge you?" They both chuckled lightly.

After Ida stopped chuckling, she said, "I should nudge you with a club. Why'd you ignore me in there? You just said 'hi' and went off talking to Alex."

"Talking about ignoring, how about you ignoring me all these years?" Tommy shot back.

"We both had our lives to live, and we both made our decisions to live those lives," Ida said flatly.

"There's no use arguing about those decisions now," Tommy said. "How has life been for you?"

"Life's been good to me. I've had a great career. I have a husband who loves me, and I love him." Her voice began to crack. Ida regained her composure. "So all in all, I'm very happy." Then she quickly asked, "How's life been for you, Tommy?"

"Oh, I can't complain; I've been very lucky. My son has turned out to be a pretty good kid, and things are going well," Tommy said, looking off in the distance. "But I've never found another Ida Freeman."

"Come on now, Tommy, I know there have been other women in your life. You've always had women falling all over you and, of course, you ended up falling on them," Ida said sharply.

"How many years has it been since we've been together, Ida? I don't know." Tommy looked intensely at Ida as he said, "But I can tell you this, everyday of every one of those years, I got up in the morning thinking of you. And every night as my head hit the pillow, I was thinking of you. You were like a shadow hovering around me all the time. I tried to work you out of my life, and I even tried to drink you out of my life, but I couldn't."

Ida threw the cigarette away and turned toward Tommy, her eyes welling up with tears as she tried to speak. "I don't know what to say, Tommy. I know I tried to cut you out of my life, and I thought that I did. But as much as I tried, I couldn't cut you out of my heart."

Outside the State Street Grill in the darkness, they embraced in a strong passionate kiss.

Inside the bar the crowd was wall to wall. It seemed like everyone was back in town for the Thanksgiving weekend. Alex and Phil made the rounds, talking to a host of old friends. In the conversations they were being brought up to date on many of the old classmates and other townies. Alex made his way over to Johnny Thompson to get a read on Johnny's feelings about Danny Fredrick. Alex hoped there would not be any incident between the two, knowing that Johnny put on a uniform and went off to Vietnam to fight. Danny Fredrick went off to Canada as a draft dodger to protest. Alex recalled how vehement Johnny had been twenty years ago when Danny came into Johnny's gas station, telling Johnny how happy he was that President Jimmy Carter gave amnesty to all those who went to Canada "so we can all be together again." Hearing that Johnny lost his temper and threw him out of his gas station, telling Danny not to come back in his business and that he better not catch Danny on the street. Hopefully Johnny changed his attitude a little.

"Hey, Johnny, can I buy you a drink?" Alex asked.

"One and done, as I always say," Johnny said in a jovial way.

Once the drinks arrived, Alex lifted his glass to make a toast. "To the good old days."

Johnny lifted his glass towards Alex, "Alex…These are… the good old days."

Both men took large slugs of their drinks. Alex spoke first, "You know, Johnny, it's really fun seeing some of the old gang again and seeing how we've all turned out. You know, I like being our age; we can do what we want. No one cares what kind of car we drive, how big our house is, what kind of job we have, and especially I'm glad no one is bragging about their kid who was so smart or gifted. We can be ourselves. We're at an age when we're back to one-on-one relationships and enjoying each other's company."

"I'll drink to that. As they say, it's better to be seen than viewed," Johnny said as he picked up his drink and took a sip.

Alex joined in and said, "How about Danny Fredrick, Johnny? You know he's here. Does that bother you?"

Johnny took another taste of his drink, smiled at Alex and said with a big grin, "Let me tell you, Alex, time is a great teacher and healer. I went off to Vietnam; Danny Fredrick and a lot of other guys went off to college to beat the draft. As a result they had good lives making a lot of money. Now I get a nice veteran's check each month. So as long as Danny Fredrick and those other guys are paying their taxes and paying me, I'm fine with them."

"That's good, Johnny," Alex said with relief.

"Yeah, Alex, but I'm not going to kiss him on the lips." Johnny said with a loud laugh.

Alex rejoined Nancy at the table, along with Phil and high school classmate Bobby Graig.

After a little small talk, Alex leaned over to Nancy and said, "Bobby Graig's two grandsons are playing for Abington in tomorrow's football game."

"That's very nice. I remember when Bobby or 'Bonehead,' as he was known as on the team. It's hard to believe his grandsons will be playing. But that was a long time ago," Nancy said in a tired voice. "But some things have changed, and one of them is I don't wait until they flash the lights before I know it's time to go home. So I think I will call it a night, Alex."

"All right, Nancy, but how about the Thanksgiving breakfast tomorrow?" Alex asked.

"One night of debauchery is enough for me, Alex. This entire drinking thing can get on your nerves, especially if you're not drinking," she said.

"Oh, come on, Nancy, we'll have a good time. You know they serve food there too. I'll pick you up at seven thirty, just like the old days," Alex pleaded with her.

Nancy stood for a moment, looking deeply into Alex's eyes. Then a slight smile appeared. "All right, Alex, I'll see you in the morning about seven thirty," Nancy said bluntly.

Alex then proceeded to gather his little band together before they started to drift off.

The little group gathered tightly around the table in the corner, the same table Alex had staked out earlier in the evening. Tommy and Ida were standing very close to each other with no outward appearance of affection. He held his glass of tonic proudly out front, chest high. However, his other hand was out of sight, nestled high on Ida's hip. For her part Ida held her drink prominently displayed with a beaming smile, anticipating the words of the pending toast, while her other hand was secretly roaming through Tommy's pocket.

Phil jumped in and began to speak, "Remember that old Bobby Darin song, "Splish, Splash (I Was Taking a Bath)? Now after a night of drinking and carousing, we look forward to a jump in a warm, comfortable bed and hope we don't have to get up every two hours to pee. See you all at the breakfast tomorrow."

Johnny and Danny were standing a short distance from each other, neither one showing any signs of being uncomfortable, as Alex raised his glass to make a toast. "I am so happy to be here tonight with you all; it's been quite an experience. I'd like to make a toast to Eddy O'Connor," Alex said loudly. They all raised their glasses; even some onlookers raised their glasses too. "We miss you, Eddy . . . almost as much as we miss your fifteen-cent beers." Everyone laughed and drank to the toast.

Alex raised his glass again, waiting for the group to quiet down. He then made a toast in a thoughtful, somber tone as he said, "To Jerry Weaver, we remember." Again all drank to the toast, however, this time quietly.

"Would you like to go to the bar for a nightcap?" Tommy asked as he and Ida strolled through the main lobby and into the spacious, grand dining room of the Radisson Hotel.

"No thanks. I have a stocked bar in the suite, which includes tonic," Ida said cheerfully.

Tommy, gawking at the high ceilings as they walked, commented, "This is a magnificent room; the intricate marble is beautiful, and the craftsmanship is equal to any I've seen in London, Paris or Rome. It's hard to believe the railroad companies spent that much money on this beautiful structure right here in Scranton."

"This railroad terminal was built when the trains were the king of the industrial age," Ida replied as they walked toward the elevators. In a few moments, they were in her suite on the fifth floor. It was a splendidly decorated room with a maroon carpet and elegant furnishings, complete with all the latest modern features and comforts. The large, marble bathroom included a large hot tub and a flat screen TV.

Tommy was standing in the middle of the room, taking in all the furnishings and amenities. Then in a proud, jovial voice, he said, "I like the way you travel, Ida."

Ida walked up to Tommy quickly, embracing him tightly and kissing him passionately for a long time. She then whispered softly in his ear, "And there's a whole lot I like about you, Tommy."

Tommy and Ida maintained the embrace as they slowly started moving in unison toward the bed, holding each other tightly, kissing passionately as they fell onto the mattress, covered with a thick, lavender down bedcover. They were swept into a comfort zone with an intense feeling of nirvana, like two old teenagers enjoying the coupling of their bodies. They swayed in each other's arms sinking into a cloudlike sensation encompassing the warmth of the fluffy, feathered cover. Few words were spoken; the only sounds were passionate moaning and whispering voices repeating over and over, "I love you, I love you, I love you."

A half hour later, Ida and Tommy were still entangled in each other's arms, and both lay in a stupor of blissful happiness. They were both completely nude and joyfully exhausted after the exotic lovemaking that would make a bridal couple envious.

After a few additional minutes of small talk, Tommy spoke in a serious tone. "We could have been doing this for years, if you would have given me a chance."

"You chose your life, and I chose mine. We've traveled different roads, and yet our paths intersect again. That's not all bad," Ida said.

"I won't rehash the long discussions we've had," Tommy said and paused for a moment. Then in a low, almost whisper, "but I remember this old poem that went, the saddest words by verb or pen are these few words: it might have been."

Ida didn't say a word; she lay in the bed now with a sober look, thinking of what to say. "Let's not go there, Tommy. We don't live in a world of 'ifs' or 'maybes'; we only have now. So let's enjoy now. . . now," Ida said in a low matter of fact voice.

"What is now . . . now?" Tommy asked as he sat up in the bed.

"Now is the present." Ida sat up, as she put on a top, next to Tommy in the bed. Glancing over toward the fresh flowers on the far table, Ida said, "See those fresh-cut flowers in the vase, Tommy? Well, those flowers are a symbol of now. I believe most women like fresh-cut flowers because they reflect the qualities of love. Fresh flowers are alive, and they seem to heighten our awareness of life; they're beautiful to look at with a delicate fragrance that rouses joy and happiness in our spirit. The similarities of flowers and love are strikingly close. Just as fresh-cut flowers in a container need nurturing and delicate attention, so it is with love. Like fresh flowers love, too, must be revitalized in the soul to remain alive and beautiful; they are both living entities present in the now. So Tommy, it doesn't matter the time or the age—sixteen or eighty-six—love can be spontaneous, revitalized, and continuously cherished just like fresh-cut flowers."

Tommy smiled at Ida with deep emotion in his eyes. He grasped her hand, pulled it to his lips, and tenderly kissed it, saying, "I've never thought of fresh flowers that way before. But as a little kid, I cut lawns for a few dollars. I saved up my money, and on Mother' Day I went to the florist in town and had a dozen roses sent to my mom. She cried when they arrived and told me I shouldn't have spent all my hard-earned money on flowers, that the flowers would be dead in a few days. I said, 'that's true, Mom. In a few days the flowers will be dead, but you'll remember them for a long time.' It's funny she never forgot those roses."

Ida reached over to Tommy, pulling him into a strong embrace, then whispered, "That's one of the many reasons I love you."

"Well then, perhaps, I should start buying you fresh flowers," Tommy said.

"I don't need fresh flowers to know you love me again," Ida said as she kissed him.

"What do you mean again?" Tommy said abruptly. "I never stopped loving you. I just didn't know if I could ever measure up to the man you wanted to spend your life with. In your heart you doubted that I would be able to provide you with all the necessities of life. Like the big house, new cars, jewelry, and whatever."

"I never said you couldn't," Ida said. Then Tommy cut her off.

"You didn't need to say it. It's what you did is what determined the life you chose, and it wasn't going to be spent with me," Tommy said.

"You were the one who wouldn't change, Tommy. I never stopped loving you, but I couldn't stand to be married to you. Everything always had to be your way," Ida said.

"My way? I would have changed. Hell I did change. I gave up my career in the pipeline business to start my own business for one reason: to see if I could be successful. I thought if I were triumphant in business, then I might stand a chance with you," Tommy said with frustration.

"I was married by that time, Tommy," Ida said in a remorseful tone.

"I know, I was married too, but it didn't last long. I was hoping yours wouldn't last long either. So I went through life hoping and dreaming that if I could make the right moves in life, maybe, just maybe, we could get together, you and I." Tommy took in a deep breath, but his voice dropped in tone and energy. "But after a while I figured you forgot all about me and were enjoying your high life in New York."

"I never forgot you, Tommy; you were always in my heart. I realized when we first met there was something about you that I adored—your smile, your eyes, your kind personality, I don't know. Maybe we knew each other in a previous lifetime. I didn't know. But I knew I was in love with you. I was torn between you and what I expected out of life, and I did have doubts about you. So I married Robert Keating, hoping we would be happy together; I would try to be a good wife, and I knew he would be a kind and loving husband, and he was. I did have some happiness, but I wasn't a good wife. There was a part of our marriage that was missing, and that part was my love for you. You were never far from the back of my mind or the pit of my stomach. I don't think Robert knew, or perhaps he just accepted it and never complained; we lived a very comfortable life together. You may have thought that our little trips to a motel were just flings for a fun weekend. But you see, I wasn't just disloyal when I was cheating with you. I was disloyal to Robert my entire married life because I loved you. I loved you then, and I love you now. I have never stopped loving you, and I will never stop loving you," Ida said as she moved over and kissed him passionately.

After their strong cuddling ceased, Tommy whispered, "I've loved you from the moment I first laid eyes on you as you strolled across the floor at O'Connor's so many years ago. You were so beautiful with your head held high, your warm, enchanting smile, and those piercing blue eyes; and you had an air of confidence about you. I knew you were special right off, and I've loved you from that time on."

"But you left me and married someone else," Ida said.

"You didn't want me, and you married someone else too. Remember?" Tommy quickly answered.

"I didn't know you felt that strongly about me. I knew I loved you all these years, and I wanted to be with you. You're the reason I kept coming back for this breakfast, making a fool of myself," Ida said.

"But I never felt good enough for you, and I doubted if I could ever live up to your expectations. When I started my plastic business, I was hoping to make it big so I could go to New York and claim you. But when it happened, I lacked the confidence to call you. I was always thinking about you and wondering if you would consider me now, knowing my company signed a big contract with GM or that our company was awarded an impressive munitions contract with the navy. Was I successful enough for you? I didn't know. I had the big house with all the trimmings. I remember after I joined the polo team, I wanted to invite you down to watch me play a few chucker's, but I couldn't muster the courage. I was still afraid to call you. At the high point of my business life, I went to New York to celebrate my company getting its trading symbol on NASDAQ, But I couldn't call you because I feared your rejection again," Tommy said in a drained voice.

Tommy picked up his head, looking earnestly at Ida. "I've tried over the years to be interested in other women, but I found there's never been anyone else for me. I knew I could live in hope...but I couldn't live in rejection."

"Tommy, I didn't reject you. We both had different aspirations and goals. We've achieved them; our life's not over. Nor is it beginning, but it is beginning a new phase of our lives together." After kissing him affectionately, she pointed toward the far wall. "Look over there on the dresser, Tommy; there's fresh flowers in our room." They embraced again, reigniting the feeling of comfort and assurance in the powerful love they shared, holding each other's bodies.

Chapter Eight

2009

After making the turn onto Holly Lane, Alex glanced down at his watch. It was 7:25 a.m. *Hmmm, a few minutes early,* he thought. *Seems to me my timekeeping is the only thing that seems to improve with age.* As he smiled to himself, his memory flashed back, reminiscing how Beth used to complain about this early morning drinking and debauchery. His mind drifted back recalling other enjoyable memories of Beth, shopping at the grocery store, buying her favorite coffee and certain vegetables she liked . . . on and on, there were other pleasant little things that floated in his mind as he slowly drove up the lane.

He pulled up into the driveway of the Bishop home, surprised to see that it hadn't changed in forty years. It was just as he remembered it, resurrecting warm-hearted memories. The house belonged to Nancy now that her parents were both gone. They had been married for fifty-eight years. Mrs. Bishop died suddenly eleven years ago, and a few months later, Mr. Bishop passed away. Nancy once commented that her father just couldn't cope or function very well separated from the love of his life. Alex recalled reading an article that pointed out widows without a male companion lived an average of twenty years after losing a spouse; however, widowers without a woman averaged less than two years after losing a spouse. Alex pondered for a minute, how long did he have without a woman in his life?

Alex was surprised as he noticed Nancy was ready and out the door, completely dressed and all buttons buttoned. She was wearing a stylish, camel-hair overcoat and dark charcoal-colored slacks with her Burberry scarf neatly wrapped around her neck. Alex took pleasure in observing Nancy crossing the driveway in her graceful, carefree style, her hair lifting slightly in the breeze.

"Just like old times," Nancy said as she opened the car door and easily slid in, fastening her seat belt and making herself comfortable. They quickly pulled out of the driveway and were on their way to Shadowbrook.

"This is a beautiful car, Alex," Nancy said lightly. "And if memory serves me right, you always liked beautiful things."

Alex kind of rocked his head in agreement and in a light-hearted way, said, "I admit this is a lot nicer than my first car, that old Plymouth convertible with the AM radio and the floor-mounted high-beam switch. I remember that car had a push-button transmission selector or, as we used to call it, typewriter controls."

"Cars have changed a lot since we were kids," Nancy said quietly. "I guess people have too."

Alex then added, "You're right, Nancy, cars and people have changed a lot, but maybe not as much as we sometimes think."

"There's a lot more computer capacity in this car than was in the Apollo spacecraft." Alex said excitedly. "Just about everything in this car is monitored or controlled by computers—the fuel mixture, the braking system, the transmission. But with all this sophistication, the car still has the same old gas pedal, steering wheel, windshield wipers, and two headlights just like it did eighty years ago."

"Speaking of people, Alex, do you remember Mr. Huffmeister?" Nancy asked.

"Huffmeister, Huffmeister . . . no I don't remember him. Who is he?" Alex asked

"Mr. Huffmeister was the janitor when we were in grade school. You remember him. He was missing three fingers," Nancy explained. "He was always nice to us."

"Oh yeah, I remember him now. He used to tell us interesting stories, like when he was a kid driving a team of horses and a wagon down to Scranton to get supplies. Back then in the winter, they couldn't get into Scranton because of all the snow in the notch in Chinchilla. I forgot all about him. I haven't heard his name in years. What about him?" Alex asked.

"When he was a kid, they used horses for picking up supplies?" Nancy asked surprisingly. "Through the notch in Chinchilla; is that how it got its name?

Alex perked up and said, "Chinchilla was originally called Leach's Flats. The little village had its own post office of the same name. Mr. Huffmeister told us there was a scorned female postmaster back in the 1800s who didn't like the Leach family at all. She knew that if she could change the name of post office, the name of the little town would eventually change too. So she developed a plan to influence her superiors and change the post office name, so it would not be associated with the Leach family. When her boss asked her who the post office should be named after, she didn't want it to seem petty or personal, and as she was thinking of a name, she was stroking her smooth chinchilla shawl. So she blurted out 'Chinchilla.' Then she concocted some story about how the local people always talked about how the winter winds blowing up through the notch in the valley made their chins chilly. The post office name was changed, and so we have the town of Chinchilla. The Leach family still has a street named after them.

"Well, anyway, I read in the obituaries that Mr. Huffmeister died last week. He was in the home for the elderly for about fifteen years. He was such a nice man. I can still see him pushing that wide broom down the hallway of Grove Street School and watching him shoveling the snow during a winter storm." Then Nancy added as her voice drifted off to a higher tone, "I was surprised how many people attended his funeral Mass at Our Lady of Snows. I guess a lot of people remembered him. He was a nice old man."

"I forgot, people around here read the 'obits' before they read the headlines. In this area the obituaries are like a social register of who's leaving this world." Alex said.

"Yeah around here they call the 'Obits" the Irish sports page." Nancy said with a chuckle.

"But it just goes to show you Nancy…in a small town everyone dies a celebrity."

"Yeah, thanks to the Scranton Times," Nancy said with a sigh. "It seems the obituaries are the only thing they print that's the truth. Even then they embellish that quite a bit." They both chuckled a little.

Alex drove down Grove Street past the old high school, then turned left at the light onto State Street through the heart of town and headed north toward Tunkhannock. A few miles out of town, they passed one of the old high school hangouts: the Glenburn Grill, which used to be the Holiday Inn Café back in the 1950s before the official Holiday Inn franchise was licensed in Pennsylvania.

"Do you remember Smitty Miller, the owner of the Holiday Inn coffee shop?" Alex asked Nancy. "That was our high school gathering place. In fact, I was there when Smitty died of a heart attack right there in the back booth. He was the first person I ever saw die right in front of me. That was about fifty years ago, I guess. But it's kind of weird going in there after all these years. I sit there and drink a coffee, looking out the old windows and watching traffic go by. It seems the only thing that has changed is the prices. I remember back then a cheeseburger was only thirty cents," Alex said in a relaxed, reflective way.

"I was just thinking how strange life is, like when Smitty Miller died. He was an older guy who lived a decent life. He was just sitting there, having a cup of coffee and in an instant his life was over . . . and that was that. Back then we were young and carefree. We had our whole lives ahead of us." Alex paused for a moment as he quietly stared at the road ahead. Then he began to speak in an affectionate, thoughtful way. "As teenagers we were just interested in what was happening in our lives. And we were always so excited about the upcoming events that had great effects on us. Who would get their driver's license next? What kind of car would our friends get? Who would go with who to the prom? Then, when graduating high school, who would be going on to college? Who was getting a job or going into the service? As time progressed, the next big event level prompted who was getting married? Who was having kids? Then, watching these kids grow up. Who got to move into their own home? Who was successful, and who was happy in life. In other words we have gone through so many major changes in life together. And now we are joining together again in retirement life where we can enjoy each other's company. We're kind of picking up where we left off in high school, except now, we have more money, and we're more interested in comfort than sex." They both chuckled at Alex's comments.

Alex paused for a moment then, looked over at Nancy with a serious look on his face, searching for her reaction to what he was about to say. "When we were little kids, I remember when Johnny Thompson's grandmother died. She was the very first person I knew who died. It was a little bit of a shock. Then other friends' grandparents died. As time went by, it was aunts, uncles, and parents of friends who died off. As time went by, the ones who were dying off were getting closer and closer to our age. Now it's our friends who are dying off. If you think about it, our kids are grown with families of their own. At this breakfast we will be meeting some of our old friends whom we've traveled with throughout life. Since grade school we've experienced the changes of life simultaneously: education, dating, getting married, having children, buying homes, and even grandchildren. We've done the most exciting things in life simultaneously, now, if you think about it, the next really big event we'll be going through in our lives simultaneously will be . . . dying."

Nancy shook her head, saying, "There you go again, Alex, with your morbid view of the future. I believe we have a lot of life ahead of us. You have the freedom to do what you want. You have your health; you seem to have enough money to do whatever you want. That's a great place to be in life. You should spend a day where I work, and you'd be a lot more grateful."

"I'm not complaining I'm just saying we're at the stage in life when I look at some of my peers and in the back of my mind, I wonder how much time he or she has left. How many heart attacks or strokes or bouts with cancer have they had? It's rather shocking when you think about it, Nancy, but it's all true," Alex said unemotionally.

"Alex, I agreed to go to this breakfast with you to have some fun. But traveling with you is like prospecting for an undertaker. So let's change the subject to something more pleasant," Nancy said.

"You're right Nancy. It's just... well... sometimes get a little melancholy driving around here, thinking of days gone by. This whole area hasn't changed since we were kids. The farms look exactly the same, even the color of the houses and barns. The old Blue Bird Diner is just the same as when were in high school." Alex paused and breathed in a deep breath, his mood uplifted somewhat, and said, "But on the brighter side, these beautiful mountains are still the same, except for the slight scar of gas pipeline running over the mountain." Alex pointed to the new pipeline snaking over a distant mountain. The pipeline would be transporting gas from the Marcella's Shale to throughout the eastern United States.

"It is still a beautiful drive out to Tunkhannock," Nancy said as she relaxed and stared out the window as they drove quietly along.

Alex was quiet listening to the rhythmic music of Deep Purple playing on the wraparound sound system; every modulation was crystal clear. The drive was so relaxing. Then as if a sudden question popped into his head, he turned with an inquisitive look on his face and asked, "Nancy, you went to college to become a missionary, and here after all these years, you are working in your own hometown. As Dr. Phil would say, how does that make you feel?"

Nancy sat still for a moment. She was startled by the question. She gathered her thoughts as she stared off at the distant mountains with a vacant look. "That's funny you'd ask me that question, Alex. I've often asked myself the same question. You know I fell in love with that young student minister, and we were going off as missionaries to serve God in the desolate parts of the world." Nancy let out a slight laugh. "But instead of converting a flock, the student minister figured he'd start to build a flock of his one, so he knocked up his girlfriend. And that put an end to my far-off missionary works and deeds. However, thanks to the Internet, I was able to reconnect with the right Rev. Rodney Williams a few years ago. It was kind of interesting. He went on to Princeton University and became a very successful and powerful minister. He's still married to the woman he got pregnant. They had a little baby boy by the name of Joshua. He was nine years old when he was tragically killed while riding his bicycle in front of their New Jersey home. He told me his wife never got over it. She became withdrawn and resentful." Nancy paused and then said in a sarcastic voice, "I think she didn't understand him."

Nancy went on in a lighthearted manner, "Fortunately for Reverend Rodney, he was able to find comfort and understanding in the arms of many attractive women. After all these years, I finally realized the man I dreamed of was a myth; he was nothing like the person I thought he would be. I realized in real life he hadn't changed that much; he was still the selfish, sex-driven man he always was. So I guess any way you look at it, he wasn't the right one for me."

Nancy squiggled a little in her chair. "He may have not been the right one for me, but he sure wasn't the last one either. Then I married Jim, that ambulance-chasing lawyer with a political ambition. What a combination! We were so young and foolish; all the boozing and drugging we did; it was a recipe for disaster. He wanted to do the right thing: work for the poor and the oppressed or mostly for the public-funded ones. I tried to be a good wife . . . ah, we both tried, but it didn't work out. As I look back, we met at the wrong time. I was not mentally stable and we didn't understand love enough. We didn't last too long together. After we split up, he got his life together, went back to his father's law firm, remarried, and lived happily ever after."

Nancy took a break for a few moments, still staring out at the distant mountains. Then she continued her saga. "It's funny; I left James for another lawyer, Tom McParland. I was so much in love with him and we got married right away. I really believed he married me just to take me away from James. Oh, how I loved Tom . . . but not quite as much as Tom loved Tom."

Nancy paused again, reflecting on the good times as if dreaming. "You know, Alex, I felt as if I was addicted to him. When he told me he wanted a divorce, I was devastated. I even considered suicide. I got drunk one night and was going to kill myself by running my car into a tree. But I didn't have the nerve, with all that religious upbringing, don't you know. First Rodney deserted me; then Tom did the same thing. I was heartbroken and couldn't believe it. He remarried and quickly had started a family. You know, I used to drive by his house for years. The pain lasted a long time and that's when I really started to drink all the time. On the outside everything looked great; I was working as a nurse in Baltimore. But in reality it was a low point in my life. The fact that I couldn't have a child seemed to me as if God was punishing me for not becoming a missionary. Now it seemed no man wanted me either. I was very lonely with no self- esteem, and then I met Chuck Clark. Or I should say, he spotted me with all my insecurities, and he embedded himself into each and every one of those dreadful feelings of mine. He set up an emotional shop there to use this negative power later on. But to me he was different in almost every way. He understood me and knew how to make me feel whole. He was witty, intelligent, sensitive, and very good-looking, although his educational background lacked a little substance. He seemed to have had a rough childhood and was mistreated as a kid, and no one understood him or appreciated him like I did. I could see the potential in him no one else could. He was full of energy and just fun to be around, always making things happen. At least that's the way it seemed at the beginning of our relationship. It was too bad his boss didn't share my optimistic view of Chuck's abilities. As it turned out, all of Chuck's bosses had strong feelings about him. That was one of the reasons they parted ways so often."

Nancy started to chuckle as she continued, "I quit my job as a nurse and went to Florida with Chuck as he started another new career, working in a carnival. Don't laugh, Alex. You can make a lot of money working the circuit. That's what Chuck told me anyway. We traveled throughout the Midwest in the summer and fall. I worked in the food department, selling candy cotton some of the time and pizza some of the time. We didn't make much money; however, Chuck with all his influence was able to get me extra hours walking around the grounds picking up the trash and then empting the garbage drums in to those large containers. This was his way to keep an eye on what I was doing. Believe me when I tell you this was the lowest point of my life. I had no self-esteem; I felt so useless. I couldn't believe I was with this freak of an abusive boyfriend. I felt like such a loser; my parents spent so much on my education and here I was picking up garbage at a carnival. Toward the fall of the year, something strange happened. The carnival company paid a bonus if you finished out the season, but for some reason when I filled out the paperwork, I put my parents' address as my permanent address. My check was sent to my parents' home. Well, Chuck wanted that check real bad . . . and he also wanted to go to New York City. So after the season, he decided to drive me home to get the bonus check and whatever else I could scrounge up. I can't find the words to express the feelings I had as we drove through Clarks Summit, seeing again the buildings and stores that were pillars of my childhood. I had to fight back the tears as we moved up Grove Street with the big, beautiful trees gawking at the brightly painted homes of people I once knew. Then we pulled onto Holly Lane in that old pickup truck with a scruffy camper on it. I was home, and I wanted to stay there. I told Chuck I wanted to talk to my parents alone for half an hour and that I was going to try to get some money from them. I told him to go over to town and get some beer."

Nancy took in a deep breath, cocked her head back, sat erect and said, "I knew if I could get in the front door, my mother and father would love and protect me. When I opened the door, they did. In an instant felt the unconditional love I knew as a child. I saw my mother and father standing in the kitchen, looking at me with tears welling up in their eyes. They both ran to me, embracing and holding me tight. I could feel the warm, strong love pulling me to them. I don't know if it was because they loved me or the way I looked—skinny, dirty, and haggard. But we cried tears of joy. They told me they loved me and would help me . . . but only if I would agree to go into treatment for my alcohol and drug abuse. I was sick and tired of being sick and tired and scared and abused, so I agreed, and we cried some more.

"When Chuck returned thirty minutes later, there was a police car in front of our house. The chief informed Chuck that I wouldn't be coming out, and there was no use for him to hang around town because Nancy was going away and wouldn't be back for some time. I never heard from Chuck Clark again."

"Now that's quite a story, Nancy. You're lucky you got away from that control freak and what he put you through." Alex said. Then he asked, "So there's no man in your life now?"

"There's no one right now. But I haven't given up. I have a busy life and I enjoy what I'm doing and who knows. How about you, Alex? Any women in your life? You've been on your own for a few years now."

"Of course there are women but no one in particular I'm interested in," Alex replied, however, he seemed to answer the question with a question.

He then started to search for the words to clarify his answer. "I've gone out on a few dates. Some well-minded people wanted to fix me up. They'd say, 'I know this friend of ours who would be perfect for you. I know you'd like her; she's so nice. If nothing else you might become friends and maybe go out to dinner once in a while.' I'd agree and meet this delightful person and it would turn out that the only thing we had in common would be we were both seniors and single. Some of these dates were like sitting next to someone on a bus. We'd have a forced conversation, and when the dinner or the bus ride ended, we'd merely say it was enjoyable talking to you, good night, and walk quickly to our respective cars. One thing I learned: no more blind dates. Now if someone wants me to meet someone, he or she has to be there too."

"Have you tried dating on the computer? I heard a lot of people have had success meeting people on line," Nancy asked.

Alex scratched his head as if he were trying hard to figure something out. "Oh, I've looked into computer dating; there are some attractive, interesting women, but they are in Harrisburg, Philadelphia, or Cleveland. I thought about for it a while, but you have to travel to meet them. Now this new person you're meeting is a learning experience in itself. You have to remember a lot of things about her. After all, you're meeting her for the first time. You've got to hear about her family, her brother, her sisters. Then there's her former husband and they all have at least one of them. And you better not have any of the bad habits or characteristics of their former spouse. And oh yes they will remind you of them. Then you must learn about her many interests and hobby's developed over time, how she lives her life—perhaps a career or gardening, baking or whatever. Then there are the children: how many are there, their names, the daughter-in- laws, the son-in-laws and the grandchildren's names. And God forbid…if one of the grand children is talented…you have to pretend you're so fascinated by it all. If you can do all that, then you have to start to explain your life story only in reverse. But you've got to drop the talented grandchild stuff. At my age I don't want to spend that much time and effort trying to find someone to grow old with. I'm already old; it's just too much work. What I would like is to meet someone from around here. Then at least we would have something in common. We would know some of same people, the restaurants, bars, and other things about the area we could discuss."

Alex sighed, looking over at Nancy with a serious look on his face and earnestly said, "You know Nancy, at my age, I've kind of accepted myself, and I'm comfortable in my own skin. I'm pretty well set in my ways—not that I'm that rigid—but I do have my opinions and tastes that I've developed throughout my life, and I'm not about to change them to accommodate someone else. When I was younger and starry-eyed, I made concessions to advance a relationship. But now I just want comfortable companionship without any hassles."

"Well, I can see you changed over the years, Alex," Nancy said.

"We've all changed, Nancy," Alex said in a relaxed manner. Then putting both hands on the steering wheel, he said in a soft, meaningful voice, "After a life of hard work and a lot of reflection, I find the simpler things in life are the most fascinating: the beauty of nature, the love of family, and the warmth of friendship."

"You're right, Alex," Nancy said as she turned and looked directly at Alex. She cocked back her head as if she were to lecture him. But, she then slowly turned, looking forward through the windshield and over the hood of the car to the distant fields. "You know life is funny, Alex," She said slowly. " Sometimes I like to visualize in my mind how we blend in nature, as if we started out as a trickle in a little stream flowing from the Abington hills, growing into a mature river, then flowing and growing and following a meandering, convoluted course that sometimes moved fast and furious, sometimes slow and peaceful, but always moving. Now our mature waters are running deeper and calmer, saturated with our experiences of a lifetime. Our river will soon be rejoining the ocean, and the cycle will begin anew—vaporizing into the atmosphere, forming into clouds, and soon raining once again in the hills forming another river of life."

"You didn't learn that philosophy in Bible study," Alex said in a surprised voice. "I could imagine you out in the wilds of Africa, teaching that religion to the virtuous hoards of ignorant, unbaptized pagans. You too have changed a lot, Nancy."

"You're right, I did want to be a missionary. I wanted to do God's missionary work in a far-off country," Nancy said. Then she thought for a moment, adding in a lighthearted way, "They say if you don't think God has a sense of humor, just make plans. Well, I had the desire to do God's work, and I started to make the plans. But God interfered, and instead of doing his work in a far-off jungle, I'm doing his work in my own hometown, working in hospice or God's waiting room, ministering to those with a number who are waiting to be called home."

Alex didn't say anything as he drove along; he was quietly taking it all in as he listened intently.

But Nancy wasn't finished. She looked again sternly at Alex and continued, "I know what I believe is not orthodox Christianity, but I do believe in a God that is everywhere and in everything. That's what Christ meant when he said, 'The rocks and stones themselves would start to sing.' I've drifted away from organized religion. They preach about how great it would be to have a spiritual experience.

"I believe the opposite, that we are the spirits having a human experience; while during this human experience we kind of exist on a plane that's similar to living in water and needing to breathe. We need religion to help keep us afloat in this material world. Religion is the buoy that we cling to. After a while some of us learn to swim, trust, and believe, and then off we go enjoying the spiritual freedom of living and exploring this magnificent world. I think we all need religion from time to time to grab onto in difficult times, and religion can be a life preserver to help us keep afloat if we lose our way. I like to think we are put on earth to learn to enjoy the swim and to explore our challenging, magical experience of life. At the end of our lives, when our spirit leaves our body, the only thing we take with us is the experiences we had during our swim in this lifetime."

Alex was silent for a few minutes, taking in what Nancy had been talking about. He didn't quite know what to say.

"You do have a unique way of looking at things, Nancy. But then again you always did," Alex said.

"How about you Alex, what are your beliefs?" Nancy inquired.

"Nancy, I'm glad you asked," Alex replied with a quick, whimsical attitude. "But we are getting close to Shadowbrook now and we can continue this discussion later."

"It's kind of odd, isn't it, Alex? You and I growing old together," Nancy said mildly as if an afterthought.

Alex didn't say anything; his mind had drifted off to other things. They were driving on Route 6, entering this familiar, small, picturesque valley about a mile from Shadowbrook. He recognized everything about this area—the mountains, the barns, the fenced-in fields, and the creek. He started having a flashback of sorts. All of a sudden he was remembering traveling this highway with his wife, Beth. How often they had driven this road. He felt a cloud of emotion filling his soul. Alex was experiencing feelings of guilt, loss, and emptiness. He recalled earlier times when he secretly desired Beth to not attend the breakfast, but she always made sure she was there, thus putting a clamp on his freedom. He now was regretting his selfishness and missing her presence, because when all was said and done, he loved her and enjoyed being with her; she was always there, caring for and loving him as no one else ever had. A slight smile appeared on Alex's face as he drove along. Beth did say she would always be near. He questioned if she was with him now in spirit, riding in this car. Alex glanced over toward where Beth would have been seated, but Nancy was there, relaxed and staring out the window.

Alex looked ahead at the highway. "Ah, the two cow heads of Shadowbrook," he said as they started crossing the bridge over the Tunkhannock Creek. "Right on top where they're supposed to be."

"What's the story about the cow heads?" Nancy asked.

"Oh, it goes back to when the original owner of Shadowbrook sold out to the Perkins Restaurant chain. One of the selling requirements was that the cow heads had to remain in public view. Of all the hundreds of Perkins Restaurants, this is the only one with two cow heads on the roof," Alex commented with pride.

He drove with delight up and over the crest of the hill past the restaurant, turning right into the golf course and banquet area. The morning sun was just above the horizon, sending rays of sparkling, golden sunlight that glistened off the vibrant green grass and trees of the manicured golf course. As Alex and Nancy drove quietly and slowly down the long driveway, they both felt a tightening feeling of excitement with the idea of seeing so many old friends.

"It looks as if there's a pretty good turnout," Alex said.

"I'm a little nervous, Alex," Nancy said in s shy voice. "There will be a lot of people and a lot of drinking just like in the old days."

"Let's face it, the real problem drinkers of our era are either sober or dead. The rest of us now drink rather sparingly, without the usual hoopla or drunk stories. It's early morning, and there's a nice breakfast buffet; and some of the guests actually eat. So let's go in. We'll have a good time," Alex said as they pulled into a parking spot.

Nancy and Alex entered the large banquet room together, trying to peer through the crowd as their eyes searched the area for friendly, recognizable faces. They marveled at the rows of long tables covered with crisp white tablecloths. Many of the tables were decorated with centerpieces of blue and white, the Abington school colors. At the far end of the room was the buffet line; a small line had formed at one end. To the left side of the large room was the bar; it had no line, but many partiers and thirsty revelers were drinking, talking, and enjoying the camaraderie of the moment.

Alex spotted Phil Whitman and his wife, Molly, at one of the decorated tables. Molly was sitting and conversing with one of her woman friends. Phil was standing next to her talking to someone Alex recognized immediately; it was Bob Parry who graduated a year ahead of Phil. Bob was of average height and build; his stomach was extended quite at bit, being restrained by his straining belt. However, he had retained his youthful looks; he was well preserved for his age, for his complexion was as clear as a teenager's and his bushy hair was brushed up into a semi round flattop. He was wearing a historic, white, varsity athlete's cardigan sweater with four blue stripes on the sleeve. (This translated into the wearer being lettered in a sport for all four years of high school.) The khaki slacks he wore appeared a little long, drooping nearly under the heel of his cordovan penny loafers. Bobby was as cheerful and witty as the high school image he portrayed. Through his life he always showed keen interest in people from across the social spectrum. He greeted people equally with a broad smile and cheerful, outwardly friendly energy. He had a knack for making people he met feel at ease, employing consideration and humor— perhaps the result of his youthful years spent working at his family-owned Summit Diner. The end results were he was very popular, and everyone seemed to know Bobby and liked him.

There was small chitchat and some gossip about events that had occurred over the years.

"It's good to see you back in town again, Alex. It's been a long time," Bobby said warmly. "You'll have to come over to the Sunrise for breakfast. Some of your old high school buddies are usually there. We have a lot of laughs each morning."

"Bobby's there every morning; I guess you can take the boy out of the diner, but you can't keep the man out of the diner. Especially if there's a good-looking waitress," Phil said with a laugh.

"I see you still have your old varsity athlete's sweater," Alex said.

"Yeah, he does," Phil said as if answering for Bobby. "It used to fit him forty years and fifty pounds ago." Phil added with a laugh.

Looking at Alex, Bobby chuckled lightly and said, "He was always jealous because I started in my freshman year."

"The only reason you started is because your old man owned the diner, and he used to give coaches free hamburgers," Phil quickly added with a laugh.

"Yeah, the hamburgers were cheap, only twenty-five cents. But my dad had to bribe them with a full chicken dinner, so I could play in the all-star dream game," Bobby jabbed right back.

"Alex, did you ever play football?" Bobby asked.

Alex was surprised by the question; for some reason he felt a little uneasy standing next to Nancy and admitting, "No, I didn't play high school football. I wasn't too athletic." He felt a little embarrassed and regretted the fact that he had never even tried out. It was the one thing in life he had wished he could do over. In his youth he longed to run out on the football field to hear the cheering crowd on a Saturday afternoon and walk into a dance wearing a lettered athlete's sweater. He regretfully missed out on that mystical sensation.

Alex wanted to change the subject, so he asked Bobby, "Aren't you in the trucking business now, Bobby?"

"I was but I sold the company, and now I'm retired without the big money or prestige. But as I've often said, I'd rather drive an old car to the country club than a new car to work," Bobby said with a big laugh.

Ida and Tommy entered the banquet room together. Ida was draped in a striking, tapered, three-quarter, navy-blue pea coat with two rows of large gold buttons, complemented by a white silk scarf. The coat had a black, fur-trimmed hood that floated gracefully on her shoulders, complementing her dark hair. The coat was partially opened to reveal a green turtleneck sweater and full-length khaki slacks with penny loafer shoes. Tommy was wearing a buckskin jacket, blue oxford shirt, jeans, and cowboy boots. Strolling across the floor, they carried themselves as a mature, affluent couple in love and weren't ashamed to show it.

They were walking toward the table where Alex and Nancy were seated. The greetings and hellos were exchanged as both couples sat down, relaxing and looking to see who all were in attendance. It wasn't too long before Johnny Thompson found his way over to their table, drink in hand, cozening and joking with people along the way.

"You're a sight for sore eyes, Johnny," Alex said as he stood up to shake Johnny's hand.

"Your eyes wouldn't be so sore if you didn't drink so much," Johnny said as they all laughed.

"Did you go out after you left the State Street Grill last night, Johnny?" Tommy asked.

Johnny took a sip of his drink, and with a big old smile on his face, he said, "Oh yeah, me and Phil DeDorie went out for a few drinks. He's eighty-two years old, drinks like a fish, and still enjoys going out at night chasing after woman. The only problem is… at his age he can't remember why."

Nancy perked up, asking, "Johnny, didn't you ever hear of early to bed, early to rise?"

Johnny glanced over at Nancy with a smirk on his face and said jokingly, "Yeah, I heard of early to bed, early to rise, but you never meet any interesting people that way." Again they all laughed.

"Johnny, aren't you a little old to be out chasing women?" Tommy asked.

"I'm a little older but I'm wiser now. In fact I bought some of that Viagra not too long ago; I called the 800 number on the package to complain about having an erection that lasted longer than five hours. They asked me how many pills I had taken? I told them I hadn't taken any yet."

Everyone laughed.

Johnny glanced toward the door as a few more people entered. "I see Bonehead coming in. I understand his grandson is a starting linebacker. They say he's a pretty good player. I just hope he doesn't use his head, like his grandfather did, as a battering ram!"

Alex was standing at the bar ordering a beer when Tommy came up, joining him for a drink. Alex was just getting the attention of the bar attendant; he ordered a beer and asked Tommy what he would like. Alex said jokingly, "You know beer is not just for breakfast anymore."

Tommy chuckled, "Yes, I know. I drank enough of Budweiser, the breakfast of champions, in my life. So today I will stay with a glass of tonic with cranberry juice, no ice!"

As the drinks arrived, Alex handed Tommy his drink. Taking a sip, Tommy smiled and said in a boastful, humorous manner, "First one today." They both chuckled.

"Well, Tommy, looks like you're having a good time this morning," Alex said. "I see you're still good friends with Ida. I guess that gives you something to be thankful for during breakfast?"

"Yes, we're still close friends, Alex," Tommy said with a twinkle in his eyes. "And I hope we will remain very close from now on." Tommy paused for a moment, then added as in deep thought, "After all these years, I think we finally understand each other a little better than we ever did before. We're both a little older now, a little wiser, and the time may be right; so we may have some good times together."

"Why did it take so long for you both to realize you were meant for each other?" Alex asked.

"It's a long story, Alex, but the Reader's Digest version is that we both loved each other all these years, and we occasionally got together, but it was a romantic encounter a kind of a good time sneak away. It was fun, naughty, and exciting, but neither of us hoped for a long-time relationship. I loved Ida right from the beginning and would have married her at any time, but I didn't think she cared for me as much as I loved her. I kind of felt like a stable boy; I was just someone that she enjoyed having around for her convenience. Like a woman of the Manor House, she thought I was a good-looking stable boy—hardworking, an excellent rider, with an abundance of ambition. But no matter what I accomplished in life, I was still just a stable boy who would never really be accepted in the society of the Manor Home," Tommy said.

"How would you get that impression? We all thought that she was madly in love with you. It was quite obvious that she came to town just to see you. Without any hint of being discreet, she blatantly cheated on her husband to be with you. We all thought she was madly in love with you, and for some reason you chose to go off on your own," Alex said.

"Well, Alex that was the confusion we lived in for all these years. Ida was the only woman I ever loved. But she wanted to live a certain lifestyle, and I wanted to be able to give it to her. So I dedicated myself to working hard and achieving a certain amount of success. When I achieved that, I would go to New York and steal her away from her trophy husband," Tommy said, and then stared in a far-off direction thinking of what to say next.

Tommy began speaking as if trying to convince Alex of his dedication to Ida. "Alex, everything I did, I did for Ida, She was always on my mind. I was constantly thinking, what would Ida think of what I was doing? If I bought clothes, would Ida like this shirt or these slacks? What type of car would Ida expect me to drive? Over the years it got to the point I was obsessed with what Ida would consider acceptable, and in my mind nothing was good enough. So I never really got the nerve to go to New York and try to win her over. Now, after all these years, I found out she has loved me all along and was hoping that I would ride up on my white horse and take her away." Tommy chuckled to himself for a moment.

He picked up his drink, and with a big smile, took a sip. Then Tommy continued in a light, jovial manner, saying, "It's funny when I think of it. I had a stable full of different colored horses; I just didn't have the nerve to saddle one up and go to New York. I just kept putting it off until I was more confident, and the longer I waited, the more confidence I needed. I guess I just hoped that if we were meant to be together, God would work it out. After all these years, I think he has," Tommy said with a confident smile.

"Now what about you, Alex? You seem to be living a good life. Are you really as happy as you seem?" Tommy asked.

Alex paused for a moment as he reflected on his thoughts and how he would answer the complicated question. "I have a great life; my kids are grown with kids of their own. I have a great deal of freedom, good health, enough money and energy to do what I want, when I want, and travel where I want. Life is very good, Tommy."

Alex again paused for a few moments, picking up his drink and staring at the contents. Then he said tenderly, "Although there are times when life is somewhat melancholy. The Christmas holidays are a little tough sometimes when I drive around town seeing the snow-covered decorations and the bright-colored Christmas lights on the houses, hanging on the trees, and draped on the bushes. That was the best time of the year for our family; it was a bonding time for us. I remember as a family decorating our house, hanging all the lights, Christmas shopping, and hiding the gifts so no one could find them till the exciting opening on Christmas morning. Listening to carols on Christmas Eve as we set up the large tree, placing carefully each of the ornaments, along with throwing on the ice cycle strips of aluminum. Hanging the stockings on the fireplace and being so happy and grateful for having such a beautiful and loving family. From the time of my own childhood, I always had input on decorating our house, but now I am more of an observer than a participant. When I visit my children and grandchildren, they decorate their own houses and have their own family traditions. For me life has changed. I don't put up decorations or plan any holiday parties. I don't have any family to entertain or lavish with gifts or welcome to my home, all decorated with

Christmas lights. I used to do all that during those happy years when my children were children."

Both men stood motionless for a moment, and then Tommy added, "I guess Christmas must be especially difficult for you, Alex."

Alex picked up his drink, taking a long, tasty swallow. He stood quietly as if waiting for the alcohol to take effect. Then looking directly ahead, he began to speak. "Oh yes, I think of her a lot at Christmas. Beth had a Christmas Squashville collection. It's a beautiful, tiny oak forest winter village inhabited by cute, little, whimsical country mice. She loved setting up that minute village each year, complete with layers of white cotton as the snow that covered the miniature community buildings. It was her pride and joy. It was fun just to see her face light up as she turned it on in the beginning of the season."

Alex paused and then said, "But it's not just Christmas that I miss her. Each time I see a commercial on washing machines, I think of how she searched for the best one. When I go shopping in the grocery store, I think of the things she'd ask me to pick up for dinner. When I have cereal in the morning, I think of her and how she liked to eat a healthy breakfast. When I hear certain music, she is in my mind, or when I see a small child, I remember how much she loved her grandchildren. When I see certain movie stars…I think of how much Beth liked them or disliked them. Certain colors remind me of her. Driving alone in the car, I miss her. So Tommy, it's not only Christmas I miss her; I miss Beth each day of the year. It's as if a part of me is missing."

"But life goes on," Alex said as if he were awaking, "and I expect to live an exciting life. That's what Beth would expect of me, and that's what I plan on doing. When traveling I sometimes envy some retired couples I've noticed. They seem to have weathered the storms of life together; they seem content and respectful, loving each other in a calm, easy manner in their golden years. That's the way it's supposed to be. But sometimes life throws curveballs. Anyway I will be with Beth in a few blinks of the eye. This life is very short."

"I agree with you, Alex, this life is very short, and it seems to be getting shorter," Tommy said in a reaffirming manner.

"Alex, I never thought of your life that way," Tommy said empathically. "Although you lost Beth, you still have a great life. You do what you want, and you travel—going on ocean cruises, skiing wherever, white water kayaking, you've even been on a cattle drive. I would imagine you probably have a few women on the side that are madly in love with you," Tommy said, trying to uplift the feelings of his friend.

Alex smiled at Tommy and started telling him something else to consider. "Let me tell you, Tommy, how I feel sometimes. Now these feelings are separate from the human emotions I have about losing Beth. This is just me when things are going good; I'm free to do what I want and life is good," Alex said as he picked up his drink and took a small sip.

Alex then focused his eyes, staring off in the distance and preparing to tell an entertaining mystical story. "Tommy, try to use your imagination for a few minutes. Sometimes I feel like I'm a young horse on a beautiful ranch in the mountains of Montana. As a young colt, I enjoy running around the large, open ranges with other young horses having a great time; life is fun and carefree. Then I notice this fine-looking, young filly running around. So I choose to be with this special, attractive one. We join up, forming a team, and we get hitched up together. Gone are my free roaming days. She and I make a great set, pulling the wagon to town and back each day. At night we are put in a barn together, eating oats and hay. It is warm and comfortable, and we enjoy each other's company. It's kind of a boring existence at times but a good life all in all. We have it good, and occasionally I do miss the freedom I once had. After years of this lifestyle, everything was fine, but then one day my teammate is gone. I'm now an old workhorse, so the boss man decides to let me have my freedom and puts me out to pasture. I can't quite jump the fences anymore, but I can run in the open ranges, enjoy eating fine green grass in the valleys, drinking clear, running water from the streams, and I'm completely free. It's a great life.

"Sometimes from a distant hill, I will look down at the horses at work pulling the wagons, and I'm glad I'm not with them. But there are times, mostly at night, when I'm all alone with the cool, evening breeze flowing, and I'll look down at the barn. I see the warm lights glowing, and I know the working horses are closed up in there. They will be up early in the morning, pulling the wagons, but on this night they are content in the barn eating oats and hay. They are warm, comfortable, and they have each other. Now I love my freedom, but sometimes at night I look down at that warm barn and think of those horses in there. And it makes me wonder."

Tommy felt badly for his friend Alex. He knew Alex was a sensitive, good person who carried his own emotional burdens and didn't share them with anyone. Tommy reached out in a rare and almost uncomfortable manner, putting his arm on Alex's shoulder, and said in a smooth, emotional voice, "We all live a private life within our own skin, that no one else is even aware off. I thought you were well-adjusted and happy. But I guess we never quite know the real-life feelings of someone else."

Before Alex could say anything else, another idea popped into Tommy's head. "How about Nancy Bishop? I've known you two were always close as kids. She would make a good partner, don't you think? I mean someone to go out to dinner with, maybe even travel a little. She's great company and a lot of fun and you know each other."

Alex looked over at Tommy smiling and nodding his head. "She is good company, and I do like Nancy a great deal." Alex halted for a moment, looking off in the distance for a few seconds, and added, "But after all these years, as the kids would say, there's no chemistry. I like to think we are very close friends and that's all. Close friends."

"At our age we don't need chemistry, we need friendship and companionship," Tommy said.

Alex smiled at Tommy, saying in a low, thoughtful voice, "You may be right, Tommy, but I was always secretly hoping to meet someone and the sparks would fly, or I'd have that electric feeling of excitement. It's been a long time and no sparks or electric feelings yet. Maybe it's just me. But I'm still a romantic."

Tommy paused for a moment, then continued, "I once saw a painting of a peaceful, isolated, small white farmhouse in picturesque country setting, and there was a note under the artwork that said, 'Visitors don't know the family problems that exist within these walls.'"

Molly Whitman was sitting at the head of the table, enjoying the morning festivities. The years had been good for Molly. Although she had been diagnosed with type 2 diabetes, she accepted it as one of those things that happen when one gets old. Over the years her beauty morphed into a distinguished, mature, attractive woman. Her hair was pure white, which was in contrast to her youthful, smooth complexion and striking, clear, dark blue eyes. She exhibited the image of an energetic, fun-loving woman who was enjoying life the best she could. She was not bashful about her opinions and was willing to share her logic with anyone who would listen. A few of her friends started to join in at Molly's table. The women sat quietly and started to nibble at the breakfast they just acquired on a recent trip to the buffet table. She was talking to one of her female friends, who happened to stop by for a quick chat. Molly was in her full party mode, laughing as she was talking.

"Hello, Molly, I hope you're enjoying the morning revelry," Alex said as he reached out both hands and gave Molly a kiss on the cheek.

"Alex, it's great to see you. I was just telling the girls, these are the good old days," Molly said loudly and laughed heartily. "We're getting a little older . . . and the days are good . . . right? Well then it's true, these are the good old days!" She again laughed.

"Do you agree, Alex? You're retired now, aren't you?" Molly asked Alex as he sat down for a quick visit at Molly's table.

"Yes, I agree with you, Molly, these are the good old days." He paused for a moment, trying to decide if he should say anything else. Then a smile appeared as he started to speak in a warm, comfortable manner. "We've been blessed with many good old days. To come back to my hometown and have breakfast at the Sunrise Café with my old high school friends is quite an experience. It seems the one thing that's changed the most around here is the cost of a cup of coffee, from ten cents to a buck and a half.'

Alex sat back, took a deep breath, and said casually, "I do think often how lucky we are to be born and grow up in this beautiful area, with all the people we know. And now we're at a stage in life when we can rekindle some of those old friendships that go back to when we were kids. I'm enjoying myself; it's a great time in life when we don't have to concern ourselves with impressing anyone with titles or deeds or achievements or hiding from our failures. We're just who we are, good, bad or indifferent. That's kind of how we were in high school, minus the big egos and without the strong sex drive."

"Well put, Alex. My, my, you've become quite the philosopher," Molly said with an air of surprise, taken back by the comments.

"We women didn't fish in those rivers or streams or climb the mountains, but we sure grew up here, and I enjoyed living here. However, Alex, I think we girls had a much milder sex drive than you referred to," Molly said with a giggle. "But that was before the pill and the sexual revolution. I remember back in the sixties when the pill came out. The pill wasn't accepted as it is today. I remember a friend of mine at Marywood College told me she had taken the pill for medical reasons. By chance her mother found them in her room and told the father. He was so mad that he slapped her face. It was the only time in her life he ever hit her, calling her a whore."

Molly paused as she gathered her thoughts. "Things have changed a lot since we were girls. I can tell you we're not like our mothers were; my mother never drove a car. My parents were so image conscious. We always had to be aware of 'what would the neighbors think." Molly started to laugh out loud as did others gathering at the table.

"Later in life we found the neighbor's family was just as dysfunctional as our family," Molly said, laughing.

Molly relaxed, taking a sip of her coffee, and then said in a serious voice, "I don't think my mother had the deep trust in friendships like women of our age do. Our friends are not always on the same social level like my mother's friends were. Nowadays we women choose our friends for certain reasons, sometimes because of their sense of humor, character, or some other trait we can relate to. The nice thing about friends is you don't have to ask someone to be a friend; they just are. We are living a different lifestyle than my mother's generation. We are not afraid of our age; we do a lot more of the things people half our age do. We like to party, travel, play golf . . . hell, I still go up to Elk Mountain skiing. This is a new generation of baby boomer women. Watch out!"

Molly finished her cup of coffee, and with a warm, wide smile she glanced over at her friend standing nearby. Handing her the cup, Molly asked, "Mary Ellen would you be a dear and please get me a refill of regular coffee?"

"Oh, I would be thrilled to get it for you, Molly," Mary Ellen replied enthusiastically. "But don't start talking until I come back," she added as she scurried off.

Molly leaned over to whisper to Alex. "Are you enjoying the lecture, Alex?"

"You ought to go on the road with this show, Molly. It's very good; you could be a stand-up act," Alex whispered back.

"Now if my own kids would listen, that would be a triumph," Molly replied.

Mary Ellen returned, handing the coffee cup carefully to Molly. "Here's your coffee, Molly . . . nice and hot."

Molly looked at Mary Ellen with a grateful smile and eyes of appreciation, saying, "Thank you so much, Mary Ellen. I would have gotten it myself but getting out of this chair . . . ah, well anyway, thank you, dear."

Molly took a sip of the coffee and then smiled, looking over at Mary Ellen as if talking directly to her when she started to speak in a whimsical tone. "It's taken us years, but we women have finally learned to say no!" Molly winked at Mary Ellen, letting her know that she was playing with words. "Not to you, Mary Ellen; thank you for the coffee. What I meant is saying no to our men and our children or anyone else we used to cow to. There is a verse of an old song that goes something like, 'Oh hard is the fortune of all womankind; they're always controlled, they're always confined; confined by their parents until they are wives, then slaves to their husbands for the rest of their lives.' Molly shook her head, chuckling to herself, then added, "We have devoted the first part of our lives to our parents, then our husbands, and then our children. Well, the kids are grown up now, our parents are gone, and our husbands can take care of themselves. We've sacrificed enough and paid our dues for many years, and now's the time for us women to enjoy our own lives. Now we're doing things we want to do, and we are not slaving as mothers and housewives doing the chores and housekeeping as we used to do. We've become liberated and independent. We have self-confidence and are aware of the world around us. We've come a long way, baby, and we wish to laugh a lot and enjoy as much of life as we can. We've worked hard raising our kids and putting up with our husbands. We've sacrificed and worked hard, giving our kids a lot more than we ever had."

Molly was smiling as she nodded her head and looked about for encouragement. "Of course they all appreciate it so much. They are always thanking us and being so generous, yeah right!" Everyone laughed in unison.

Molly started to laugh a little, looking around for one of her friends who seemed to be missing; she then spotted the woman just sitting down at the table and yelled over to her, "Brenda, how's your 'gratitude tree' doing?"

"Nothing yet, Molly, it's still kind of bare," Brenda Cummings said, smiling.

What's a "gratitude tree?" someone at the table asked.

Molly chuckled again, trying to control herself, as she went on to describe her pet project, "I was complaining about my kids awhile back, about how ungrateful they are, and I got to thinking of this generation of kids. I get a kick out of our kids today; they all have brilliant, talented children, but their parents are irritable half-wits."

"As parents we made sure they had a comfortable life, made sure they had what they wanted; we gave so much more than we had, and we spent a small fortune educating them. Now that they're on their own, well let me say, ah . . . they all seem to have poor memories. So I've made up what I call 'gratitude trees,' and I gave a few of them to friends who have grown children. It's a simple thing, just a broom handle about 24 inches high mounted on a block of wood. It has paper clips fastened to it, so you can attach letters and thank-you notes from your grown children when they go out of their way to let you know how much they appreciate all that you've done for them. The gratitude tree is a trophy piece to display just how much our grown children show, in little ways, their gratitude and admiration for all the sacrifices we've made. Now if one of your kids sends you a thank-you card, a letter of appreciation, or a note of thanks for the good advice, you can clip these little paper trophies on your beautiful 'gratitude tree.' There's also special colored clips for checks or cash they may send to you for whatever reason. When the tree is in full blossom, it's so beautiful," Molly said with a chuckle.

"Well, I've had mine up for over six months, and it still looks like a flag pole," Molly said in a tone of humorous disgust.

Those at the table laughed heartily, some asking where they could get such a practical gift.

Molly continued discourse like she was running for public office. "Well now, we're in a time of life with no more babysitters to worry about or rigid schedules of what has to be done on certain day. The days of regimentation are over. When we had children around, the meals had to be served at a certain time. The laundry had to be done on a certain day; everything had to be ironed and then put away. Now I do the laundry when I want. If I need something, I grab it and iron it and put it on and out the door I go. Cleaning day is when I have a little time to clean up. I used to go food shopping for the 'order' on Fridays. Cooking for one or two seems like such a waste of time, so we just go out to eat. Now I hardly have any food in the refrigerator. Now I am spending more time doing the things I want, and you know what? I'm liking myself more and more. Sometimes I'll watch an old movie in the middle of the afternoon just because I want to, and sometimes I may stay up till four in the morning playing on the computer or surfing the Internet. I do miss some of the phone calls I no longer get from my mother, my older brother, and friends who are all dead now. When I was younger, I used to daydream about what future life was going to be like. Now I daydream what my future in heaven will be like."

Molly took a sip of her coffee and reflected on what she just said. She put down her coffee and patted her mouth with her napkin, being prim and proper, to ensure no coffee remained on her lips as she readied herself to continue.

Smiling at Alex, she patted his hand gently and said, "Now this talk doesn't apply to you men, Alex, but us women need to stick together." Then she mischievously glanced around her little group, seeking approval. "It's true women share their feelings with girlfriends much more than men do. We can empathize in ways that men can't understand and can only imagine. We like to talk and tell all kinds of stories over and over again. We talk about our husbands, our children, brothers, sisters, and anyone else we know. Being able to shar fun times with quality friends is a wonderful time of life. When there's good news or a reason to party, we like to share in the celebration and, at our age, without envy or too much criticism." Molly turned her nodding head around, wearing an innocent smile. Then she took on a serious manner, saying, "But more importantly, in the sad times of hurts, pains, heartbreaks, deaths, and loneliness, that's when it's so important to have good women friends. I once read, 'A true friend is someone who listens and cares when no one else even knows you have a problem.' After all these years, I've learned to maintain friendships sometimes in life it's better to be kind than it is to be right. Friends are so unique and special to each of us. Our friends are our life supports."

Molly sat for a moment staring off toward the far end of the banquet room. She had a large, peaceful smile as she began to speak. "I am very happy to have the friends I have. We like to go out and have a lot of fun together now that we're mature, or at least be a little bit more patient and understanding. We drink more than we used to, but we laugh a lot more than we used to. It's like we were in high school again; we don't care who has what. We can kick back and relax. We have enough money to do what we want. We've learned that money only buys things . . . not joy or happiness."

One of the women sitting at the table said, "Molly, I wish I was more like you. I like the way you look at life."

Molly was caught off guard as she looked over at the woman and said, "Marian, it's all in your attitude. I knew this woman friend of mine . . . her husband was dying and the thought of being lonely bothered her so much that she brought a date to her husband's funeral. Now that's a positive attitude."

After the laughter from the group, Molly adopted a more serious tone. "I've noticed as I got older that it's easier to be positive; you can care less of what others think about you. Your decisions in life are much easier, such as where are you going to live. Having children, worrying about your husband's career, even paying the bills . . . these decisions are already made. I try to live a positive lifestyle. I learned a long time ago we have choices to make in life. It's a simple choice; how do we handle information we receive? Lordy, lordy, we're inundated all the time with negative news. It's prevalent and frightening. And if you allow this negative bombardment to influence you, you'll end up with a negative attitude that's so depressing. But if you choose to develop a positive attitude, believe me, honey, you'll feel better. But this battle against this powerful negative input is an uphill struggle. Now for example, if you go to the library, you'll find hundreds of books on how to develop a positive attitude. There are no books on how to think negatively, because thinking negatively is natural, and it comes easy with no effort at all. All you have to do is sit around and complain how tough life is and watch a lot of TV. The media will supply you with the rest. Then you'll be stuck on the lonely, miserable road of depression. And that's a bad place to be. Or you can change your attitude, and choose another way in life. It takes a lot of work to develop an attitude of gratitude, and thus live a positive, happier life. But it's simple, my dear, and it all starts with the appreciation of all our blessings, no matter how small they may seem . . . but the end result will be a richer, happier life. This attitude thing has worked for me. It's made a happier life for me and those around me."

Allie Wilkes joined in the group. She had apparently just departed the bar, carrying a fresh drink in hand and appearing to be a little tipsy—rather odd this early in the morning even for this crowd. Allie was an attractive forty something native of the area; she seemed in fine physical shape. Her father was a successful, well-known attorney in Scranton. She lived in his shadow, using his influential name often and his money even more. She had been married twice with a host of affairs that added to her notorious reputation. She was not well liked nor respected for various reasons, including being a boring, loud-mouthed drunk and of course a bossy snob.

"Well, Molly, what are we talking about this morning?" Allie's slurred voice asked.

Molly held her stature for a moment. Then with a warm smile that was intended to conceal what she was thinking, Molly said in a sweet, mild voice, "We were just discussing the merits of alcohol."

"Now that's one subject I know a little about," Allie said, picking up her glass as if offering a toast. After taking a sip of her drink, Allie confidently held her glass toward Molly as in a mock salute and said, "Please continue your discussion of this miraculous social lubricant."

"Oh yes, alcohol is a social lubricant enjoyed by a multitude of people on many occasions and festivities. This morning many folks are enjoying their bloody Mary, glass of wine, beer, or whatever else they are drinking and having a lovely time. But there is another dark side of the effects of alcohol. Medically speaking as a nurse, I know that most accidental deaths are alcohol-related, and many premature deaths are related to drinking too much. I've read that booze has ruined more lives than any other single source, and when you think about it, alcohol has caused more divorces, broken up more families, ended more friendships, and destroyed more careers than any other single reason," Molly said in a cool, matter-of-fact manner.

Molly then looked warmly over at Allie and said, "And of course it's also considered by some as a miraculous social lubricant, isn't it, dear?" Molly sat motionless with her warm smile gazing over at Allie.

"Yeah, whatever you say, Molly," Allie said as she got back on her unsteady feet as she walked oddly away. "Well, I'm going back to the bar for another drink. No lectures over there, just laughs."

"Oh, there'll be a few laughs here," Molly said as Allie walked away. "Oh yes, dear, as soon as you're out of range of my voice." The group chuckled.

"Now, Molly, you shouldn't be too harsh with Allie. Her dog had to be put down a few months ago, and she hasn't been the same since," Ann McGowan, a close friend of Allie's, said.

"Oh, I'm sorry to hear that. I'm sure she must have loved that dog very much," Molly said.

"Rainbow was more than a dog to Allie. He was her everything; she loved him more than anything in this world. She never had any children. So to Allie Rainbow was her child, and she loved him just like any other mother would love a child," Ann continued in support of her friend Allie.

Molly took a sip of her coffee before she responded. Then she smiled over toward Ann McGowan and said, "Ann, dear, I am sure Allie loved Rainbow with all her heart. But to compare the love of a pet owner to that of a mother is not quite fair. Now we all love animals; I have two border collies that I adore. Over the years I buried some of the best friends I've ever had in my backyard. I loved those collies dearly. But to compare them to a child? I don't think they are on the same level or on equal basis. Pet owners love their pets, and I'm one of them. I can tell you I loved my pups, especially at the end of the day when I walked in the door and they would run up to me. It was a wonderful feeling petting them, loving them, and taking care of them. But parents love their children, and there's no comparison. One thing's for sure, pets are a lot easier to love, and they seem a lot more grateful. But they are not the same. There's nothing like the loving feeling of holding your own baby in your arms; looking in amazement into those beautiful, dependent little eyes while feeding your baby a bottle; or the thrill of holding on to the tiny hands of a one-year-old as she takes her first step and watching the expression of excitement on that beautiful baby face. None of my loving pets ever asked me, why are the clouds white or is there really a God? Can I have a cookie? I never hoped to see my grand puppies play soccer or Little League baseball or see their excited faces on Christmas morning. I never saw one of my pet's report cards or watched them take the keys of the family car and drive off. I never expected to help any pets get dressed on prom night or attend their weddings. To me pets bring love and warmth to our lives. But children bring a certain perspective of life with a deeper awareness of where we come from and a peek at the future. As a parent there is some pride and amazement in seeing the miracle in the life we created and how this person will help make this a better world to live in."

"The problem with this world is the people who are living in it. Today people are so selfish and materialistic they don't seem to care about anybody," an anonymous voice said.

Molly looked over toward the direction of the comments. She smiled and said, "Now, dear, it's been my experience that most of the hurt feelings and misunderstandings we have in life are what many people do unintentionally. Very few people intentionally want to hurt someone else, but we all do hurt people by unintentional actions. It may sound strange, but perhaps some of the most wonderful people who have ever lived are with us on earth today. And I may add, we may have some of the worst people that ever lived on earth with us today also. I believe we all are born pretty much the same. What determines if we are considered good or bad people are the activities and deeds we do. Those who do good things and good deeds are considered good people; those who do bad things and deeds are considered bad people. When we peel away the curtains, masks, smoke, and fog of deceit we should not be judged by what we feel or what our intentions are, but rather we should be judged by what we do. Simply put, people who do good deeds and feel good about themselves are considered good people; those that do bad deeds are usually unhappy people and considered bad people. It's rather simple, but it seems to be true."

Molly chuckled to herself for a moment and then looked around at the table of listeners. "Of course at our age I have a lot of nurse friends who for one reason or another are single. I warn them to be careful of getting hooked up with any man nowadays." The group at the table had confused expressions as they glanced over at each other. Molly continued, "Yes, I tell them to be careful because a lot of men our age are looking for women not for love but to take care of them, and nurses can do a lot of things, including changing their diapers in their old age."

Molly glanced over at Alex with a warm, affectionate smile and said, "We've found out over the years that kind and considerate men are the most valuable."

Alex's face turned a bashful red as he said, "You must be talking about your husband, Phil."

Johnny was standing at the bar by himself, drink in hand, when Tommy walked over to join him. "You look like I need a drink. So tell me, Johnny, do you still date lady luck at the casinos?" Tommy asked him.

"You might say I'm kind of an Indian lover." Johnny said joking. "I believe in giving back as much as I can to the Indians. They now own those casinos." Johnny chuckled as he continued, "Things are kind of reversed now: the white man used to give the Indians token gifts and hope they wouldn't lift our scalps off our heads; now the Indians comp us with cheap gifts and take our shirts off our backs."

Tommy laughed and ordered a drink. As he was standing at the bar, he turned and seriously looked at Johnny and asked, "If you won the lottery for, let's say, a hundred million dollars, what would you do, Johnny?"

Johnny looked into Tommy's eyes and said in a cocky voice, "I'd go down to Atlantic City, check in at the Trump Plaza, give them the check, and tell them, 'Let me know when that's gone.'"

"Oh, they'd let you know when it's gone, all right; you could bet on that," Tommy said, smiling. "And that is one bet you'd win, Johnny."

Johnny became serious as he looked down the bar and began speaking, "You know, Tommy, we all want to do what we like to do. I worked hard all my life for my family and spent all my money on them. Look what it's gotten me. I'm all alone to do what I want. Now I'm looking out for me, and quite frankly, I like to play the blackjack table. At the beginning of the month, I get my retirement money, and I pay my bills. I don't want to go out and spend money on dinners, drinking, or chasing women. I don't spend money on new cars or expensive clothes. I have what I need, I've already spent enough money on my family, and now I'm spending the way I want. My entertainment is gambling, so I spend all my spare money doing what I like, playing at the casinos."

"Well, Johnny, I guess we're all going to do what we want to," Tommy said.

They both took a sip of their drinks, thinking quietly for a moment. Neither of them talked about their wartime experiences with anyone. When they discussed Vietnam between themselves, their conversation was usually brief and to the point. They didn't dwell on the past nor complain about the present. They shared a concealed, emotional bond that seemed to unify them in an odd, subconscious level. Neither understood it at all.

"It's been a long time since we wore an Army uniform," Tommy said as he noticed young Jim Ryan walking across the large room. Private Ryan was home on leave and was wearing his desert camouflage uniform. As the young soldier made his way through the flock of partiers, some would shake his hand; others patted him on the back and inquired how he and his family were doing. It appeared as if the entire community was proud and interested in their young soldier warrior.

Johnny held up his drink, looked over at Tommy, and said, "They didn't treat us like that when we wore a uniform."

"That's true, Johnny, but we went off to fight in Vietnam, a faraway place that few people knew anything about. That young warrior over there in uniform went to war because we were attacked at home and the World Trade Center was destroyed," Tommy said.

"Kind of interesting that one of the first people killed on 9/11 was from Clarks Summit, Laura Lee DeFazio. She was on the United flight that flew into the towers on that morning. There's a plaque to honor her on Depot Street just across from the Sunshine Café," Johnny said. "I knew her and her parents; they were nice family. Her dad used to come into my gas station all the time. Years ago, after Eddy died, her father bought Eddy O'Connor's Bar."

"I am happy to see that young people in uniform are getting the respect they deserve," Tommy said as he took a sip of his drink. "You know, after all these years, we old veterans are starting to get a little recognition and consideration. Recently I started to wear one of those black baseball caps that say 'Vietnam Veteran.' I noticed when wearing that hat, people seemed to be a bit more friendly and considerate. When I'm out shopping, the clerks always seem to be friendlier, and sometimes I even get a discount. Many times men and women working in the store will tell me they too are vets and relate a story about themselves or a loved one. Or out of the blue, some very ordinary guy who's a vet will come up and strike up a friendly conversation. Most people are very proud of being in the service, and they usually tell a short story of when they served. Looking at them, you'd never think they flew a B17 or served on a submarine. Sometimes they'd tell me where they were stationed; it's really fascinating to meet some of these guys, especially the old ones. Tommy paused for a moment, turned, and looked directly at Johnny, asking in an inquisitive voice, "Just think about it for a minute, Johnny. When you and I were born in 1944, the war was still going on. Many of these little old guys wearing those black hats are the unsung heroes who fought the Nazis and Japanese. If they had failed, right now you and I would be living under a swastika flag, and for sure we wouldn't be here sipping drinks."

Tommy took another drink of his beer. Then in a lighter tone, he continued, "But the real reason I like my hat so much is that it saves me on speeding tickets. I've been pulled over a half dozen times, but when the cop comes up to the window and sees me in my Vietnam Veteran hat, well, he smiles and checks me out. Then he tells me to slow down. It kind of makes me proud to be a veteran . . . if you know what I mean, Johnny."

Johnny said curtly, "Vietnam was the most intense part of my life. I hardly ever tell anyone I served in Vietnam. I go on as if nothing ever happened. I've told you about my uncle John T who died on the Bataan death march in the Second World War. Everyone says I look just like him; in uniform we did look like twins. To this day I won't drive a Japanese car. In my store we rented videos, but I would not allow any Jane Fonda video in the place or any antiwar movies. I used to enjoy bugging the antiwar crowd. I had a big movie poster of John Wayne in *The Green Berets*. And of course I always had the American flags flying. I am proud to be a Vietnam veteran, but I don't need to wear a black baseball hat to prove it."

Tommy thought for a moment, then in a philosophical manner, he said, "For me, Johnny, I like to see those veterans wearing black baseball hats that tell a little about them. It warms my heart seeing some old guys with WWII hats, and it makes me wonder about what they saw and did. And when I see veteran hats from Korea, Desert Storm, Iraq, Afghanistan, and other military units, I stand in awe. Sometimes I look at those vets wearing those hats, and I think of the friends they served with who didn't come back and didn't get the chance to grow old. And when you think about it, Johnny, we owe them a lot; without veterans we wouldn't have a country."

Tommy continued speaking in a resolute tone. "I once saw a bumper sticker that read, 'What do we owe our veterans? Reply: Everything!'"

"Ah, you're right, Tommy," Johnny said in an accepting manner. Then after some thought, he added, "But I'm still not comfortable wearing one of those hats. Oh, I agree with your motive, but I don't think it would work for my hairstyle." They both chuckled without saying more.

Johnny's attentions changed abruptly; he suddenly appeared startled as he looked across the banquet room. His eyes focused on a young women walking toward him. His face was drawn without emotion, his body rigid, even his breathing seemed to be frozen.

"Hi, Daddy," Johnny's daughter said as she approached him smiling, head held high, posture erect, presenting herself proudly for his acceptance. She was well dressed in a denim and sheepskin jacket with brown, knee-high, fur-trimmed boots and walked nobly as if she had not a care in the world. She was a plain, unnoticeable-looking woman in her early thirties, but there was something attractive about her. She could pass as a schoolteacher, a nurse, or a young housewife. Without another word to her father, Terry smiled gracelessly at Tommy while extending her hand in greeting. "Hi, I'm Terry Thompson; it's very nice to meet you. My father is sometimes at a loss for words," she said with a confident, friendly voice.

Tommy was also taken aback and pleasantly surprised at the sight of his friend's daughter. He would have predicted that Johnny's daughter would be quite different. Others had told him that Johnny's daughter had been heavily involved in drugs and had been in trouble most of her life. She had been in prison for over two years on drug and shoplifting crimes. Rumor had it that as soon as Johnny's money ran out so did the leniency of the legal system. Tommy was somewhat confused; he was expecting to meet a hard-core female criminal complete with all the features one would see on TV. However, Tommy was surprised to see this well-groomed, fine-looking woman greeting him. She didn't have a tattoo showing, no purple hair, not even a pierced nose. He noticed she had a serious but pleasant facial expression; at a glance one could tell she had experienced life and was comfortable being who she was.

Tommy snapped back to reality, returning her greeting with a warm smile. He took her hand and grasped it with both of his, saying affectionately, "It's so nice to see you again, Terry. I'm Tommy Wilkinson, an old friend of your dad's. The last time I saw you, you were in diapers."

Tommy then stepped back, taking a full look at her for a moment, then added, "My, you've grown into a beautiful young lady."

"Oh, yeah, I remember you now. My father used to tell stories about you," Terry said.

"Some of them may have been true," Tommy said, smiling.

Johnny was taking this all in, still not saying a word for a moment. Then he spoke as if she was expected and welcome. "Hi honey, when did you get in?" Johnny asked in a warm, caring manner.

"The other day. I've been staying with Mom for a few days," Terry said.

"Let's go over to the empty table over there," Johnny said as he pointed to a table in the corner. Johnny then motioned to Tommy to join them.

After a few minutes of small talk and light conversation, Terry became more serious. "Dad, I need a little money."

The pleasant, smiling features of Johnny's face changed into a serious, searching frown. "How much do you need?" Johnny asked without emotion.

"Not much, about a hundred and fifty should be enough," Terry said like a salesclerk would ask for payment.

"So the real reason you came to find me at the breakfast was just for money?" Johnny asked in a cold voice.

"No, Daddy, I came to see you," Terry said with a chuckle. Then she added with a smirk, "And to get some money."

"Well, the apple didn't fall far from the tree," Johnny said with a mocking tone. "You're just like your mother; all she wanted was money. When the money ran out, so did she."

"There's more to life than money, Daddy. Maybe that's what mother was looking for," Terry said in a cold voice.

"Yeah, she was looking for more than money, all right," Johnny replied in a tough tone.

"There you go again, Daddy, back to your money God. That was always so important to you. That's all you cared about. In your gambling all you wanted was more and more money, and we ended up with less and less," Terry argued back.

"I earned the money. I worked like a fool sixteen, eighteen hours a day. I earned it, and I plan on spending it the way I want. I've spent a fortune on you and your mother between doctors, lawyers, and bribes, and what good did it do? So now I'm spending it on myself," Johnny railed back.

This verbal hostility was getting to Tommy, making him a little nervous, so he tried to change the current of the conversation. "Johnny," Tommy said ginerly, "there are people taking notice."

Tommy then turned toward Terry, asking in a mild interested voice, "Are you working now, Terry?"

Terry smiled over at Tommy and said, "Yes, I am working, although it's very difficult to get a job when you're a convicted felon. But I was able to get a job as a waitress at the Golden Corral. I kind of like it there."

"Tell us about prison," Johnny abruptly injected. "What it was like?"

Terry stared at her father for a moment with hatred in her eyes. She quickly turned and smiled in a relaxed manner as she started talking to Tommy. "Prison life is a lot better than being locked up in the county jail. At least in prison you can work, go to the commissary, and go outside in fresh air. But county jail, you were stuck in a cell with nothing to do all day. It was very depressing."

Terry then looked over at her father, saying, "Daddy, do you remember when you used to come to visit me in the county jail, how depressing it was?"

"I can tell you, Mr. Wilkinson, it was a horrible experience. I remember when I first arrived at prison. When we were led into the intake, that's when reality set in. I had to strip naked, then bend over and spread my cheeks as the guards watched my every move. It was so humiliating." Terry reflected for a moment, then continued, "It was then I started looking back on my life at all the little decisions I made as a kid—to be cool, to fit in, taking chances and the excitement of taking chances on doing something illegal. I did a lot of things that were wrong and illegal; some were much worse that I was convicted for. I couldn't believe I went to jail for the small things they finally pinned on me. But I was convicted and sent to prison. When I arrived, I was put in admission with the scum of society, murderers, child abusers, and thieves. I was there for a few weeks before I popped out to the general population. Then the life of a numbered inmate began. They issued me everything I needed: a prison uniform we called states, soap, and even a toothbrush. I remember each inmate got two rolls of toilet paper per week. You had to carry a roll under your arm and make sure no one stole it. I felt so alone, and I knew I had to take care of myself, so one of the first things I did was to pick a fight with another inmate—just to establish my territory and just to let them know, don't screw with me."

Johnny sat staring into Terry's eyes as he listened to his daughter share some of her life experiences that were shocking and painful for him. This was the first time she had opened up to anyone about her experiences, but she felt tranquil and informative telling her story.

Terry then began speaking confidently with brightness in her eyes. "Life there wasn't as bad as you may have seen on TV. We didn't live in cells; actually it was more like a college dormitory, although it was very overcrowded, and the constant noise would drive you crazy. But everyone had a job to do, and I learned that if you were a student, you didn't have to work a job. I didn't want to clean toilets or work in the laundry, so I told them I had dropped out of school. I became a full time student. I could lie in bed until noon, then go to class in the afternoon, and I enjoyed relearning some of the things from high school. But you never forget where you are. You have to be always looking over your shoulder. I learned a lot of self-control and to just walk away from conflicts. Sometimes in the middle of the night, I'd wake up panicky, shutter with a sickening feeling, just hoping I was dreaming this nightmare."

"How long were you there?" Tommy asked.

"Just over twenty-six months; it seemed like a lifetime going in, but as I look back now, it didn't seem that long." Terry smiled slightly as she continued to speak in a light, whimsical manner. "When I think of it, I'm almost glad I was sent to prison; it may have saved my life. Down deep in my heart, I knew I was on a road of self-destruction, and prison was a kind of roadblock or at least a detour. Anyway it gave me a second chance at life. Being a prisoner was terrible in so many ways. Just taking a shower was a nasty event; some women could be absolute pigs. There were a few nice women there without a criminal background, because of an accident or prescription drugs or a white-collar crime like embezzlement. But some of the inmates became like family to me—we became very close, we shared secrets of our souls, and I'm still in contact with a few of them. I had to make friends the best way I could just to get along. Food was the one thing we all had in common; it was a kind of motivation thing that brought us pleasure, and it helped maintain a little sanity in our lives. I experienced hunger like I never knew; in the big house you learn how to deal with it. I learned to become quite a good cook with the microwave." Terry laughed, waving her hands. "There should be a prison cookbook with all the great recipes you can prepare in a microwave. Have a little mayonnaise with some chips of cheese, and you could cook up best-tasting Southern fried chicken you've ever tasted," Terry said proudly

"Where would you get food to microwave?" Johnny asked.

"If we were good, we could shop the commissary every two weeks and buy fast foods," Terry said.

"What would you use for money?" Johnny asked coldly.

"I didn't get any money from home," Terry replied sarcastically, peering directly at Johnny.

Terry then regained her pleasant attitude and said, "We were paid twenty dollars a month, but the real currency used in prison was envelopes or, as we'd call them, 'lops.' With six lops you could buy a Snickers candy bar. For a cigarette it cost five lops."

"If you worked a real prison job, wouldn't you get paid more money?" Johnny asked.

"I didn't want to take a chance and get a maintenance job, cleaning the bathrooms. During visits some inmates would swallow drugs in balloons; later they would shit them out in the shower. I didn't want any job that involved cleaning up that stuff."

Again Terry paused for a moment and then continued telling her story. "I forced myself not to think of the outside world, and I decided to try to make myself be happy as possible, I looked for the humor in our lives and the funny stories some of the mates would tell. I had to concentrate on what positive things I could find while in prison, and that was tough, but it made life better. I did a lot of walking in prison; that was my way of clearing my mind and burning up energy. The system tried to control my mind, and in doing so they would control me. I had to remember that I was person not a number. I realized I had to build myself back up to become a better person. I was determined to take command of my future and make sure

I'd never go back to that place again. I want to be a good parent to my daughter, have a normal life, and enjoy my freedom."

"That's quite a story, Terry. I'm glad you're here this morning and telling us about it," Tommy said. He paused and asked, "Was it difficult getting back in society again?"

"To tell you the truth, Mr. Wilkinson, I had mixed feelings about coming home. Although some of the COs, or corrections officers, were the meanest, cruelest people I've ever known and I wanted to get away from them, I believed I was different from these women. One thing I noticed in prison, none of the inmates ever expressed remorse for anything they did. It was because they were under the influence of drugs or booze while they committed the crime, like killing someone or robbing a store. Some of the mates were used to being in there and were comfortable with the fact that most of their lives had been behind bars. They had no desire to be free with all the outside responsibility of providing for their own livelihood."

Terry took another deep breath, then continued, "To tell you the truth, I was a little scared myself and had anxiety spells just thinking of getting out. My head wanted to leave immediately, but my heart had a slightly different opinion. You've got to remember, I had been living in a controlled environment, being told what to do and when to do it. I didn't have the stress of the outside world. I didn't have to worry about working, the boss, paying all the bills, making sure everything was done around the house. I was afraid of what was I going to do when I got out; I was panicking about my future. I was used to a prison system of life; I knew what I had to do, and that was that. I had I no bills to worry about, no clogged toilet, no one expecting too much of me. Just go along and get along. I felt free of the stress of living the outside life with all the responsibility; in prison just follow the rules and life's okay. Many people in there think that way, and that's why they recycle back. It's a structured lifestyle that some people feel comfortable in."

"How has it been since you've been out?" Tommy asked.

"I remember the drive home; it was so calm and peaceful. How quiet it was, seeing the new cars, the green mountains, and the delightful scenery. I was full of excitement, listening to my music and talking freely. I'm still adapting to freedom. I find myself asking permission to do almost anything, like lighting up a cigarette or going to the bathroom, because in prison I had to ask permission for everything. I'm a lot more patient than I used to be. In prison we waited in line for everything, sometimes for hours. Now when I go to the grocery store, I'm happy to stand in line and wait my turn. All in all I am so happy just to be free; although loud noises still peak some anxiety in me, and every time I hear a set of keys jingling, a rush of fear runs up my spine, because all the COs had large key chains as they strutted their authority. Of course at 4:00 p.m. and 11:30 p.m. I never forget that I had to be in my bunk for count time."

Terry then stared off into the distance, thinking for a moment; then she said in a thoughtful way, "You know, in prison people read a lot of books, and there's an old prison superstition that if you start to read a book and don't finish it . . ." Terry said, paused for a moment, and then in a serious, convincing expression, said, "you will be back in prison to finish it. Well, I made sure I read every page of every book I opened. Believe me, there are no books for me to go back to finish."

Terry paused for a moment, and then with a large smile, she continued in a lighthearted manner. "Being a felon does have its advantages. As an ex-felon, I am now entitled to all kinds of grants for college, business, and housing, even for dental work. Just Google it, and you can see as a felon I'm entitled to more benefits than a decorated war hero."

"It sounds like you've got your life together, and I wish you all the luck in the world, Terry," Tommy said.

"Are you going to join us for breakfast, honey?" Johnny asked in a loving way.

"No thanks, Dad, I have a few things to do before dinner. I just need the bucks, Dad, then I'll shoot out of here," Terry said affectedly. She then added, glancing over at Tommy, "It was so nice to see you again, Mr. Wilkinson, and thank you so much for your kind words of interest and encouragement."

"Thank you for sharing your story with us, Terry. It was quite fascinating," Tommy said as he stood to shake her hand.

Johnny stood up, reaching in to his back pocket, and counted out the money Terry requested. Handing the cash to her, Johnny said warmly, "Here, honey, I hope this is enough. I love you," he said as he bent over and kissed her gently on the cheek.

The two men stood silently staring at Terry as she walked across the floor and out the door. "Johnny, your daughter is quiet a remarkable girl, I mean, young woman," Tommy said.

"Yes, she is," Johnny said sadly. "If I could believe she would change and that she has learned from this prison experience, but I heard it before, and I believed it all before."

Johnny's eyes stared intensely at her as she walked away. Then, as if speaking to himself, he said in a unemotional voice, "If she could only understand the terrible pain and harm she has caused our family. She seems to be concerned about one person . . . herself. I lost one child because of drugs, and I worry about what lies in front of her. I'm afraid she is going to go right back where her friends are, the drug world, and they usually die off in their mid-thirties."

Phil Whitman walked over to the table where a few elderly people were seated; among them was Mr. Ziak. Mike Ziak had changed more noticeably in his later years. His hair was now completely white, and he seemed to be physically smaller than just a few years ago. His posture had also diminished; he sat at the table somewhat hunched over, sipping on a cup of coffee, as Phil approached. He exchanged pleasantries and greetings with Mr. Ziak and the others seated at the table, including a few retired teachers.

Phil was upbeat as he shook the hands of those seated. He then looked around the room and said half jokingly, "I was hoping to see some of my old high school friends, but when I look at their faces, it seems as if their parents showed up instead." There was some mild laughter and nodding of the heads at the table.

Mr. Ziak spoke quietly but used all his voice so he could be heard, "Hey, Phil, I see your old buddy Johnny Thompson is over there at the bar. Some things haven't changed, but I wish he would." There was again some light laughter at the table.

Phil chuckled, asking "How are you doing, Mr. Ziak? Is life treating you good?"

"At our age, Phil, it's better to be seen than viewed," Mr. Ziak said jokingly.

"You seem rather lively, Mr. Ziak. You still have your wit about you and your bright Gleem toothpaste smile," Phil said supportably.

"I do take pride in my smile, Phil," Mr. Ziak said boastfully. "After all these years, my teeth are still bright white, and they still sparkle a little. You know, they're like the stars in the sky; they come out at night.

Phil laughed again. He then sat down to talk to his old colleagues and friends. "Well, how do you guys like retirement?" Phil asked.

Someone at the table yelled out, "For Mr. Woodstone his retirement week consists of six Saturdays and a Sunday to rest." Everyone laughed.

Mr. Ondish, a high school teacher for over thirty years, answered, "Oh, I noticed a big change in the way people treat you once you're retired. As a teacher in this community, I had a stature in our town. Even out of school, if I went to the store grocery shopping, people would come up to me and say hello and ask me questions. They were respectable and interested in my opinion. Now that I'm retired, I've noticed a distinct change in the way I am treated. Now when I'm in the store, a lot of people I've known slightly just walk by not saying a word; now I'm lucky if I get a thank-you from the checkout person while I am paying for my groceries. It seems to most people that if you're not a contributing member of society, then you are of less value and less interest."

John Williams, an owner of a small business in Dalton, then spoke up. "I think retired people are very valuable." He lifted his beer high in the air exulting his opinion. "Over the years I have hired many retired people, and let me tell you they are the best workers you could ask for. They seem happy to come into work, and they never show up with any hangovers. They are there to do a job, they do it right, and they don't take lazy shortcuts. They work every hour they're paid for, and they don't care about company politics; they are not worried about becoming a boss. I wish all my employees would retire, so then I could hire them back to work and perform on the same level as my other retired people."

Bob Parry joined in, sitting down with a cocktail in hand, what appeared to be a manhattan straight up with a lemon twist. Although no one said anything about his early morning imbibing, it didn't go unnoticed. A few eyebrows were raised, and there were a few gawky stares at the drink. But none of that bothered Bobby. He took a slow, methodical sip, smiling with his eyes closed and clearly demonstrating the pleasure he achieved from the forbidden, early morning cocktail.

After he finished his sip, he opened his eyes with an expression of complete satisfaction and joy. He looked around the table to share his happiness. "Like so many wonderful holidays, Thanksgiving morning comes just once a year. So once a year I have my little treat of a Southern Comfort manhattan up with a twist, just one of the little pleasures of growing old."

"Is that the only pleasure you have in getting old?" Someone at the table yelled out.

Bobby took another small sip of his drink, smiled and continued talking to whomever would listen. "I remember when I was a youngster, I was so excited what life had in store for me, and I wanted to learn and prepare myself as much as I could for the unknown future. Then in middle life, I wanted to experience all this lifetime had to offer. Now as I look back, it was a crazy ride; I experienced a lot, suffered a lot, and now I'm trying to figure out what life is all about. I seem to have come full circle dealing with various kinds of people, and now I'm back to my old friends. I'm trying to remember what my life was all about.

"I'm now a father of grown children, and I'm glad that the hard part of that job is over. I'm also a grandfather, and I love being a grandpa. I once saw a bumper sticker that made me laugh; it said, 'I wish I had my grandkids first.' We grandparents have a special love, and I cherish it; there's nothing like it. My grandchildren love me, and I love them so much; we spend precious time together in a special, loving relationship. But no matter how wonderful it is, we are like two different species, loving each other and fascinated with each other but not truly understanding each other.

"But when I am with my old buds I grew up with, I'm back being just me, my soul, my own personality. Instantly I can communicate with these friends in a way I can't describe. When I see their eyes, their smile, their posture, and hear their voice, I feel like my spirit returns to my younger days of carefree happiness, being silly, and seeking fun as we did in high school. If you think back to high school, friendships were of paramount importance before careers, marriage, houses, and children. Then life led us in separate directions, making our marks and footprints in life. The in-between years of life are over now. We've all succeeded, failed, or just treaded water. It really doesn't matter much now. We are currently at a time in life where friendships are so very important again; after all we no longer have the responsibilities we once had. We no longer have careers or houses to buy, and our children are all grown; they have children of their own, and they all have strong opinions of their own too. So now's the time to surround ourselves with our old friends and enjoy what life has left for us."

Bobby took another sip with a smile, only this time he was considering how to answer. "There are many pleasures of growing old. In old age Thomas Jefferson commented, 'Tranquility is the greatest good of life.' For me, I start out each day having breakfast down at the Sunrise Café on Depot Street. Now this place will never make *Gourmet* magazine as a fine place to dine or even a good place to eat, but it's a fun place to have breakfast. It also has won the prestigious Abingtons 'friendliest booth' award. We all know Dawn, the proprietor of the little bistro, is there at dawn each morning with a bright smile, coffeepot in hand, ready to pour a hot cup. Although the prices are printed on the menu, the cost varies depending on the mood of the owner and is usually rounded off the nearest dollar. Very few ever complain or even notice. As I sit down in a booth, I am joined with any of an assortment of friends who happen to be there that morning. These are people I grew up with, that I've known all my life. Some of the guys left the area over forty years ago and now are retired and come here to live or visit. We have breakfast and talk about the glory days of high school and other adventures of life."

Bobby paused for a moment, looking around at those listening as he shared a mystery of life. He continued as if preaching, "Do you realize how great it is forty years after high school to talk and laugh about some of the things that took place back in our teenage years? With some of the people who were with you when it actually happened! To relive the funny stories and events, gossiping about friends you grew up with so long ago. It's kind of like being in our old bodies but returning in spirit and mind to our active high school days, carrying on, joking, and laughing like we did when we were back in school. Very few people are blessed to share in this wonderful experience. Under the right conditions, you can grow older; but if you're real lucky and with the right friends, you can live longer enjoying the spirit of your youth. Having the right friends at our age is a good reason for growing old."

Someone spoke out for the table, "It's okay for you, Bobby; you're a member of the country club. You live the good life."

"I am still a member of the country club, but I lost my business a few years ago and almost all my money. I have a few bucks to live on. I realize how non-important money is," Bobby said, shooting right back.

Bobby looked in the direction where the comment came from. "You all remember Ralph Kessler; he was worth over thirty-million dollars when he died a few years ago. Do you know how much he left behind?"

There was silence for a moment; then Bobby answered his own question, "All of it. There are no U-haul trucks in a funeral procession. I've found out there's no correlation between happiness and money. Bobby took a deliberate sip of his manhattan, savoring the moment. He then smiled and added, "Remember, the one who goes to heaven with the most intriguing episodes of life wins."

Ida and Tommy were standing next to each other and making small talk along with Danny Fredrick. The trio was engrossed in light conversation with some giggling and chuckling.

Phil noticed the merry conversation going on and leaned over to Johnny, saying, "Those three appear to get along pretty well, considering Tommy stole Ida from Danny years ago."

"Yeah, it's a little strange. They were both after Ida. Danny seemed to be worried and complaining all his life about what was fair and just. Tommy enjoyed living life, taking it as it comes. Looks like Ida chose the one who lived life with a smile, which is hard to do at times. I think people seem to like to be around people who are fun to be around."

"Johnny, I'm glad you didn't lose your keen ability to detect the obvious," Phil said with a chuckle.

"Well, Sherlock Whitman, it will be interesting to see just how long the mystery couple stays together," Johnny replied.

"The real mystery is, Johnny, how much longer any of us stay together here on earth," Phil said in a whimsical voice.

"You're right, Phil. I've noticed on holidays I don't make as many phone calls as I did years ago; most of my relatives and a lot of our friends are on the other side now. We've had a good life growing up here." Johnny paused for a moment, staring off in the distance, then asked quietly, "What do you think life's about, Phil?"

"Well, Johnny, I believe our life is a result of four factors: our environment, our decisions, our experiences, and our motivation to pursue a life in reality but always groping for the clouds of dreams," Phil said as if he was talking to someone else.

"In other words, Phil, you don't have the foggiest idea what's life's about either?" Johnny asked.

"Not the foggiest, Johnny," Phil said with a smile.

Alex was sitting alone at a large table, reflecting on the weekend and how it was shaping up. He was joined by Danny, who sat down quietly with a drink in hand.

"Would you like to me to go over to the bar and get you a drink, Alex?" Danny asked before he sat back to relax.

"No thanks, Danny, I think I had enough for the morning," Alex said, greeting Danny with a warm smile.

Danny smiled as he glanced around the large reception hall. He seemed pleased with himself as he said, "I'm glad I came in this weekend. It's been a long time since I spent any time here."

Danny then slipped into a quiet, melancholic mood. Staring off toward the end of the room, he said thoughtfully, "The last time I was in was for my parents' funeral about twelve years ago. They both died within a few weeks of each other, and it seemed like one long funeral. I didn't know if I would ever come back to this town after their funerals. It didn't seem like I had much to come back to. I believe you can return to where you grew up but you can never go back."

"You're partially right, Danny. You can't go back in time, but you can go back to a place where you felt comfortable being young. To see the old buildings, streets, homes, trees, and various other landmarks that were there during the young, fun, and learning years. That's an experience worth the effort, " Alex said.

Danny replied with a scornful voice, "It's all well and good for you, Alex; you've had a great life. You been successful; you haven't experienced the things I had to put up with in my life."

"Danny, you remind me of a guy who told me he was born a pessimist, even his blood was B negative. And you're right, Danny. I didn't live your life; I lived mine with my successes, losses, and frustrations. I learned that life is not a straight line, and no two lives are the same; we all have joys and tragedies. In most people's lives, if you were to put tears of joy in one cup and tears of sorrow in the other, they'd both weigh about the same."

Alex stood a stern look at Danny and continued, "I believe we are all given problems by outside forces; it's how we handle the problems that makes us what we are. Problems can make us stronger, smarter, and wiser. We learn and grow solving problems. But so many people look at problems as 'poor me' and hoist a flag of misery into their life. Remember, Danny, misery is a self-inflected condition and can be long term."

"I'd like to be like you, Alex, but I can't," Danny said coldly.

"You're correct on that point, Danny. If you say you can't, you'll always be right," Alex said in a growing voice of irritation. "'I can't' is the laziest, most destructive phrase in the English language. Those who use it live a restrained, limited life, lacking the joy of viewing the future. Is that the way you want to live the rest of your limited life, Danny?" Alex asked.

"I don't know, Alex. When I come back here, I get strange feelings," Danny said sheepishly. "I had my own life to live; I wanted to make it on my own, to be a success and then come back. I admit I didn't want to keep in touch with the friends I grew up with because I felt I was a failure. "Maybe it has caused some hard feelings."

Alex reflected for a moment, then he said, "I understand what you're saying, Danny. Over the years I've noticed the lack of dialog or communication in a relationship creates a void that's ripe to germinate suspicion and fear into large, imaginary clouds of resentment. It's followed by a long time of emptiness and silence, and that silence can grow into a powerful wedge of division. Fortunately a few words of interest or kindness usually evaporate this difficult situation.

"Remember, Danny, this is your hometown," Alex said in a cheering-up voice. "This is where you grew up. This is where real friends are, the ones who know the real you."

"The real me?" Danny chuckled in a frustrated voice. "Think about it for a minute. Who is the real me, Alex? Many people remember me as my senior picture in the Cliff's yearbook. That's one image of me. Sometimes I think we're all just images, separate from who we really are, our true being, or as some call it, our soul. We are kind of like human pictures viewed by those who know us. To the bartender, I'm a drinker at the bar. To my friends, I'm a friend. To a bank clerk, I'm a customer. To a doctor, I'm a patient. To my grandchildren, I am Gramps; to my children, I am Dad; and to my wife, I am her husband. The person that I'm perceived to be is the one viewed by all those who come in contact with me. And I try to fit the image of the viewer. I try to be a good tipper to the bartender; to the bank clerk, I try to be considerate and make sure my bills are paid; to the doctor, I respect and follow his directions. To my grandchildren, I try to play that image as grandparents do; and I try to be a good father and respect my grown children. To my wife, I try to be loving and a good husband. But it seems as though I am the man behind the curtain, trying to adjust to the image of who I am dealing with at the time."

Danny paused for a moment, picking up his glass of beer and taking a sip. Then he continued, verbalizing his thoughts. "But when I come in contact with my old friends, it's like they are windows in the house of my life. They see through all the additions and all the walls I have built over the years. These windows, or my friends, see into the real interior of me, the way I am."

Danny had a puzzled look on his face as he turned to Alex and asked, "Does that make any sense to you, Alex? Or was that just too much early morning drinking on my behalf?"

"I understand a little of what you're saying, Danny," Alex said. "It seems as though we are perceived by others as to who we are . . . by those who come in contact with us . . . and how they look us is how they value us. That makes sense; just look at all the jewelry and designer clothes with signature logos. The cars we drive, the houses we live in are all to establish an image of who we are or whom we want the outside world to think we are. Sometimes we put a false value on ourselves, because a false value is generated by others. But we're in this stage of life where true friends and loved ones who know and care about us are not interested in the image; they are interested in the person. It's kind of like looking at a friend's beautiful house and realizing it's not the dwelling that we're interested in, but it's the friends who live inside—the people not the building, the spirit not the body. Our body ages through life and dies, but our spirit experiences life and then goes on."

"I know what you're trying to say, Alex. I'm at a time in life where I'm a little fearful about the future. I'm a little confused in what lies ahead. I worked hard all my life, been married a few times, and my children are grown. They both live in different parts of the country. Now I 'm facing life ahead, and things have changed so much.. I have enough money to do what I want. My health is good, and I feel like I'm in my forties. But I don't know what to do. I golf a little and fish a little, but it's not enough to occupy my time. No one wants to hire me, and I don't know if I want to work. My wife Debbie's attention is focused on her children and grandkids; we've become more like brother and sister than husband and wife. I want to do something, but I don't know quite what. I want to live and do things I enjoy but I don't know how. I'm losing interest in life, and that scares me. I feel as if I am living an empty life."

"Danny, you've always questioned authority even as a kid, but you got suckered in by false powers that you thought could solve life's problems. You believed certain entities like the right government, certain people, or even money could control life. That's living without faith, and without faith the future life is rather bleak. Change your beliefs and change your attitude, and you'll change your life or what you have left of it."

"Hmmm," Danny said as he sat thinking about what Alex had just said.

Alex smiled at Danny and added, "Don't discount your relationship with Debbie; over time physical passion morphs into contented companionship. And that's a good thing."

"You have friends, Danny; we are still here. We are your friends from your youth. We've come to accept you and ourselves," Alex said with a smile.

"It's those friends that I have a difficult time relating to. I wish I could do better in that area. It's just that I have a hard time trusting in them. So many other people let me down in life," Danny said as if asking a question.

"We all like to have friends; remember 'to have a friend you must be a friend.' Good, honest communication is important in friendship; a positive personal dialog is a way of building positive relationships. I once read that silence is the wedge of division," Alex said.

Alex paused for moment and then continued speaking, "You know, Danny, there's a lot of people trying to find out who they really are; they go to shrinks, they practice yoga and seek other spiritual outlets. Maybe we find out who we really are after we leave this life. Now wouldn't that be something."

Phil meandered to the table, sitting down to join Alex and Danny. "So what are you two discussing? The secrets of life?" Phil asked in a whimsical tone. Then he added with a chuckle in his voice, "It's funny, I came here this morning expecting to see some of my old friends, but it looks like their parents showed up."

"We're just reflecting on life a little," Alex said. "There's been a lot of changes since we graduated from high school. When we were in high school, computers were owned by large institutions, and no one ever dreamed there would be one in every home."

"Not to mention the Internet, with e-mails and Facebook. We live in a fantastic time," Phil said.

"Don't forget the cell phone, the greatest cheating tool for having an affair," Danny said.

"It's also the number one way to be found out. Because of pictures in the phones and there's a record of all the calls made, to whom, how long, and when," Phil said.

"Yes, well some technology isn't always good for everyone," Alex said lightly.

A short time later, Nancy and Molly joined the group at the table, with coffee cups in hand, fitting right into the conversations. "We were just talking phones and about all this new technology that's all around us, and how it's changed our lives," Alex said to Molly.

"We still have a landline phone at home," Molly said, staring off for a moment. Then she said as if thinking out loud, "But the only ones who used to call on that line have all passed on. I guess we keep the old phone line for sentimental reasons. No one ever calls either one of us on it."

"Cell phones have changed everyone's life," Nancy said.

"Oh, I don't care for all this new computer stuff. Flat screen TV is as far as I want to go, because I can still watch some of my favorite old shows on cable," Molly said.

Molly took a sip of her coffee and continued, "There is always something changing in our lives, and some for the better. But there are some things I wish wouldn't change, like the characters we grew up with. Now I like watching old movies and reruns of old TV shows like Dean Martin, Johnny Carson, and *Barney Miller*. The humor was simple, fitting, and funny. Nowadays I'm embarrassed to watch nighttime shows with my grandchildren. Even the cartoon shows are shocking like the show *Family Guy*. It's funny but not appropriate for small children or good-living Christians."

Phil sat next to Molly, picking up on what she had just said, and added, "The comedy shows are being replaced all the time, but we have not been able to replace the TV heroes we admired as kids, like the Lone Ranger, Captain Midnight, Roy Rogers, and the Duke, John Wayne."

Tommy and Ida made their way to the table and seemed to be in a jubilant mood. "I see the whole gang is here," Tommy said, smiling as he glanced over at everyone. He then noticed someone missing. "Except Johnny, here's not here."

"Johnny's not here because he's not all there!" Phil yelled out, laughing.

Then Johnny's distinctive voice was heard saying, "Well, Phil, I see you're still here but rearranged a little. I noticed your hair has stopped growing on your head and is now growing out your big ears and nose. And I noticed your shoulder muscles have dropped to your stomach."

"Well, Johnny, some things haven't changed, like your hairstyle," Phil wisecracked.

"Your head hasn't changed either; it's still as big as it always was," Johnny snapped back.

Although the group was laughing at the bantering, Nancy felt compelled to smooth the water a little. "Where have you been, Johnny? Not outside smoking, I hope."

"We used to think it would stunt your growth," Phil said, "But in your case, Johnny, it stunted your brain."

Johnny ignored Phil's comment and looked directly at Nancy. "I went out for some fresh smoke."

"How much do you smoke a day, Johnny?" Nancy asked.

"Oh, I cut way back. I'm down to smoking about two packs a day," Johnny said.

"Johnny, that's over ten dollars a day going up in smoke, and it's so unhealthy," Nancy said in an astonished voice.

"No, I buy smoking tobacco and have a little machine; I roll my own for about fifty cents a pack. But you've got to remember; when I started smoking we were just kids. As a kid I thought, by the time I grew old they'd find a cure for cancer. So I never stopped smoking; who would have thought they wouldn't stop cancer? I guess I was misled. As Groucho Marx used to say, 'If I knew I was going to live this long, I would have taken better care of myself,'" Johnny said as he sat down confidently.

Johnny put on an air of cockiness as he added, "I've noticed the people that tell me how unhealthy smoking is are all fat. But I don't say anything to them. I just look at them and smile."

Phil started to chuckle, saying, "With that smile, they may not want a smoke. But I bet they'd want a drink." Everyone seemed to chuckle at Phil's remark.

"Speaking of drinking," Alex injected, "I remember when happy hour was when drinks were half price. Now happy hour for me is nap time."

Tommy chimed in, "Yeah, I know. For me an all-nighter means I don't have to get up to pee."

Ida injected merrily, "It wasn't too long ago when we used to laugh at the old saying 'At least we have our health.'"

Alex injected, "Yes, sixty years ago life seemed so big and unimaginable, and now it seems so short and limited."

Alex was taking it all in, observing everyone as they all sat around the table, talking and laughing just like the old days. Naturally one would expect them to look their age, and they did; but they were acting as youthful friends, laughing and frolicking as they did back in high school.

Johnny laughed and said, "Well, I intend to live forever, and so far so good!"

"All things considered, I believe we all have had a pretty good life," Alex said.

Phil nodded his head in agreement with Alex, saying, "There's an old Irish saying 'You've lived a good life if you dance at your granddaughters wedding.'"

Johnny spoke up, saying loudly, "My grandparents were Irish immigrants, and they were in the iron and steel business. My grandmother did a lot or ironing and my grandfather did a lot of stealing." Again everyone laughed.

"Did anyone see Sandy and Ralph Sawyer?" Nancy asked.

"They were married right after high school, I think," Tommy said.

"They were both as ugly as sin," Johnny added.

"Well, I was talking to them, and they seem very happy. They showed me pictures of their children and all are so beautiful," Nancy said.

"That's because they didn't use their faces when making the kids," Johnny said as everyone joined in laughing.

Nancy was laughing and having a wonderful time; she was taking in all the fun. She glanced over at Danny just to ensure that he too was enjoying himself. Hoping to draw Danny into the conversation, Nancy said, "I'm having a great time this morning; after all these years, isn't it great to have all of us here together again? After all we've been through in life, you're still my dearest friends."

Danny smiled slightly, saying, "Yes, it's great to be together again. I remember when I was young and excited, I wanted to learn whatever I could about what life had in store for me. Then in middle life I wanted to experience all life had to offer; now with white hair I'm trying to remember what my life was all about."

Tommy said jokingly, "When we were young, it was important to learn about life; in middle age we thought it was important to know life; now it's important to reflect on life. Soon it will be important to just to remember life."

Phil spoke up in a serious matter-of-fact manner. "This is a great place to grow up, and as we write the final pages of our life's book, I think there's comfort in being near your birthplace— the familiar landmarks, the roads we traveled that helped shape our lives—and in feeling the serenity of realizing that we lived a wonderful life and that this is a great place to end our journey on this planet."

Johnny picked up on what Phil was saying. "It wasn't long ago when death was a shock; now it's common and almost expected. Life is now kind of like playing musical chairs. When the music stops, who will be leaving next?"

"This is not a funeral or a wake," Tommy said to change the darkening atmosphere. He then looked over at Phil and asked, "Phil, do you know the difference between a Irish wedding and an Irish funeral?

Phil smiled with a perplexed look and replied, "No, I don't, Tommy."

"Well, at the funeral there's one less drunk," Tommy said, laughing.

"I was just thinking," Alex said.

"Take it easy until you get used to it, Alex," Johnny laughingly yelled out.

"I've been thinking that Tommy's right. We're not at a memorial service; we're at a party. We all still have a lot of pages left in our book of life. Try to visualize, as the river of life flows closer to meet the ocean, the water gets deeper and calmer, blending the salt and fresh waters together as perhaps our bodies become closer to the spirit life that lies ahead. We are near, but we're not there yet."

"I've been an educator all my adult life, but I believe the best teacher in the world is time, and I want to use the time I have and do a lot of living," Phil said loudly. "I may have a few miles on this old body, and my kids look middle-aged now, but I'm still young at heart. I don't want to spend time thinking what I wished I had done. I have my health, money and energy; all I need is the courage to do it."

"It's about time you started spending some of that money you've hoarded all your life," Johnny said jokingly.

"This is hard to say, Johnny. But you're right," Phil said, smiling over at Johnny. "I've lived sparingly all my life, but I made sure my kids had all the brand-name stuff, Ralph Lauren clothes, Nordica skis, North Face jackets, and all the rest of that brand-name stuff. They dressed like royalty while I shopped in discount stores for my clothes. But now the blue suede shoes are on the other feet, and I'm buying what I want. I just bought a large, flat screen TV. I'm getting rid of that old ten-speed bicycle of mine and buying a semicustom-made for over five grand."

Phil was on a roll; he glanced over at Johnny again, smiling and saying loudly, "Just to demonstrate how much I've changed, Johnny, I'm going to buy you a drink! And the way you look, I need a drink."

"Looks like the fresh water is going to reach the ocean rather quickly; I'd better take that drink before we spot surfers on the beach," Johnny said as they all chuckled.

Alex was taking in all the light bantering and laughing going on with the group; out of the corner of his eye, he noticed an elderly man walking toward them. At first Alex didn't recognize the figure, but when he noticed the book in his hand, he knew it was Jake the barber. As Jake made his way across the floor, Alex noticed he was dressed in an oversized sport jacket with a slightly faded, whitish dress shirt and an out-of-style tie. He had changed radically over the years, which was rather shocking to Alex, for Jake the barber was now completely bald. It was like seeing a revered car mechanic riding a bicycle. He had also lost his masculine stature; he no longer was the erect, broad-shouldered, former football player but just another round- shouldered senior citizen. However, the features that hadn't changed over these many years were the twinkle in his eyes and his rapturous smile, which were in earnest when he approached the table.

"Hello, everyone," Jake said as he dipped slightly, showing a warm, friendly sign of affection and respect for the group. "Alex, I have something for you," he said, handing to book over to Phil with a notable sign of respect.

"Thank you, Jake. Sit down and join us for a few minutes," Phil said as he shook Jake's hand.

There was some small talk among the group with Jake joining in. All were in good spirits, laughing as they waited their turns to add to the pages of history recorded in the diary.

Nancy asked lightly, looking over at Johnny, "Johnny, you're kind of quiet. How about a penny for your thoughts?"

Phil yelled out, "Nancy, you'd be overpaying."

Johnny injected quickly, "With you, Phil, every time someone says something, you've got to bellow in; it's like kicking the jukebox."

"I would like to get the last word in before you take your 'dirt nap,'" Phil said, laughing.

"Just remember, Phil, he who laughs last, thinks slowest," Johnny said.

"How do like retirement life, Johnny?" Nancy asked.

"Well, I think this retirement stuff is greatly overrated. It seemed so far off such a little while ago. Now it's here. This friend of mine told me now that he's retired, he gets half the money and twice the wife," Johnny said laughing.

Johnny Thompson glanced at the others standing around idly talking waiting, for their turn to write whatever was on their minds in the book. Johnny took a sip of his drink and put it on the table next to him. He then slowly and quietly walked over to the table to scratch his feelings and opinions into this book. For him this was almost an annual event. After all, he lived in the area and attended the football games each year. His oldest son played on the football team, an average player but good enough to play varsity his junior and senior year. But those happy years were a long time ago.

Johnny sat solemnly, looking around only once to see if anyone was paying attention. This was not the usually flamboyant Johnny as he picked up the pen to write.

Hello,

This is Johnny Thompson again. It's been a few years since I wrote anything in this book, and I don't know what to write now. I used to think I knew a lot about life and people, but I found out I don't. As I look around here today, I see many happy people, laughing and sharing good times with friends. That used to be me. I had it all at one time; I knew everyone and was surrounded friends and well-wishers. I worked hard becoming successful in business. I played hard, trying to be a good husband and father. I devoted my life to my wife and children, and now it looks as if that was all in vain. I look back at all the things I provided for them, all the money I lavished on them, the small fortune I spent on doctors, lawyers, judges, and cops, trying to maintain a normal life. Now it all seems to be a complete waste.

So now I am all alone, questioning what happened, where I went wrong, and what I could have done differently. Divorce in this stage of life is so difficult. If this happened when I was younger, I think I could have planned for the future.

But now in the September of my life, I'm facing the final years alone, and this is difficult. When I look in the mirror, I can't believe anyone would want to be with me. I still love Melody and still miss being with her; she was the love of my life. I don't know if she is really happy now with her new boyfriend; I guess time will tell. It feels so bad to be the one left behind. I wish she and I could just get along together. I can always dream. Then I look at my children struggling now more than ever, trying to get along in this life. I can only hope and pray they will steer themselves clear of the booze and drugs that have ruined their lives so far. If I could only help them, but I don't know what to do anymore.

I would like to be happy, but happiness seems to be evading me. I must look toward the future.

My most active business life is over, but I am not through yet. I am still in real estate, buying and selling. So I will keep busy and make the future the best I can. Life's not that bad . . .

And I hope to be back again!

Johnny, 2009

Alex walked over to the table; he hesitated for a moment, staring down at the book. He appeared troubled, as if he were thinking of something to write. He sat down and picked up the diary, flipping through the pages and reading briefly some of the inscriptions of years gone by. After a few minutes, he picked up the pen and started to write.

Dear Diary,

It's been a long time since I last wrote in this book. So many things have changed, and yet so many things remain the same. I find it interesting and revitalizing that Eddy's place is still here, although now it is known as the State Street Grill; it too has changed, but the address and basic structure still remains. So it seems like many of my friends have changed, but the soul in their eyes is the same as I remember when we were young. We all had different life experiences, and we all weathered our individual storms of life; but the basic core of these long-lost friends seems to be intact. To me, these dear friends kept their individual perspective and integrity of life, and continued to be the same, basically good people I knew back in high school.

Over the years I sometimes regretted leaving this area to follow an elusive career, but as I look back, I believe, for me, it was the right thing to do. I loved growing up here, but I wanted to see what life had to offer on the other side of the mountains. I ventured out and did what I wanted to do, although there were many times I would have preferred different results. But I am blessed, having married my soul mate and raised three wonderful kids, who gave me six of the greatest grandchildren anyone could ask for. I am so fortunate to come back to my hometown to enjoy the full circle of life and blessed to share the twilight years with friends. I am truly blessed and eternally grateful.

Alex, 2009

PS: It ain't over yet!

Danny walked slowly over to the table. He turned around looking over at Alex and the group, sitting, talking and laughing with each other.

Hello Diary,

Needless to write, it's been a long time since I have written anything in this book. Life is strange, and I've lived an interesting one, and now I'm back here where it all began. Although I've lived in other areas of the country, this place is still home to me. Strangely I'm still friends with the kids I grew up with. I know I am different than they are, but they accept me the way I am, and I am grateful for that. I believe it's important to be accepted by those who really know who you are.

I am glad I came in this weekend to see life as I once knew it. Although many things have changed, many things remain the same. The Summit Hill, the Catholic church, and the Summit Diner seem about the same. O'Connor's is now the State Street Grill, and we've all changed in appearance, that's for sure, although our personalities seem about the same.

I have had difficult times in life when I missed this place. As I look back, I can see where I made the big changes in my life, and they came about because of little decisions, like going to a concert, where I met my first wife, and playing in a band instead of going to classes. There are a few things I regret not doing: not finishing collage and not going in the Army. Although I argued with and at times hated Johnny Thompson, he did go when drafted. I do like and respect him, go figure. (Just kidding.)

I do enjoy coming in and seeing everyone, and I love it here, but it is not the place for me to live. Whatever it is, I look forward to going back to my home in Connecticut on Monday.

It's been fun!

Danny

It was Ida's turn to put her pen to work; she was smiling, anticipating what she would soon be writing. Ida stared at the book for a moment, smiled, and with pen in hand, started to compose her thoughts and feelings.

Dear Diary,

This is perhaps the happiest of times, and I am really enjoying this weekend. I am so pleased I came to this weekend breakfast. Back in New york things are coming to an end, and I have mixed feeling about that. My life will be changing no matter what I do. Now I have an opportunity to be with the one I have loved all my life. I know it has been a long time, but I believe our happiness is upon us. I have loved Tommy Wilkinson all these years, and I am not ashamed to write about it today. I am so happy!

I must remember all those other great people here today whom I also love and enjoy being around. They have been like family to me. I am so grateful to know all of them. I've been blessed to be friends with some to the funniest, nicest, screwiest people in the world. I hope to spend more time with them, especially now that I will have more free time. Tommy enjoys being around this area; hopefully we will have some great times ahead.

Again, I feel so happy just to be here today. This is a great Thanksgiving breakfast.

Love,

Ida

When Ida was finished, she rose from the table and walked directly toward Tommy, smiling. "Your turn, Tommy," she said, adding with a chuckle, "I'll read it when you're finished."

Tommy smiled at Ida, touching her hands as he passed. "I'll write something sweet."

He then continued to the table, sitting down and starting right in.

Hello Diary,

Life is good. I have found the love of my life, and I am very happy. This is one of the best weekends of my life. I am here with old friends and my long-lost love. Who could ask for more? I do hope the future will be as pleasant as this holiday weekend, but I doubt it. Life is full of twists and turns, and I have had my share of it all on my road of life.

I do wish all my friends would find the happiness I am experiencing. As I look back on my life, I believe success is 90 percent drive and determination and 10 percent luck; and happiness is 90 percent attitude and gratitude and 10 percent luck.

Oh well, no need to lecture in this book. I am happy to have grown up in this time, this area, and with these friends. I look forward to some good times ahead. (Especially with Ida!)

Tommy

Everyone was sitting around the large table gibber-jabbering when Phil noticed that no one was writing in the diary. "Has everyone written in the diary?"

"Oh, I better go over now and get that little ritual done. I'm glad Johnny has already scribbled his words of wisdom; now for once I'll have the last word," Phil said as he got up and started walking over to the diary table.

Johnny's head perked up, and with a big smile and a loud voice, he said, "Phil, if you want the last word, you'd better take a dictionary with you, so you'll know how to spell it!"

Phil looked back at Johnny and replied with a quick, verbal jab, "I went to college, and I taught school; I know how to spell, Johnny."

"Yeah, Phil, we all know you got book leaning, but we also know how smart you are. So you better take the dictionary," Johnny said laughing.

Phil didn't reply to the last comment. He opened the book, glancing over the entries of the others, and on a clear page started to write.

2009

Greetings Diary,

This is a great breakfast year; for me it was a special time, seeing my dear friends and old classmates coming in for the weekend. We are now at an age where many of our friends and classmates are departing this earth. Just in these last few years, cancer and other disease have taken so many away from us. It's very difficult going to these funerals of the kids I met in grade school, knowing them all my life, or seeing some of them even now crippled with disease or in bad health. There are many curveballs in life that I've seen thrown into some people's lives— financial reversals, spouses leaving coldly after thirty or forty years of marriage, then the sad death of a classmate or lifelong friend. Sometimes it feels like I'm like watching a movie of our lives; you see some characters dying off and the dilemmas of others. We know the end is coming, but we just kind of watch to see what happens, hoping our ending is off in the distant future.

On a happier note, I see that some of my friends are enjoying life. They are in good health, and have the time, the money, and energy to do what they want. For the lucky couples, these golden years are the best time of their lives. They love each other and care for each other; they don't have to worry about anyone stealing their spouse or so many of the temptations and difficulties that younger couples face. I am grateful to have Molly; she is still my best friend and the love of my life. I hope we have a great future together.

I hope everyone had a great time and we do this again next year with the same people enjoying life.

Phil

PS: If somebody teaches Johnny to read, I wrote this without a dictionary.

Nancy was the last to take up the pen. While the others talked and joked, she quietly walked over to the table.

Dear Dairy,

This is a wonderful Thanksgiving weekend. I am so grateful to be here, sharing good times with friends I have known and loved all my life. As I think back on all the years that have passed since we started writing in this journal, I reflect on many mixed emotions. I don't regret the past, and I am comfortable with the present. I am so grateful for having experienced an interesting life and now being surrounded by wonderful friends.

I don't know what the future has in store for me, but I look forward to having an enjoyable life and hope I continue to share these good times with my good friends.

Again I am so happy to be here, rekindling the loving friendships of my childhood.

Nancy, 2009

PS: Thank God for this great weekend.

Alex stood up, clinking his glass to get the attention of those at the table. "I'd like to make a toast," Alex said nervously as he glanced around the table. He took his drink in hand, lifting it high; and with his eyes welling slightly with tears, he began to speak in a powerful, emotional voice, "To all of us who have made it this far in life and are now sharing a new phase of life. May our upcoming experiences be filled with the same thirst for adventure that we possessed so many years ago, as we first wrote our thoughts and feelings on the pages of our breakfast diary. We've enjoyed great lives, although some seem greater than others." There was a chuckle from the group. "But in our little group, we should always remember the Jerry Weaver we knew and loved, and the many Jerry Weavers who gave up their privilege of writing on the pages of life so we could write ours. May we have an appreciation for what God has in our future, and may we be surrounded by good friends, good cheer, and happiness until we meet again . . . in this life or the next."

The group embraced each other, promising to keep in touch. Everyone seemed to be happy for the event and happy to be together again.

Exit

Alex was quietly walking toward the coatroom to retrieve his overcoat, when he heard a low, distinguished female voice, "Hello, Alex Flynn."

He casually turned to see just who was calling his name. He was pleasantly surprised to see a quiet, attractive woman generating the most beautiful smile he'd seen in quite some time. At first he didn't recognize the woman with the radiant complexion and the reddish-blonde hair, but with one look into her eyes, he immediately realized who she was. She was the friend of his younger sister, Marie. Alex hadn't seen her in years but instantly recognized her striking, turquoise-blue eyes. He remembered her hanging around with his sister years ago, but he didn't have any interest in her; she was much too young. But now she was a striking, mature beauty.

"Hello" was all Alex could think of saying. He was awestruck. He was trying to think of something clever to say, but no words came out. He felt like a klutz, but he couldn't take his eyes off her.

Fortunately for Alex the unknown beauty walked toward him with her hand extended. She maintained her affectionate smile while speaking in a warm, pleasant voice, "Hi, Alex, I'm Kathy Foley. You may not remember me. I was a friend of your sister Marie's."

Alex regained his composure and started thinking clearly again as he grasped Kathy's hand with both of his. "Yes, I remember you very well, Kathy. You lived over on Stone Avenue, and you had an older brother by the name of Brian. He was a real character and a good ball player."

"Yes, that was my brother Brian, all right," Kathy said as the smile disappeared from her face. She bowed her head slightly as she said sadly, "Brian passed away a few years ago of cancer. It was a real loss. He had a beautiful wife and three great kids."

"I'm sorry to hear that," Alex said tenderly.

Kathy snapped out of her momentary slump, again looking at Alex with a beaming smile. "Thanks to Facebook, I was able to reconnect with Marie. She said she likes living in Cincinnati but still misses the Abingtons."

"Do you live in the Abingtons?" Alex asked.

"Yes I do now, but we lived in Atlanta for many years. When my husband got sick we moved back in the area. I was married to Jim Olgeman; we had two grown boys. They both live in the South." Kathy said and again her expression became sorrowful. "But a few years ago Jim fell down the basement steps and died shortly afterwards."

Again Alex was at a loss for words. "How tragic." Is that all he could think to say?

"It was a real shock, and I had a very difficult time for a while," Kathy said meekly. "Fortunately I had a lot of great friends and family who helped." Kathy paused for a moment, and then asked, "Are you familiar with Wayne Dyer?"

"Oh yes, I have read a few of his books, *Making the Shift* and *Manifest Your Destiny*, and I've met him personally after one of his lectures. He's put a different spin into my life," Alex said.

"He's changed mine too. I've read a bunch of his books myself, and my favorite book is *There's A Spiritual Solution to*

Every Problem. I don't know what I would have done if I hadn't learned how to live a new kind of life," Kathy said.

"And life does go on. God has a plan for us, although it seems confusing at times," She said as she raised her head with a slight smile again, peering into Alex's eyes. "And I understand you also know what it's like to lose someone you've loved?"

Alex looked into Kathy's deep intriguing eyes and felt a bolt of spiritual connection. He was overcome with emotion and bewilderment. She too felt something unexplainable—a strong feeling aroused in her as if she had known Alex all her life and an astonishing sensation of connecting with his soul. They both were frozen in time, trying to adjust to this sudden, sparkling encounter.

Kathy was one of those people who look directly at you when she talks to you. She spoke in a kind, persuading tone to Alex. "To love and be loved by someone is a beautiful experience, and I believe love does go on even on the other side. I believe they want the very best for the ones they left behind. They want us to live a great life and to be in love again." She smiled again with an air of confidence, saying, "And somehow I believe they play a part in making the arrangements."

Alex was frozen but managed to say in a feeble, stuttering voice, "I know what it's like, but I never . . .ah . . . never thought . . ." He couldn't finish what he wanted to say.

"You don't need to say anything, Alex. I understand," Kathy said faintly in an angelic voice as she fought to hold back tears.

"I was going to say," Alex paused for a moment as he gathered up his nerve and continued, "I was going to ask you if you would join me for a coffee, or a drink or anything you'd like?"

"I'd love to have some champagne now," Kathy said in a light, whimsical way.

"That's fine with me," Alex replied happily. "Would you join me at the bar?"

Kathy agreed and was so happy that she was beaming with delight as they strolled toward the bar. Alex commented lightly, "So you like champagne?"

"Not particularly," Kathy said joyfully.

Alex looked perplexed at Kathy and said, "Then why did you say you wanted champagne?"

Kathy turned toward Alex, extending her wide smile, flashing her bright, white teeth and peering into his soul with her turquoise-blue eyes, in a voice of confidence said joyfully, "I wanted champagne… to celebrate."

They stopped walking, turned toward each other and grasping hands, they kissed in the middle of banquet room at Shadowbrook.

Alex felt a magic sensation through his body. He was in kind of a shock. This woman he had just met, he kissed in public in the middle of a banquet floor, and he was thrilled. He was so lightheaded with joy and happiness. His knew his life had changed; he suddenly realized he was in love again. He was overcome with euphoria. With a most heartfelt voice, he said just above a whisper, "Kathy, I am so happy you are here this morning. Meeting you has made this by far the greatest Thanksgiving breakfast."

The End
Of this Story

Made in the USA
Lexington, KY
16 December 2013